SWEDISH MYSTERIES

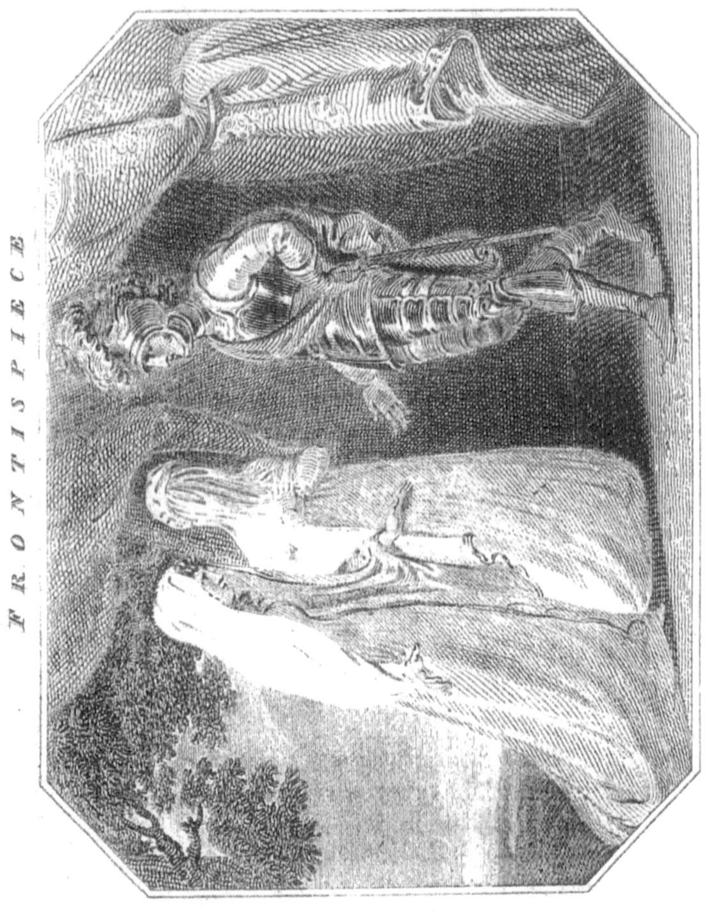

Frontispiece to the first edition (1801)

Gothic Classics

SWEDISH MYSTERIES,

OR,

HERO OF THE MINES.

A Tale.

THREE VOLUMES IN ONE.

BY

ANNA MARIA MACKENZIE

Edited with a new introduction and notes by
Janina Nordius

——"He who reigns, but climbs to care;
Tho' safe his throne, he finds no softness there;
Dangers, and doubts, and toils his moments seize,
Hang on his business, and perplex his ease."

FIELDING'S MEROPE.

Kansas City:
VALANCOURT BOOKS
2008

Swedish Mysteries by Anna Maria Mackenzie
First published by William Lane in 1801
First Valancourt Books edition 2008

Library of Congress Cataloging-in-Publication Data

Mackenzie, Anna Maria.
Swedish mysteries, or, Hero of the mines : a tale / by Anna Maria Mackenzie ; edited with a new introduction and notes by Janina Nordius. – 1st Valancourt Books ed.
p. cm. – (Gothic classics)
ISBN 1-934555-47-9 (alk. paper)
1. Gustav I Vasa, King of Sweden, 1496-1560–Fiction. 2. Sweden–History–1397-1523–Fiction. 3. Sweden–History–Gustav I Vasa, 1523-1560–Fiction. I. Title. II. Title: Swedish mysteries. III. Title: Hero of the mines.
PR4971.M37S94 2008
823'.6–DC22
2008017728

Published by Valancourt Books
Kansas City, Missouri

Composition by James D. Jenkins
Set in Dante MT

10 9 8 7 6 5 4 3 2 1

CONTENTS

INTRODUCTION

"[A]s ignorance continued longer [in Sweden] than in more southern climates, so truth was there concealed under fabulous and superstitious tales, long after it had shone with sufficient splendor on a great part of the rest of Europe," Sarah Scott writes in her 1761 *History of Gustavus Ericson, King of Sweden* (xii-xiii). Her comment typically reflects eighteenth-century Britain's general notion of the backwardness thought to exist in this remote and little known "Gothic" outskirt of Europe before the reign of Gustavus Ericson Vasa in the first half of the sixteenth century.[1] By the turn of the nineteenth century, however, Sweden had not only become a modern state, but also gained a more prominent place in British public consciousness. It had risen to become one of the most powerful nations of Europe in the mid-1600s, only to again lose its influence and the greater part of its European dominions in the early 1700s; Swedish scientists like Linnaeus and Celsius had achieved wide fame; and, more spectacularly, in the climate of political unrest that pervaded Europe after the French Revolution, its king had been dramatically assassinated during a masked ball in 1792. As the transformation of the country from alleged barbarism to enlightened but complicated modernity was thought to have begun during the reign of Gustavus Ericson, it is perhaps understandable that a writer of gothic fiction would find early sixteenth-century Sweden an intriguing a location for a novel—quite on a par with those more traditional haunts in continental France or Italy usually favored by gothic novelists.

One writer who obviously did so was Anna Maria Mackenzie, whose *Swedish Mysteries, or, Hero of the Mines: A Tale* was published in three volumes at William Lane's Minerva Press in 1801. Setting her novel on what Robert Miles has called the "Gothic cusp" enabled her to explore the tension between past and present that is always more or less explicitly at the heart of first-wave literary gothic (*Ann Radcliffe*, 87). That Sweden was thought at the time to be quite literally the original home of the ancient Goths—a belief which, though debated today, was suggested by the name used for the southern part of present-day Sweden, Gothland (Sw. *Götaland*)[2]—may only have made the choice of setting even more appealing to Mackenzie.

On the title page of the first edition, *Swedish Mysteries* is presented as an anonymous translation "from a Swedish Manuscript," allegedly written "by Johanson Kidderslaw, Formerly Master of the English Grammar School at Upsal." The name and affiliation of the supposed author sound sufficiently odd to a Swedish ear to suggest that they are mere inventions, made up to allow the writer to pass off his or her work as a fake translation. But it was not until 1814 that a Minerva Press catalogue attributed the novel to Anna Maria Mackenzie, one of Lane's most successful writers of fiction in the historical-gothic vein (Blakey, 201).[3]

Swedish Mysteries is one of Mackenzie's more interesting contributions to that genre, but it is also one of her least known works, due to the extreme rarity of the first and, it appears, only edition until now.[4] The fact that it has been so hard to get hold of may also explain why it has gone virtually unnoticed that, besides relating a tale of gothic horror and suspense, *Swedish Mysteries* has also left its mark on a quite different, if lesser known, literary tradition. For the eighteenth and early nineteenth centuries saw a series of fictionalized accounts dealing with the so-called Swedish revolution in the early sixteenth century, most of them dramatizations for the stage, and all of them idealizing Gustavus Ericson, the leader of the revolution and later king of Sweden. Mackenzie's novel was clearly inspired by this tradition, but it also added a set of new plot elements and characters to the story, elements which were later incorporated into subsequent versions of the Gustavus Ericson lore. Yet what makes *Swedish Mysteries* stand out from these other texts is not only that it is to my knowledge the first English *novel* on the topic, but also that Mackenzie was the first to exploit the story's gothic potential, conspicuously projecting upon the figure of Gustavus and the situation in early sixteenth-century Sweden the concerns current in British late eighteenth-century gothic fiction.

A word of warning: as some of the events in *Swedish Mysteries* are discussed in some detail below, especially in the section "*Swedish Mysteries* as Literary Gothic," readers wishing to keep up suspense while reading Mackenzie's text are recommended to save that section for last.

Anna Maria Mackenzie and her Critics

Anna Maria Mackenzie belonged to the growing group of women writers who took up a literary career as the popularity of novels and novel-reading began to boom in the latter half of the eighteenth century. Born Anna Maria Wight, the daughter of an Essex coal merchant, she married a Mr. Cox who died after losing his money, leaving Anna Maria to provide for their four children (McMullen 205; Summers, *Gothic Quest*, 172-173). Between 1783 and 1809 she published at least fifteen novels, possibly more; in a dedication in *Feudal Events* (1800) she claimed to have published 28 volumes, and in the preface to one of her late novels, *The Irish Guardian* (1809), she refers to "her humble attempts in the literary line" as "an occupation, which has formed the amusement (and in some degree the employment) of more than twenty years" (I, [i]). The difficulties arising during these years from her "confined education, and want of patronage" she only conquered, she claims, by her "ardent love of writing" (I, [i]). Some of her novels were, like *Swedish Mysteries*, initially published anonymously or under a pseudonym, as for instance *The Neapolitan* (1796), whose author was given as Ellen of Exeter; others were published under the various names of Mrs. Cox, Mrs. Johnson, and, from 1795, Anna Maria Mackenzie.

As a woman writing for a predominantly female readership, Mackenzie was not unaware of the low esteem in which the novel was still held in certain quarters, for she complains in her 1809 preface to *The Irish Guardian* about novel writing being "considered as the lowest of literary pursuits" (I, ii). But just as Jane Austen would do a few years later in *Northanger Abbey* (1818), Mackenzie fervently defends the genre and its readers against what she perceives as both unfair and gendered criticism. Leaving no doubt about the gender of the "censurers" she is referring to, she claims to have "heard *all* Novels condemned, by more than one censurer, as totally unworthy the perusal of a sensible man" (I, iii). And although she admits that in "some instances" the criticism bestowed on novel writers might be justified, there are still, she insists, enough "examples of beautiful writing" to "do away much of [the] prejudice so strongly maintained" against the genre (I, ii). While Austen was to praise the works of Fanny Burney and Maria Edgeworth as proof of novelistic excellence, the titles Mackenzie lists to the same effect in her 1809 preface may be lesser known today; but to readers at the time they were probably, if not as famous as the works of these two writers, at least as familiar as the examples of "horrid" novels Austen would go on to list in a later chapter of *Northanger Abbey*.[6] Besides three titles by Jane West—*A Gossip's Story* (1796), *A Tale of the Times* (1799), and *The Infidel Father* (1802)—Mackenzie mentions Frances Jacson's *Plain Sense* (1795) and *The Saracen*, a translation from the French of Sophie Cottin (1805), as examples of novels to admire.[7]

These novels, we are to understand, exhibit the qualities that to Mackenzie were requisite of good literature, and would also meet the special standards she apparently set for women readers: "a purity of sentiment, a professed abhorrence of every insinuation [. . .] that can alarm the rectitude of mind so indispensable in a virtuous female,—a steady adherence to true, not fastidious delicacy, [and] firmness of principle, with an avoidance of every subject which may lead to abstruse and unnecessary points" (I, iii). She expressed a similar concern for her young female readers many years earlier, in a note, "To the Readers of Modern Romance," prefaced to *Mysteries Elucidated* (1795), where she also commented on the vogue for the gothic novel. With the same apparent modesty as made her, in the preface to her 1809 novel, refer to her own "moderate endeavours" as "a lambent moon-beam" when compared to "the brilliant sun" of other writers (I, ii), she pays tribute to Ann Radcliffe's "genius" and "brilliant imagination" in the prefatory note to *Mysteries Elucidated* (28). Yet this praise does not stop her from finding fault with Radcliffe's flirting with the supernatural: "Let every mystery thicken in the progress of the story, 'till the whole is elucidated, but let it be without the intervention of super, or preternatural appearances. Dreams and apparitions savour too much of the superstition which ought never to be encouraged," she writes. Rather than seeking to "derive fame by [her] success [. . .] in alarming the timid," Mackenzie speaks up for another "kind of writing, founded [. . .] upon historical facts," as being better cut out to provide both amusement and moral examples to be emulated by "the young and ductile mind" (28-29). Yet having thus stated that "historical anecdotes are the most proper vehicles for the elucidation of mysteries" (29), she treats these anecdotes with the utmost liberty when it comes to adding characters and episodes wholly of her own invention, and notwithstanding her declared concern for the sensibilities of her readers, towards the end of her career her novels tended increasingly to incorporate elements borrowed from German-inspired horror gothic.

When Mackenzie complains about the low status afforded to the novel genre, she was presumably writing from her own experience. For although some of her novels were highly praised by the reviewers,[8] others were apparently less lucky. Commenting on *The Critical Review*'s assessment of *The Neapolitan* (1796) and *Dusseldorf; or, The Fratricide* (1798), Lorraine McMullen notes that it is in particular Mackenzie's "gothic tendencies which *CR* most dislikes" (206). This seems also to be the bias that informs *The Critical Review*'s short commentary on *Swedish Mysteries*, included in the April issue of 1802. The reviewer objects to the "gloomy" narrative—"gloom" being as we know one of the most frequent catchwords associated with the gothic—and, lumping the novel together with "its brethren," he assumes rather aloofly that it would "amuse for two or three months those who search after novelty."

It is of course vain to speculate whether the reviewer would have been more enthusiastic, had he known who was the author of *Swedish Mysteries*; but it is quite clear from his comments that he did not have access to this information. For, finding fault with the novel's "turgid" language as well as its gloomy narrative, he declares that these two aspects taken together are enough "to warrant a belief that it is the offspring of some northern author." The remark is as formulaic as the ethnic stereotype on which it draws, and says probably more about the reviewer than about the author of the novel; yet it is a fact that Mackenzie can be stylistically uneven, and a few aspects of her style in *Swedish Mysteries* may deserve some comment. She has for instance a tendency to write rather long sentences at times, adding subclause to subclause in a way that demands the reader's full attention. Yet this is compensated for by her liberal use of dialogue which reads easily and vividly enough, even though as in most novels of this kind it includes quite a few archaisms in order to create the wished-for illusion of "Gothic" times. There are the occasional unhappy formulation (the "positive negative" given in answer to a request, [115]) and periphrastic phrase (the "frosty particles" in the opening chapter [9]), but on the whole Mackenzie's diction causes no problems. She weaves a complex plot of interrelated mysteries and untangles them all to satisfaction. Some of the explanations we get may, to be sure, seem rather surprising, or even contrived, as that of Ursula's inconsistent behavior in the convent of St. Frances, or when we learn of Ulrica's crush on Gustavus just after we have witnessed her cruelty to his mother and sisters. Readers may also raise an eyebrow at the puzzling reference to an "unexpected interview," supposedly interrupting Ulrica's "power of utterance" in chapter two of the third volume (222). As there is no interview or conversation to which the phrase could possibly refer, and as the preceding paragraph gives a clear impression of being a summary, we must conclude that Mackenzie for some reason or other had to cut down her text at this point, leaving the gap imperfectly sewn together.

But these are minor lapses, and do not seriously interfere with our appreciation of her narrative. Like most women writing for a living at this time, Mackenzie wrote and published fast, and it was perhaps unavoidable that this would sometimes show in her texts. In general, she writes with verve and gusto, and she has a flair for concocting spectacular plots which would keep her readers happily on their toes until all the mysteries are resolved.

The "Gustavus Ericson" Tradition in History and Fiction

The reviewer for *The Critical Review* concludes his short comment by predicting that after its expected short span of popularity, *Swedish Mysteries* would "be forgotten," just "like its brethren." Insofar as the first vogue for gothic began to give way to other literary tastes in the early nineteenth century, the reviewer can of course be said to have been right. Before that happened, though, *Swedish Mysteries* seems to have inspired, more or less directly, several new versions of the Gustavus Ericson story, for which Mackenzie ought to receive her due credit.

The story of the young nobleman who was elected king of Sweden after defeating the Danish king Christian II in the early sixteenth century, and who subsequently brought about the Lutheran Reformation in Sweden, was already well known in Mackenzie's Britain. It had been retold throughout the whole eighteenth century, not only in fictional dramatizations for the stage but also in a number of more or less imaginative histories, written in English as well as other European languages. The British interest in Gustavus Ericson was, as Margaret Omberg has pointed out, largely a consequence of the popularity enjoyed by his grandson, Gustavus Adolphus. The latter's fame as a "champion of European Protestantism" helped to draw attention to the elder Gustavus, who was generally hailed for having "not only liberated Sweden from Denmark but the Swedish Church from the power of Rome" (21-22).

In recent historiography, the view of Gustavus Ericson is that of a rather typical Renaissance prince aspiring to absolutist rule—tough-minded, quite brutal in enforcing his will, and prepared to strike hard against former allies if it suited his purposes. Hence whereas the epithet "tyrant" has traditionally been reserved for the deposed king Christian in Swedish historiography, Gustavus Ericson may in the view of later historians like Lars-Olof Larsson have been quite well qualified for that title himself. Yet this was not how he appeared in the older historiographic tradition that began to emerge already during his own life, and which was probably partly based on the king's own words as dictated to his first chronicler Peder Swart. In this tradition, which lasted well into the twentieth century, Gustavus is portrayed as a benevolent paternal figure, caring for his people and the good of his country; in particular, his adventures as a young man hiding from king Christian's troops in Dalecarlia have long been part of the romantic lore cherished by this tradition. Nor was this idealizing view a feature of Swedish historiography only: most of the fictional and nonfictional accounts of his life written in English as well as other languages tended to glorify the person and achievement of Gustavus.

Of the more influential histories available in English can be mentioned Samuel Pufendorf's *The Compleat History of Sweden*, translated into English from the German in 1702. Pufendorf held a position as national historiographer in Sweden for a few years in the late seventeenth century, yet how far his several works on Swedish history influenced Mackenzie or, indeed, the perhaps most well-known writer on Swedish history in eighteenth-century Britain, the French abbot René Aubert de Vertot, is difficult to say. Vertot's *History of the Revolutions in Sweden*, published in French in 1695 and translated into English the following year, was reissued in numerous new editions throughout the eighteenth century. Yet when Sarah Scott wrote her already mentioned *History of Gustavus Ericson, King of Sweden*, she polemicizes in her preface against Vertot whom she apparently did not always find quite reliable, drawing instead on Pufendorf's *Introductio ad Historiam Sueciæ* as well as a number of other sources, most of them in Latin (Scott, xiii-xiv). That Mackenzie, with her "confined education," should have consulted these Latin sources does not appear very likely, but it seems beyond doubt that she included information from Vertot, and most likely Scott as well, when drawing up the plot for *Swedish Mysteries*.

At the time Mackenzie was writing, there were also at least two plays in English centering on Gustavus Ericson's revolution: Catharine Trotter's *The Revolution of Sweden: A Tragedy* (1706) and Henry Brooke's *Gustavus Vasa, the Deliverer of his Country: A Tragedy* (1739). The latter had been banned from the stage under the Licensing Act of 1737 but was nonetheless—or perhaps precisely for this reason—reprinted numerous times throughout the eighteenth century. That Mackenzie knew Brooke's tragedy seems quite clear, as there are obvious loans from it in her novel.[9] Whereas *Swedish Mysteries* seems to be the first prose novel dealing with Gustavus Vasa and the Swedish Revolution, yet another play appeared only a few years later, when William Dimond's *The Hero of the North* was performed in February 1803. It was taken up again in 1810, apparently with no changes except for the title which was now given as *Gustavus Vasa, the Hero of the North*, and the subtitle "An Historical Opera" added to the printed edition of the following year (Omberg, 30-31).

In her insightful discussion of these three plays and their indebtedness to Vertot and to each other, Omberg comments on the striking difference between Dimond's opera and the works that came before it. For while Trotter's and Brooke's ambition seems to have been to dramatize on stage the history of the Swedish revolution with at least a token degree of faithfulness to the account given by Vertot, Dimond's "melodramatic plot" relies on a "gallery of largely fictitious characters" and seems initially to have "little relation" even to Brooke's play (32). Yet if we consider Mackenzie's *Swedish Mysteries* in relation to these plays, we will find that many of the elements mentioned by Omberg as new to Dimond's *Hero of the North* may well be loans from Mackenzie's *Hero of the Mines*. The blizzard in the opening scene and other stereotyped touches of local color, the traveling patriots finding a shelter from the storm in the cottage of an honest miner, the romantic connection between Gustavus and the daughter of his old friend and teacher, and the confinement of a young woman in a convent are just some of the elements that Dimond seems to have taken over from Mackenzie. Omberg notes Gustavus's transformation into a "man of feeling" in Dimond, evident not only in his role as lover but also in his "unusual reaction to the carnage of the battlefield" (33); this is likewise a conspicuous feature of *Swedish Mysteries*, where the hero "lament[s] the misfortune" of the Danish soldiers who happen to fall victim to his own troops (93). That Dimond's Gustavus is "no rebel leader but a dispossessed king," as Omberg observes (33), may also come from Mackenzie's novel, where the hero is consistently represented as "the lawful heir to Sweden's Crown" (57). Hence, even though as Omberg notes, a closer look reveals a number of instances where Dimond seems after all indebted to Brooke (33), there is still enough evidence to suggest that *Swedish Mysteries* may be the missing link between Brooke and Dimond. That Dimond in other circumstances is known to have "us[ed] the work of other writers freely" would only seem to corroborate this assumption (Omberg 39n42).[10]

Nor was Dimond's opera the last to celebrate the growing myth of Gustavus Ericson. In 1813 appeared the first books of an epic poem called *Gustavus Vasa*, by the seventeen-year-old William Sidney Walker. Begun on a grand scale but never finished, Walker's *Gustavus Vasa* does not, however, show any particular influence from Mackenzie, and he himself refers in his "Notes" to Vertot and Pufendorf as his major sources. But the fact that he began planning the poem at age eleven, as he says in his preface, gives yet another indication of the topicality of the Swedish revolution throughout the first decade of the nineteenth century. In 1821, moreover, appeared yet another novel on the same theme, *The Festival of Mora: A Romance*, written by Louisa Sidney Stanhope. Stanhope adds yet another set of fictitious subplots to the story, while at the same time taking care to reproduce the historical data known to her as faithfully as possible. Like Mackenzie she weaves her tale around a number of mysteries, which are, however, almost overshadowed by the excessive sentimentality and nationalistic overtones abounding in her narrative.

Historical Background

The historical background to *Swedish Mysteries* can be found in the turbulent and more than a century long period of the Kalmar Union, which did not formally come to an end until Gustavus Ericson acceded to the Swedish throne in 1523. The Kalmar Union was initiated in 1397 by Queen Margaret of Denmark and Norway, who in 1388 had also become queen of Sweden. When she stepped down in favor of her adopted son, a document was drawn up at the Swedish town of Kalmar, stating that Denmark, Sweden, and Norway should in future be permanently joined under one monarch. The union was to be based on federal principles: the monarch was to be elected, preferably from among the sons of the previous king, as was the established custom in Denmark and Sweden (Norway was already a hereditary country); and the three countries were to present a united front against common enemies, while preserving a certain degree of independence in administering their own affairs.[11]

Although the agenda behind the Kalmar Union was clearly to put an end to the conflicts that until then had raged within and between the Scandinavian countries, it did not take long until hostilities broke out again. Popular discontent with the oppressive regime of one of the union king's local representatives in Sweden triggered a major uprising in the 1430s. Yet the primary aim of the Swedish factions who on this and later occasions in the fifteenth century rebelled against the Danish union kings was not to abolish the union. Many of the leading families in Scandinavia owned large properties in more than one of the three countries, and rather than centering on issues of nationality, the controversies that arose tended to concern the distribution of power, whether between the monarchy and the privileged classes, or between the leading families themselves. Hence, although the opposition in Sweden from time to time proceeded to elect their own administrators (*Sw. riksföreståndare*) in lieu of the union king, and even made one of the administrators king of Sweden during three separate periods, recent historiographers tend to regard these conflicts as civil wars rather than as national wars of liberation.

It was not until 1501, when a group of leading Swedes rebelled against the Danish union king John (known as Hans in Danish), that support for the union began to wane among the Swedes and the revolt took on the character of a conflict between two separate countries.

King John died in 1513 and was succeeded in Denmark and Norway by his son Christian II, and in Sweden, where Sten Sture the Younger had been elected administrator the year before, the resistance to Danish sovereignty continued.[12] Though Sten himself does not figure in *Swedish Mysteries*, he is frequently alluded to, sometimes being referred to as "the Regent" (a translation of the Swedish title more or less equivalent to "administrator") and sometimes, incorrectly, as the "the lawful Monarch of Sweden" or its "martyred King" (6). Yet whatever his own aspirations may have been, Sten Sture was never elected king of Sweden. A controversial politician, his appointment to the post of administrator was largely due to the support he held among the peasantry, who in Sweden were politically independent to a degree not common in other European countries; but several members of the national council who formally appointed him remained suspicious of his political ambitions. Recent historians have seen Sten Sture as a clever politician, as hungry for power as most of his political enemies, but in Swedish post-1523 historiography, and especially in the romanticizing tradition prevailing in the nineteenth century, the younger Sture was idolized as a national hero. This, then, is also the picture we get of the deceased administrator in *Swedish Mysteries*.

The struggle for power between Sten Sture the Younger and

his political opponents in Sweden continued throughout Sten's time as administrator, alongside and intermingled with the ongoing conflict with Denmark. Among Sten's fiercest enemies was the archbishop Gustav Trolle (see *Swedish Mysteries* p. 134), who like most of the leading clergy at the time possessed considerable worldly and political power. Sten Sture accused the archbishop of conspiring with Christian II, and when the Danish king attacked Sweden in 1517, Sten charged Trolle with treason and had him deposed from his office and imprisoned. With the deposition of the archbishop, the conflict ostensibly took on the character of a war about religion—or at least this seems to be how Christian wanted it to appear when he renewed his attacks on Sweden. For, with support from the pope, Christian made the Danish archbishop excommunicate Sten Sture and his followers, and lay Sweden under an interdict.[13]

But worse was to come, as Christian continued his efforts to subdue the rebellious Swedes and overthrow the Sture party. Another attack on Sweden in the summer of 1518 failed, as Christian was defeated by Sten Sture's army outside Stockholm. The event has been remembered primarily because the hostages Christian demanded as a guarantee for his personal safety during a planned meeting with Sten Sture were treacherously abducted to Denmark. In retrospect the most famous among these hostages was the young nobleman Gustavus Ericson, like his fellow hostages probably taken prisoner because Christian hoped for an opportunity to persuade them to side with himself and the supporters of the union in the internal politics of Sweden, rather than support the Sture party. In volume one of *Swedish Mysteries*, Mackenzie makes her hero relate how he escaped from his relative Erik Eriksen Banner, under whose surveillance he had been staying at the castle of Kalø (Calo) in Denmark, and fled to Lübeck (Lubec), an account which seems to reproduce fairly faithfully the story as known by her time (see Vertot, 76-77, 87-89).

Of far more decisive import, however, was Christian's third attack on Sweden a little more than a year later, when Sten Sture's army was defeated and scattered outside Bogesund in Västergötland in January 1520, and the administrator himself mortally wounded. Following Sten's death a few days after the battle, the

Swedish national council negotiated with Christian and acknowledged him as king, and on 4 November 1520 he was crowned at Stockholm by Gustav Trolle, now reinstated as archbishop. The events that followed only a few days after the coronation have been remembered in Swedish history as the Stockholm Bloodbath and earned the new union king the byname Christian the Tyrant.

As part of the deal with the national council, Christian had agreed to a general amnesty and invited the Swedish nobility and leading members of the clergy to the coronation festivities in Stockholm, among which groups were found many of his former political opponents. On the fourth day of the celebrations, the doors to the castle were locked and archbishop Trolle read out an indictment accusing the deceased Sten Sture and his followers of heresy. An ad hoc tribunal was called, and almost a hundred people were executed in the square outside the castle, many of them citizens of Stockholm and their servants, but also two bishops who had supported the deposition of Trolle, and a number of other noblemen, among whom was Gustavus Ericson's father. The dead bodies were left in the square for a day or two before they were burnt in a great fire south of the city. Sten Sture's remains were disinterred and thrown into the same fire, and his widow was brought as a prisoner to Denmark, as were also Gustavus Ericson's mother and two of his younger sisters. Before Christian left Sweden after this massacre to return to Denmark, he made a tour of some of the major cities, executing former followers of Sten Sture as he went along. On passing the Cistercian monastery at Nydala in Småland, he had the Abbot and several monks drowned in a nearby lake, since he suspected them of supporting his political enemies. The event made it quite clear that, notwithstanding his previous shows of support for the Church of Rome, as far as Christian's ambitions for Sweden went, they were political and not religious.

It is in the wake of these traumatic events that Gustavus Ericson enters the scene of Swedish politics as a major figure, while trying to muster support for the rebellion against king Christian that would soon end the Kalmar union for good. At the time of the Stockholm massacre Gustavus Ericson was a young man, probably in his twenties. He and his parents had been closely allied with Sten Sture, to whom they were also related by family ties: the administrator's wife was the half-sister of Gustavus's mother. Having returned to Sweden from his Danish captivity after the death of Sture, Gustavus tried to win support for the resistance against Christian in the southern province of Småland and the city of Kalmar. Yet having failed there, and distrusting Christian's promise of amnesty, he did not attend the coronation at Stockholm but stayed hidden at one of his father's estates in Sudermania (Södermanland) until after the Bloodbath. It was only at the end of November 1520 that he traveled in disguise to Dalecarlia in the hope of persuading the population there to rebel against King Christian.

The main action of *Swedish Mysteries* takes place between Gustavus's arrival in Dalecarlia, where he would win his first adherents, and his ascendance to the throne as king of Sweden two years later. He did not meet with immediate success in Dalecarlia, but after the population of Mora (and not Hedemora, as Mackenzie mistakenly assumes) had decided to make him their captain, this village became the first hub of Dalecarlian resistance against Christian. After a successful attack on the Dalecarlian mining center, Kopparberget, the rebellion was underway. For the rest of the Dalecarlian section, Mackenzie draws liberally on the rich store of anecdotes that over time began to emerge around Gustavus's stay in Dalecarlia. Most of these stories concern the short period before the breakthrough at Mora, when Gustavus was still on the run from Christian's supporters. The incident of the richly embroidered collar that reveals the noble birth of its owner is part of the anecdotes recorded in Peder Swart's chronicle, and so is that of the treacherous Peterson whose wife helps the fugitive to escape his pursuers; yet Mackenzie changes the details in her novel by fictionalizing the characters involved.[14]

As Christian's reputation for tyranny grew, his remaining supporters in Sweden began to desert his cause by and by, and more rapidly so once the ever successful Gustavus had been elected Swedish administrator in August 1521. A number of major cities were taken by the insurgents during the following winter, but Stockholm and a few other cities on the Baltic coast remained under siege, supported from the sea by the Danish admiral Søren Norby operating from the island of Gothland. In this situation Gustavus sought and received help from Lübeck, the leading city in the Hanseatic League which at this time dominated the Baltic trade. The negotiations with Lübeck were partly conducted by Berend von Melen, commander of the German mercenary troops that went over from Christian to Gustavus early on in the campaign. Mackenzie uses the historical von Melen as the basis for a highly fictionalized character appearing in *Swedish Mysteries* under the name Sir Bernard Milan, while an all but identical form of his name—Van Melen—is given to the Dalecarlian peasant-*cum*-miner who rescues Gustavus from the snow storm in the opening scene.[15] The only incident involving Sir Bernard that bears any likeness to events related in historical sources is the scene in volume two where the forces newly arrived from Lübeck refuse to march under his command, demanding instead that Gustavus come down to Söderköping (Sundercoping) to take charge of the troops.[16]

In March 1523, after years of warfare, the situation changed suddenly as Christian was deposed by the Danish aristocracy and succeeded by his uncle. In this situation the Swedes called a meeting at Strängnäs and elected Gustavus their king on June 6, 1523. Two weeks later the Danish garrison in Stockholm gave up and the new king could enter the city in triumph on Midsummer Eve. During Gustavus's thirty-seven-year long reign that followed, Sweden was transformed into an independent state with a centralized modern administration and a strong monarchy, made hereditary at the instigation of Gustavus. The transformation was by no means an altogether smooth process, and Gustavus who proved to be a tough ruler fought down several domestic rebellions during his years in power. The Lutheran reformation of Sweden began a few years into his reign, and although the reform was unpopular with many of his subjects, it helped Gustavus to strengthen the power of the crown by reducing the influence of the Roman Church, and to pay off his debt to Lübeck by confiscating Church property.

Swedish Mysteries *as Literary Gothic*

Readers in Mackenzie's Britain would have thought of *Swedish Mysteries* as a "gothic" novel simply because it dealt with so-called Gothic times. But for readers in the twenty-first century, to whom the term "gothic" is more likely to connote a heterogeneous but compelling literary genre than a historical epoch, the gothicism of *Swedish Mysteries* resides above all in the thematic and stylistic characteristics we now associate with early gothic of the first wave. The fictional worlds in these narratives are invariably haunted by the anxieties of the society that produced them: most jarringly the fears of a relapse into the barbarous and oppressive practices of a past just recently escaped from, but also the growing unease about what new terrors might be held in store by the modern age. Mackenzie's novel is no exception, and in using the story of the young Gustavus Ericson as the basis for her novel, she is able to explore these contemporary fears without "alarming the timid" by including supernatural elements, which practice she had so vehemently objected to in her preface to *Mysteries Elucidated*. Instead she holds the attention of her readers by weaving a complex web of mysteries and historical drama; but while the mysteries are all solidly of this world and punctiliously elucidated at the end, it needs to be stressed again that many of the so-called "historical anecdotes" on which she bases her plot are highly imaginative, for Mackenzie stretches her license to invent fictitious characters and events to the very limit.

The mysteries pertaining to the birth and subsequent fate of Mackenzie's character Catherine Sleswic is a case in point. A supposed orphan, Catherine is secretly in love with Gustavus, who however has eyes for no one but her friend Sigismunda, daughter of Catherine's guardian Marienburg. Despite Gustavus's professed feelings, his old friend and mentor Marienburg mysteriously insists that he marry Catherine rather than Sigismunda, and his reasons are only gradually revealed to us during the course of the second and third volumes. For it appears that Catherine is the daughter of Marienburg's sister by Magnus, Duke of Saxe Lunenburgh; yet due to the plotting of a rejected suitor of her mother's, Sir Gormund, her parents were separated before her birth, and her mother abducted to a convent and forced to take the veil when Catherine was still a baby. Mackenzie's representation of the nun St. Alexa who eventually turns out to be Catherine's mother seems to owe not a little to Radcliffe's Olivia in *The Italian* (1797), notwithstanding her ambivalence towards this writer voiced in her preface to *Mysteries Elucidated*. *The Italian*, with its abundance of mysterious monks glimpsed in shady ruins or cathedral cloisters, may also have inspired the scene at the end of *Swedish Mysteries* where Duke Magnus, walking through Stockholm, is approached by "a dark and slowly moving figure emerging from a low door, leading to a side aisle of the Cathedral" (274). "Its height, although diminished by a bend of the shoulders, the groan it uttered as it closed the iron door, its black drapery, and musing melancholy attitude" captures the attention of the Duke, who soon discovers him to be "a Friar of one of the most rigid orders Stockholm contained" (274).[17] Needless to say, the mystery is swiftly explained as the friar turns out to be the once wicked Sir Gormund, now repentant and anxious to set things right by confessing his sins. Having in this manner reinstated Catherine to her proper social position and made Sigismunda die a tragic death, Mackenzie is free to marry Catherine to Gustavus at the end of the novel, presumably hoping thus to align her invented story with historical facts. However, her fictitious Catherine has nothing but the name in common with the historical Gustavus Ericson's first wife, Catherine of Sachsen-Lauenburg.[18]

This brief account of the mysteries relating to Catherine's supposed orphanhood should be enough to show Mackenzie's skill in creating sensational plots out of the traditional sets and props of gothic fiction. It is evident that her expertise is more in the traditional conventions of the genre than in any intimate knowledge of Sweden, for the dashes of local color she provides are clichéd and often inaccurate, and her notions of geography seem likewise a little shaky (see the explanatory notes). In portraying the locals, she resorts—when not dealing with her major characters—to ethnic stereotyping in much the same way as did the reviewer for *The Critical Review*. The miner's wife Mrs. Van Melen is, for instance, "like many others in the frigid zone," said to be "in the constant habit of drinking spirits" (12), which propensity also shows in her outer appearance: "Her aspect was heavy, and her manner exhibited neither wonder nor compassion." Mackenzie also draws on Vertot and Brooke for apparent local color, setting her opening scene among the mines of Dalecarlia, where Gustavus Ericson arrives in disguise to muster support for his uprising against Christian. In contrast to her precedents, however, Mackenzie introduces a note of lurking terror as her hero seeks shelter in "an old copper-mine, long since disused" (7), for he soon concludes, on inspecting "the rugged walls of his retreat" and "the impending ruins that nodded above," that their "threatening aspect seemed to forbid his stay" (9).

Perhaps this is the scene that makes Frederick S. Frank refer to *Swedish Mysteries* as a "subterranean Schauerroman," a novel of the type that promises "[h]orrendous incidents in an underground of no return including the imminent possibility of live burial" (221-222). This characterization of Mackenzie's novel is however rather misleading; for once the author has set the tone of latent terror in the opening scene, the narrative quickly moves on from subterranean Dalecarlia to other settings, leaving Mackenzie free to explore a spectrum of gothic conventions more specifically concerned with such horrors as, it was felt, ought rightly to belong to a barbarous past.

One of the most common themes in gothic fiction, from Horace Walpole's *The Castle of Otranto* (1764) onwards, is the threat of sexual assault that tends to hang over the heroines, and from which they are saved, if lucky, by a more considerate suitor. While this theme is by no means unique to the gothic, it has nonetheless a clear bearing on the genre. For by contrasting the libertine would-be rapist with the much preferred sentimental lover, these novels—often written by women—in fact make a statement in favor of modernity. The libertine rake, once a popular character in the aristocratic culture of restoration drama, becomes in gothic fiction an icon of the feudal past, a period when heartless tyrants were free to exercise their arbitrary power over their hapless subordinates. In contrast, the sentimental hero is made to stand for a new ideal of manliness, more suited to a modern and enlightened age—an ideal where self-will and brute force are replaced by sympathy and consideration, and where moral virtues are as highly valued as noble birth or prominent connections.[19]

Hence, it is no coincidence that Mackenzie makes Christian a libertine and Gustavus a sentimental hero in *Swedish Mysteries*. Sigismunda, said to be "dearer than life itself" to Gustavus (15), becomes the object of Christian's "infamous design" (40). When she rejects his proposals, he resorts to "terror" as the only way to achieve his goal, and professes "his natural bias to revenge, declaring, that whoever incurred it by an opposition to his will, should be, and were, when opportunity assisted, the certain subjects of it" (41). Gustavus on the other hand is represented as the typical sentimental lover, for large parts of the novel on the brink of abandoning his military campaign against Christian for the sake of assisting his damsel in distress. When at a crucial point in the narrative Gustavus finds his beloved Sigismunda dying from starvation and neglect in a convent to which she has been abducted, he behaves quite according to protocol: we are told how "a film came over his terror-struck eyes" at the sight of her condition, "his senses failed, and the great Gustavus sunk helpless by the side of his lost, his murdered love!" (179).

Yet if Mackenzie's Gustavus outshines King Christian in modernity when it comes to the cultivation of feelings and the right attitude to women, this is nothing compared to his purported progressivism in religious questions. In *Swedish Mysteries*, as in most British gothic fiction written from an expressly pro-Protestant perspective, anti-Catholicism is a major theme; for even though the reformation movements in both Sweden and England had as much to do with politics as with religion, in Protestant propaganda the rites and practices of the Roman Church were soon becoming associated with a backward and oppressive past. As it was the historical Gustavus Ericson who enforced the Protestant reformation in Sweden, albeit not until several years into his reign, Mackenzie makes her hero a fervent Lutheran who vigorously challenges the alleged superstition and bigotry of the Catholic Church. For Gustavus, we read, "was a *Christian* on the purest principle, and had already meditated the establishment of Luther's doctrines as soon as he should be authorized by regal power to support and mildly enforce them" (171). In contrast, many of the villains in the novel are deeply involved with such Catholic forces as, we are told, "conceived themselves justified in defeating, by every possible means, the pious endeavours of enlightened men" (45).

Gothic fiction tends generally to dwell less on the merits of Protestantism than on the supposed corruption of Catholicism, the latter topic clearly yielding more opportunities for writers to concoct spectacular or frightening episodes. *Swedish Mysteries* is no exception, for Mackenzie has her characters routinely condemn the "foppery, glare, and superstition of the Romish Church," its "superfluous ornaments, unessential ceremonies, and [. . .] anathemas [. . .] hurled against those who could not afford to pay for sinning" (217). Moreover, as we have seen, she also follows the convention that represents Catholic convents as covert detention centers, where innocent victims are imprisoned at the will of their enemies. The threat of confinement in St. Croix hanging over Catherine in the first volume materializes with a vengeance for her fellow-sisters at St. Frances later in the novel. If they are not, as Sigismunda, locked up in a dungeon and starved to death at the instigation of a jealous rival, they are, as her co-sufferer St. Alexa, forced to take the veil against their will—"dragged to the altar" when "weakened and exhausted by monastic rigours, which extended even to merciless flagellations" (257).

To readers familiar with the horrors threatening the protagonist at the end of Matthew Lewis's *The Monk*, the drawn-out episode where King Christian orders Gustavus's mother and sisters to be burnt to death at the stake, "laden with the heaviest chains," may well have suggested an auto-da-fé arranged by the Inquisition (74).[20] Yet Christian's dominant trait of personality in Mackenzie's novel is not so much his allegiance to Catholicism as his unparalleled "barbarous despotism" and "tyrannic cruelty" (5-6), which is said to affect the whole population of Sweden. "Not a Swede whose property, principles, or situation could excite the envy, jealousy, or avarice of the invader, but suffered in various instances," laments the indignant Gustavus (56-57). Christian's followers apparently take after their master, for his "marauding Danes" are said to commit "the most cruel excesses in several undefended villages, inhabited by peasants of the poorest and most helpless description" (171). The murders of the monks at St. Frances, an episode probably inspired by the killings at Nydala in 1521, is just one of the example of random brutality Mackenzie lists to demonize Christian's regime.

For Christian is represented as a "detestable usurper" (16) said to have "usurped the lineal succession of Sweden [. . .] and *murdered* its Monarch" (13). Usurpation had by this time become a standard motif in literary gothic,[21] and Mackenzie seems just to have taken over and used to her advantage Brooke's disparaging the Danish king as the "Usurper of *Sweden*" in his tragedy.[22] Historically, her version of the story is of course not quite correct, as Christian had been formally recognized as king of Sweden by the Swedish national council; nor was there any "lineal succession" to usurp, as Sweden was not a hereditary kingdom at this time. But Mackenzie is not a stickler for detail; representing Christian as a usurper helps her to lionize Gustavus as "the just heir to those kingdoms that were usurped by his bitterest enemy" (23). As already noted, the idea that Gustavus Ericson should have any hereditary claims to the Swedish throne seems to be Mackenzie's own invention, probably inspired by Gustavus's kinship with the younger Sture.[23] Yet though incorrect, this idea was later repeated by both Dimond, in whose play Gustavus is referred to as "king" of the Swedes (Act I.i), and by Stanhope, who consistently refers to him as "the royal Gustavus" (I, 2ff).

Mackenzie's demonising of Christian and hailing Gustavus as "the lawful heir to Sweden's Crown" seems in many ways to duplicate a story she had told with great success before, in her 1790 novel *Monmouth*. In that novel she champions the Protestant duke of Monmouth, natural son of Charles II and, in Mackenzie's view, rightful claimant to the British throne after the death of his father. The novel gives us Mackenzie's highly romanticized version of Monmouth's short-lived and unsuccessful rebellion against his Catholic uncle, James II, in 1685. Her unequivocal backing of the Protestant candidate against his Catholic antagonist clearly shows the extent to which she partakes in the dominant discourse favoring established state Protestantism that informed the political climate in post-1688 Britain. It is the same discourse that informs her narrative of political events in sixteenth-century Sweden, for when she reverses the Monmouth situation and presents her readers with a pretender to the Swedish throne explicitly denounced as false, this claimant is not only generally wicked and corrupt but also linked with the Catholic forces in the novel.[24]

Mackenzie probably based her character of Fitzer on the historical "Daljunkern" (the term means "the young man from Dalecarlia"). For claiming to be Sten Sture's son Nils, Daljunkern got the support of the Dalecarlians for an uprising against King Gustavus in 1527, and Fitzer, likewise claiming to be Sture's son, is at the end of the novel said to be in Dalecarlia at the head of "a powerful insurrection" (299). Like his historical model, Mackenzie's Fitzer is said to belong in the Catholic camp (cf. Vertot, 226): his aunt is the Abbess of a convent, used by the nephew as a handy prison for people he temporarily wants out of the way. Fitzer introduces his prospective detainees to his aunt as "secret favourers of the doctrine of the Reformation" in order to ensure their "rigorous" treatment (45). That such a person should be the rightful heir to "the murdered King," as Mackenzie chooses to call Sten Sture, is obviously unthinkable in the stereotyped system of religious values that informs her text. Hence, as speedily as the historical Gustavus Ericson dismissed the purported Nils Sture as an impostor, as expressly does Mackenzie make the falsity of Fitzer's pretensions a basic premise of her narrative.[25]

But even if Mackenzie mobilizes the traditional religious stereotypes of gothic fiction to distinguish between her ruthless usurpers, false pretenders and lawful claimants to the throne in sixteenth-century Sweden, it helps her only so far in championing the Swedish "Revolution," as Gustavus's uprising against Christian was often called. For from the mid-1790s, a set of new and more acute worries had also begun to loom large on the horizon of the British reading public. As Robert Miles has discussed, the Terror in France would have evoked memories of similar violence in Britain's past history, which no more than the French Revolution could be blamed on Catholicism or the political interests of the Roman Church. The Civil War and the execution of Charles I in the mid-seventeenth century, and the more recent Gordon riots in London and Bath in 1780 are significant examples ("The 1790s," 55).

Mackenzie is clearly aware that her readers might get the wrong associations when reading about Gustavus's revolution, and she leaves no stone unturned to assure her readers that *her* hero is by no means to be associated with either the revolutionary violence reported from France or the Protestant excesses of the British Civil War. Her account of the 1520 "massacres" at Stockholm seems clearly designed to remind her readers of the executions reported from France a few years earlier—the streets "echoing the shrieks and groans of unhappy senators and their mourning relatives"

(216). Yet, as this is so obviously an event where Gustavus and his family are the sufferers rather than the perpetrators, the horrors described do not reflect negatively on the future king. Quite to the contrary, when Gustavus turns up in Dalecarlia a fugitive from Danish captivity at the beginning of the novel, he is explicitly referred to as an "unhappy emigrant" (5), a term which to an English reader in 1801 would immediately have suggested one of the many refugees seeking a safe haven in Britain from the revolutionary violence in France.

In her effort to exempt Gustavus from all association with excessive revolutionary violence, Mackenzie's rhetoric comes very close to that of the conservative Whig politician Edmund Burke, who lamented the extinction in France of "the old feudal and chivalrous spirit of *Fealty*" in his 1790 *Reflections on the Revolution in France* (78). This ideal state is contrasted to the "anarchy" recently exhibited in revolutionary France, where "[l]aws [are] overturned; tribunals subverted; industry without vigour" and "the people impoverished" (39). Yet, as we are told that the "loyal patriot" Gustavus is permeated with

> the love of liberty;—[but] not *that* which gives to rapine, sacrilege, and murder their diabolical powers of action—[and] not *that* which tears asunder the beautiful tie that binds an affectionate people to their lawful Sovereign—nor *that* which plucks from contented poverty its little earnings, perverts the decision of justice, and makes the decrees of a wise legislator subservient to its own nefarious purposes (8),

we are apparently meant to rest assured that his is a revolution conceived entirely under the auspices of Burke's spirit of fealty.

The revolutionary violence in France left quite an imprint on gothic fiction in the 1790s. It was widely believed in conservative circles in Europe at the time that the French Revolution was the result of a secret conspiracy by political radicals, bred by the Enlightenment, and that there were secret societies in both Germany and England clandestinely plotting against governments and established religion, whether Protestant or Catholic.[26] Despite—or perhaps because of—such sinister apprehensions, secret societies became a favourite topic in German horror tales; translated into English, these tales became popular also among British readers of gothic and spawned quite a number of followers. Mackenzie was quick to capitalise on the popularity of this trend, and possibly inspired by James Boaden's play *The Secret Tribunal* (1795) she represents a number of her characters in *Swedish Mysteries* as members or otherwise associated with the so-called "Free Judges" of a mysterious "Secret Tribunal." In contrast to her vehement incrimination of Roman Catholicism, however, Mackenzie does not seem to have a clear ideological agenda when dealing with this theme; for even though almost all of the main characters except Gustavus are at some point threatened by a summons to the Tribunal (whether fake or not), the characters represented as actually belonging to that institution tend to stay aloof from the worst villainy exemplified in the novel. Hence it appears that the hyper-secret Free Judges are mainly included to sound the background note of unspecified but portentous terror in Mackenzie's so-called historical romance; but the fact that they *are* there places her narrative solidly in the later phase of the first wave of British gothic fiction beginning in the late 1790s.

And that is why *Swedish Mysteries* is so solidly a *British* novel. For although there were indeed several works in English dealing with the career of Gustavus Ericson by Mackenzie's time, and although all of them perhaps to some extent reflected domestic and contemporary British concerns, Mackenzie's novel remains an unusually clear example of the way gothic fiction of late 1790s Britain can be read as an index of current anxieties existing very much then and there.

JANINA NORDIUS
Göteborg

March 15, 2008

ABOUT THE EDITOR

JANINA NORDIUS is Associate Professor of English literature at the University of Gothenburg. She has published *"I Am Myself Alone": Solitude and Transcendence in John Cowper Powys,* as well as articles on various topics including Gothic and colonial fiction.

NOTES

1 I use the English name form Gustavus Ericson when referring to the Swedish king Gustav. The patronymic Eriksson (Ericson) was the form generally used during his own life, whereas his family name Vasa began to be used by historiographers from the late sixteenth century.

2 The notion that the Goths originated from Sweden occurs as early as in Olaus Magnus's *Historia de Gentibus Septentrionalibus* (*History of the Nordic Peoples*, 1555).

3 Neither "Johanson Kidderslaw" nor the inverted form of the name has been found in Swedish bibliographies. (Johanson would not be used as a first name in Swedish.) Nor is there any evidence of there having been an English grammar school in Uppsala during or before Mackenzie's time.

4 To my knowledge, there are no more than a handful of copies of the 1801 edition still extant. A search of world libraries turned up only the copies at the British Library, Corvey Collection, Yale University Library, and University of Alberta.

5 *Burton-Wood* (1783), *Joseph* (1783), *The Gamesters* (1786), *Retribution* (1788), *Calista* (1789), *Monmouth* (1790), *Danish Massacre* (1791), *Slavery* (1792), *Mysteries Elucidated* (1795), *The Neapolitan* (1796), *Dusseldorf* (1798), *Feudal Events* (1800), *Swedish Mysteries* (1801), *Martin and Mansfeldt* (1802), and *The Irish Guardian* (1809). Montague Summers lists 16 titles in *A Gothic Bibliography* (London: Fortune Press, 1941), leaving out *Joseph* but adding *Almeira D'Aviero* (1811), which appears to be only another title for *The Irish Guardian*, and also *Orlando and Lavinia* (1792), which title is however not attributed to Mackenzie in the British Library's Integrated Catalogue, nor in the English Short Title Catalogue.

6 For Austen's praise of Burney's *Cecilia* (1782) and *Camilla* (1796), and Edgeworth's *Belinda* (1801), see chapter 5 of *Northanger Abbey*; for the "horrid" novels, see chapter 6.

7 *A Gossip's Story* and *A Tale of the Times* went through at least three editions, and *The Saracen* and *Plain Sense* at least two.

8 *Calista* (1789) was praised in *The Critical Review*, and *Slavery* (1792) and *Mysteries Elucidated* (1795) in *The Monthly Review*, according to McMullen (206).

9 The name Augusta for Gustavus's mother seems to be a loan from Brooke, as do Mackenzie's two re-workings of the "testing of Gusta-

vus" scene, mentioned by Omberg as Brooke's addition to the story (26-27). In one, Christian threatens to execute his mother and sisters if Gustavus continues obstinate during his Danish captivity (1: 62); in the other, it is Gustavus's friend Marienburg who has to choose between saving Augusta and her daughters, or saving Gustavus and the revolution (1: 84-86).

10 The remark concerns a comment made by Dimond in his preface to *The Doubtful Son* (1810), where he admits to borrowing freely from Beaumarchais.

11 The content and validity of the Union document have however been debated among later historiographers.

12 Although not belonging to the Sture family, Sten Svantesson took the name Sture in order to share some of the goodwill enjoyed by a previous administrator called by that name.

13 Laying Sweden under an interdict meant prohibiting all religious offices to be performed in the country.

14 Swart's chronicle was probably written while Gustavus was still alive, and it is believed that the king himself may have taken an active part in its composition. Although not published until 1870, the chronicle was according to Omberg known in manuscript form much earlier (37n15), and may thus have been available to Vertot, who also relates these anecdotes (118, 122-124).

15 The name of the German commander varies in the historical accounts available at the time: Swart (whom Mackenzie would presumably not have read in the original) calls him "Bern van Melen" (50); Pufendorf uses the name "Bernard de Melen" (177), and Vertot that of "Bernard de Milan" (155).

16 The episode is mentioned by Swart (50), Vertot (167-168) and Scott (189).

17 Cf. the assassin gliding about the cathedral in the opening section of Radcliffe's *The Italian*, and the mysterious monk appearing at Paluzzi in the novel's first chapter.

18 The historical Catherine of Sachsen-Lauenburg was indeed the daughter of a Duke Magnus, but she did not grow up a supposed orphan in Sweden, and had never met Gustavus Ericson prior to their wedding in 1531.

19 For a discussion of shifting ideals of manliness, see Philip Carter, "An 'Effeminate' or 'Efficient' Nation? Masculinity and Eighteenth-Century Social Documentary," *Textual Practice* 11, no. 3 (1997): 429-443.

20 In the last chapter of *The Monk* (1796), Ambrosio learns that his accomplice Matilda "must expiate her crime in fire on the approaching

Auto da Fé," and "shudder[s]" himself "at the approaching Auto da Fé, at the idea of perishing in flames" (425).

21 For examples of gothic usurpers, see, *e.g.*, Walpole's *The Castle of Otranto* (1764), Clara Reeve's *The Old English Baron* (1777), and Radcliffe's *The Castles of Athlin and Dunbayne* (1789).

22 See Brooke's list of characters.

23 Mackenzie may be taking her cue from Brooke but adding the usurpation-succession motif to his story. For although Brooke does not make Gustavus a legitimate "heir" to the throne, he calls him "first Cousin to the deceased King" in his list of characters, the "deceased King" apparently referring—incorrectly—to Sture.

24 To British readers, Mackenzie's introduction of the pretender theme would presumably have evoked memories of the two Jacobite rebellions in 1715 and 1745; yet her treatment of it clearly suggests her unwillingness to condone the appropriation of Gustavus Vasa as a Jacobite icon common in certain circles at the time, as revealingly discussed by Niall MacKenzie in "Some British Writers and Gustavus Vasa," *Studia Neophilologica* 78 (2006): 63-80.

25 Both Vertot (224ff) and Scott (270) assume that the man who claimed to be the late administrator's son was a false pretender. This remained the established view for a long time, although recent evidence seems to suggest that he may indeed have been Nils Sture (see Larsson, *Gustav Vasa*, 161).

26 See, *e.g.*, John Robison, *Proofs of a Conspiracy against all the Religions and Governments of Europe, Carried on in the Secret Meetings of Free Masons, Illuminati, and Reading Societies* . . . (London: T. Cadell and W. Davies, 1797).

WORKS CITED AND CONSULTED

Part of this introduction appeared, in an earlier version, in Janina Nordius, "Gustavus Vasa in a Gothic Mirror: Anna Maria Mackenzie's *Swedish Mysteries,*" *Moderna Språk* 101, no. 1 (2007): 9-22. My main sources for the historical background to Gustavus Ericson and his time, in the introduction and the explanatory notes, are two books by Lars-Olof Larsson, *Kalmarunionens tid*, 2nd ed. (Stockholm: Prisma, 2003) and *Gustav Vasa: Landsfader eller tyrann?*, 2nd ed. (Stockholm: Prisma, 2005). Neither of these has so far been translated into English. For details concerning especially the older history of Scandinavia and Germany, I have also occasionally consulted an early edition of a Swedish standard encyclopedia, *Nordisk Familjebok*, 2nd ed. (Stockholm, 1904-26), as well as the *Encyclopædia Britannica Online* (2007). For definitions of words and phrases in the explanatory notes I have when needed turned to the *Oxford English Dictionary Online* (2007). Other cited works are listed below.

Blakey, Dorothy. *The Minerva Press 1790-1820*. London: The Bibliographical Society, 1939 [for 1935].

Brooke, Henry. *Gustavus Vasa, the Deliverer of his Country: A Tragedy. As it was to have been acted at the Theatre-Royal in Drury Lane.* London: R. Dodsley . . . , 1739.

Burke, Edmund. *Reflections on the Revolution in France*. 1790. Oxford: Oxford University Press, 1993.

Carter, Philip. "An 'Effeminate' or 'Efficient' Nation? Masculinity and Eighteenth-Century Social Documentary." *Textual Practice* 11, no. 3 (1997): 429-443.

Dimond, William. *The Hero of the North: An Historical Play*. London: Barker, 1803. New ed. *Gustavus Vasa, the Hero of the North: An Historical Opera*. London: Barker, 1811.

Frank, Frederick S. *The First Gothics: A Critical Guide to the English Gothic Novel*. New York: Garland, 1987.

Mackenzie, Anna Maria. Preface to *The Irish Guardian, or, Errors of Eccentricity*. London: Longman, Hurst, Rees, and Orme, 1809.

———. "To the Readers of Modern Romance." In *Gothic Readings:*

The First Wave, 1764-1840, ed. Rictor Norton. London: Leicester University Press, 2000, 27-30.

MacKenzie, Niall. "Some British Writers and Gustavus Vasa." *Studia Neophilologica* 78 (2006): 63-80.

McMullen, Lorraine. Entry for "Mackenzie, Anna Maria." In *A Dictionary of British and American Women Writers 1660-1800*, ed. Janet Todd. London: Methuen, 1987.

Magnus, Olaus. *Historia de Gentibus Septentrionalibus*. Rome, 1555.

Miles, Robert. *Ann Radcliffe: The Great Enchantress*. Manchester: Manchester University Press, 1995.

———. "The 1790s: The Effulgence of Gothic." In *The Cambridge Companion to Gothic Fiction*, ed. Jerrold E. Hogle. Cambridge: Cambridge University Press, 2002.

Naubert, Benedikte. *Herman of Unna: A Series of Adventures of the Fifteenth Century* . . . . Written in German by Professor Kramer. 3rd ed. 3 vols. London: Robinson, 1796.

Omberg, Margaret. "Gustavus Vasa and the Myth of the Mines." *Studia Neophilologica* 67 (1995): 21-39.

Pufendorf, Samuel. *The Compleat History of Sweden, From Its Origin to this Time*. London: Joseph Wild, 1702.

Robison, John. *Proofs of a Conspiracy against all the Religions and Governments of Europe, Carried on in the Secret Meetings of Free Masons, Illuminati, and Reading Societies* . . . . London: T. Cadell and W. Davies, 1797.

Scott, Sarah. *The History of Gustavus Ericson, King of Sweden: With an Introductory History of Sweden, from the Middle of the Twelfth Century.* By Henry Augustus Raymond [pseud.]. London: A. Millar, 1761.

Stanhope, Louisa Sidney. *The Festival of Mora: A Romance*. 4 vols. London: John Richardson, 1821.

Summers, Montague. *A Gothic Bibliography*. London: Fortune Press, 1941.

———. *The Gothic Quest*. 1938. London: Fortune Press, 1968.

Swart, Peder. *Konung Gustaf I's Krönika*, ed. Nils Edén. Stockholm: Ljus, 1912.

Review of *Swedish Mysteries; or, Hero of the Mines: A Tale*. Translated from a Swedish Manuscript, by Johansson Kidderslaw. *The Critical Review* 34 (April 1802): 476.

Trotter, Catharine. *The Revolution of Sweden: A Tragedy*. London, 1706.

Vertot D'Aubeuf, René Aubert de. *The History of the Revolutions in Sweden, Occasioned by the Change of Religion, and Alteration of the Government in that Kingdom*. Done into English by J. Mitchel. 1696. 7th ed., London: A. Ward, E. Curll, J. and P. Knapton, T. Longman, J. Brindley, C. Hitch, C. Cobbett, R. Caldwell, R. Wellington, and J. New, 1743.

Walker, William Sidney. *Gustavus Vasa, and Other Poems*. London; Longman, Hurst, Rees, Orme, and Brown, 1813.

NOTE ON THE TEXT

This is the second edition of Anna Maria Mackenzie's *Swedish Mysteries, or Hero of the Mines*. It is based on the text of the first edition, published in three volumes as a fictitious translation from an anonymous Swedish author at William Lane's Minerva Press in 1801. With the exception of the few alterations indicated below, the new edition retains Mackenzie's idiosyncratic style and often inconsistent spelling and punctuation.

The 1801 edition contains quite a few printer's errors, the most conspicuous being the faulty pagination of twenty-four pages in volume three, and the misnumbering of one of the chapters (chapter four) in volume two. In addition to these mishaps, there are also a number of minor errors in the text proper (missing or obviously faulty letters, quotation marks or punctuation, and in one case a missing preposition) that seem clearly to be typographical rather than authorial. These have been silently corrected in the present edition. I have also replaced the running quotation marks in the left margin, used in the chapter epigraphs, with the standard opening and closing quotation marks used in modern texts.

The spelling has been regularized in the cases of two proper names. King Christian's queen is thus called Blanch throughout, as this is how her name is mostly spelled in the 1801 text, with the exception of a section in volume two where she is Blanche with a final e. Likewise, Duke Magnus and his dukedom have consistently been spelled Lunenburgh, which is the far most frequent spelling in the first edition, although volumes two and three occasionally have the variant spelling Lunenburg, without the final h. In one place in the second volume (indicated in an explanatory note) I have moreover substituted the name Von Hemert for Van Melen, the latter being mistakenly referred to as the protector of Sigismunda at this particular point. In the same volume (and likewise indicated in an explanatory note), I have inserted the name Sigismunda in a clause where the grammatical subject was clearly missing in the 1801 text, an omission which rendered the sentence nonsensical. Ulrica Landen's servant Caroline is in one place in volume two called Carolina; this I have regarded as a typographical error and silently corrected.

As *Swedish Mysteries* is a novel, Mackenzie obviously deviates from and makes her own additions to historical facts on a number of occasions. Readers wishing to trace the places in her text where fiction departs from facts are referred to the explanatory notes at the end of the book.

SWEDISH MYSTERIES,

OR

HERO OF THE MINES.

A TALE.

IN THREE VOLUMES.

TRANSLATED FROM A SWEDISH MANUSCRIPT,

BY

JOHANSON KIDDERSLAW,

Formerly Master of the English Grammar School at Upsal.

> ——— "He who reigns, but climbs to care;
> "Tho' safe his throne, he finds no softness there;
> "Dangers, and doubts, and toils his moments seize,
> "Hang on his business, and perplex his ease."
>
> FIELDING'S MEROPE.

VOL. I.

LONDON:
PRINTED AT THE
Minerva-Press,
FOR WILLIAM LANE, LEADENHALL-STREET.
1801.

Title page of the first edition (1801)
(reproduced from the best available copy)

Swedish Mysteries

Volume I

SWEDISH MYSTERIES.

CHAPTER I.

> "To bow and sue for grace
> With suppliant knee, and deify his power,
> Who, from the terror of this arm, so late
> Doubted his empire—that were low indeed,
> That were an ignominy and shame beneath
> This downfall!"
>
> MILTON.

AT the commencement of a tedious Scandinavian winter, a noble Swede sought refuge among the frozen mountains of Dalecarlia, from the barbarous despotism and unjust usurpation of Christian, King of Denmark and Norway; and, accompanied by one servant, to whose honesty he confided the little portable treasure his sudden departure allowed him to collect together, had passed through Sudermania, Westermania, and Nerecia, in the utmost peril of pursuit.

Already had he reached a little inn near the frontiers of Dalecarlia, when misfortunes of a new and unexpected nature gave a blacker tinge to the dismal future. His servant, whose fidelity in every former transaction admitted not a doubt, was missing; and, upon the coolest deliberation, his betrayed master found every reason to imagine himself divested of that support a few valuables might have procured. This was a distressing occurrence, and in some circumstances would have warranted an expression of rage, and a diligent search after the ungrateful villain; but our unhappy emigrant, whose fortitude was tried in much severer points, had scarcely leisure to attend to the consequences of this transaction, any further than as they might tend to an abridgment of the means necessary to existence.

The tyrannic cruelty of Christian, who was guilty of the most atrocious actions to the family of this injured hero, by assassinating his father, and confining his mother and sisters without a prospect, almost without a hope of release—nay, it was the predominant sentiment of his soul that they also had shared his father's fate, and this sentiment was ever present to his mind; nor could the sense he retained of his own treatment lessen his abhorrence of a wretch who, without even a plausible motive, had confined him in a loathsome prison in Denmark, from which he had been recently delivered by the generosity of a disinterested Dane. Added to all these incentives to revenge, was the deposition and death of Steen Sture, the Regent, or rather the lawful Monarch of Sweden, which every friend of that martyred King attributed to the diabolical Christian, and formed another link in that chain of circumstances which induced this indignant soldier to trust the adventitious hospitality of strangers, rather than crouch to an haughty tyrant, whose policy, upon his mounting the treacherously obtained throne, would have conciliated the adherents of his murdered predecessor by the most liberal offers; many of whom, induced by a love of ease, which, however, they failed to experience, and allured by the largesses bestowed upon Christian's friends, readily acknowledged his sovereignty. Not so our gallant patriot; he disdained those terms of amity and preferment which, if acceded to, struck at every sacred and honourable principle, and to preserve which he had travelled in a mean disguise through a great part of Sweden proscribed, and diligently sought after by his bitterest enemy.

But, contrary to his expectation, he now found himself beyond the *immediate* influence of those fears, which were by no means inconsistent with true courage, since to fall into Christian's hands at the very moment when the accumulated injuries he had suffered from that usurper, rendered him an object of suspicion and hatred to the jealous Dane, would be to defeat the noblest hopes that ever warmed a human bosom—hopes which, while they guarded his soul against the torpor of despair, gave energy to the determination of a well-governed mind. Certainly the present moment afforded but little encouragement for the exercise of a glowing imagination, since he had evils of various descriptions to combat against before a firm basis could be established for those hopes to rest upon; nor could this gallant stranger turn with confidence to any friend powerful enough to protect his person, or defend his cause:—even the sinews of war were for the present denied him, nor could he just then form any feasible plan for the certain furtherance of his designs, while subject to such numerous inconveniences; but, released from the apprehensions of being discovered that night at least, whose obscurity promised a temporary security, he wound among the hardy trees which clothed the stupendous mountains of the north, and enjoyed a degree of that liberty so congenial to his soul: but while the vigour of an active spirit preserved its unvaried tone, fatigue and extreme cold acted so powerfully upon a wearied frame, as to oblige him to seek some shelter.

The evening was nearly closed, when he threw an eager eye over the inhospitable tract before him. Trees of every hardy description were scattered about the different heights, among which he could perceive no vestiges of a human residence. That there must be cottages in this vicinity appropriated to the use of the miners' families, he was well aware, but in what direction to seek them he knew not; and even the heart of a Swedish warrior began to sink under the idea of passing a night in those frozen wilds, when he was suddenly cheered by the appearance of a light passing through a hollow in an opposite eminence, which, till guided by this favourable circumstance, he had not noticed.

Happy to discover what he conjectured would afford a defence from the cold, if nothing more, he hastily entered the recess, which ran a considerable way under the rock. Towards the middle of this cavern he discerned a tremendous cavity, that proved to be an old copper-mine, long since disused. Here then, while secure from the barbarians who traced his steps, till they were lost among the prodigious firs that rendered useless their keenest endeavours to discover him, and defended from an easterly wind, which blew the falling snow in the face of the dejected traveller, he felt a comparative degree of ease—a degree of ease which was soon disturbed, if not destroyed, by a contemplation of the past, the present, and the future.

Attached by the most powerful ligaments to a gracious and betrayed Monarch, whose cause he had defended, whose conduct he had revered, and whose person he loved, our generous emigrant felt the bitterest resentment agitate his loyal heart against the wretch who so recently precipitated the suffering Steen's fate, to which the harrowing remembrance of his own unfortunate family added a still keener pang. Long had this loyal patriot reconciled by his conduct the *amor patriæ* with his most zealous attempts to guard the sacred rights of his royal master; and proved how incompatible is any endeavour to separate the interest of King and people. It was certain that the warmest energies of his soul were tinctured by the love of liberty;—not *that* which gives to rapine, sacrilege, and murder their diabolical powers of action—not *that* which tears asunder the beautiful tie that binds an affectionate people to their lawful Sovereign—nor *that* which plucks from contented poverty its little earnings, perverts the decision of justice, and makes the decrees of a wise legislator subservient to its own nefarious purposes.

His ideas of liberty were perfectly consonant with those he entertained of the monarchical rights and privileges, and proved (by the fire of his zeal for the claims of Sweden) his own illustrious descent from her ancient Sovereigns; but, alas! his indignation was ineffectual—his title to universal respect set aside—himself a wretched outcast, and the brave exploits he had performed in favour of the people he loved, brought forward by the vindictive Christian as proofs of a dangerous, at least a contumacious spirit; and in support of this plea, the tyrant thought to avail himself of a subject's opposition to his will, concealing from a timid conquered nation the terms on which that Nobleman might have recovered a limited influence in Gothland—namely, to give a tacit consent to Christian's elevation, to take an active part in the defeat of his opponents, and to express a decided approbation of Steen's terrible fate.

No wonder that these proposals were rejected with a detestation that gave the usurper an excuse for his cruel conduct, or that proscription and every sort of persecution should follow an offence so unpardonable; for well he knew he had nothing to expect from a lenity which, if ever indulged, was ostentatiously assumed to cover some latent mischief: but *he had escaped*, and this was a circumstance of congratulation to our hero, who, in revolving the causes he lamented as irreparable, forgot not to rejoice in the possibility of shaking the pillars of a throne so ingloriously filled.

Wearied with the unsatisfactory discussion of points so important to his interest, and so poignant to his feelings, the tired wanderer, with a sigh, impelled by various causes, rose from his sheltered seat, and, invited by the first glimmer of a sickly dawn, cast an eye of curiosity round the rugged walls of his retreat, whose threatening aspect seemed to forbid his stay, while the impending ruins that nodded above, soon determined him to seek a safer asylum, when a recollection of the light, as it had been seen on the preceding evening, pressed upon his imagination, and he could not help wishing to find out the motive for an appearance which indicated the proximity of something human. But in vain was every attempt he made to develop the mysterious business—not the smallest resemblance of more than one outlet presented itself; and, wearied with a search so dangerous, he quitted his subterraneous residence, after sixteen hours' stay in that dreary abode; for now the symptoms of excessive hunger became too powerful for controul, and his next concern was to discover some means of renovating a system that, however inured to bodily hardships, felt in a forcible degree the necessity of immediate support.

Upon leaving a habitation, which the warm vapours that rose from the earth rendered not only tolerable, but comparatively comfortable, he found the change scarcely to be endured. The frosty particles, from which he had already suffered much inconvenience, rendered every effort to travel eastward nearly impossible; and to return might hazard his safety, for he was fully sensible of the importance his detention would be to those of his pursuers who might yet be lingering among the vallies, and all he could do was to search for a cottage near the old mine.

While thus employed, he was alarmed by the voices of men hallooing to someone before them, that seemed to proceed from behind the rock which covered his late retreat; and, turning suddenly round, beheld a party of people, who were too far distant to be distinguished in any other way than as travellers in an inhospitable region, and too probably the very enemies he was so solicitous to shun. While endeavouring to trace their course, as they wound among the masses of stone which, detached from the vast protuberance above, lay in confused heaps, he suddenly lost all traces of them, and this he attributed to the snow, which now began to fall in great abundance.

It was true, this circumstance was much in favour of his escape; but it might prevent the discovery he aimed to make, as the thickness of the atmosphere rapidly increased. Thus cruelly situated, the bewildered Swede reluctantly gave way to despondency, and felt half inclined to submit to a fate, from which he saw no means of deliverance.

Several hours had already passed since he had quitted the mine, and unfortunately, in losing sight of it, he lost every trace of its direction. Added to his present distress, an unconquerable supineness stole upon him, which soon arose to a state of lethargic debility; and although he knew it was a general prelude in those climates to death itself, he could not resist its potent influence, but, sinking upon a heap of snow, gradually lost all perception, and every faculty gave way to the dangerous indulgence.

CHAPTER II.

> "Thou know'st but little
> If thou dost think true virtue is confin'd
> To climes or systems.—No, it flows spontaneous,
> Like life's warm stream, throughout the whole creation,
> And beats the pulse of every healthful heart."
>
> BROOKE.

FROM a torpor which threatened the extinction of vital action, the feeble invalid awoke to a situation that excited every inducement to wonder and gratitude. The barren mountain, and loaded trees bending beneath their accumulating burden, no longer disgusted with a chilling aspect his fainting soul; and although still shuddering with excessive cold, a kindly warmth played about his heart, invigorating the animal spirit, and slowly diffusing its reviving powers through the half-frozen system. Heavily, and with a doubting eye he surveyed his present asylum, and turning with some difficulty from the recumbent posture he was placed in, met in the honest countenance of a peasant who stood near, a very hearty indication of the pleasure he felt in beholding a fellow-mortal snatched as it were from the brink of destruction. The stranger would have spoken, but was prevented by the hospitable cottager.

"I see your purpose, my friend," he cried, "but no thanks—I have done my duty; you was in distress, and I could assist you. So far all is well.—Come rise; perhaps you can bear the heat without any injury."

The grateful Swede now clasped the hard discoloured hand that was extended for his assistance, and advanced to a fire, whose blaze (the stove being open in front) reflected itself in the coarse but shining furniture of a miner's cot, which, contrary to the general appearance of those smoky habitations, wore an air of cheerful cleanliness.

He had now leisure more fully to discriminate objects; but every other idea was absorbed for the moment in admiration and astonishment while observing a young female, who, on his arising, suddenly retreated, as though loath to attract the notice of a stranger. Her figure, and what he could discover of her countenance, as her profile struck him, indicated something so extremely superior to the inhabitant of a Dalecarlian abode, as to induce a high degree of curiosity in our hero, which her sudden departure, if it did not destroy, at least protracted.

It now was necessary for him to understand by what means he became the object of Van Melen's compassion, for so was his deliverer named. To his questions upon this head, which were applied with an intermixture of the most grateful acknowledgments, he was informed that the group of men he had mistaken for his pursuers, were only some miners who always passed their Sundays with their families, and lived the rest of the week in the mines—that when they sunk from his sight, it was in pursuit of their usual occupation.

Van Melen was one of the number who belonged to a mine contiguous to the recess he so recently quitted, and which was lately known to contain some rich veins of copper ore. He then proceeded to say that, in consequence of a sudden sickness, to which those who exchange a frosty air for the unwholesome vapours of a recess, impregnated with the most pernicious effluvia, are commonly subject, Van Melen was obliged to reascend; but finding his complaint unabated, he determined to return to his cottage, which fortunately happened to be near the spot where this unconscious sufferer was calmly breathing out his existence, who little imagined he was so near a comfortable shelter, owing to the intervention of some prodigious larches, among which it stood.

At the sight of a poor creature, whose complaint the miner perfectly understood, he almost forgot his own infirmity, and with the help of his son, who accompanied him, conveyed the body to their abode; and after rubbing it with snow, and using the common applications, they had the satisfaction to see their endeavours rewarded by the partial recovery of their patient.

Van Melen, having finished his little, but interesting recital, summoned his wife and son to procure some refreshment for the stranger, who had now an opportunity of seeing more of this good man's household. Mrs. Van Melen betrayed the appearance of one that, like many others in the frigid zone, was in the constant habit of drinking spirits. Her aspect was heavy, and her manner exhibited neither wonder nor compassion: yet with this appearance that of her dwelling did not accord; and her guest, who well knew that neither gentleness, cleanliness, nor elegance of deportment was to be expected in a province so remote from the higher order of life, was willing to attribute all he saw of the second named virtue to the young woman, whom he looked for in vain. In the son he beheld the same dull expression which characterized his mother; nor did the face of Van Melen itself differ from the others, now that animation had subsided, which his success in recovering an exhausted creature had created. Indeed the obscurity, labour, and danger of his employment were too apt to deaden every feeling, as well as to give a cast of insensibility to the features; but under this gloom Van Melen preserved the beautiful virtue of charity unimpeached, as well as an ardent love of his unhappy country, and possessed no less a degree of self-denial in shunning, as far as in him lay, the earnest thanks of his guest. When the little repast was placed upon the table, that Nobleman naturally expected he should again behold the lovely apparition that had so recently vanished.

"You have a daughter," he cried, upon finding there was no seat unoccupied; "where is she?"

"I have *no* daughter, stranger," answered the miner, with a cold repulsive accent.

The stranger was silent. There was a mystery which, indebted as he was to Van Melen's hospitality, forbade any present indication of curiosity, and he strove to forget the cause that raised it. A portion of the simple viands was now conveyed to an inner room, and the meal passed without any further hope of explanation.

As Van Melen continued rather indisposed, he sent Peter to supply his place in the mine, and when his wife was withdrawn, took occasion, in his blunt manner, to speak of the dangerous and threatening circumstances which involved a country he loved to enthusiasm.

His auditor listened to the plain yet forcible observations of his entertainer with an emotion that his utmost coolness and intrepidity could not entirely restrain; and when the cottager, in a vehement, unguarded way, expressed his detestation of Christian's cruelties, the gallant hero, forgetting, in the moment of patriotic zeal, his own danger, exclaimed—"Perish the villain, to whom our devoted country owes its wretchedness!—he who has usurped the lineal succession of Sweden—abused its privileges—imprisoned its loyal adherents—and *murdered* its Monarch!"

Amazed at these spirited incautious observations, Van Melen gazed with a doubtful sort of hope upon his guest, whose impassioned accents and crimsoned cheek seemed to declare a readiness to unite in the cause which already filled every Dalecarlian with an eager wish for its support. He even felt assured there could be no danger in confessing how very desirous his countrymen were to come forward on an occasion so important to the nation.

"We are all ready," said Van Melen, "to march at a day's notice; but where all are equally ignorant of military skill, none can be found to act as a leader."

"And yet," cried the zealous loyalist, "there is one," and his eye almost blazed with the ardour of his feelings, "there is one, my friend, who would joyfully lead you on to victory!"

"It may be so, stranger," answered Van Melen, "but where is he to be found? Deprived, both by situation and employment, from applying to this warrior, how can he know our wishes and intentions?—Besides, although I believe the whole province, if they would declare as much, are of the same opinion, yet there would be much trouble, and danger too, in learning their sentiments, and where is the heart that would not tremble at making the experiment?"

"Here!" cried the stranger, striking his agitated bosom, "here palpitates a heart that burns for revenge, nor can it ever shrink from the means which may gratify it!"

Van Melen started. The presence of his animated companion created a sort of reverence for which he could not account, and his soul caught a spark of that fire which glowed upon the hero's countenance, banishing the native phlegm and dulness of a northern peasant, and rendering him worthy of a soldier's confidence. At length impatient to know the quality of the man he had so happily preserved, yet dreading to be thought officious (for that he was of noble extraction Van Melen doubted not), he ventured to ask if he would take upon himself the command of the Dalecarlians, after attempting to sound the opinions of such as had not yet declared themselves.

The stranger paused. It was an eventful task, big with danger, "but," decided his intrepid heart, "replete with glory.—Yes," he cried, "I will undertake the arduous business: Christian, prepare! A vindictive adversary steps forth to assert the rights of fallen majesty and an injured people!"

CHAPTER III.

"Let's join our battle with a force may glut
The front of death, and choke him with himself.
As fiercely as destroying whirlwinds rise,
Or as clouds dash, when thunder shakes the skies."

CAIUS MARIUS.

The spirited conversation of Van Melen and his visitor was now most critically interrupted by the entrance of his wife, who told him another stranger entreated to be admitted till the following morning; for that in his way to Hedmora, the chief village of Dalecarlia, he unfortunately had lost the beaten track, which the snow had completely obliterated.

Ever ready to assist a fellow-creature, Van Melen would have nodded assent; but upon turning towards his guest, he remarked a striking alteration in his features. It was too late, however, for deliberation; the stranger entered, and was beginning to express a sense of obligation for the consent Mrs. Van Melen thought proper to accelerate, when suddenly interrupting himself, he darted across the room, seized the hand of the astonished Swede, who, on the point of retiring, was stopped by this rapid action, and exclaimed—"It is he—it is my long-lost, revered *Gustavus Ericson!*"

A name so dear—so infinitely valued by all who suffered under Christian's tyranny, and which had reached even the northern extremities of Sweden, operated with indescribable effect upon the honest miner. He saw this almost worshipped hero sheltered by his own humble roof; he had saved this first of men from an obscure death; he was partially admitted to the noble General's confidence, entitled himself to his warmest gratitude, and stood a joyful witness of an interview which would have touched a more insensible heart than Van Melen's.

No sooner had Gustavus recognised in the aged stranger a well-tried friend, and one whose presence recalled scenes of anguish, sorrow, and disappointment, than he turned for a moment to hide the tear his unimpeached courage deemed a weakness. This consequence of a meeting so painfully pleasing was fully understood by Marienburg, whose generous heart trembled to the truest touch of sincere friendship; and well he knew that the intelligence which he must communicate to his beloved Ericson, would harass with deeper agony a soul, on which the keenest arrows of disappointed affection had exercised their power; but amidst the broken sentences and unconnected expressions of congratulation that this meeting gave rise to on the part of Marienburg, Gustavus soon discovered a certain awkwardness, and a restraint unusual in the manners and address of this candid veteran. There was but one motive to be assigned for it. Of the sad situation of his beloved relatives he was but too well acquainted; nor did he suppose that in so short a time as had elapsed since he had quitted his prison, any event could have taken place respecting them, to justify his fears for their safety.—But Marienburg had a daughter, who was dearer than life itself to the Swedish hero, and with whom he could have been almost contented to lose the very memory of his royal descent, had not her parent, with a Roman steadiness, subverted every attempt made upon his parental feelings. In every other instance Gustavus displayed the noblest command of his passions;—in this the contest became too powerful for opposition; and ever alive to the recollection of an object so dear, yet so firmly withheld from his pursuit, he ventured to pronounce the name of Sigismunda.

All the delight which animated Marienburg's features, vanished at the mention of his child; and casting an agonized look upon Ericson, he confirmed by an ominous silence the fears of this ardent lover. At length—"Cease," he cried, "Gustavus, nor disappoint my noblest hope by an indulgence of this lingering weakness! In a moment like this, no puerile sentiment ought to debase the ardour of a hero, or check the generous enthusiasm of true patriotism. Honoured from an early period by the confidence of your noble father, and entrusted with the education of Sweden's lawful Monarch, for such I deem Gustavus, it shall never be told of Marienburg that the aggrandizement of his daughter could be a leading consideration with him; when the Prince, who would promote it, must by such an event not only degrade his dignity, but hazard his establishment in the hearts of his adherents. No, my Lord, you must now admit of no softer ideas than those which revenge for your unprecedented wrongs, and those of your country, shall inspire."

"Strange inflexibility!" returned the conquered Ericson; "but I submit; and yet would you but speak of——"

"Sigismunda—it is of her you would ask?—Well, then, she is no longer in her father's power—Christian has summoned her to the Court. She is now at Stockholm, and it is to be feared her ardent attachment to your mother and sisters has rendered her an object of jealousy to the detestable usurper, although the ostensible motive for her residence there is that of attending the Queen. I see you are disturbed at this intelligence, my Prince; but let this fresh outrage act as an additional stimulus to the cause which demands your immediate interference. Think not, because this heart swells with the bold design of crushing, through your concurrence, the power of a tyrant, that it is impenetrable to the tenderest paternal feelings!"

Marienburg hesitated.

"No, Gustavus, I would only wish to prove by my conduct that all private considerations should give way to the grand principle of promoting the public weal. There is a species of selfishness in every mode of acting, which tends merely to individual gratifications, and it shall ever be Marienburg's care to keep up the proper distinction."

There was an energy in the countenance and voice of this extraordinary man that went to the soul of his brave pupil; and although he had circumvented his youthful hope, and denied to his impetuous wishes an almost portionless bride, yet so high was his opinion of Marienburg's integrity, and so unlimited was the veteran's influence over Gustavus, that no resentful expression, no sullen complaints followed this contradiction of his heart's sweetest affections; and while languishing for a fuller explanation of Sigismunda's situation, he made a successful effort to change the subject, and the distress of a mother and two beloved sisters were next adverted to.

On this head Marienburg could give no comfort, or even information. That Christian detained them in some strong fortress was past a doubt; but whether in the environs of Stockholm, Nyhopping, or Gottenburg, or even Denmark, remained an entire secret to the aged adventurer, who, learning from private intelligence that Gustavus intended to reach the northern confines of Sweden, had followed him thither, passing on the road Christian's emissaries, to whom, as it proved, he was unknown, and with a degree of resolution, which no common circumstances could appal, pursued this interesting object of his highest hopes and expectations.

It then was mentioned in the course of conversation, that the light Gustavus had observed at the further part of the mine, which, owing to the direction of the metallic veins, was worked horizontally, till, exhausted of its contents, they had perforated it perpendicularly, was carried by Marienburg, who deviating from the common track to Hedmora, (or, as it is sometimes written, Herdenora) had taken up his lodging in an insular part of it, where by the assistance of a tinder-box, some brandy, and a cake of bread, he passed some hours in a tolerable way, and, more fortunate than his friend, discovered on the following morning a passage which led to the abode of another miner, who civilly shewed him the track he had mistaken, but from which he had again so far diverged as to get close to Van Melen's hut.

With grateful acknowledgments for the comfort his friend's society promised, Ericson mixed repeated declarations of his intention to accompany him to Hedmora, for the purpose of sounding its inhabitants; and after settling that Van Melen, who, from the beginning of this discovery, was fallen into a profound sleep, should inform his friends of the reason they had to expect assistance from Gustavus, they drew nearer the stove, and attempted to lose the succeeding hours of a long Swedish night, in the repose so necessary to the renovation of their exhausted bodies, and which they might possibly miss on the following night.

CHAPTER IV.

> "It is wisely ordered in our present state, that joy and fear, hope and grief should act alternately as checks and balances upon each other, in order to prevent an excess in any of them which our nature could not bear."
>
> BLAIR.

EMBARRASSED with a variety of conflicting thoughts, and too ready to devote the silent hour of midnight to painful recollection, Gustavus soon gave up every idea of sleep. The probably dangerous events which Sigismunda's residence in a Court so dissipated as Christian's, might reasonably be supposed to create, were increased by a high-raised imagination to evils of the most horrible magnitude. Even Christian himself was known to be particularly attached to every female whose beauty was in the style he affected to admire; nor could the subtilty and hypocrisy of his favourite Ulrica (a woman whose turbulent and ambitious disposition rendered her a terror to all on whom she cast a suspicious eye) do more than induce him to conceal as much as possible his preference of others.

The bare idea of Sigismunda being in either instance an object of admiration or jealousy was intolerable to indulge; and he wished to annihilate both space and time, as much at least as might yet interfere before he could effect his daring purposes. While thus anxiously, though uselessly employed, a murmuring of female voices from the innermost apartment changed, or rather interrupted, the course of his meditation. He listened, and plainly distinguished the nature of Mrs. Van Melen's request to her companion, which was, that she would suffer her to sleep, if she did not intend to take any herself.

The answer was given in a low weeping tone, that struck Ericson as being familiar to him; and the remembrance of the female he beheld in the morning, awakened that curiosity which more momentous circumstances had suppressed.

There was nothing in the half-soothing, half-reproaching accents of the drowsy dame from which he could gather any satisfactory intelligence; for, inebriated as she was, those accents soon became inarticulate, and then totally ceased, and with it the hope Ericson had conceived of again hearing a voice that seemed to remind him of his dearest interests, till he was once more surprised with an exclamation that distinctly closed with the words—"*Unhappy Sigismunda! Sigismunda!*"

"Oh! who," cried the amazed lover, "in that obscurity knows aught of a name so dear—sacred as it is to a parent and friend!" and then looking upon Marienburg, who was calmly sleeping—"It cannot be!" thought Gustavus; "no, he cannot have brought her hither—deception is not in the practice of a Marienburg! But she weeps—she complains.—It is—it is Sigismunda!"

He then, rising, was about to enter the room, which he now felt assured contained so much of his earthly treasure; but suddenly hesitated. It was an infringement upon female delicacy; for even the retirement of a peasant, supposing it was no otherwise ennobled, had something in the eye of strict honour almost sacred in it: but a glimpse which he caught of a lovely woman reclining pensively against the bed on which Mrs. Van Melen was profoundly reposing, allowed no motive in favour of propriety to operate, and springing forward, he was about to catch the hand of an object so desirable, who, starting up, discovered—not his beloved Sigismunda, but the companion of her youth, the gentle Catherine Sleswie—an orphan, whose reputed father had fallen in battle, which circumstance endeared her so much to Marienburg, such was the ostensible reason he gave, as to secure her an asylum in the family of that benevolent man.

She immediately recognised the person of Gustavus, over whose insensible form, when he was brought to the cottage, she had mourned with the truest friendship, if not with a yet warmer incentive.

Incapable of governing the emotions of his heart at a meeting so unexpected and so portentous, he awoke Marienburg by the impetuosity of his exclamations.

Not less surprised, though more collected, the veteran entreated from Catherine her motive for leaving his daughter, and becoming an inmate of Van Melen's cot.

She could only articulate the names of Christian and Ulrica; then bursting into a flood of tears, convinced the unhappy father there was yet a pang in store for him superior to what he had ever experienced; till at length growing somewhat more composed, she informed her eager auditors, that on the day Marienburg quitted Stockholm, she was commanded to leave that city; and when she expostulated with Ulrica upon the cruelty of sending her from Sigismunda, that haughty woman deigned to give no other answer than a menace of perpetual confinement, if she left not the Court within a short period.—"Thus," continued Catherine, "I was obliged to quit the friend whose society has ever been my delight, and this without even one parting interview; for the King, whose motive I am totally ignorant of, added to this cruel decree, that Sweden itself should afford me no protection. Alas! in what instance could Catherine Sleswie be an object of Christian's resentment, or why should he prohibit my entering the apartment of your daughter?"

Marienburg sighed, for he could give a dreadful interpretation of this conduct, and the looks of Gustavus declared a similar fear.

"But why are you here?" cried the impatient Ericson.—"Oh Catherine! why so decidedly give up every opportunity of being useful to that dear creature? Had you no friend in Stockholm who could have protected you from the power and knowledge of Christian?"

"Indeed no, my Lord: certainly, were that the case, I should not have taken so long a journey; but the only person I could trust was Madam Schewellen, at Upsal, and my intention was to apply to her for shelter till I could discover my guardian:—but she was absent, and I was tempted to accept the offer of a good woman, who meant to travel to Hedmora. Again I was disappointed, for she was induced to stop short on her journey; and as we could not both be conveniently accommodated at the house of her relation, I was sent forward to this place to wait for her; and such is my dread of that savage, Christian, that it seems as if even this obscurity was insufficient to conceal me from his power, and I engaged Mr. Van Melen's secrecy on the subject of my being here. At Upsal, perhaps, or Hedmora I should have nothing to dread; but here, indeed, I must have been insecure, for the wretches, sent in pursuit of the noble Gustavus, gave me hourly terror, as I beheld them scattered among these desolate mountains; and when you, my Lord, was reviving from your temporary death, I withdrew from your ardent gaze, dreading I hardly knew what."

When the timid Catherine had closed her little recital, Marienburg, who could scarcely forgive her groundless fears, turned to Ericson.—"Sigismunda is in danger, my friend; but so is Sweden, and till the latter is liberated, nothing can be done for the former. True, I can go to Christian—I can demand my daughter; but will the tears of a helpless old man, unsupported by more powerful auxiliaries, avail with one, who sports with every endearing, every affectionate tie?—No, I will first go to Hedmora. Catherine shall accompany me thither; and while you are making your party good among the miners, I will represent the horrors of our situation to the spirited Dalecarlians."

"Yes," answered Gustavus, with an energy that entered the soul of Marienburg, "we will both unite our endeavours to crush that monster, and free——"

He would have named Sigismunda, but substituted instead of that loved title the word *Sweden*; and then suddenly breaking off, awoke his sleeping host, to whom he communicated as much of their intentions as might be sufficient to furnish him with additional motives for rousing his companions to a full sense of the miseries, both public and private, that threatened the whole state, of which they composed a part.

Although happy to discover in the person of Marienburg an

honourable protector and safe companion, Catherine's heart trembled at the bare mention of reaching Hedmora without any other guard than him; added to which, the idea of travelling for many miles over the frozen surface of a country, exposed (in the track through which their route lay) to the keen and boisterous winds that streamed along the narrow defile, or poured over the barren tops of those hills that intervened between the mines and Hedmora, (for the plantations of beech, oak, and fir extended not more than a mile from Van Melen's cottage, and all beyond was one uninterrupted waste of shining white)—these difficulties were more than she could bear to contemplate, especially as, in her journey hither, she had already endured fatigues which, as a helpless female, she dreaded to renew. But there was no appeal against the terrible decree—no kind friend to interpose in a case so delicate. Ericson she fancied understood and commiserated her situation, but he was silent; a sympathizing look, a sigh of pity were the only proofs he dared give of his dislike to this arrangement; while Marienburg, to whom the imbecility of feminine feelings was either wholly unknown, or who totally disregarded their effects, urged the strong necessity there was for his hasty departure; and Catherine, without further opposition, while the tears trickled from her eyes, prepared to leave the friendly cottagers.

Upon hearing of an intention so inimical to the inclinations of her gentle companion, Mrs. Van Melen, who had heard part of this conversation, now entered, and, in her way, began to paint the inconveniences she must endure in a journey undertaken on foot, and in such an inclement season; but a look from her husband had its common consequence, and she sunk into her usual state of listless inattention, mindful of little more than the few occupations which came under her directions, excepting the pleasure of supplying her company with a liberal portion of that spirit, whose potency had disarmed her own countenance of every trait of sensibility and animation.

From this strongly recommended spirit the unhappy Catherine turned with disgust; and after partaking with her friends of a coarse breakfast, she joined the ready Marienburg, and entered upon a peregrination from which her sick heart revolted with terror; but her apprehensions in the present instance were rather too premature, for the day was bright; the snow had hardened to a consistency that made walking neither disagreeable nor dangerous; and our travellers, as they faced the eastern blast, found its influence rather bracing than overpowering, while, to shorten the length of their first stage, the good veteran employed his favourite ward (for so she might be styled) in giving him further particulars of her recent ill-treatment at Stockholm; and when they arrived at a cottage recommended to them by Van Melen, Catherine began to think the task she had undertaken neither impracticable nor even difficult. The accommodations were more than tolerable, and their hosts almost generous.

Gustavus, whose eye had traced these valuable friends to a considerable distance, sighed as the hill, which bounded the visible horizon, hid them from his view; and too much impressed at that hour by private calamity to advert to those public ones which filled the mind of Van Melen, he sent him among the miners, to sound them respecting their readiness to join his cause, and then, retiring to the inner room, indulged himself with a retrospect of those peaceful hours which, marked with happiness, flew lightly, and (ah, how swiftly!) bore with them every hope of a return, since, from the inflexibility of Marienburg's principles, there was much to fear, and still more from the arch villany of those who kept, as was really suspected, a helpless virgin from her natural protector.

It had been settled by the gallant Marienburg to dispatch, by the earliest opportunity, a trusty messenger to Gustavus with the intelligence of his arrival at Hedmora; and as he had no reason to expect this information under a fortnight, Ericson passed the intermediate time in visiting the mines, and, under the borrowed appellation of Linden, to gain a more decisive knowledge of those tempers and dispositions which he sought to bend to his purpose.

This he was happily enabled to do with the concurrence of Van Melen, who, in his first embassy, had every reason to be pleased with its result. Another powerful auxiliary to the force of elocution was added by the familiarity which occurs from mixing in the same manual employments; for the descendant of a Prince—the just heir to those kingdoms that were usurped by his bitterest enemy—even the noble Gustavus Ericson condescended to become an inhabitant of subterranean regions, and, sinking from the face of day, to equallize himself with a race of beings poor, but not despicable,—obscure, though not mean, and distinguished by that sort of courage which stamps the actions with a nobleness that in higher situations would claim and receive unbounded applause. Possessed, from watchful observation, of the clue that led to a development of these characters, our hero saw in the success which attended his cautious advances to their confidence, the most flattering prospect of profiting by their future assistance; for, without suspecting the integrity or quality of their new partner, they heartily coincided with him in every opinion he established, as well as agreed to every project he hinted for the promotion of their own wishes.

By this time Ericson began to look out for the messenger who was to announce the safety of his beloved friends; and as he chose not to repose in the unwholesome obscurity wherein he passed his days, it became his usual custom every evening to climb a neighbouring eminence, for the purpose of descrying, if possible, the expected courier; but no such object met his wearied eye, and the time elapsed without any appearance of intelligence, till at length, from the intenseness of the weather, he was led to imagine no one would engage in an employment so disagreeable; for although it was customary for the Swedes to pursue their travels even by moonlight, yet to a spot so desolate as that Van Melen inhabited, he supposed no one would willingly direct their solitary steps: and Ericson saw little probability of his desire being gratified till a more favourable period should arrive.

CHAPTER V.

"Oh send me to some lonely, desert wild,
Wide as yon bright ethereal high expanse!
There let me wander, friendless and forlorn,
To find the charitable herds of beasts,
Driven from the faithless commerce of mankind."

Havard.

While Gustavus was impatiently arranging the disposition of those incidents which still prevented the satisfaction he so earnestly coveted (for already four months were gone over without the smallest intelligence from Hedmora), the hapless Catherine was experiencing all the horrors of a fate that equalled her most terrifying ideas, and which fell more oppressively on her by preluding its operations with a deceitful calm; for the appearance of every thing at the cottage where they were to pass the night, was such as to give even an idea of cheerfulness, and she drew near a comfortable stove, which dispersed its warmth through the little room set apart for decent guests.

With a grateful sensation Marienburg saw and was pleased with his companion's evident thankfulness for the comforts she enjoyed; and although their supper consisted only of some dried fish, cakes of barley bread, and brandy (the two first of which their good friend Van Melen had furnished them with, and the latter, which was sparingly taken, they were supplied with by the host), still the idea that so much of their journey was passed over without much difficulty, gave a relish to the fare it otherwise might have wanted, for they were on the morrow to strike into the public road leading to Hedmora; and, notwithstanding it was incumbent on them both to shun, as much as possible, every avenue that might lead to a discovery of their persons or intentions, yet self-preservation forbade any further continuance of the path they had hitherto chosen, which led from the cottage to desolate wilds that were truly impassable, excepting at the height of the summer solstice.

A view of Hedmora, as its spires were distinctly observed on the edge of the eastern horizon, gave to Catherine and her fellow-traveller the reasonable hope of seeing a speedy termination to their present pilgrimage; and, as soon as the sun was advanced sufficiently high to qualify, in some measure, the severity of the season, they quitted the civil Dalecarlians, and cheerfully bent their course towards a wide and bare valley, which lay between the town and the mountain they were now descending. The scene which spread itself on all sides to the high acclivities that surrounded them, refined as the atmosphere was by a penetrating frost, gave a new pleasure to Catherine; and she indulged the ideas they created in silent ecstacy, till a rising wind dissolved the sweet enchantment, which, bringing with it a heavy fall of snow, pierced even through the furs that Mrs. Van Melen had plenteously supplied her with.

Catherine shuddered, drew them more closely about her, and looked at Marienburg with a dejected and foreboding aspect.

He pressed her hand, but spoke not, although his trembling nerves declared him an equal sufferer with herself.

"Have we far to go, dear Sir?" she asked.

He turned his head aside.

"You are extremely cold," added she: "I can spare this outward cloak. Do be persuaded, let me fasten it about you."

"Poor girl!" said the shuddering Marienburg, "I *am* cold; but your attention shall not be so sadly rewarded; keep the cloak, my love; you will want all the comfort it can yield before you reach Hedmora."

Surprised at his melancholy accents, she examined his countenance, and was shocked to perceive a visible alteration in it. Even his steps faltered; and the vigorous pace, which but two hours before Catherine's nimblest exertions could barely equal, now sunk into an almost imperceptible motion. It required much more resolution than his timid friend could boast, to look forward to the probable consequences of this delay. Several passengers had met them on sledges, which began to be generally used, but none were going towards Hedmora, and she threw a hopeless look upon the road already passed: but not an object, excepting two or three stags, and several rein-deer, that were bounding across the valley, appeared to cheer her sinking heart.

From Marienburg's manner she could deduce no comfort: the hero was subdued, and nothing remained of all that spirit which informed his language, actuated every motion, and sparkled in the penetrating eye, but a faint attempt to hide his debility from the anxious Catherine, whose terrors he endeavoured to pacify by ascribing his present weakness to a transient cause, and locking his arm within her's, strove to assume a livelier air; but his pace, his countenance, his deep, though half-repressed sighs told a tale of sorrow to the youthful sufferer, and Hedmora, with all its fancied comforts, hidden as that was by the falling snow, became an object of regret rather than hope; even the tears, which a mournful view of their present situation induced, could not with safety be indulged, so keenly did the freezing blast condense every liquid exposed to its fury.

While despair contributed to benumb the torpid senses, no wonder that our wretched travellers felt less capable of warding off the excessive cold that acted upon their enervated limbs; and the fate of Gustavus, when Van Melen first discovered him, rushed upon Catherine's mind with horror totally uncontroulable. She saw herself, in imagination, exposed to all the misery of a slow but certain death—and with the most plausible reason, for it was already too dark to see a furlong distance; and even were it possible to support her trembling companion to the gates of Hedmora, she could no longer trace the road that led thither, which soon was entirely obscured. Certainly her heart was deeply impressed for the sufferings of Marienburg, who, sinking on the frozen snow, declared he could go no further;—but Catherine was no heroine; the distress of one she revered was severely felt, and would have produced the strongest exertions in his favour, had there been a possibility of being useful to him; but the pains *he* suffered served only to produce the most agonizing reflections upon the similarity of their situation, and while she pitied him, her own afflictions were doubly aggravated. The kindness of their landlord at the cottage was now remembered by Catherine with a thrilling transport, for, added to their little stock of provisions, he insisted upon Marienburg's acceptance of a small flask of spirits, and she immediately pressed him to take a little.

He shook his head, but complied with her request.

While she was in the act of holding the flask to his lips, her attention was caught by the voices of people at no great distance.

"Courage, dear child!" cried the poor invalid, "that sound is westward of us."

"It approaches! Yes, I am not deceived!"

Catherine listened. She scarcely breathed—she forgot the spirits—she forgot Marienburg. Ah! who could blame her in a moment like that? The tender heart may feel even for fictious distress, may give a tear to real sorrow, may enjoy with peculiar delight the happiness of a friend; but, under the pressure of immediate calamity, shrinking from the near prospect of death, how different are our feelings, how pungent our emotions, how compressed (if I may be allowed the expression) every wish, every hope, which, generally speaking, are at that instant all centered in self. Such, at least, were

Catherine's sensations; yet, when accosted by a man, who occupied a large sledge, which he stopped on perceiving her approach it, she could not articulate a word till the arrival of several more, filled with people, going towards Hedmora, gave a complete turn to her ideas. She felt confused, abashed, and terrified. The first and chiefest evil was done away, that of perishing by excessive cold; but how to answer properly to their interrogations of who she was, and how she came thither, was too difficult a task for the poor creature: and when they reiterated their questions, she could only lead them to Marienburg, who was too weak to say more than that they had missed the conveyance which would have taken them to the town, and therefore hoped they would carry them to that place. To this request a ready assent was given; and Catherine, released from her worst fears, could now attend to her good friend, supporting him on the sledge, and procuring him such assistance as their situation allowed.

On arriving at Hedmora, the friendly Dalecarlians, not content with conducting them to a tolerable house at the entrance of the town, recommended Catherine to the landlady, by whom she was supplied with every comfort her weak state demanded; nor was Marienburg forgotten, every application his debilitated frame required being readily offered, and as gratefully received.

For several days succeeding his arrival at Hedmora, Marienburg's situation was truly alarming; but as his complaints chiefly originated from the cold that had acted so forcibly on his aged limbs, they soon gave way to the comfortable restoratives of warmth and sleep, and his active mind again recovered its vigorous tone.

Catherine beheld with a sincere pleasure this favourable amendment in her friend, and cheerfully took possession of a lodging near a small building denominated the Council-hall; and this apartment he proposed to share with her as her father, for so he chose to style himself to avoid suspicion.—One difficulty still threatened to defeat the accomplishment of his plan, and this was of no small magnitude, namely, that of an introduction to those of Hedmora, whose influence might be supposed to affect the lower orders of people; and till this could be completed, he chose not to hazard the sending a messenger to Ericson.—At length the regular appearance of a veteran in the outward hall, whose countenance and figure were calculated to command respect, attracted general notice, and the nature of his business was enquired into by a member of the Council. A confused remembrance of this person's features struck so forcibly upon Marienburg, that he hesitated in his answer.

The interrogator was equally surprised, and the names of Marienburg and Fitzer burst spontaneously from the lips of both; an explanation immediately followed, and Fitzer presented his friend to the Assembly as a man to whom he owed obligations of the most singular nature. Thus was Marienburg's hope of pleading his cause before the heads of Dalecarlia most unexpectedly established, and he made no scruple to commit every particular of his intended negotiation to Fitzer, whom he formerly recollected as execrating the very name of Christian; and though the character of this man was such as would not justify any dependance upon his integrity in private affairs, it had little to do with the matter in question.

Luxurious, impetuous, and unable to resist the impulse of violent passions, he had brought himself under the cognizance of the civil law, from the sentence of which Marienburg had formerly employed his utmost power to free him; and this more from the respect he owed Fitzer's father, than any pity that young man's situation could have inspired. How he became a member of that Assembly was a subject of astonishment to his friend; nor did Fitzer's explanation at all abate it, since he only said it was Christian's pleasure to send him thither upon a particular embassy, and, as one of the Council was absent, he was permitted to supply that gentleman's place till he returned. It was evident Fitzer chose not to be explicitly circumstantial on this head, and Marienburg dropped any further enquiry.

The plan in favour of Gustavus's claim was soon brought forward. Several Dalecarlians of distinction promoted the business with incredible celerity, while those who, content to preserve their possessions by a slavish submission to the usurper, would hear of no terms of emancipation, attempted in the public debates to set aside or prevent every overture made by Marienburg towards the deposition of Christian. Upon these occasions Fitzer, with a boldness common to his character, scrupled not to urge the necessity of striking at the root of a power, which sooner or later threatened the extinction of their choicest privileges; and while Marienburg, with his newly acquired party, admired the fearlessness of a spirit, apparently bent upon the restoration of their lawful rights, those of the opposite side were struck with astonishment by a conduct so adverse to that which had procured him a seat in their little senate.

During these frequent altercations a sort of intimacy was begun (for, notwithstanding her residence with Marienburg, this man had never before met with her) between Catherine and Fitzer. He praised her attachment to Marienburg's family. Of the sufferings Sigismunda was suspected to endure, he spoke with a generous resentment, and pitied Catherine for a separation, which he doubted not went very near her heart.

Pleased with a sympathy so congenial to her own sense of the injuries her friends sustained, the unsuspecting girl betrayed the dearest secret in her possession, and Fitzer learned from her incautious communicativeness, not only her own exact situation, but that of Gustavus, with his attachment to Sigismunda, and the motives for his residence in the mountains, with every particular incident she could recollect during her residence at Van Melen's. As a part of this information was given in Marienburg's presence, he felt displeased at a confidence so unlimited; and although every hope of success depended upon Fitzer's endeavours to secure it, he thought there could be no necessity for trusting circumstances of a private and delicate nature to one whose carelessness respecting his own interest had nearly effected his ruin; and it had ever been a maxim with this cool decider, that an implicit reliance ought only to be allowed in cases of an exigence strong enough to demand or justify it.

Struck with this visible dislike of her blameable loquacity, Catherine felt the error she had been guilty of when it was too late for rectifying her folly, and, after Fitzer's departure, submitted with a silent consciousness to Marienburg's strictures upon female imbecility, the government of the tongue, and the ill consequences attending indiscriminate communications; and as ingenuous minds are apt, by way of reparation for little errors, to speak worse of them than they may deserve, Catherine, after a short pause, confessed her extreme penitence for the oversight she had been guilty of, and promised in future to observe in Fitzer's presence an invincible taciturnity. Marienburg smiled at this remarkable resolution, but wished it had been taken prior to the occasion for it.

A few days after this little event, it was determined, by the friends of Gustavus, to send a deputation from Hedmora to that Prince, with every offer of assistance his party could possibly procure. Delighted with a mission so agreeable to his desires, Marienburg joyfully undertook to perform it; and as the river Dala was hardened sufficiently to bear the sledges, that method of journeying was deemed most easy, as well as expeditious.

To this arrangement Catherine made a very natural objection, that of being left among strangers, for, comparatively speaking, the residents of Hedmora, however hospitable, were totally unfit for the protection of a young and helpless female; but in this instance she had to suffer an unexpected contradiction from her respected guardian, who (although warmly alive to the honour, interest, and personal safety of Catherine Sleswie, and even instigated by deep and to her unknown motives to provide for her security) was impelled, through the exigence of his business with Gustavus, to put a stern negative upon her request to revisit Van Melen's cottage: but this denial he afterwards qualified, by promising to get her once more conveyed to Upsal, at which place she might expect to enjoy a quiet asylum, till the purpose for which he was induced to leave her, should be gloriously accomplished. With this assurance Marienburg contrived to satisfy his disappointed ward, and immediately joined Fitzer and his companions, and under the auspices of an almost brilliant moon, they entered upon the Dala.

As Marienburg accompanied Fitzer in the largest sledge (on whom the conduct of their journey rested), he gathered his furs about him, and sunk into a sort of doze; but from this he was speedily roused by the voices of several people, who he now discerned were on the banks of the river; and was considerably surprised to hear Fitzer order the sledgeman to turn towards the shore. This symptom of useless curiosity appeared exceedingly unnecessary, and he entreated his companion to lose no time in attending to trifles; but the request was wholly disregarded, and Marienburg now turned his attention to the before-mentioned group of men, who were then standing near the water's edge, on a spot between the mountains, which skirted at intervals the frozen Dala, when, to his utter amazement, he was abruptly requested by Fitzer to step on shore.

"To what purpose?" exclaimed the astonished Marienburg; "we have much farther to go before we need quit the river; Van Melen's habitation lies to the west of yonder mountains."

"Possibly," cried Fitzer, with an ominous coolness, "but we *must* alight here. A power, from whose decree lies no appeal, commands obedience."

Speechless through a variety of sensations, Marienburg sat for a minute motionless—even the faculty of thinking seemed torpid; but a sudden and horrible suspicion soon darted through his mind, and the *decrees* referred to involved *more* than life, for they struck at his honour. He looked at Fitzer, and beheld such traits of obdurate, even ferocious cruelty warp his features, as convinced him he was the dupe—nay, victim of a designing villain.

"I have enemies," cried the wretched old man;—"and *you*—yes, you—whom I once loved and protected—you, in whom I but now confided the dearest secret of my heart, are chosen to confirm the decrees you hint at."

"We lose time," observed the hardened wretch, and almost dragging the aged Marienburg from his seat. "Yonder, perhaps, you may encounter faces still more hateful than mine!"

"Yes, and not less known," rejoined his prisoner, who, on his nearer approach, discovered among those apparently waiting to receive him, Buxi and Rodar, two servants that some years back had served him with fidelity, and who quitted the household of Magnus, Duke of Saxe Lunenburgh, to find peace and tranquillity in that of Marienburg, who, it may be noticed, had formerly been an ill-treated and determined opposer of that violent Prince, in consequence of which animosity Marienburg experienced at different intervals the bitterest effects of a malice, which wanted only the addition of uncontroulable power to be completely gratified: and this addition he had recently procured, by obtaining a distinguished post in a Society, once the scourge and pest of Germany, of which

Baron Bock gives a correct and wonderful account.* That Magnus was a Member of that horrid Tribunal was a circumstance which appalled the very soul of Marienburg, who was a native of Lunenburgh, consequently still more amenable to its Prince in every light. Struck with a retrospection of the past, and dread of the future, the unhappy friend of Gustavus gave up the most distant hope of promoting that nobleman's interest; and he agonized under the idea of being suspected of treachery, or even carelessness, while he deeply lamented the fate of Catherine, which he now began to suppose would be involved in his.

As every thought of resistance must have been madness in a

* Perhaps it may be necessary to observe in this place, that the origin of Free Counts, or Free Judges, may be traced back to the year 800, when Charlemagne, son to Pepin of France, became possessed of the imperial diadem, the nature of whose commissions was both public and private. Respecting sorcery, magic, and sacrilege, enquiry was made with the utmost secrecy; but all other crimes admitted of public examination. In general, too, persons of known probity were chosen in each district, who were solemnly sworn to examine the supposed crimes of the accused, and on their report sentence was definitely passed. To these extraordinary commissions, the Secret Tribunal, which was posterior, bears a perfect resemblance, whose Free Judges also were bound by a terrible oath to deliver up their nearest relative, without exception, if cognizable by the Tribunal, and, if condemned, to put them to death wherever they found them. This Society was known in the year 1211; but towards the end of the fourteenth century its power rose to a degree so formidable, that it was dreaded throughout Germany, and it became extremely rare for any one to escape them; for the Free Judges, not being known, used to go by night, and nail to the criminal's gate or wall the citation of the Tribunal: and after this ceremony had been three times performed, if he obeyed not the summons, the unhappy creature was soon destroyed by those whose business it was to execute the horrid decree, and this was generally done by hanging him with a willow branch, but never by a rope, to the first tree they came to; but if they were obliged, through particular circumstances, to stab the criminal, they fastened the corpse to a tree, in which they left the weapon, to shew it was the work of a Free Judge. It is true, their power extended no farther than the frontiers of Germany; but instances have been known when the unhappy object of their vengeance, who thought himself perfectly secure in a neighbouring nation, has found his death when least expected, by being pursued even to a country where this tremendous mode of execution was not tolerated, though none has occurred of the apprehension of those by whom it was committed.

case so decided, and as the genuine pride of an exalted soul could not stoop to parley, or make the smallest attempt to conciliate a monster of Fitzer's description, Marienburg observed a profound silence during the continuance of their journey, which, notwithstanding the severity of the season, he found reason to suppose pointed towards Saxony.

CHAPTER VI.

> "Affliction is the wholesome soil of virtue,
> Where patience, honour, sweet humanity,
> Calm fortitude take root, and strongly flourish."
>
> MALLET.

To account for this diabolical treatment of a man, whose integrity and purity of principle, added to a discriminating benevolence, had secured him the esteem of the worthy, and the respect—nay, love of his dependants, it will be proper to investigate Fitzer's antecedent conduct, with the motives by which that, as well as the present was influenced, and also to give the movements of the master-wheel in this horrid business.

We have already noticed the obligation that deep designer was under to Marienburg, on whose credulity his late concurrence with him in the plot against Christian so fully imposed, as to do away any prejudice arising from a recollection of former errors; but, agreeably to the suggestions of a corrupted heart, which, restless, and designing in all its pursuits, found fresh subjects for mischief even in the source of his own safety, Fitzer made no scruple to attempt the chastity of his benefactor's daughter; and, irritated by the severe reception his vile intention merited, as well as fearful of the consequence, should Marienburg become acquainted with his atrocity, he suddenly quitted Stockholm, and at Lunenburgh (to which place, with a hope of meeting some employment suitable to his own ideas, he directly travelled) Fitzer became acquainted with a circumstance that roused his intriguing genius to a full exertion of its powers; for the premature death of Steen Sture, which happened soon after Fitzer's arrival, being announced to him, with its train of suspicious accompaniments, he almost immediately arranged a plan which, through the medium of the rash and credulous Dalecarlians, who were ever ripe for a revolt, he conceived might be crowned with success.

Fitzer had been educated as a page in Steen's Court, and through the seeming pliability of his disposition, obtained the partial attention of that affable Monarch, till his subsequent conduct rendered Marienburg's utmost power necessary to clear him from the imputation of ingratitude, even treachery. On Steen's former kindness, then, did the artful Fitzer ground materials for his plot; and in consequence of his ancient friend's benevolence, was enabled to travel with a speed suitable to his purpose to Hedmora, the residence of the principal Dalecarlians, two of whom fortunately, as he then conceived, had witnessed, while on a visit to the Court of Stockholm, Steen's goodness to his unworthy favourite. Thus strengthened by the importance of his auxiliaries, Fitzer ventured to announce himself as the son of the murdered King.

To this astonishing assertion many objections were started, nor could they be fully overruled by the Pretender's consummate art. However, attracted by his modest deportment, specious manners, and an assumed self-denial of the honours and privileges due to a member of their little Society, of which he was pressed to make one, the Dalecarlians granted to the semblance of worth what they denied to his pretensions. It was at this juncture, when party prejudices were daily strengthening, and the restless spirit of some of his opposers seemed inclined to take up a cause which promised a change, the well-digested system of which the appearance of Marienburg threatened to overturn; and Fitzer found in the cause which he pleaded, the candour of his proposals, and the wisdom of his address, a total defeat of his *own* schemes, unless it were possible to counteract those of Ericson's ambassador.

The first idea that occurred on this momentous head, was to go with the stream; and, while he contrived to retain the confidence of his staunch friends, he appeared to promote and forward the plan in favour of Gustavus, stipulating only with the Assembly for their secrecy respecting his original intentions, and politically declaring he would secede from those intentions, through a consciousness that Gustavus could plead a superior right from his great skill in matters of state. Thus secured, he now found leisure to form a new scheme, in which the destruction of his noble coadjutor was to be involved, whose removal, he doubted not, would pave a way for the completion of his protracted wishes.

During Fitzer's short residence in Saxony, he had become acquainted with Rodar and Buxi, the two men whom we mentioned as once serving in Marienburg's establishment; but who, in consequence of an overture from Magnus, with the offer of a lucrative post, as an amends for the injuries they complained of while in his service, were again returned to Lunenburgh; and from the hints they contrived to drop, Fitzer understood they were inferior Members of the Secret Tribunal, of which the Prince was a Free Judge. That Marienburg, through the suggestions of Magnus, was amenable to that power, was unknown to Fitzer; till accidentally meeting the Saxons at Hedmora, he understood they were in pursuit of the devoted patriot. This was an event so far above his utmost hopes, that he could scarcely conceal the delight it created in his wicked heart; and he lost no time in settling with these indefatigable hunters of their own species, the mode of his seizure. It was certain that, according to the duties of their office, they were justified in taking him immediately away; but as Fitzer's intimacy with these men might give the colour of suspicion to his particular connection with Marienburg, he persuaded them to lay in wait for him at a distance from Hedmora, trusting to his own versatile genius for such an excuse, respecting the business on which they were to meet Gustavus, as should completely satisfy the Dalecarlians.

Had Marienburg continued at Stockholm, the ministers of vengeance would have finished their work in a more decided manner; but understanding, after their first summons of the devoted man, which was placed against the wall of his house at Stockholm, that he had quitted it prior to the citation, and, having procured a knowledge of his route, they arrived at Hedmora about a week after him, and had actually prepared a second citation, which on the following day was to have appeared on the door of their victim's lodgings, when, upon an accidental encounter with Fitzer, Buxi mentioned the name of Marienburg in a way that excited suspicion as to the tenor of their business with him; and as Rodar was not perfectly clear as to the extent of the commission, which possibly did not include Dalecarlia, they thought Fitzer's plan a safe and sure improvement, nor refused to wait till they could avail themselves of it. Thus then was the hapless veteran betrayed, by the integrity of a loyal heart, into a situation of all others the most painful to an active and zealous spirit.

The uncertainty of his beloved Sigismunda's fate, the danger of Gustavus, the helpless state of Catherine, the importance of his own freedom to Sweden, at a crisis when the safety of *all* depended upon the success of the expedition he had planned, were circumstances that rose in their utmost horrors to his perturbed mind. Magnus of Lunenburgh, too—*he*, whose malice in every possible shape haunted him both publicly and privately, and whose misconception of Marienburg had been a source of the bitterest contention between them, *he* would now be empowered to satisfy the vengeance of a rancorous heart. Concluding then that his ruin was certain, the aged prisoner beheld the Castle of Lunenburgh (for after a tedious journey he discovered Lunenburgh to be his present destination), as it made a prominent feature in the enchanting view before him, with only one sentiment—that within its walls one true friend to Gustavus and his interest, would meet a ready fate; for he was led to suppose that his trial as a criminal, amenable to the power of the Secret Tribunal, would be decided even before he could reach Saxony; in consequence, his first interview with one of its Free Judges would be the termination of his existence. How great then was his surprise to find, upon his entrance into the Castle, a reception bordering upon civility from Colonel Klopstock, who was Governor of that fortress, and allotted to his prisoner a tolerable, though well-secured, apartment for his abode; but the mystery was soon explained. Magnus was still at Hernosand, and his general orders respecting Marienburg were, that he should be decently treated during an absence which the season, added to other circumstances, rendered peculiarly disagreeable to the Duke. In this confinement, then, we shall leave the unfortunate Marienburg, and return to the objects of his heart's dearest affection.

Of these claimants Sigismunda Marienburg, his lamented daughter, maintained the foremost ground. Her situation, when he left Stockholm, has already been partially delineated; and as the characters of her detainers were unequivocally infamous, he trembled for the fate of his child. Her principles, so truly opposite to the practice of Christian's Court—her spirit, which could yield to no duplicity of conduct in others, so totally unfit for the *contest*, which a noble adherence to those principles would, he well knew, be frequently repeated—and her person so exactly calculated, by its majestic loveliness, to gain the Monarch's admiration, and excite his mistress's jealousy, were all brought forward to increase the pungency of Marienburg's fears, and raise the most painful suggestions in the paternal bosom.

The situation of Catherine Sleswie was another theme for cruel reflection. Her present danger, and his own confinement, defeated a project which once was the second wish of his heart; for however incredible it may appear, that a father, and that father a Marienburg, should neglect the interest of an only child, even to the exclusion of her heart's tenderest hope, for the aggrandizement of a stranger, it is most certain that, from the day in which Catherine Sleswie became his ward, he determined to effect an union between her and the illustrious Gustavus, and this resolution accounts for the constant opposition he had hitherto made to the wishes of that enamoured Prince.

Sigismunda, who had long seen and secretly lamented an attachment which her father's solemn injunctions and her own prudence rendered dangerous, even impossible to encourage, found in the species of self-denial she practised, a consolation for the violence done to her earliest affection in the praise of her beloved parent. Of his motives respecting his interdiction of a suit, the success of which must eventually bring the highest honours upon his house, she presumed not to judge; and modestly persisted in rejecting the passionate advances made by Gustavus, who, while he accused her of pride, obstinacy, and indifference, saw not beneath the veil, with which discretion enveloped her chaste and delicate feelings, a love as ardent, though more governable than his own, and which, from the moment he became an object of Christian's jealousy and revenge, imbittered every future hour.

To Catherine Sleswie alone was the important secret known. She only had witnessed the agonizing pangs of this wonderful woman, whose sweetness of disposition and manners gave her, in the estimation of her young and timid friend, a distinction above comparison.

Marienburg saw the cruel conflict;—he could not be ignorant of his daughter's sentiments, and his heart bled for sufferings himself had inflicted; but there was no medium, nothing in all the round of possibilities which could meliorate the decree already given, and from an opposition to this decree the discretion of Sigismunda decidedly revolted.

The cruel treatment of Gustavus by Christian, and his consequent escape, were communicated to our heroine, who heard her father's resolution to pursue, and assist the noble fugitive with a pleasure she sought not to conceal. Her heart beat high with the hope of seeing her country restored to freedom by the object of her cherished love, and a latent idea stole across her mind that the determined contradiction of Marienburg to his suit *might* originate in the uncertainty of his situation. Catherine, to whom she revealed the half-formed wish, heard her with a marked and melancholy silence, shrinking as it were from any further disquisition of a subject on which neither could satisfactorily decide. But the time was hastily advancing when disappointments of a very different complexion were to occupy the attention of our young friends. A message, which in its nature and manner carried the force of a command, arrived from the Court of Christian to Marienburg, inviting Sigismunda to pass a few weeks in that scene of dissipation. His heart shrunk with horror from a compliance with this mandate, and it was not till it had been twice repeated, that he suffered her to go, accompanied by his beloved ward.

The ostensible reason given for this request was, that the Queen, who, deserted and neglected for the ambitious Ulrica, passed her days in solitude, sickness, and grief, had expressed her wish to be indulged with the society of Sigismunda—a comfort she had before enjoyed, when, as Principal Woman of the Bedchamber, her mother had some years prior to the present epoch attended that ill-treated Queen; but so far from obtaining a situation she would have rejoiced to fill, Sigismunda was not even permitted to approach the Queen's residence, but with her companion Catherine, was constrained to attend the unprincipled Ulrica, whose jealousy fixing on young Sleswie as the object of Christian's regards, she banished her as before mentioned, when the poor girl had no alternative but to seek the protection of a lady she had been taught to consider as her father's sister.

It was not in Marienburg's power to avail himself of the intelligence sent him by Sigismunda, previous to Catherine's departure, that in consequence of her unequivocal expressions of horror for the fate of Ericson's family, she had been threatened with similar punishment.

He would have recalled this daughter so precious to his peace, and actually made application to Christian for that purpose; but that flagitious Monarch, who had deceived the vigilance of Ulrica by a pretended admiration of Catherine, covered his infamous design upon the still lovelier Sigismunda, and the excuses he made for retaining his child proved to an unhappy father that her danger was extreme; for *he* was not to be the dupe of such specious art; and, convinced that the path of extrication for Sigismunda must lie through the heart of Christian, he took the steps already mentioned to dethrone him, at the same time gratifying the friendship and loyalty of a noble heart in his endeavours to serve Gustavus.

From the time Catherine had quitted her beloved companion, that persecuted maid began to feel the dangers of her situation. The pride and half-jealous manner of Ulrica, contrasted with the fawning, though secret attentions of Christian, were equal subjects of her dislike. The freedom with which she had censured his barbarous conduct towards the mother and sisters of Gustavus, convinced him that, from her good opinion of his humanity, no advantage could be gained; nor could the most splendid offers, he imagined, avail from one who was in the practice of almost unprecedented barbarity. By terror, then, only could he hope to succeed, for the open contempt which accompanied her reception of his most cautious attempts to conciliate her favour, was a certain sign that her aversion was insurmountable; yet it was worth while to try the force of persuasion before he put it beyond his power to soften her stubborn soul, for, although repeated observation almost induced a hopelessness of success, the grand trial had not been made, and Christian, whose passions stuck at nothing which dared to impede the accomplishment of his wishes, made use of Ulrica's accidental absence to plead his abominable cause.

The indignant silence which followed his unequivocal confession, encouraged him to repeat and enlarge his infamous proposals; till, perceiving indubitable marks of resentment in her blushing cheek and resentful eye, he began to fear his vanity had misled him, and would have changed the ground of his battery. But it was too late; the pride of offended modesty surmounted even that fear which an offence given to the Majesty of Denmark, Sweden, and Norway might be supposed to create; and although she considered herself as deserted by every protecting friend, and forgot in the important moment that Power which made potentates tremble, she couched her refusal in the most spirited and bitter terms, which Christian considered as the most decided and irrefragable symptom of grounded hate. To begin, therefore, his operations of an opposite tendency, he scrupled not to avow on the following day, in her hearing, his natural bias to revenge, declaring, that whoever incurred it by an opposition to his will, should be, and were, when opportunity assisted, the certain subjects of it.

A furious glance, which met the withdrawing eye of Sigismunda, explained the terrible denunciation. She trembled, and the more when Ulrica, before whom this declaration was made, and who conceived that it had for its object the temerity of Sigismunda in pleading for her imprisoned friends, malignantly took the same side of the question; and our unfortunate heroine read in the indignation of the former, and visible triumph of the latter, her own wretched destiny, hourly expecting farther tokens of that resentment which began its plan of cruelty in the discharge of Catherine. But, unlike that timid maid, she suffered not the threatened storm to deprive her of her usual foresight and fortitude. The first idea that occurred was to inform Ulrica of the true motive which urged the King to such a vindictive behaviour; but delicacy, even prudence forbade such a step. Would the mistress of Christian attend with patience or feeling to a tale that struck at her ambition, her authority, her love? Would not the natural disposition of that bad woman shew itself in accumulated injuries to the innocent supplanter of her interest with her paramour? Besides, what form of words could she chuse, that would not militate against the modesty and dignity of her own character, while they conveyed the full force of Christian's proposals?—This idea then became totally abandoned, and Sigismunda determined to wait in silence, till fresh insults, or the accomplishment of her dear father's plans, respecting the overthrow of Christian's government, should render a different conduct necessary.

CHAPTER VII.

"You have deserv'd from me
————More than reward can answer.
Were the main ocean crusted into land,
And universal monarchy were mine,
Here should the gift be plac'd!"

DRYDEN.

It was not therefore with sufficient cause for uneasiness that Marienburg contemplated the sad situation of his adopted child, Catherine Sleswie, who left, as she then was, to the merciless arrangement of his artful enemy, stood in a predicament equally dangerous with that of his beloved Sigismunda. Both, he had reason to dread, were objects of the most hateful passions, and both eventually deprived of every mortal succour.

For the fate of this unhappy young woman his heart endured a thousand pangs. The grand design he had formed in her favour would be effectually frustrated, and the train of circumstances he had promoted, and partly created, as it were, for the advancement of this favourite purpose, be rendered of no effect;—how far his prognostications were justified, remains to be shewn.

For several days succeeding her guardian's departure, Catherine encouraged sensations, composed of hope, mistrust, and even suspicion of Fitzer's integrity. She was but a superficial observer of human nature, its bias, or corruptions. Her life, from the first year to the last six months of it, had been passed under Marienburg's protection, in the endearments of friendship, and an attainment of such accomplishments as were deemed equal in those days to the female comprehension.

Mysterious as were her guardian's limited disclosures, when questioned particularly as to her possessions and destination, they made no lasting impression upon her youthful and happy heart. She had not been used to reason, to discriminate, to develop the obscurity of intrigue, or the designs of the cautious; but in the Court of Christian, at the toilet of Ulrica, a system of manners so culpable were displayed, that awakened the dormant spirit of enquiry into those causes, of which she beheld such heterogeneous effects. It was true that, in consequence of Fitzer's pretended pity for her situation, she had followed the impulse of a naturally unsuspecting heart, and discovered more of that situation than was consistent with the caution it required; for although she knew him from Marienburg's report, that could not justify her loquacity. This defalcation then, from the delicacy of retention, was singular, and she proposed to avoid it in future. In consequence, therefore, of her internal debates respecting the motives for Fitzer's remarkable attachment to the cause of Gustavus, she felt herself inclined to doubt, and even to fear; nor when the subject of these new-raised emotions appeared, to assure her of Marienburg's junction with Gustavus, and to inform her *he* was commissioned to guard her to Upsal, could she throw off a certain presentiment of evil, which mixed with her ardent wishes to be once more in safe and honourable hands; and Fitzer beheld in her varying countenance and half-reluctant preparations to accompany him, the latent symptoms of distrust, and inwardly gave her credit for a prescience so natural.

Catherine, made wise from experience, kept to herself every indication of suspicion, independent of those above described; for well she imagined that any expression of dislike to her companion, and the mode of journeying he proposed to adopt, would but heighten her own difficulties.

The winter solstice was now fully arrived, and Catherine found herself upon the eve of an expedition, to be chiefly performed by night, for the days were so contracted as to afford but little assistance to the traveller. As every advantage was procured for her comfort and accommodation, which the nature of the climate would allow, there was little to be dreaded on a journey to Upsal; but a new and pungent alarm soon destroyed the tranquillity with which she looked forward to her future residence in that city. Of the road which led from Hedmora she knew nothing, till they had passed the defile leading to the mines; but of that she had formerly quitted to stop at Van Melen's, she wanted no information. With an anxious heart then, and trembling lips, she enquired of Fitzer his motive for leaving this well-known track, after travelling several miles in a right direction, for one immediately foreign to Upsal. His answer was short, ambiguous, and evasive. She repeated her question, but to no purpose. A trifling excuse, an insidious smile, and an ardent pressure of the hand convinced Catherine of her conductor's treachery: all caution now forsook the unhappy creature; she burst into tears, and, casting a look of anguish upon the bright and desolate scene around, shrunk fearfully from an investigation of her future fate.

To remonstrate, to entreat, to command, she felt would be useless. The wily arts by which her revered Marienburg had been lured to his *destruction*, (for so depictured her affrighted imagination), were now practised upon *her* inexperience. The looks of Fitzer appeared to her, when direful suspicions changed their import, as conveying something too horrid for reflection; and to his request that she would not weep, lest her tears might prove a serious inconvenience in a frost so intense, her answer was, a mental prayer, that the cause might cease with the effect; but, however probable might be the suggestions of a heart put upon its guard by ominous appearances, it was by no means the intention of her conductor to give her any just motive for the terror his looks excited.

Certainly her abode at Upsal, and under the protection of those she considered as her natural friends, would have rendered abortive that part of his scheme which related to the disposal of Marienburg; for, although it was in his contemplation, at some future period, to make her honourable amends for the temporary alarms she then endured, he could not think of trying to obtain her hand, while supposed to be the betrayer of one she so affectionately esteemed. A Convent then was Fitzer's security; and that of St. Croix, near Eroson, a Bishop's see, within forty miles of Stockholm, held out irresistible advantages to Fitzer.

The Abbess was his aunt, whose affection to her nephew gave to such of his excesses as had reached her knowledge, the softening appellation of youthful follies, which a maturer judgment would correct.

To this lady then he *knew* the unfortunate Catherine might be safely consigned, and had already arranged in his own mind such circumstances respecting her history as, he was sure, when represented to Mother St. Magdalen, would effectually bind her over to his interest, and render futile any endeavour of Catherine's to clear herself of the imputation of indiscretion, respecting a preference to the family of Gustavus—a family, which his aunt's adherence to Christian and his government stigmatized as rebellious, and even the pest of all civil society. Added to all this, he proposed to represent herself and Marienburg as secret favourers of the doctrine of the Reformation, which of itself was enough to ensure to the suspected heretic a mode of treatment rigorous, if not cruel, from those who conceived themselves justified in defeating, by every possible means, the pious endeavours of enlightened men; but, with the strictest injunction to keep her from any communication with the world, he meant to be very particular in guarding the Abbess against every severity in the performance of her duty, as *that*, he politically considered, would only harden the heart he wished to conciliate: and as he already felt as much affection for the devoted girl as was compatible with his own selfish designs, he now, during the rest of his journey, put on a more open and benign countenance, consulting her ease and comfort in every particular the season and his private intentions would admit; but the alarm was given to Catherine's foreboding soul, and she wrapped herself up in an impenetrable reserve, nor could all Fitzer's attempts to introduce a sort of conversation rouse her from a gloomy and impolitic taciturnity.—"By observing a strict silence," argued she mentally, "I shall escape the danger of having my words misapplied, and be more at leisure to seize upon every unguarded word he may chance to utter, even perhaps to the discovery of his disposal of my dear guardian."

Thus decided Catherine, but she decided wrong; her silence grew disgusting and infectious. Fitzer caught the clue she gave him, and they travelled almost equally dissatisfied with each other's society, till the distant appearance of Eroson was faintly seen amidst the shining waste that lay on one side, and the frozen Maelar, a lake that bordered this little city.

As it would have been extremely improper to introduce Catherine to the Lady Abbess till she was prepared for her reception,

Fitzer stopped at a little inn which stood near the Convent, and within two miles of Eroson, with an idea of leaving her in the care of two trusty Saxons, whom he had chosen from the guard appointed for Marienburg.

Catherine beheld this arrangement with an indifference that sunk almost to apathy. Helpless, and nearly hopeless of any happy change as to her destination, she viewed his departure as a necessary promotion of his culpable intention, nor considered the guards to whom she was consigned, but as ministers of undeserved vengeance; for Catherine had fully decided on Fitzer's motives respecting his conduct to those she loved, namely, that every act of cruelty to Christian's enemies would be eventually a recommendation to that Monarch's notice. But again Catherine was mistaken—Fitzer had higher pursuits than to court favour; nor could she possibly suppose he meant to supersede the tyrant, by declaring himself the son of Steen Sture—a purpose he had only suspended, not laid aside.

Thus given over to her own melancholy cogitations, she sat with her eyes fixed on the stove before her, nor heeded the desultory and unintelligible discourse of her companions, who, clamorous for the refreshment which a long and abstemious journey over the frozen wilds made absolutely necessary to either party, were lamenting to each other the stupidity of a Swedish hostess, that could not understand the extent of a demand made in the Saxon language, while they appeared to envy the superior situation of their prisoner, before whom she was busied in placing such viands as her scanty cupboard afforded.

However incompatible with the dignity of ancient heroism, we are obliged to confess that Catherine refused not to partake of the notable dame's provision. Her spirits were languid, and her whole system enervated; but a moderate use of the comforts within her power gave renovation to the latter, and to the former a degree of their usual elasticity; even the evil she foreboded, lost something of its terrors, and the present inconvenience diminished in magnitude:—so true it is, that both body and mind depend in a certain measure on the respective vigour of each, with regard to their several functions.

As the Convent of St. Croix was seven miles distant from the inn, Fitzer's absence was prolonged to a degree which gave Catherine a faint gleam of hope, that he had left the conduct of her remaining travels to the Saxons; and she was actually employing her invention upon the surest means of working upon her apparently stupid hostess, to induce her either to promote her escape to Upsal, or openly to demand assistance of several Swedish boors (who happened to be collected round the stove) to guard her thither; but while balancing between the above-mentioned schemes, a sudden noise at the door of the house destroyed the fabric her ready hope had raised, for it announced to her imagination the arrival of Fitzer; and the train of apprehensions she had so hastily dismissed, again returned to darken the momentary prospect of deliverance. Deprived then of the sweet illusion upon which fancy had thrown the most brilliant tints, Catherine resumed her sullen demeanour, nor would turn an eye upon the unwelcome intruders, who she conceived (for they nearly filled the little apartment) were auxiliaries called in by Fitzer, to prevent any attempt she might have made in his absence to provide for her future security.

As Catherine momentarily expected to be summoned to quit the poor asylum, it created a surprise to find herself neglected by a company who seemed wholly intent upon providing for their own wants; and she timidly raised her head to an object that stood between her and the small light which remained of the quickly closing day.

The appearance of this figure, wrapped in a large fur coat, gave an indefinable motion to her heart. She trembled, even gasped for utterance. There was something in its air, something in its impressive manner she could neither understand nor account for: at last it turned away, seated itself on the further side of the room, and seemed absorbed in a reverie which no one attempted to interrupt.

Catherine sighed. The earnestness which marked its first notice of her, had given rise to a sudden fluctuating expectation; but it subsided, and the next alarm she received was from the voice of Fitzer, who, abruptly entering, told her, in an ungentle tone, that they must depart on the instant, for their sledges were ready, and there was no time to lose.

At this shocking intimation Catherine cast an imploring eye

upon the surrounding guests; but it rested upon the stranger, who caught the agonizing gaze, and returned it with a steady look. She blushed as she slowly passed him, while Fitzer seized her hand, and urged her forward.

"I cannot—I will *not* go from this place," exclaimed the reluctant maid, as she dropped into a seat beside the door, "till you can prove your right to force me from my natural friends!"

"Force!" repeated a voice, the tone of which, so awful, so indignant, shook even the soul of Fitzer, as he quitted the hand he had till then strenuously detained, "is it owing to *force* then that *you* are *here*?" added the energetic stranger.

"*Me!*" cried the agitated Catherine, observing the strength of his question, nor heeding Fitzer's disorder, "do you know the unhappy——"

"No more of this," interrupted her persecutor, "as you value my good opinion. We shall be late; the Abbess expects us!"

"*Your* good opinion?" returned Catherine, bursting into an agony of grief. "Cruel deception! Oh Fitzer! where is Marienburg? You possessed *his good opinion* too!"

"Fitzer from Hedmora!" vociferated the stranger, "and Marienburg of Stockholm! Say, villain!" and he catched the amazed hypocrite by the throat, "where *is* Marienburg, the good, the unsuspecting, the deceived veteran?—Say, thou tool of a base monster! what dungeon hides that virtuous man? His angel daughter too, and this blameless creature, must all be sacrificed to the despotism and lust of that tyrant?"

Conscious that this friend of the unprotected was mistaken as to the source of his treachery, Fitzer, after making a successful attempt to disengage his throat from the furious gripe, would have cleared himself of the pointed accusation; but the sight of Catherine pleading for his antagonist's support, and the readiness with which he accepted it, put Fitzer so entirely off his guard, that he attempted to snatch the terrified girl from her defender, who, with one hand firmly clasping her's, and with the other drawing an enormous sabre, pressed on the yielding Fitzer, saying, at the same instant, with an air of indescribable dignity—"Now arm thy sword with added vengeance, and take a sure aim at the heart of *Gustavus Ericson!*"

The Saxons had beheld the whole transaction without thinking it necessary to interfere in a point about which they could decide nothing; nor did they chuse to do it, from an idea that the scuffle might arise from an old quarrel, in which they could have no concern, till seeing the lady in the hands of this stranger, they rushed to the support of their master; but the *name* of Gustavus, a name so well known, and so generally admired, struck terror to their hearts, and, without comprehending the right he might have to defeat Fitzer's designs, they shrunk from the contest, and even beheld him the captive of his potent conqueror, without making one effort towards his deliverance.

An interference so providential and so successful, claimed Catherine's pious gratitude. She sunk upon her knees in an ecstacy of sublime devotion, and, after a short but fervid aspiration to Heaven, arose to express, by every means in her power, the sense she had of Ericson's generous goodness.

If *he* felt not the ecstacy which a similar benefit conferred upon Sigismunda might have excited, Gustavus, however, experienced a high satisfaction in redeeming a deserving young woman from the toils of an incorrigible offender against almost every virtue; but his delicacy would not arrogate to the act he had performed that grateful distinction with which she treated him. Waving, therefore, a subject which employed Catherine's highest eloquence, he proposed to have her conveyed to Upsal by some of his friends, while himself, with the rest of his companions, would conduct his prisoners to a place of security.

CHAPTER VIII.

"We've neither safety, unity, nor peace,
For the foundation's lost of common good.

— — — — —

Now could this glorious cause but find out friends
To do it right!"

OTWAY.

To avoid the too often repeated subterfuge of the romantic historian, in straining every natural incident to produce amazing revolutions and critical (not to say impossible) events, it will be necessary to trace those which brought together two beings involved, as it were, in similar circumstances, so far, at least, as the vindictive and cruel spirits of their merciless persecutors could effect; and to do this, we must advert to the situation in which we left Gustavus, as well as touch upon those scenes in which he had formerly borne an active part.

The anxiety induced by Marienburg's unpropitious silence, grew at last too formidable for the fortitude of our hero to suppress. The daily, or rather nightly, excursions performed by hardy Swedes, who occasionally travelled within a small distance of the mountain from whence he usually took his observation, was a convincing proof that something more important than the season retarded the intelligence he was so desirous to obtain; but while, under the name of Linden, he continued his hard and slavish employment in the mines, an incident occurred, against which the foresight of Gustavus had failed to provide. Of his quality, and the motives which induced this exalted man to become the companion of peasants and labourers, Van Melen's wife was kept in total ignorance; and as she was too often in a state that forbids discrimination, while it deadens even curiosity, the task was not difficult: but it unfortunately happened that, in continuing the disguise he first wore when he came to the cottage, he retained with it the linen he had worn in better days, the collars of which (as was the custom of those times) were richly embroidered. This uncommon appearance struck even the heavy perception of Mrs. Van Melen, who mentioned it to the superintendent of the mines, a person of sense, good-nature, and property. These combining circumstances uniting with a suspicion that he was some illustrious unfortunate, to whom he had the power of dispensing the comforts and protection of his hospitable habitation, induced Von Hemert to offer them to Ericson.

Struck with the advantage such a connotation might realize, Gustavus thankfully accepted the invitation, and quitted the mines, with a full assurance to Van Melen of soon returning to claim the assistance of the miners.

Van Melen shook his head; he knew Von Hemert's principles, *knew* his attachment to Christian, who (in consideration of a probity which even the wicked respect, and fail not to encourage, when it can be made subservient to their intentions) had given this honest man the superintendency of the mines in that part of his usurped dominions. Guided, therefore, by a sense of gratitude for a lucrative post, and the trust reposed in him, it was very unlikely, in Van Melen's estimation, that he should favour a claim that must strike at the safety of his benefactor. But of this the suspicious miner gave no oral hint; and Gustavus, after a long and secret consultation with his steady adherent, departed for the house of his new friend, under the impression of fresh hopes, and determined to send a courier immediately to Hedmora, for the purpose of learning tidings of Marienburg, his ward, and what measures had been taken to forward his own pretensions. But, however vivid were the colours his ready fancy had thrown on this change in his situation, a very short time proved sufficient to sully their lively tints, and a very little more to deface them entirely.

The candid manners and liberal principles of Von Hemert soon conquered every scruple of Gustavus as to trusting him with his real name and business. The superintendent listened with an attention which, in the eye of a disinterested observer, had a cast of horror in it. The enmity of Ericson against Christian flowed with its wonted energy; and the shudder which visibly affected his hearer, at the strength of expressions that required a full knowledge of that Monarch's baseness to justify, was considered by the unsuspecting sufferer as a testimony of Von Hemert's abhorrence of the Danish usurper: but the cold and ominous silence that followed this warm disclosure of Ericson's sentiments, chilled his ardent feelings, and a sensation of censure, respecting his own imprudent communication, flushed the noble Swede's cheek.

In Von Hemert's bosom different passions were at variance. Pity and esteem for our hero's qualities and sufferings were powerfully counterbalanced by gratitude to the Dane, and a strong sense of the trust reposed in him. The oath of fealty, too, which had been solemnly given, found also another insurmountable bar to Ericson's hopes; and he could scarcely conceal his chagrin, when this worthy subject of a treacherous monster laconically articulated his obligations to the man so bitterly reprobated.

"You know not," cried the empassioned Gustavus, "the numerous motives I have to curse that execrable being! Hear me, Sir," perceiving evident marks of impatience and disgust in his varying countenance and shifting attitude; "if usurpation, tyranny, and murder—the murder of a father, cannot excuse the suffering son, and loyal subject, in giving vent to his ardent resentment, then is Gustavus reprehensible before his friend!"

"*Murder!*" reiterated Von Hemert, while horror succeeded the symptoms of displeasure, "I knew not that self-defence, and the usual consequences of national opposition to the Sovereign against whom it has been raised, could bear so harsh a term, since the mischief arising from such an opposition ought, at least, to be equally imputed."

"But what are the principles on which Christian grounds his claim?—Are they not those of——"

"No more, my friend; we enter not into disquisitions that *must* be useless. If you can patiently detail your family's wrongs, without wounding my ears by unnecessary vindictiveness, I shall be enabled to judge, in some degree, of your motives for this intemperance."

"Be it so," returned Ericson, while the deep glow on his cheek evinced the pride of a noble heart, that almost disdained to make the concession which prudence urged as necessary to his purpose.

"It would be perfectly useless to attempt," cried Gustavus, after a solemn pause, which he employed in recollection, and an endeavour to reason down the objections his degraded dignity was prompt to make—"it would be perfectly useless to urge to a friend of Christian *my* legal title to the throne he has usurped, as an ostensible stimulus for this application, and yet it *is* one—a motive sacred, just, and honourable; but to a feeling heart I shall present claims still more forcible than that which a prejudiced mind would contemn and reject—claims that, if disregarded, would brand me as a tacit parricide!

"It is possibly unknown to you, a resident so far distant from the late dreadful scenes of action, that, in consequence of some great advantage gained by Steen, our lawful Monarch, Christian thought proper to invite him to a conference; but, reasonably suspicious of the Dane, Steen refused upon any other terms than those of his repairing to Stockholm in person, which was agreed to, upon the condition of having six noble hostages sent to Copenhagen as pledges of his safety.

"Von Hemert, can I keep the bounds of moderation while confessing that an aged mother, a valiant father, three blooming sisters, and——" here his voice trembled, and his eye kindled with a blaze of insulted dignity, "Gustavus Ericson composed the devoted number that was to swell the triumph of a—— a—— But I proceed.—His end was then attained, and, regardless of consequences, he carried us to Denmark, where a strict—nay, cruel imprisonment confirmed to us the sentiment we had previously entertained respecting our detainer's character. The spirit of my father could not brook a treatment so inimical to his notions of honour and humanity; and, in an audience he demanded of Christian, the pride of birth, the importance of his late situation, and the consciousness of his superiority, deprived his remonstrances of prudent caution; when irritated by the majesty of a spirit he could not imitate, this vile, this——"

"But not to *me* vile!" interrupted the superabundantly grateful Von Hemert.

"What," cried Gustavus, again transported beyond the rule himself had laid down of patient forbearance in this recital, "what words—what gestures can express the detestation of—— yes, of a savage and remorseless tyrant, who condemned this noble soul to immediate decapitation, for daring to assert his own grand and sacred prerogative?"

Rage and filial piety now took possession of, and wrung every fibre of Ericson's heart.

"Yes, Von Hemert, in *my* presence, before a son loaded with chains! God! what a moment! Can I forget the mild reproving eye, the tranquil countenance, which pity for the impotent distraction of an almost execrating son could not effectually disturb, while he exhorted me to avoid that fierceness of expression which had precipitated *his* fate? Before *my* face a father sunk beneath the arm of an executioner! His blood, that pure stream which had fed a heart nearly allied to perfection, flowed to my feet; when Christian, who beheld with a seeming insensibility the horrid scene, dropped, as if unconsciously, a piece of linen into the crimson fluid, and——(now may I not curse him, Von Hemert?)—and taking up the stained handkerchief, threw it carelessly against *my* eyes, to unite, perhaps, a parent's blood with the tears of his child!"

A convulsive shudder now impeded articulation, while the violence of his emotions, and that indescribable somewhat which irradiated his impressive features, stamped the seal of truth on this sad relation, and created in his pitying hearer every contrary sentiment that worth, and villany could excite. Gustavus, after wiping away the filial tear, which gives dignity even to true courage, proceeded, unchecked by Von Hemert for any unguarded anathema which the subjects he had yet to discuss occasionally extorted.

"There yet remained more victims, my friend, to be sacrificed upon the altar of sanguinary vengeance. Neither my mother nor sisters knew as yet of their irreparable loss; confined in a distant part of the Castle, they could only lament, and forebode future evils. No means offered by which I could convey the intelligence my heart yet trembled to communicate. That they were then alive, I could only hope; and had very little foundation even for that, when I considered the barbarity which gratified itself at the expence of a gallant veteran's life. The subsequent conduct observed by Christian, relative to this event, amazed, while it confounded, my almost shattered reason; for, so far from the punishment my temerity led me to expect, I was freed from my chains, and, after a period of about three weeks, was permitted, although strictly watched, to visit the dear relatives I had given up for lost, to whose earnest interrogatories respecting a husband's and a father's safety, my heart refused the answer truth suggested; but the cool, intrepid fortitude of his consort soon rendered every attempt to conceal it of no effect, for, fixing a steady and tearless eye upon my half-averted face, she exclaimed—'*You know*, Gustavus, what tenderness for us would teach you to conceal.' And looking upon her weeping daughters—'This must not be, my children; it is an imbecility unworthy the offspring of the illustrious Gustavus Ericson! Blessed spirit!' she continued, lifting up her hands and eyes, 'communicate a portion of thy heroism to thy feeble descendants; and thou, Gustavus, shame not the grandeur of thy principles by a weakness, at which a true-born Scandinavian would blush!'

"This was the reproach of a matron, given at the moment when she *more* than suspected herself to be the widowed captive of the monster who had murdered her husband. As she asked not the particulars, which I could scarcely recount, I entered upon the subject of that indulgence which restored me to such estimable society; but my mother, as if inspired by a presentiment of what was to follow, adjured me to resist the allurements of a tyrant.

'Trust him not!' she exclaimed. 'Refuse his most trifling requests! There is a design, a black concealed design in all he says, in all he does. Thy noble father stands first in the list of assassination, a list in which Royalty itself is included. Go, my child, provoke not the Dane's jealousy by too long a stay. Fear not for thy mother—she is safe; her children too——' (here she extended her arm, as if to press the distressed creatures to her soul, as they wept at her feet—'these precious heirs of a father's virtues and misfortunes are safe; with *me* they may know sorrow, but never guilt, and Heaven will *not* abandon them!'

"This great behaviour, so contrary to what my notion of feminine tenderness had led me to expect, produced its desired effect; and before I quitted the dear prisoners, I was enabled to give a mutilated account of my father's death, which was received in a way that confirmed my reverence for a mother, who ennobled her station by the energies of her principles, while for my sisters I felt the softest compassion.

"The motives which induced Christian to treat me with such a flattering distinction, soon became apparent. Fresh actions commenced between the Swedes and Danes, in one of which our royal master lost his life. To the treachery of Christian was this calamity attributed; and so heartily was he detested for it throughout the Swedish dominions, which, from that black event, became subject to his power, that he thought it necessary to strengthen it by a coalition with some of its most dignified natives.

"The prognostication and caution of my dearest mother now established themselves, and my hatred against the self-named Monarch yet became more potent. To dissimulate was impossible; it militated against my own sentiments and those of the parent I adored; and when, in consequence of a heartily expressed refusal of the terms he mentioned as necessary to my entire liberation, this artful deceiver again immured me in a close dungeon, where light itself was denied, I felt proudly satisfied with a lot that proved my determined opposition to an inhuman foe;—it was then I experienced the full effects of a tyrant's hatred, and, as if to punish that integrity which dared his utmost fury, Christian sent me the horrid information of the intended execution of my mother and sisters, as the certain fruit of my own obstinacy."

"And *this man*," interrupted his shuddering auditor, "is the benefactor, the friend of Conan Von Hemert!"

This apostrophe was music to the soul of Gustavus; it announced his victory over a sensible mind, and little more of his sad but true representation seemed necessary to establish a just and extorted indignation against the crimes this good man disdained; but more freely did he express his abhorrence of Christian's behaviour to those hostages who had nobly pledged themselves for their beloved Steen. Against this species of villany he loudly declaimed, and seemed ashamed of that attachment to Christian which his own honour held sacred, while the object of it spurned as a weakness (at least his actions expressed as much) that conduct by which he profited.

To the sufferings so faithfully delineated, Conan paid the tribute of a tear. His idea of Augusta's heroic virtue, her husband's mild submission to a cruel fate, the sorrow of their blooming girls, and the manly grief of Gustavus, was consonant to the feelings of humanity, and the spirit of true Christianity, as taught by Luther.

Ericson beheld and gloried in the interest his cause obtained with this worthy and prudent being.

"Still unconvinced of my stedfastness," observed Ericson, "Christian again liberated the man who owed to him such unprecedented injuries; and under the care of Banner, a Danish Nobleman, I was permitted to enjoy both air and exercise, but with the strictest limitation respecting any knowledge of my unfortunate relatives, prohibiting the slightest enquiry concerning even the certainty of their existence, and charging the generous Dane, upon the penalty of six thousand crowns, not to permit the escape of his prisoner. The horrid massacres and desolation which, on my emancipation from prison, became a constant theme of terror and pity, rendered the partial liberty I enjoyed, more irksome than pleasant. Not a Swede whose property, principles, or situation could excite the envy, jealousy, or avarice of the invader, but suffered in various instances, and my heart burned with a desire of revenge against their persecutor; but so critically circumstanced, it was impossible to achieve any design of importance.

"The noble Banner, whose generous confidence in my honour deserved the highest esteem, not only remained inflexibly silent as to my family, but prevented by his incessant watchfulness any probability of obtaining the ardent desire of my soul; and for some time I remained hopeless of an advantageous change in my situation, which, distinguished as it was by every attention in the fortress of Calo, in Jutland, commanded by Banner, yet wanted the blessing of liberty to make it desirable.

"If ever the shadow of duplicity could attach itself to the actions of Gustavus, this was the period in which his conduct might be thought to justify such a suspicion; but suspend your censure, my friend, till subsequent events shall obliterate that suspicion. From the known inflexibility of Banner, I deemed every attempt to reconcile him to a scheme I had formed for my escape, as utterly fruitless; and being, since my arrival at Jutland, indulged with greater privileges, I one day quitted the fortress of Calo, under the pretence of hunting, and returned to it no more. On the third of my departure the gates of Flensburgh presented a formidable obstacle to my purpose. Without a passport, and amenable to Christian's recent edict, any further prosecution of my intentions appeared highly improbable; but by the favour of a Saxon merchant, who took me as a temporary servant—— Yes, Von Hemert, the lawful heir to Sweden's Crown has been reduced to—— Pardon the pride of painful recollection—I will proceed!——With this merchant I safely quitted Denmark, and after a short stay at Lubec, was discovered by the generous Banner, who had pursued me thither. At first he exclaimed with great warmth against my seeming ingratitude in leaving him burthened with such a tax upon his property and character, as my flight would necessarily fix upon him; but, influenced by the First Consul of Lubec, my representation of the motives which had withdrawn me from Calo, and his own re-established high opinion of the ill-treated Gustavus, he consented to return, with a pretence of being unable to trace my steps. The reception his noble conduct met with I learned from its consequences, as an immense price was set upon my person; and, under the disguise of a peasant Dane, I heard myself denounced a traitor to the Triple State of Sweden, Denmark, and Norway.

"At Lubec my cause was in good hands, as the Regency, to whom I was known, declared in my favour, promising, if I could procure the protection of any other Power, they would lend every assistance to that cause.

"Assured of success, and grateful for their kindness, I quitted Lubec for Calmar, a city garrisoned chiefly by Germans; but the principal officers were most of them my fellow-soldiers in the late Administrator's army. With these men, who were acquainted with my birth and connections, I immediately joined, expecting nothing less than an approbation of my plan; but a doubtful mistrust increased on every countenance, while I was rehearsing my inducement for attempting a revolution,—nay, so cold, so cautious was their treatment of the warrior they had once almost idolized, that I disdained any further development of my plan, but hastened to these mountains, in the hope of inflaming the peasant breast with such sentiments as might enforce an obedience to the commands of their lawful Sovereign."

Here Gustavus ceased, while, with a penetrating eye, he examined the changing countenance of his expected adherent.

To a tale so eventful, the full and undivided attention of Von Hemert had been given; but in the long and serious silence that followed this communication, no symptom occurred which could confirm the anxious hopes of our hero, who, in his haste to come at the Dane's sentiments, omitted to enumerate a thousand dangers, and an infinitude of disappointments he had endured previous to his journey to Dalecarlia, both at Stockholm, and at an old family castle in Sudermania, the peasants near which, satisfied with the possession of some of their ancient immunities, refused to take up arms against the Monarch by whom they were continued; but eager to ascertain the success he had too prematurely reckoned upon (for the influence of Von Hemert over the miners would make Ericson's task more easy, as their *ungoverned* vehemence in his favour might do as much mischief eventually, as a direct opposition might probably create) he waited in painful suspense the momentous result. What then were his sensations when Von Hemert, roused from his profound meditation, and heaving a deep sigh, solemnly uttered the words—"*It must not be!*"

CHAPTER IX.

"Enliv'ning hope and fond desire
Resign the heart to spleen and care;
Scarce-frighted Love maintains her fire,
And rapture saddens to despair."

JOHNSON.

"*It must not be!*"—What a mortifying decision for Gustavus, at the very instant too when, in defiance of a latent foreboding, he strove to congratulate himself upon the acquisition of another friend; but the tone of voice, the troubled features, and retiring footsteps were fatal proofs of his disappointment.

"I am truly concerned," cried Von Hemert, in a cold but unsteady tone, "for the sufferings which gratitude to the inflicter prevents my resenting; but I cannot reflect upon the situation in which Christian found me at Flensburgh, where I was left wounded by the Swedes, without feeling emotions of thankfulness for the service he rendered me, in protecting me from those who were then my enemies, and, after his elevation, procuring me this profitable post: *I* therefore am bound, by the strictest ties, not to interfere in a case so important to his interest!"

"But *I* am held by no such bonds!" exclaimed a person, who, unknown to Von Hemert, had overheard a large portion of Ericson's narrative from an adjoining apartment.—"Myself, my house, my vassals are and shall be devoted to the cause of the noble Gustavus! You are surprised, my friend," addressing our hero, as he advanced to the entrance, where stood a Swedish Officer, "at this address; but——"

"It is Peterson!" interrupted our hero, while he embraced the intruder.—"This offer will indeed make amends for my late disappointment!" and then, turning to Von Hemert,—"But *you*, because the claims of gratitude forbid any actual exertion in my favour, will not *therefore* be my enemy?"

"Forbid it, justice! forbid it, humanity!" said this friendly man.—"No, Gustavus, those claims you hint at require no such sacrifice; command my services in every other instance. I must soon visit Stockholm; it may then be in my power to learn somewhat of your family, or——"

"No more, Von Hemert," cried Peterson; "long ere you bring intelligence of them, I trust my gallant Prince will be seated on the tyrant's throne! Retain your cold and cautious principles! Peterson acts by no such selfish rules; his heart is the seat of truth—of honour; but your's——"

"Dictates the words of truth, and feels even more than those words convey."

As Von Hemert articulated this interruption, he fixed a look upon Peterson, sarcastical, yet calm.

Gustavus lost not the expression; but charmed with the ready zeal of Peterson, he attributed Von Hemert's visible mistrust to the natural character of his feelings: and, after gratefully thanking this good creature for his benevolent attentions, departed, at the instigation of his new patron, for Lincopping, where his family resided.

Once more then did the heart of Gustavus beat high with the assurance of a most powerful assistance, and once more did he encourage a hope that his friend Marienburg might be employed in a similar way with himself; for Peterson had recently assured him that the Dalecarlians, through the influence of a person, whose description answered that of the veteran, were in a state of insurrection, and could their force unite with those *he* should be enabled to procure, the great example would doubtless be followed by those at Flensburgh, and others.

Thus supported, and inwardly rejoicing at a view, the accomplishment of which might bring freedom to his family, if yet in being, and the purest gratification of his long suppressed wish—an union with Sigismunda, Gustavus listened with increasing confidence and rapture to the schemes of his ardent auxiliary. No longer the proscribed and unfriended mark of a tyrant's vengeance, no longer mortified by an opposition to his various wishes, Ericson found in the vehement Peterson a supporter of his claims and desires, whether as respecting his right to the Crown of Sweden, his beloved and ever-lamented mother and sisters, or the idolized Sigismunda Marienburg, his affection for whom made a part of his constant themes, while conversing with this new and zealous friend, by whom he learned that she was removed from Stockholm to some place of security. Impatient to realize one of the many plans he had adopted for the completion of his choicest purposes, Gustavus, after a short period had elapsed, solicited of Peterson the assistance he so often and so eagerly proposed; and in the presence of Madam Peterson urged the necessity of an immediate junction with the peasants of his district, of whose decided attachment to Ericson's cause so much had been said.

"I cannot just now," returned Peterson, glancing a threatening look at his wife, "enter upon a subject which requires the utmost privacy."

The look was understood, and she quietly quitted the room. There was a rudeness in Peterson's conduct towards this respectable woman which caused a temporary disgust in the heart of Gustavus, and he determined to offer all the amends for her husband's abruptness that his situation would allow, conceiving himself amenable, in some degree, for the concern which settled on her features as she slowly withdrew.

As if relieved from some apprehension which the presence of Madam Peterson created, his friend directly entered into the full spirit of Ericson's affairs; and it was finally agreed that an attempt was to be made in a few days, the success of which should entirely confirm the hopes and expectations this ardent Swede so completely raised.

Scarcely was this arrangement made, when the appearance of a Danish officer, whose principles and post declared him the ally of Christian, put a speedy end to the conference; and on the following day Ericson, accompanied by some of those adherents Peterson had recommended, arrived at the inn which Catherine occupied, on their way to a village named by Peterson, as containing numbers of those whose allegiance to Christian was, by his cruel conduct, totally annihilated.

Triumphing in the unexpected deliverance of Catherine, and the detention of her persecutor, Gustavus hastened back to the abode of his friend, where he proposed to leave Fitzer and the

Saxons till he had accomplished the business that led him towards Eroson; and after explaining the cause of this extraordinary appearance, adjourned to an apartment where Madam Peterson waited to take her coffee with him previous to his return. It was then Gustavus proposed to offer some apology for the undeserved affront the manner of Peterson had so fully given upon his account; but in the moment he began it, that gentleman's introduction of the Danish Officer to his Lady gave the conversation another turn.

As the business which so closely united the interest of Ericson with that of his patron could not be discussed in the presence of the stranger, our hero readily allowed for a certain taciturnity and awkward constraint in Peterson, which was utterly inconsistent with his usual open, not to say impetuous, manner; but to the particularly reserved and confused behaviour of his obliging hostess he could grant no such indulgence. Even the etiquette of hospitality was devoid of that elegance which usually graced the dispenser of it. A neglectful inattention to the duties of her place marked every action. If addressing an insignificant question to her husband, a penetrating look at Gustavus declared her thoughts to be at variance with her words. Deep sighs, sudden changes of countenance, and even a starting tear, all declared the agitation of a labouring mind; but when Ericson arose to bid her farewel, she caught his presented hand with an eagerness that would have raised the vanity of almost any one but the object of this extraordinary movement. Seated between her husband and his visitor, any attempt to rise, and follow Gustavus would have excited suspicion as to its cause; but Madam Peterson regarded not the dread of censure, but abruptly leaving the table, she pursued the astonished Nobleman till he reached his horse, and in hurried whispering accents exclaimed—"*Beware of Peterson!*"

Gustavus started.

"*Of Peterson!*" he repeated; and was about to demand her reason for this strange, and as he imagined, unwarranted caution, when she hastily added—"Go to my brother Plesban!" and instantly retired.

Confounded at the suddenness of this intimation, and the dreadful thoughts it inspired, he cast a vacant eye upon the road before him, when the approach of a troop of soldiers gave a different turn to his ideas. They wore the Danish uniform, and apparently directed their course to the house of his entertainer.

The motive which had impelled Madam Peterson's extraordinary address was rendered sufficiently plain; and, while he blessed her disinterested friendship, he knew not what method to adopt, to escape the toils of her treacherous consort: for if the troop, which he now beheld dividing into parties of two or three, and carelessly sauntering in different paths, were deputed to secure his person, any attempt to avoid them, with only the assistance of a few followers, however it might evince his rash intrepidity, would bear no marks of cautious courage. This manœuvre, then, he thought proper to shun; and as the suspicion Gustavus entertained, could not, he imagined, be immediately realized, he practised a mode of behaviour not much less dangerous, though perhaps not so directly fatal. Quitting, therefore, his first intention, he redelivered his horse's reins into the hands of a soldier; and at the moment Anna Peterson thought him almost beyond danger, her very soul was chilled at the reappearance of a hero, whose virtues, misfortunes, and cause rendered him an object of the most friendly attachment.

With far other sensations did Count Struensee and her husband receive the noble warrior. They had seen the arrival of the troop appointed to secure Gustavus, and those very few adherents his merits had secured; and as their plan was (if he did not fall into the ambush they had appointed) to have him seized in his bed, they were still more pleased to find he had, by his stay, given a better probability to the confirmation of their hopes, than if the prior scheme had taken place.

When Anna considered how ineffectual were the steps she had taken towards her favourite's preservation, her fortitude forsook her, and she burst into tears when he addressed her. Gustavus knew how to appretiate this friendly warmth; while Peterson and his visitor, who dreaded nothing less than the true motive for those tears, attributed them to a preference disgraceful to the virtuous Prince, and dishonourable to herself.

The mind of Peterson was in a tumult. The superior elegance and manly perfections of Ericson had, from the second day of their meeting, been considered by that bad man as subjects of his wife's unguarded admiration. Judging with an illiberal meanness, of which such souls alone are capable, he had converted every expression of esteem and respect into those of a criminal nature; and this jealousy was the prior source of an action, which had the ostensible covering of loyalty to Christian for its basis. No wonder then that a reception so striking should alarm that selfish bosom, or that it should produce in Peterson's conversation a bitterness of irony which Gustavus could neither understand nor submit to; but a look from Anna, while it gave another pang to her tyrant's heart, carried such intelligence to that of Ericson, as convinced him his danger was extreme, while it suggested (so, however, he translated it) the necessity of a prudent forbearance.

To the sarcastical observations, therefore, of the unguarded Peterson, respecting his sudden change of resolution, he gave slight and unsatisfactory answers; and the advance of night, while it gratified the sanguinary betrayer, brought no hope of deliverance to his agitated victim. Madam Peterson was retired; and Gustavus, without one decided motive, unless it was to see in what manner the newly arrived Danes were disposed of, went to the outward gate, under a pretence of viewing the state of the thaw, which was recently begun, and which, if continued, would render travelling exceedingly difficult: but all around was perfectly still; no vestige of any thing human was seen near the premises, and again the dependance of Gustavus on Madam Peterson's information was weakened.

Somewhat better satisfied with his situation than before, and willing to impute Peterson's abruptness to something independent of himself, he was about to re-enter, when, through the dusk, which was rendered still more dense from the proximity of lowering clouds, he fancied he beheld within a few paces of him two or three figures, who seemed as if shrinking from observation. The circumstance was suspicious; but a stranger to fears of a common description, he was determined to watch the event of this appearance, when Ericson dimly discovered several horses, whose motions the men seemed endeavouring to restrain. Again suspicion, not wholly devoid of terror, arose to combat his re-established opinion of Peterson. It was plain his presence had not been noticed; it was possible, therefore, some light into their schemes might be obtained by his preserving the strictest silence, nor did his curiosity long remain ungratified.

"Certainly," cried one of the men, in a low tone, "this project will not succeed; and if we should be discovered?"

"Fool!" cried a second, "or coward rather, are you afraid of *one* man?"

"This good sabre," boasted the first, "if he would but appear—— Hush! some one comes this way."

" 'Tis Iwan," exclaimed another voice.

Gustavus almost trembled. Iwan was one of his most faithful followers, and had quitted the mines with him. Was Iwan then treacherous?—"Too true he is," thought the unhappy Ericson, who the next moment distinguished that favourite's voice, as he saluted the others by the appellation of "fellow-soldiers," adding his fears that their enterprise would not be attended with success.

"Yes," replied another, "that is Redman's opinion, but he is wrong; we are in the service of our lawful Prince, and——"

"If we do not conquer, we can *die* in it!"

This last assertion was Iwan's—that Iwan who had often sworn to support Ericson to the latest moment of his existence.

"And such," in a low tone, articulated our disappointed chief, "are the friendships of the lower class." Peterson, too, a gentleman, one from whom he had received unexpected and unasked protestations of assistance, he also was probably actuated by the same grovelling sentiments.

"There is no distinction then," concluded Gustavus, "but in the exterior; both act upon the same wicked principle, and from both *I* am equally a sufferer!"

A deep, unconscious sigh that followed this decision, alarmed the conspirators.

"We are discovered," said Iwan, "and he will be lost."

"*He* shall *not* be lost," vociferated the enraged Prince, "while this good sabre holds! Come on then, treacherous Iwan, and take a just reward!"

"*Friends!*" exclaimed the astonished Iwan, avoiding the stroke intended for his destruction.

Gustavus dropped his weapon, and in the next moment raised

his yet faithful follower, as he was sinking on his knees before the delighted Ericson.

"Away!" cried Redman; "the family is alarmed. This instant mount, my Lord!" presenting a fleet horse to his master.

Gustavus vaulted into the saddle; the rest, who held themselves in readiness, took to their impatient steeds, and, following Iwan, were soon beyond the power of their expected pursuers, while every shadow of doubt respecting the trusty leader, was effectually destroyed by his present conduct; and it remained, as a mere matter of curiosity upon Ericson's mind, to know by whom this plan of his escape was suggested. With honest, though blunt encomiums on Madam Peterson's generosity, Iwan declared that to her alone was his Lord indebted for his safety; for on her quitting the room after she had given those dangerous tokens of her sensibility, it appeared that she sought for Iwan, and briefly informed him of the Prince's danger, and then charged him to prepare every thing for an immediate departure.

These orders were punctually obeyed; nor needed there much dispatch, as they had been commanded by Gustavus to keep their horses ready for an instant's warning. But just as they were silently taking possession of the ground appointed by Madam Peterson, as a place of rendezvous, where they might secrete themselves till she could inform Gustavus of his danger, they observed a soldier creeping behind some palisadoes, as if employed in watching them, and this accounted for the application Ericson made of their threats as relative to himself. Thus then was his gratitude engaged towards Anna Peterson, who, in despite of opposition, suspicion, and its consequent dangers, had so happily exerted herself on his behalf; and by so doing, he feared, would fix a stigma on her character, never to be erased.

As soon as Gustavus could properly consider himself as a free agent, he determined to revisit the sincere, cautious, but friendly Von Hemert, whose conduct, steady, yet cool, formed a contrast with that of the impetuous and treacherous Peterson, so infinitely to that hypocrite's disadvantage. Accordingly, after taking a route contrary to the one he intended, and leaving his attendants by the way, he secretly returned to the path leading to his friend's habitation, whose countenance, at this unexpected arrival, evinced the warmth of hospitality, while its placidity was deeply tinctured by a shade of melancholy, which the beam of pleasure Ericson's appearance created, could not disperse.

Gustavus, whose skill in physiognomy was extremely superficial, accused his own readiness in following Peterson, as the cause of this increasing gloom, and he felt the awkwardness of guilt while hinting at a palliation of his conduct. Von Hemert saw the ingenuous struggle, and with the utmost candour allowed for a situation which required every exertion, and demanded every endeavour to amend it.

"But you are unhappy, my friend," cried Ericson; "some misfortune, independent of mine, affects you. The serenity which used to distinguish Von Hemert, is destroyed. Is it true that *he*, who possesses the allegiance of that valuable heart, is no longer in a capacity to enjoy it? Has Christian——"

"I know nothing recently of Christian but by report, which report, if rightly founded—Oh, Gustavus! how truly are you to be pitied!"

"Pitied!" exclaimed Gustavus.—"Report! what report can produce so mean a sentiment as *pity* for the Prince of Sweden?"

"Alas!" cried the compassionating Conan, "how soon must the lightning of that ardent eye be quenched in tears of——"

"Thy caution is torture to the soul of Ericson! Explain, Von Hemert—is Marienburg, is Sigismunda, Catherine, or—— Oh shame! the lightning is already quenched!" So saying, he dashed off a tear—"or the dear relatives I left in dangerous confinement, any way involved in this painful mystery?"

"I have had intelligence from Denmark," hastily replied Von Hemert; "it speaks terrible things—it involves most of the parties you hint at: but be patient, my Lord; the papers I speak of are not in this house. They are by this time at Upsal, with Catherine Sleswie;—to-morrow you may have them. Not another word on this subject!" perceiving his vehement attempt to speak.—"Night wears; some rest is necessary: *I* will accompany you to Upsal; till then rest satisfied."

"*Rest!* Oh Von Hemert! you stuff my pillow with the sharpest thorns, and then counsel me to *rest!*"

"I have done wrong, my Prince! forgive me! Could I extract

those thorns by a recital of what you seek to know, Gustavus should not ask in vain; but it would only increase an impatience that is already too painful."

Conan, indeed, had acted wrong. He was no judge of human nature, nor could he give a false elucidation of his feelings; yet, true to the motive which inspired his resolution, he combated the pressing remonstrances of Ericson with an energy that proved successful; and after a small refreshment, which was imbittered by the present circumstances, Von Hemert sent a messenger to the retreat in which Ericson had left his friends, and then with the utmost difficulty induced the agitated hero to retire, for the purpose of obtaining a few hours' repose.

CHAPTER X.

"Life, fill'd with grief's distressful train,
For ever asks the tear humane.
Oh! hear that lonely widow's wail;
See her dim eyes, her aspect pale!
Heard you that agonizing throe?
Sure this is not romantic woe!"

LANGHORNE.

FROM the rapid succession of hope and disappointment which marked this epocha of Ericson's political and domestic progress, it would seem as if an omniscient Providence had but proportioned them to the strength and spirit of his noble principles. At this eventful period, duty, friendship, love, and even personal safety were threatened with accumulated dangers. To preserve any one of these claims was doubtful; to guard them all impossible, more particularly if the important business, which involved his grandest interest, was yet sedulously attended to; but in this, as in every other incident of Ericson's fate, he lost not the end in the means. The overthrow of one project was but the foundation of a future; and from every disappointed scheme, his vigorous imagination deduced fresh strength, new invention, steady resolution, and cooler intrepidity. To a weaker mind his present embarrassments and distresses would appear insurmountable; but if he indulged for one moment a despairing idea, it only originated from the uncertainty of not knowing exactly what to dread, or if the evil he was taught to expect, did not strike at every *precious* dependance.

Soon, however, the rising morn dissipated the most comfortless of these fears. Catherine, he understood, was safe at Upsal: from *her*, he was led to believe a solution of this mystery would be obtained: and, contrary to Conan's system, the lighter evil of certainty would supply that of a doubt, which *might* create more horrible sufferings than the former would inflict. Thus persuaded, he beheld the spires and towers of Upsal with a steadiness, the result of dispassionate reasoning and renewed fortitude.

Although unchanged as to his loyalty, and still persuaded there was merit in his attachment to Christian, Von Hemert scrupled not to acknowledge Gustavus as his friend; and, although the Monarch's proscriptions remained in full force, ventured to Catherine's retirement, accompanied by the subject of them.

No sooner did the grateful Sleswie perceive her deliverer (whose disguise was insufficient to mislead her) enter the avenue of pines that led to her asylum, than she ran to meet him. Gustavus dismounted, and with Von Hemert followed her into the vestibule. Catherine then, modestly apologizing to Conan for leaving him, conducted Ericson to a large sitting-room, at the farther end of which a figure caught his eye, whose appearance spoke volumes to his feeling heart.—It was *Marienburg!* or rather the shattered remains of what was Marienburg.

"I was told," cried Gustavus, as he grasped the emaciated hand of the feeble veteran, "that Catherine Sleswie possessed the means of wounding my soul; instead of which, she bestows a cordial on my grateful heart, for even this picture of debility is precious in the estimation of friendship."

"Are you alone, my Lord?" said Marienburg.

There was a coldness in this address that chilled the empassioned fervour of our hero: he turned to Catherine; she was weeping, but that effusion was countenanced by the scene before her.

"I *have* a companion, Marienburg," he answered, while hardly knowing how to act.

"Can he be trusted, my Prince?"

"Yes."

"Then introduce him, love."

Catherine ran to execute this commission, and Marienburg beheld in Von Hemert a former favourite, the contrast to Fitzer and all bad men.

His reception of this gentle man was cordial; but from what the Prince could collect, his presence was not unexpected.

Gustavus watched every turn of Marienburg's features; he saw, without being an adept in physiognomy, that some important discovery hung upon the lips of the old man. The coldness he first noticed, gradually changed to an affecting solemnity, which, to an accurate observer, appeared tinged with a sense of guilt; and that distant manner which chilled the fervour of a long-desired meeting, seemed to originate in a far distant cause to the one he had reluctantly adopted.

"Be seated, my dear friends; and you, ever-precious and long-lamented object of my affectionate allegiance, prepare to execrate the wretch who, while his heart beat with the strongest sensations of loyalty to his Prince, has forfeited every title to all but his deepest hatred."

"It cannot be Marienburg who thus accuses himself?" said Ericson.—"It cannot be *me* he has so cruelly injured?"

Marienburg was silent, apparently struggling with the emotions of an almost exhausted heart. Catherine had reclined her arm upon her guardian's couch, endeavouring to conceal the tears she could not stop. Von Hemert cast a pitying eye upon the half-prostrate veteran, as he indulged what heroic courage, not yet wholly conquered, would have restrained; while Ericson, with an anxious attention, which barely admitted respiration, hung suspended between the most agonizing doubts.

"I have a long and shocking story to relate," resumed Marienburg, "the heads of which Catherine committed to paper, and sent to Van Melen's; from him we learned you had taken refuge with the good Von Hemert, who last week returned them, with an account that you had quitted his protection—a circumstance that Catherine knew not of when you so generously rescued her from Fitzer. Upon the subject, then, of those papers I would be explicit; yet nature, worn out with recent severities, forbids——"

"I cannot," interrupted Gustavus, "any longer endure this torturing uncertainty! Some dreadful catastrophe doubtless attaches to these mysterious papers. I will be master of my fate—I will read what Marienburg's infirmities cannot permit him to explain!"—So saying, he took from Catherine, who presented them with a trembling hand, the mandates of his destiny, and retired to a distant apartment to peruse a scroll, every line almost of which was calculated to astonish and torment.

From what he then read, we shall endeavour to arrange the events that followed Marienburg's confinement in the Castle of Lunenburgh, to the present period.

It appeared, from his own representation, that till the day of Saxe Lunenburgh's arrival at his capital, the aged prisoner met with every practicable civility from Colonel Klopstock. The Duke's presence was rather unexpected by Klopstock, who imagined he would stay till a thorough change of season; but fearful of the approaching thaw, which would render travelling both difficult and dangerous, he supposed the Duke chose to avoid an inconvenience so important before the frost broke up.

The hints which Marienburg had previously received, added to the motives that he was aware would stimulate Magnus to revenge himself by employing the powers of the Secret Tribunal, gave his ancient captive but little reason to hope for any favourable change in his affairs. He could not but recollect that, in consequence of opposing Magnus in a case of seduction, (such was the opinion conceived by Marienburg), which, during his residence at the Court of Lunenburgh, that Prince had disgraced himself by engaging in, and which had been attended by circumstances of a cruel import, that the years following this event had passed in an uniform endeavour, on the Duke's side, to harass and distress the noble-minded Marienburg—nay, the very incident to which he owed his present confinement sprung, as he supposed, from this grounded hate, and he looked upon Fitzer with his companions as mere agents in the criminal transaction. All, then, he now could expect, was a full condemnation by that awful Tribunal, and he hourly awaited the fatal summons; when, after two days of anxious doubt, the entrance of the Governor, with an open paper, gave a tremulous emotion to that heart which was so soon to lose the throb of existence.

"Listen!" cried Colonel Klopstock; "I am commanded by this order to send you to Christian of Sweden. I pity you, Marienburg—Christian is a savage! He waits with greedy impatience every opportunity to gratify his sanguinary passions: a rich sacrifice lingers but for *your* presence to make it complete!—The mother and sisters of the great Gustavus (whom Heaven inspire with the means of revenge!) will grace your fall; for he removed them in his own train from Copenhagen to Stockholm, where he now is."

"Horrible!" cried the devoted man. "Must the execution of those virtuous women swell that monster's list of crimes? But I am ready, Sir—the Duke's commands shall be obeyed; at least I shall see, and perhaps embrace, the illustrious Augusta and her chaste offspring;—even this will be a pleasure I expected not to taste, suspecting, as I have recently done, that they were already immortalized."

Pleased with, yet pitying, a spirit so cruelly treated, the Governor delivered his prisoner over to the guard appointed to convey him to Stockholm; and this alteration in his destiny arose neither from compassion nor a sense of injustice in Magnus, who both knew and detested the character of Christian; but sensible he could bring forward no lawful plea for impeaching Marienburg as an object of a Free Judge's vengeance, and secure of his intention to dethrone the Dane, he hastened from Hernosand to make the arrangement, and felt fully satisfied with the delegate he had chosen for his infernal purpose. No gentleness of disposition, no relenting consideration had prevented the operation of a personal revenge. Upon the nature of his offence against Christian the Duke founded his expectation of a secure and seemingly honourable retribution in the punishment of Marienburg, the whole of whose treasonable practices he had, through Fitzer's information, conveyed to Stockholm, where an agonizing trial of that good man's principles awaited his arrival.

It was not without a severe pang the aged prisoner beheld the walls of that palace, from whence he had too much reason to dread his innocent child had been dragged to meet a horrid fate; and when he enquired, with a trembling heart, for that beloved daughter, the short and undecisive answer he received sounded like the mandate of her death.

Marienburg was allowed but little time to indulge in a hopeless grief; for on the morning succeeding a rapid and fatiguing journey, he was summoned to appear before Christian.

To convey any idea of the agony a wretched parent must endure while beholding the triumphant persecutor of his child, and the self-established tyrant of an oppressed people, ready also to sign his own death-warrant, can only be done by a description of the scene which determined in some degree his fate. The aspect of Christian, proud, cruel, and unrelenting—the presence of Ulrica, whose eye gleamed vengeance against the veteran—the awful silence that followed Marienburg's entrance, interrupted only by the clank of his own chains, and those of other unfortunate victims, who, he judged, were then approaching to receive *their* doom, failed to impress his mind with any sensation so affecting as that caused by pity for his dear daughter; and when the Monarch, in bitter accents, reproached him for his attachment to Gustavus, he turned a calm and impressive look upon the conscious King, while he slowly pronounced the name of "*Sigismunda.*"

"And what of Sigismunda, thou hoary-headed villain?" exclaimed Ulrica.—"Is she not the offspring of a *traitor*? Can aught good or honourable be the produce of a stock so base?"

"She is *virtuous*, Ulrica!—Not even the examples of Christian's Court could contaminate so pure a spirit!"

"Ha! foolish dotard, enjoy the illusion. Facts, stubborn facts shall soon overwhelm thy weak belief!"

"Away, Madam, with this woman's war of words," cried Christian; "and thou, Marienburg, listen to the first and last overtures I shall make, to which, if thou consentest, freedom, honour, and almost regal dignity shall be the reward of thy compliance; but if our proposals are refused, death, in its most ignominious forms, shall be the consequence to thyself, and those thou best lovest. We are aware of thy amazement, and will not keep thee in suspense. Inform us where the traitor Gustavus is concealed, or by whom protected, and Christian will be the friend of Marienburg."

"And Marienburg the *murderer* of Gustavus!—Oh Christian! is it not so? No, Sir, that must never be! Thou hast sported, it is indeed too probable, with the happiness of my child. Thou art striking at the life of her parent; take it—'tis thine, I know, and thou must have thy due; but, Gustavus, Oh great and glorious hero!" lifting up his hands with an air of exultation, "safe mayst thou ever continue from the grasp of violence and oppression!"—His voice now sunk from the tone of triumph to that of dejected humility, and he added, "Delay, I beseech thee, my fate no longer. Marienburg must suffer; in pity then suspend not the mortal blow; my soul is weary of this bad world—it seeks to be at rest!"

"Away with him!" said the enraged Monarch; "he shall have the pleasure to *die* for Gustavus!"

"Save him! Oh save the hero and the friend!—Not Marienburg, but *I* will *die* for Gustavus!"

"From whence," asked the condemned veteran, with the quickness of terror, "from whence cometh that voice?"

"From one who shall not be disappointed!" answered Christian; and throwing back a curtain to the right of his throne, disclosed, laden with the heaviest chains, Augusta and her hapless daughters, who had been brought in his train from Copenhagen. "Now see," continued the monster, "the value of that sacrifice thou hast made to obstinate prejudices—nay, it is not yet too late. This noble matron—those weeping virgins ask thee to give them life and liberty!"

"'Tis false, Christian! we ask no favour independent of Ericson's interest. Think not of *us*, old man; preserve thy faith to Gustavus—*we are free!*"—So saying, Augusta proudly wrapped her chains about her, as if deriving dignity from the cause for which she wore them.

"Aye, free to die, Augusta," exclaimed Ulrica; "thy distinction will soon be lost in the dust!"

"No, foolish woman, thou judgest wrong; the grave is our refuge and our reward! There even the taunts of Ulrica shall no longer be heard! Secured by that, even Christian cannot persecute us! Our boast is thy dread; the boast of virtue is in the prospect of futurity.—Can Ulrica say as much?"

Stung with the force of these reflections, and piqued with the majesty which fetters only rendered more conspicuous, Christian made a sign to the guard who were appointed to lead the prisoners away. An agonizing shriek from the daughters of Augusta, on beholding that heroic mother silently surrendering herself to the soldier, who respectfully took her by the arm to lead her off, convinced Marienburg how inefficient the most exalted sentiment of patriotism is, when acted upon by such complicated motives for weakening its noble propensities.

Christian was too deeply read in the operations of the human heart not to perceive the effect this distressing scene had upon his prisoner. He saw the struggle of compassionate tenderness with the sterner virtues, and properly attributed the tear, which channelled itself on the furrowed cheek, to its real cause.

"Proceed," he cried to the reluctant guard; "we will gratify this zealous adherent to a traitor, by destroying that *traitor's* dearest connections! Strike off the women's chains, and lead them forth to execution!"

Marienburg turned his eye to a court which opened to the Hall of Audience, and, in an agony no pen can describe, beheld the apparatus of death exhibited in various shocking forms, which the mother of Gustavus approached with a Roman steadiness, casting from time to time looks of encouragement and smiling tenderness upon the innocent and reluctant sharers of her fate.

Already was the fire kindled for a sacrifice so noble; already Augusta had mounted the funeral pile, while her lovely children, in all the distraction of duteous affection, heightened by the horror of their own expected sufferings, were ineffectually contending with the executioner deputed to kindle the fatal flame, and who patiently bore their agonizing taunts, while the eldest madly caught from his hands the lighted brand, and hurled it against the diabolical author of this cruel tragedy; another enfrenzied victim clasped in her trembling arms the chains which had fastened those of a mother, moistening every link with the tears that fell from her fixed and overflowing eye.

"Christian," exclaimed Marienburg, "I yield! Save those innocents—Gustavus is yet in thy power; easily mayst thou conquer him; save but those innocents, and he will thank thee for their preservation!"

"Villain! thou injurest him!" cried Augusta; "*my son* cannot be conquered! Fellow, obey your King's commands!"

"Not yet, proud woman—wait *my* leisure; but speak, Marienburg, where is Gustavus? Speak, or death!"

"At Hedmora, or near it, protected only by a superior Providence and his own matchless courage.——Now, Marienburg, thou art *indeed* a traitor!" added the self-accuser.—"Bring me Sigismunda, and then let me die!"

"What," said Ulrica, who had steadily witnessed with unfeeling cruelty the dreadful scene, "what, not stay for Augusta's thanks?"

"My curses, rather!" denounced the unfortunate mother; and the next minute beheld her, with her helpless children, fall victims to the basest of the human species.

* * * * *

As if satisfied with this display of perfidy, cruelty, and almost unexampled malice, Christian remanded the speechless Marienburg to prison, who, totally overcome by various sensations, fell into a stupor of grief, which appeared to render him at least a harmless enemy; and he was permitted to quit Stockholm, emancipated from his chains, (to the great disappointment of Magnus), accompanied by several friends, who anxiously waited the termination of his business; and, compassionating his sorrows, guarded him to Upsal, where, when the assiduity of Catherine had restored in some degree his powers of thinking, he traced the heads of this terrible business, and mourned the loss of Sigismunda, about whom Christian had preserved an inflexible silence, and they jointly execrated the barbarity practiced upon the family of his noble friend.

CHAPTER XI.

"I grieve, yet dare not shew my discontent;
I love, and yet am forc'd to practise some deceit;
I do, yet dare not say I ever meant;
I seem stark mute, yet inwardly do prate."

Ashmol Museum, Mss.

"And the monster yet lives unpunished who has effected such diabolical villany! Oh my mother! didst thou *indeed* prefer the glory of thy family, the honour and claims of thy son, to thine own precious life, and that of my sweet murdered sisters?——Christian, beware!——Gustavus swears revenge!"

With this apostrophe the hero closed Marienburg's narrative; and after struggling to regain his usual fortitude, which had nearly forsaken him, he joined his sympathizing friends, and fully exonerated the doubting Marienburg from every degree of blame, whose tears, as he embraced this much-tried friend, evinced the joint expressions of pain and pleasure.

The apparent security in which Gustavus laid his plans, and pursued a regular mode of enforcing them, became a subject of astonishment even to himself, as well as to those whose ardent attachment to his cause made them tremble for the consequence of a tyrant's revenge, which, they dreaded, was only suspended, till it could fall with a more destructive power upon their darling hero; but neither Gustavus nor his auxiliaries could develop a mystery that lay too deeply involved for that soul of honour, or his generous adherent, to fathom. It was evident, from the accounts he obtained, through the medium of several friends, (who retained, by a pretended zeal for Christian's interest, their usual influence with that Monarch), that his designs against the throne of Sweden were not unknown, and that the dreadful catastrophe, in which the barbarous Dane openly exulted, had even been precipitated by Ericson's defiance of his royal adversary; but that he should stop at such a signal instance of vindictiveness, and seem satisfied with tearing away by the roots every sweet domestic attachment, without following up the suggestions of his cruel will, by sending an army to destroy a competitor, who was in no condition to cope with the Sovereign of a conquered country, was such an error in politics, which, while it excited our noble warrior's wonder, encouraged in a similar degree his hope of success, as well as served to convince him of Heaven's interference in his favour.

Too deeply, indeed, lay the motive for this amazing neglect of Christian, who, impelled by a weak and slavish subjugation, beheld the effect of this imbecility without the power of controul, which, wonderful to say, originated with Ulrica Landen. Even *she*, who could behold unmoved the heroic Augusta and her innocent daughters suffering tortures, which she well knew would pierce the heart of Gustavus with the keenest pangs, employed all her fascinating arts to stop the career of vengeance which was rolling towards the enemy of her confessed adorer; and by dint of false representations, pretended schemes for detecting the plots of Ericson, so as to involve the whole combination of his friends in the same destruction, and even devising feigned plans for the seizure of his person, she procured to him a continuance of that liberty he so well knew how to employ.

On the motive which could induce such an extraordinary conduct in Madam Landen, we can only observe at present, that even the death of those unfortunate victims was not exactly wished or intended by her, who, influenced by the same cause which proved the present safety of Gustavus, had previously stipulated with Christian to spare their lives; but irritated at the unbending virtues of Augusta, mortified at the grandeur of her sentiments and correspondent manners, and conscious of her own degraded situation, she could not repress the bitter irony of a spirit which derived no support from internal principles, and too late regretted the consequence of her cruel pride.

In delineating the features of this violent woman's character, their expression may possibly appear contradictory, and almost *unnatural*, to the discriminating reader. Would to Heaven, for the honour of humanity, such features were never suffered to disfigure its countenance!—But as the business of a good painter is to copy faithfully, even to the representation of deformity, so must, at least so *ought*, the biographer to observe the same justice in his descriptions; and if in some the sombre shade predominates even to the injury of the piece, they will, it is to be presumed, be properly contrasted by the fairer tints which mark the noble and innocent of our better characters.

It is not to be supposed that Christian yielded an implicit credence to Ulrica's assertions and inventions; but habituated to a servile concomitance of opinion, he chose not to hazard the peace, which a just and vigorous opposition would have much more easily secured, by the smallest contradiction of that will his better judgment would have despised, and Ulrica triumphed in the attainment of her present wishes; but mistaken in the means of procuring lasting felicity, she only protracted what she could not avoid, and, during a long and iniquitous course of vice, found the balance between certain good and real evil so unequally preponderate, as to afford no encouragement to a continuance in error.

Thus indebted to one he had with much reason considered as his bitter enemy, Gustavus meditated on every plausible means for the increase of his army, and strove to strengthen his cause by making its success an object of future felicity to the people, whose happiness he solemnly determined to promote. Indeed, the rapid advance of summer, which in northern countries permits hardly any spring, gave to our hero all the satisfaction his heart, big with unutterable resentment, could possibly imbibe.

The time was approaching when an annual feast of the surrounding villages was to be held at Mora; and by the advice of Madam Peterson's brother, the good priest to whose care she had recommended Ericson previous to his last escape, and in whose company he now sought to wear away the time which neither Marienburg nor the anxious Catherine could render pleasant, from an idea which their connection with his lamented Sigismunda created, he determined to put his cause into the hands of the numerous assembly that were to meet on that occasion.

Marienburg, who saw and appropriated his reluctance to continue with those whose society was calculated to remind him of his affecting losses, submitted to this deprivation; but Catherine, deeply impressed with an increasing sense of her noble deliverer's worth and wrongs, would modestly intimate her wish to obtain more of his company.

Marienburg sighed at the recollection this wish gave birth to. He contemplated the extreme improbability of realizing that scheme, the completion of which he scarcely ever lost sight of; but Ericson's unshaken attachment to Sigismunda, which preserved itself amidst every blow his hopes had endured, and the evident indifference he still manifested towards Catherine, would scarcely suffer the smallest hope of success.—Another mortification began also to render his remaining hours still more painful. While subject to the changes of an eventful life, and not greatly skilled in the emotions of the female heart, no idea of Catherine's encouraging a sentiment of affection for Gustavus had ever given strength to his intention respecting their union; but now, since the service Ericson so happily rendered the grateful maid, every word, every action in which the feelings of her soul were portrayed, discovered to Marienburg his error, and threatened, in *his* opinion, the torture of disappointment to her fondest hopes.

"Were she but beautiful—did she but surpass my daughter!"—This was the thought of the moment. Sigismunda, perhaps a victim to those who had triumphed over paternal agony, could he bring her forward in the light of competition, or in any other than that which frequently wrung the fibres of his aged heart? Even Catherine, much as he esteemed her, and dear as her interest was to him, sunk in the comparison. Mysterious and important motives had placed her claims before his daughter's. It was due to honour, justice, and the integrity of his soul; but in no other instance, where her peace, her happiness, or safety was concerned, did he hesitate for one instant to promote those rights.

Erroneous were Marienburg's sentiments as to Ericson's sense of personal charms. True, the majesty of Sigismunda's figure, and her commanding graces, stood far before those of Catherine, who, with sufficient pretensions to loveliness, possessed a softer and inferior line of beauty; but with the gallant hero those advantages availed but little. Through the fire of Sigismunda's eye, and the quick changes of her sprightly countenance, he discerned a soul similar to his own, formed for deeds of heroic import, and in her's loved the virtues of his own bosom. The difficulties attending this unfortunate passion were not to be conquered by any means hitherto used for that purpose; and Gustavus plainly understood, from Marienburg's serious silence, when that subject was hinted at, that, were Sigismunda safely restored to her father's arms, *his* acceptance as a lover would be no further advanced. Yet how little was he acquainted with the real motive for a conduct so inexplicable—a conduct which added to his reluctance to enter upon any subject with this incomprehensible parent, tending to his disastrous love! To Catherine his predilection had long been known; she had witnessed the struggles of Sigismunda, the determined opposition of her father, and the ardent love of Gustavus—of itself enough to discourage any attempt upon a heart so tender and so fixed; nor could she dare to whisper to her *own* any cause for that perturbation which agitated her spirits when in his presence, or when his worth, his sufferings, and noble claims were made the subjects of conversation:—but the adventure at Eroson, the sorrows he had so lately endured, and the more than uncertainty which attended his suit with Sigismunda, awoke the almost unsuspecting maid to a full sense of her own situation. The *lover* of Sigismunda, that dear, lost, inestimable friend, shall *he* be the object of Catherine's hope?

"The *lover!*—Yes," said Catherine, "and the *beloved* of her, whose affection and tender goodness to Catherine Sleswie deserve no such return! Oh shame to thy sex, ungenerous girl! Detest, abhor the grovelling sentiment which would impel thee to harbour an inclination so improper! Gustavus and Sigismunda!—Worshipped names! May they soon extend their influence through Scandinavia—may the diadem of Sweden be the portion of that godlike hero—and may she, so dear to my heart, share his glory and happiness!"

"My noble child," cried Marienburg, who had overheard the ardent apostrophe, "thy goodness shall, so I would hope, be rewarded.—Not Sigismunda—whom all-gracious Heaven restore to her aged father!—not Sigismunda, but Catherine and Gustavus must give tranquillity hereafter to Sweden, and by their mild and wise government restore felicity to her oppressed subjects!"

"Impossible!" exclaimed Catherine in wild amazement; "a thousand impossibilities forbid it!—My origin——"

"Is illustrious!—it nearly equals Ericson's. Motives, hereafter to be explained, forbid the union you hinted at. My child (if she be living) must not soar so high; she is *Marienburg's daughter*, and, I trust, will think as he does. Certainly I could have wished you still insensible to his merit; for much I dread the tenacity of a spirit which would be deeply wounded by a knowledge of my wishes, and I feel infinite pain in the apprehension of your disappointment, and the violence done to modesty. But rest satisfied,—your secret remains with me. Eager to correct the mistake of your generous enthusiasm, I have disclosed my intentions prematurely; but I cannot retract. It is now my earnest prayer to exist but till I see my child, and likewise view Gustavus and Catherine Monarchs of Sweden; but this a creature so feeble dares hardly to expect, and perhaps Ericson himself may supersede my wishes, for he must not be compelled."

"Compelled!—horrid idea! My more than father, if you wish to see your poor orphan in the repossession of her own good opinion, forget that she ever entertained so presumptuous a thought!"

"Nothing *can* I remember to your dishonour, my love; for you have acted greatly. Let this business sleep. We are surrounded by dangers; the result is known only to Him, who gives the arrow its proper mark, and wields the sword to extirpate evil!"

Alas! for Catherine, could such a business *sleep* in a bosom so agitated—could *she*, who till then considered herself as solely dependant on the liberality of her ancient friend, for the advantages of an education given her in a Convent at Upsal, and who never considered her origin in a light superior to that of a Lieutenant in the late King's service—what could Marienburg mean by giving her a claim almost equal to that of a regal one, and then to prefer her in an instance of such magnitude? She was well acquainted with the grandeur of his principles; she knew that an attention to self formed no part of his inclination; but was it in the nature of mortality to reject an establishment that would place his descendants on a line with Kings?

In vain Catherine strove to give this extraordinary conduct a natural solution;—every motive defied her keenest scrutiny, and she could only conclude that the enthusiasm of his character had tinctured his age with a degree of insanity: and this strange decision, while it destroyed the illusion of imagination, placed her hopes and prospects in the exact state they were previous to his information. But it could not regulate the tone of her affections; once persuaded of the tendency they had taken, she could lament the numberless and dispiriting reasons there were for weakening—nay, destroying this fatal propensity, and the seeming impossibility of conquering it by a superior judgment; and as if eager to ascertain the humiliating difference between herself and Sigismunda in a similar situation, the remembrance of that noble creature's resolution to give up a Gustavus as a sacrifice to duty, failed not to torment her, while it raised a momentary wish to equal such heroism.

Grown rather more attentive to the index of the heart, Marienburg beheld with real anxiety in her fading countenance, the consequence of Catherine's attachment; for every meeting with Ericson seemed to throw his wishes to a remoter distance.

To Von Hemert, whose prudence gave the fullest security, he had committed his important intentions before that gentleman's departure, and whose answer to the communication he saw every day gradually verifying.

"Gustavus," said this accurate observer, "possesses a constancy of spirit which no unexpected circumstance can totally alter. His love of your child makes a part of his virtues, for it is grounded upon generosity and justice. Indebted to *you* as the author of so many grand acquirements of education, and the friend of his noble claims, there is no reward, for so I *know* he thinks, adequate to such disinterested goodness, but that of ennobling your daughter's descendants; besides, in loving Sigismunda, he loves excellence itself. How then can you suppose that the cold, comparatively *cold* claim of mere interest will supersede such incentives?—Nay, even the prosecution of his present pursuit would stifle every attachment less strongly founded than that you lament. The late horrid losses, too, which he has sustained, can leave little else upon his mind, if we except his long-established passion, than a sense of extreme grief and fell revenge. You urge the singular deliverance of Catherine from Fitzer as attributable to something more than friendship—no such thing, Mr. Marienburg; he would have done as much for a Danish peasant, if convinced she deserved it. Depend upon this, while Sigismunda exists, the offer of an Empress's hand would be rejected, and, indeed, I think his noble submission to *your* will deserves the highest reward humanity can receive!"

"True indeed," thought Marienburg, "is this representation; and Oh, how much indebted to this good, but unpresuming, man is Ericson! How much unlike the treacherous Peterson's crackling blaze of pretensions is this character! Governed through life by *one* sentiment, which, while it attaches him even to a tyrant, ministers to the virtues of *that* tyrant's enemy, and does him every effectual service in his power, independent of his duty. A warm friend and a harmless foe!"

This eulogium was due to Von Hemert; it was due to his merits, and the acknowledged sense of his attachment to Gustavus. Convinced, therefore, that till the exact issue of his child's fate was obtained, and the effect of the intended invasion known, nothing respecting Catherine's establishment could be decided on, Marienburg endeavoured to correct the error his zeal for Ericson's interest had occasioned, by leading her thoughts as much as possible from the painful subject. Even his own infirmities were no longer attempted to be concealed; and in the attendance, which he rather promoted than repressed, of that affectionate girl, she found an employment that had its use: reading, transcribing of papers, and conversation, were all encouraged by the anxious old man, who severely repented the effusions of a heart, not much accustomed to such mistakes. No longer would he point out to Gustavus the perfections he strove to magnify in Catherine—no longer check the animated and affectionate turns this faithful lover gave to discourses which began with Catherine, but ended with Sigismunda—nay, he would sometimes suffer his ideas to dwell on the glory of an union so honourable to himself, and so delightful to the beloved parties; but with the departure of his friend these ideas faded, and were succeeded by a horrid train of images, the consequences of such a gratification. A tremendous oath infamously forfeited—an innocent heiress of greatness wronged, as he termed it, of her natural rights—no amends made for a duplicity of conduct which then would have no excuse—faith to the dead outrageously violated, and justice to the living egregiously injured—so many deeds so important, soon destroyed any pleasing delusion which paternal tenderness might naturally encourage, and his first resolution revolved in its usual course.

In the week preceding the feast of Mora, Gustavus bade adieu to Marienburg and Catherine.

"I go," said he, "my friends, in the full assurance of punishing Christian, and recovering Sigismunda! The good Plesban, who has lately entertained a priest belonging to the Convent at Eroson, speaks of a lady confined there by the savage Ulrica."

"At Eroson!" Catherine faintly repeated, while she shuddered at the recollection of her situation at the inn of that place, when condemned, for aught she knew, to a fate far worse, in her estimation, than that which Gustavus erroneously supposed to be Sigismunda's, and from which he so generously freed her—"at Eroson, my Lord?—Can it be possible?" she exclaimed. "And could no innate presentiment point to St. Croix as the prison of our beloved friend, no attempt be now made for the dear creature's emancipation!"

Ericson sighed.

"The will of Heaven, Catherine," observed Marienburg gravely, "permits not the accomplishment of our dearest wishes for nobler purposes than their attainment could produce. If Sigismunda be at St. Croix, she is comparatively safe. Her honour, her delicacy, her character can receive no contamination from a temporary residence among those who are concerned to preserve the purity of their inmates. *I* am well acquainted with the fortitude of my child's principles, and am certain she will never fall a sacrifice to superstitious bigotry through any temptation which its tinsel grandeur or pretended claim to monastic happiness may hold out. If *I* am satisfied with such a destination, no one else ought to be concerned. It is true, Gustavus *may* attack the Convent, and bring my daughter from thence by force; but will such an infringement on the laws of civil and ecclesiastical society redound either to *his* honour or *her's*? Will a violation of the forms of delicacy and decorum advance his suit with one so tenacious of their observance? No, Catherine, Ericson will not tarnish *his* glory or *her* character by such a step! A few weeks' occurrences may throw a very different light upon this business, and what would now be subject to the severest reprehension, may then be not only justifiable, but meritorious."

It is more than probable that Marienburg's disbelief of an assertion, in which Gustavus chose to place an implicit faith, gave such a frigid cast to this cold and cautious address. Be this as it may, our hero chose not to contravert sentiments so diametrically opposite to his own; but proceeded to avow his confidence in the Minister's information, while his active love was already forming plans for Sigismunda's release.

"That your daughter is confined at Eroson," he said, "relieves my heart from a great portion of uneasiness. Indeed, this intelligence ought to comfort us all; nor have I the least doubt but the good Marienburg will live to bestow his paternal benediction upon Gustavus and Sigismunda, joint Monarchs of Sweden."

The tears of Catherine, and the sigh of Marienburg, were tenderly, but falsely appropriated by Ericson on this occasion; and he rushed from their presence to conceal the pang their sensibility created.

Upsal now became disagreeable to Catherine, and she prevailed upon her commiserating friend to exchange his residence for a small house near the suburbs of Stockholm, which her fervid imagination forgot to estimate as both dangerous and improper for either of them.

Its vicinity to the palace Marienburg considered as hazardous, but neither Catherine nor himself could be objects of a revenge already, he feared, too deeply glutted; and, complying with Miss Sleswie's wishes to be nearer the scene of Ericson's future glory, which he plainly understood, although the plea of renewing her former acquaintance was only brought forward, the good old man readily acceded to those wishes, and he once more considered himself as a citizen (although beyond the walls) of Stockholm.

CHAPTER XII.

"Oh were I sure my dear to view,
I'd climb the pine-tree's topmast bough,
Aloft in air that quivering plays,
And round and round for ever gaze."

Song of the Laplander.

Enraged at the facility with which Gustavus had escaped the snare so artfully managed by Peterson, that restless intriguing being applied to Fitzer, who, it may be remembered, was left in his hands as an enemy to the cause *he* so recently supported. To be the foe of Ericson was a sure recommendation to Peterson; and many days had not elapsed before he was so completely duped, as to trust Fitzer with an embassy to Christian, explaining, as far as they knew, the particulars of Ericson's escape, and exonerating at the same time Count Struensee, who, in consequence of Peterson's information, had already transmitted to the Court at Stockholm his intention to produce Gustavus as a prisoner to the usurper.

Rejoiced to find himself once more at liberty, and certain that his credentials would give him importance with Christian, Fitzer determined to secure that Monarch's confidence as an auxiliary to the design he still meditated: nay, he went so far as to imagine a possibility of bringing over, through this medium, some of Christian's warmest adherents. Filled, therefore, with the most groundless and improbable hopes of supplanting the Dane, he assumed, on his appearance at Court, an air of self-consequence, and actually, by his artful representations, gave the King room to suppose he had gained an acquisition in the treacherous pretender.

To follow him through the various manœuvres he practised while aiming to substantiate his claim as son to the late Steen, would be a tedious, nay almost an impossible business. The rebuffs he met, the mortifications he experienced, and the dangers he often incurred by venturing too far with those who were not to be duped by the finesse he practised, might have discouraged a more cautious designer; but depending upon the ground he yet maintained with Christian, and strengthened by the acquiescence of those whose just abhorrence of the tyrant forced them to accede to any measures that promised a change, Fitzer continued to forward his plan by every probable means, even while gratifying his luxurious propensities in the Court of him whose interests he was actually endeavouring to destroy.

Of this extraordinary circumstance Gustavus was quickly informed. Detained by the various difficulties which attended his negotiation at Mora, the intelligence of Fitzer's escape, and reception at Stockholm met the enraged Ericson while concluding his arrangements with the different inhabitants of various distant villages, where he found nothing to complain of in their professions and consequent behaviour.

Elate with the increasing strength of his growing army, he only waited the arrival of those Dalecarlians whom Van Melen's representations had warmed with eagerness to engage in his cause. No sooner had that honest peasant declared the real name and quality of him they had formerly worked with under the name of Linden, than their ardour became ungovernable. No representations of Von Hemert could keep them to their duty. The mines resounded with—"*Gustavus for ever!*"—"*Down with the tyrant Christian!*"—and while the friendly heart of Conan responded to the first acclamation, justice, or rather prudence, revolted against any encouragement of the latter.

At Hedmora the treachery of Fitzer became another source of

assistance to Gustavus. One of the sledgemen, who was not in the cruel secret, beheld with indignation the capture of Marienburg; for, as cunning sometimes outwits itself, Fitzer, trusting to the natural boorishness of those fellows, scrupled not to engage this man instead of one more properly tutored for this purpose; and after his arrival, which did not take place till Catherine's departure, he disclosed all he knew of that transaction.

To such as had been entrusted with Fitzer's aspiring intentions relative to the Crown of Sweden, this treachery appeared in a heinous light; and they scrupled not to express their detestation of an act which marked a constitutional depravity in its most odious colours. Others, who had been attached to Marienburg, and saw deeply into the specious arts of his betrayer, felt still more powerfully drawn to Ericson's cause, and openly expressed their approbation of every successful step taken by his friends.

With a resolution so favourable to his hopes Gustavus was speedily acquainted; and as soon as his business at Mora was completed, he proposed to return to Dalecarlia, and finally arrange every thing with his auxiliaries previous to a decisive onset: even the day was fixed for a coalition of his friends in those parts, who were to accompany him to Hedmora, not improperly judging as to the effect so many worthy veterans might produce upon a number that yet hung back from a hearty declaration in his favour.

Already the last evening approached that Gustavus was to pass at Mora, already was Iwan brightening the steel ornaments of a superb suit of armour, the united gift of his peasant friends—a gift he dared not refuse, as it would have indicated in *their* opinion a spirit of pride incompatible with his expectations from them. A very few hours intervened between the setting sun and the given time of his departure; and Gustavus, whose mind was torn by a thousand afflicting remembrances, gladly turned a willing ear to Iwan's notable observations. The honest fellow loved his Lord; he had been told of his numerous misfortunes—he knew his claims, and heartily subscribed to the justice of them. To draw, therefore, the pensive hero from his mournful reflections, Iwan departed from his natural taciturnity, and attempted to signalize himself as a wit. Gustavus smiled while he approved the motive, and Iwan had the satisfaction of beholding the temporary improvement in his master's countenance with an honest consciousness of having occasioned it; when, suddenly assuming an air of recollection, he followed his topic, which was a general ridicule of the Romish Clergy, who were daily becoming more obnoxious to the supporters of the Reformation, and objects of contempt to its inferior orders, by a more particular reference to an individual of that sect.

"And now I think of it," cried the happy Iwan, "one of them wanted to get his cloven foot under my Lord's table;—'but no,' says I, 'no bloodsuckers *here*; go to your King Christian—*he'll* give you employment enough!'—How the Priest marvelled at this refusal! Well, then it was—'I must be admitted—thy Lord will be pleased to see me—I am sent by Father Plesban.'

"*Father* Plesban!" repeated Gustavus, who had fallen into a reverie which this name alarmingly interrupted.

"Yes, yes, my Lord, that was his excuse; it was he that made my Lord so uneasy a little while since; but *I* sent him off—he'll not come again—no, no, he's gone back with——"

"Fly! pursue him!" cried the agitated Prince; "bring him hither—his embassy is probably of moment to the life of your master!"

Iwan would have argued this point with his leader, and actually began to suggest the difficulty of finding a person whom, seven hours before, he had threatened with corporeal punishment if seen by him near Mora; but a threatening glance left no inclination to disobedience, and dropping the cuirass, he precipitately engaged in the hopeless pursuit.

Too fatally certain that the Priest had brought some intelligence of Sigismunda, as Father Plesban, in consequence of this man's prior information, was deputed to make enquiries at Eroson, Gustavus could neither restrain his anger against Iwan, nor his eagerness to ascertain the truth of those fears which placed his beloved maid in a situation that forbade even the encouragement of hope, this impassioned lover, neglecting, in that unhappy prepossession, even the advancement of his own glory, madly quitted the spot in which his auxiliaries had already begun to assemble, and mounting his charger, stopped not till he reached Mr. Plesban's residence; but how was his chagrin increased to find him absent, and that it was supposed he had taken the road to Ericson's temporary habitation.

Still more wretched than before in the idea that he should by this rashness be effectually deprived of the mournful satisfaction he yet dreaded, our hero lost no time in measuring back the tedious distance, while the opening dawn convinced him of the necessity he was under of meeting the whole of his friends by sunrise in a plain near Mora. Distracted with a variety of claims on his noble and generous principles, he could hardly rejoice in the appearance of his troops, drawn up in the highest order on the appointed spot, while the brightness of the rising day threw a radiance upon their leader's arms, and illumined every cheerful countenance. Instinctively, as it were, he was drawn towards these valuable adherents, whose universal shout, when they perceived his approach, rekindled the flame of patriotism and honourable ambition in his swelling heart. Advancing close enough to distinguish the persons of this warlike assembly, he caught a glance of Iwan, who pressed forward to obtain his notice with an eagerness that implied success.

"I have seen," cried the poor Iwan, as he drew the Prince's horse on one side, "I have seen Father Plesban; he was afraid that confounded Priest might make some mistake, and so he came to seek my Lord himself. I asked the good gentleman to tell his business, but—"

"Silence, fool! only say *where* he is!"

"Why, that indeed your servant knows not; for I was so eager to relate my success, that I left him immediately after, though I have some notion he is gone to Mr. Marienburg's, as he turned towards Mora."

It was in this critical moment that Gustavus experienced the torture of contradictory sensations arrived at their climax. To quit, through an impulse he dared not acknowledge, a generous people assembled for the united purpose of aiding his pretensions, and crushing a tyrant, at the very minute when his presence was essential to this grand and important purpose, would for ever destroy that interest he had so sedulously promoted, and weaken to a fatal degree their veneration for a character hitherto unimpeached; and yet on that very instant might hang the destiny of Sigismunda!—a destiny which the fiat of a parent would probably revoke, could Marienburg be induced to present himself at the Convent previous to the day appointed for his daughter's utter seclusion; for not a doubt remained upon his mind as to the nature of Plesban's intelligence.

While these perplexing suggestions rushed upon him, the little army was arranged in the utmost order by a deputed officer, and only waited the word of command from their Prince, who mechanically began to march at the head of a chosen detachment, with a latent hope that he might encounter either the Priest or Plesban, by one of whom he meditated to send his earnest entreaties to Marienburg to visit the Convent at Eroson; for the idea that, as a professed Lutheran, Sigismunda was not amenable to the Romish Church, so fully possessed him, as to obviate every difficulty respecting her exoneration from its power, when claimed by her natural protector, unless defeated by the schemes of his detested enemies, Christian and Ulrica. But the hope which accompanied the first idea soon lost its basis, as the route they were obliged to pursue diverged from that leading towards his friend's residence; and the last effort Gustavus could make for the accomplishment of this cherished desire, was to charge Iwan with a commission to the benevolent Clergyman, which *he* was to convey to Marienburg, expressing the suspicion and wishes of his Lord, with a charge to follow the small army to Hedmora.

While Ericson was thus vainly tormenting himself with conjectures, fears, and decisions, and not wholly unsupported by that latent power which derives strength from every attempt to forward our designs, and bestows, during its vigorous exertion, a degree of patience and consolation, he judged very erroneously of Sigismunda's unhappy destiny; for instead of the monastic, yet safe confinement his imagination suggested, that peculiarly unfortunate young woman was contending with a situation far more dangerous and distressing in its consequences to her peace, her character, even her life, than the one he so positively marked out for her—a situation which Mr. Plesban, disappointed in his indefatigable enquiries, had accidentally discovered, the disclosure of which he was induced to trust with Father Peter, of whose discretion and humanity, although in favour of the new sectaries, he entertained no doubt; but, mortified with the unwary Iwan's reception of the good Priest, he determined, in defiance of a severe indisposition, personally to convey tidings so important and so tragical—a purpose which the impetuous Gustavus, by his late excursion to the friendly Minister, so rashly defeated.

Thus unluckily superseded in his intention, Plesban, who felt extremely reluctant to wound the heart of a parent, avoided Marienburg's retreat; and stopping to recruit himself at an inn, was detained by an increasing illness till Iwan had returned from his successless embassy:—for Sigismunda's father, unable to collect, amidst the confused suppositions and exclamations of Iwan, any certain elucidation of his Lord's meaning, (to oblige whom the blundering messenger chose, unauthorized, to visit Marienburg on his road from the Minister's), could only promise to visit Plesban, under an idea that, from his representation, the obscure accounts of Iwan might be properly explained.

With this incongruous information the Prince was highly dissatisfied; but, convinced that, till possessed of regal power, any attempt on *his* part to emancipate his beloved, would be attended with no certain success, while the injury *his* cause would receive by such procrastination was indisputable, he gave up the secret wish of his soul, and with an ardency of spirit bordering upon despair, resumed the former purpose of his heart, to conquer or die!

Arrived at Hedmora, he was immediately joined by Van Melen at the head of the miners and peasants of Dalecarlia, who conducted him through the town with such marks of welcome as approached to adoration; while many of the higher order, whom fear and policy had condemned to silence, now mingled with the partisans of Gustavus. Even those who were still under the influence of Fitzer's pretensions, chose not to stand aloof, but tacitly coincided with their countrymen in behalf of our hero; nay, when, in consequence of a prevailing report that the Danes were about to invade their province, the coldest amongst them united in a common cause, and warmly declared their sentiments and resolutions to oppose the efforts of Christian and his natural subjects.

Enchanted with this confirmation of his hopes, Gustavus led his warlike band against the Governor of that province, whose attachment to Christian, and the strictness with which he had performed the savage Monarch's edicts respecting a persecuted people, rendered him a monster of depravity in the soldier's estimation; nor could the native clemency of their commander restrain the fury which exercised itself, not barely upon the conquered Governor, but every Dane who was unhappy enough to fall into their hands.

To his plea of sparing an enemy that was not otherwise obnoxious than from a natural attachment to *their King*, they answered, *that* reason was sufficient, and Gustavus felt the force of this motive too powerfully to refute it; though while the Chief underwent the punishment due to his crimes, the Prince could not but lament the misfortune of those who suffered a similar fate, unstained by similar enormities. But it was not his business to damp the ardour of his adherents, who, transported by the success attending this first onset, looked up to Gustavus as their saviour and deliverer, professing their readiness to follow him to the gates of Stockholm, even to the palace of Christian itself; and the propriety of extending a plan which, however encouraging in its outset, teemed with innumerable difficulties, became an object of serious consideration with the victorious Swedes.

During the little banquet which closed their more sober councils, Bernard Milan, a noble Lubecker, who had previously enlisted under Ericson's colours, brought back to our hero's imagination the mournful remembrance which war and its consequences had in a faint degree stifled. A toast was demanded—he gave *Sigismunda Marienburg*. The sparkling eye and crimsoned cheek of the youthful warrior while he passed the important toast, convinced Gustavus he had a rival; but, too generous to feel the pang of jealousy against his gay competitor, Ericson only sighed to the sacred name which till that moment lay buried in his heart; and breaking up the company, retired to vent the feelings of his soul.

CHAPTER XIII.

"Virtue, I grant, is often try'd
By sickness, sorrow, envy, pride,
Nor is asham'd to mourn;
But trial strengthens, conscience cheers,
Of death and woe prevents the fears,
Assaults to victory turn."

Dr. Fordyce.

Leaving Gustavus to the performance of those military operations which justly procured, or rather established to him, the character of an intrepid, yet prudent warrior, we shall advert to the fate of her whose supposed misfortunes coloured his brightest expectations with a cheerless hue, and who, the reader may remember, we left exposed to the jealous caprice and remorseless cruelty of Christian and his mistress. Kept in utter ignorance of Gustavus, and the consequence of her father's leaving Stockholm, Sigismunda began to consider herself a devoted object of unprincipled villany, deserted by her natural friends, and left only to the helpless efforts of her own fortitude, (so far helpless, as it could oppose neither the cunning nor open violence of her enemies), she saw no possibility of escaping the evils by which she was pursued.

A sullen malignity had now usurped the expression of ill-concealed admiration in Christian's eye; while the still more open indication of dislike and contempt rendered the countenance of Ulrica equally disgusting, who, since the departure of Catherine, had transferred her suspicions from her to Sigismunda. She also found another motive for indulging this rancorous hatred against the innocent daughter of Marienburg. It is true that, allured by the splendid offers and situation of Christian, she had consented to supersede his injured Queen in her honours, and the affection of her royal consort; but she considered those honours and that affection too dearly purchased, since, as the ostensible, though illegal companion of a Monarch, she could not indulge her unbounded desire of criminal admiration, nor take the steps which unbridled passion suggested for the attainment of a beloved object.

To explain this hint, it will be necessary to say that, previous to her conquest of Christian, while the majesty of a fine, but rather masculine figure secured the adoration of the dissipated and unthinking, she had selected from the youth of Stockholm, *him* only of them all upon whom her artful blandishments were entirely lost—Gustavus Ericson; and who even censured the boldness of a carriage that others affected to admire.

Stung with a neglect which the grossness of her ideas could neither excuse nor account for, Ulrica endeavoured to find a more plausible reason for this treatment than mere indifference; and soon discovered, in the beauty and perfections of his tutor's daughter, a motive in this attachment which eagle-eyed jealousy quickly discovered. She beheld the defeat of her own wishes, and from the moment of that development, Sigismunda became an object of this unprincipled woman's secret hatred.

About the time of this unwelcome disappointment, Christian arrived at Stockholm, and fell a ready sacrifice to the bright commanding looks of the imperious dame, whose revenge was soon most exquisitely gratified in the disgrace of Ericson and his family; nor was the brutal conduct of Christian to those noble sufferers falsely attributed to that bad woman, who triumphed in the agonies her tenderness might have mitigated, if not wholly prevented.

Abandoned to the indulgence of every malignant passion, a still more exquisite gratification presented itself in the possession of her unconscious rival, whose influence she now dreaded, with the more reason if the attempts of Gustavus to dethrone Christian should succeed; for, although inflated with his conquest of Sweden, the haughty Monarch looked not to any future faction as capable of disturbing his quiet, Ulrica saw deeper into the probability of an invasion:—she knew the detestation her paramour's cruel despotism had raised in every honest bosom; she was informed by her emissaries that Gustavus had escaped, and that even the mines of Dalecarlia echoed with the claims of Ericson. Should he therefore succeed, no doubt but his choice of a Queen would fall upon the hated Sigismunda.

"Oh perish first!" cried the revengeful Ulrica, as this idea pressed for admission, "perish the whole race of Marienburg, rather than that pernicious individual should be thus honoured!"

How little was Sigismunda aware of a rancour so implacable, and how far was she from deciding on the true motive for Ulrica's conduct! Perhaps had it been freely discussed, her regret for the real cause would not have exceeded that which she supposed originated in Christian's recent partiality; for it never occurred to her that Catherine had ever been an object of Ulrica's jealousy.

During a painful interval, which was passed by Christian in forming plans for humbling what his own vile principles induced him to term a proud, insulting manner,—by Ulrica, in considering how she should dispose of the intended victim,—and by Sigismunda in fruitless lamentations, or ineffectual plans to obtain her liberty, a report of the schemes of Gustavus began to circulate in Stockholm so seriously as to alarm the usurper; and as if every petty consideration fled before an object of such magnitude, his severity to Marienburg's daughter was no longer apparent; even Ulrica remitted her usual frigidity, and Sigismunda beheld the alteration with the liveliest satisfaction. All the purposes of her filial and friendly heart were again revived; and as the genial change advanced, she found, with her hatred and terror, even her late excessive fears subside. Hope again dawned in her bosom, which Ulrica's increasing kindness rendered more brilliant; and the company she had hitherto shunned as abhorrent to the purity of her ideas, became less offensive, in the expectation of soon quitting it for ever. Often as her opinion was demanded as necessary to the establishment of an hypothesis, or the decision of an argument, did she wonder at the facility with which it was adopted by Ulrica; and although tempted to reject, with an honest indignation, the dangerous sentiments avowed by that refined voluptuary, no expressions of resentment followed the unguarded declaration.

To a change so unexpected and so astonishing, no certain cause could be appropriated; but as Sigismunda's heart was the seat of kindness, it expanded to a treatment that promised such advantages, and this more from its characteristic benevolence, than any effect even of lucrative benefit to herself. Indeed the candour of her own principles betrayed the caution which ought to have been excited by this signal carriage; for with all the distinction so amazingly shewn to her amiable prisoner, Ulrica diminished in no degree her usual restrictions, nor ever suffered Sigismunda to leave the palace without proper attendants, although she was not only permitted, but even commanded, to appear at the various amusements devised by a Court, who sought, by every means in their power, to convince a jealous Monarch that the luxuries of peace were more congenial to their sentiments than the harassings and dangers of a civil war; and by thus acting, escaped the suspicions which fell upon those who dared to express a different mode of behaviour.

The partiality of Ulrica, which almost forced Sigismunda upon a line of conduct at which her delicacy revolted, began to disgust when it ceased to gratify. No proposal for returning to her father's habitation—no permission to attend the deserted Queen, gave stability to the hope, of late so vivid; a circumstance too that again aroused her suspicions, and, though it owed its existence to her own unguarded warmth, chilled her ardent expectation.

The pretensions of Gustavus, and the fate of his unhappy family, who, notwithstanding they had trusted themselves as hostages to the protection of Christian, were spoken of at Stockholm as likely to be included in the list of his inhuman sacrifices, haunted her imagination with a violence not to be confined by prudential motives; and availing herself of her recently acquired consequence, she ventured freely again to reproach the King with his impolitic and cruel conduct, in confining the relatives of a man whose injuries were sufficient to shake the pillars of a doubtfully established throne.

Thrown from his guard by this ill-timed remonstrance, Christian conveyed his sentiments of Sigismunda's indiscretion by a frown so dark, so malignant, as more than equalled his usual reception of her entreaties on this subject; for this repeated offence was of a nature still more stimulative of resentment than her former ones: and she saw too late the consequence of her generous interference. Ulrica, who disguised her indignant astonishment with greater facility, although deeply wounded by her attachment to the race of her still adored Gustavus, coolly endeavoured to change a subject which so fully betrayed the feelings and partiality of Marienburg's daughter; but as if determined to try the strength of her power, she followed it by an earnest request to attend the Queen, whose wrongs were another call upon her benevolent heart.

"You wish then," cried Ulrica, "to exchange the pleasure of a splendid Court for the gloomy residence of peevish discontent! Go then, ungrateful maid! and repent, when perchance it will be too late, the folly of such a preference; but do not suppose," and she affected to be highly displeased, "do not imagine that the caprice which urges you hence, will find the gratification it may expect in that lady's society."

Too happy in this unexpected permission to notice Ulrica's concluding hint, Sigismunda hastened to prepare for her short journey; for, scandalized at her consort's conduct, the Queen had left Stockholm to seek in retirement the peace which solitude encourages, where, in the enjoyment of sacred contemplation, she strove to forget her palpable injuries. To this hallowed retreat our innocent heroine looked for a recovery of her own good opinion, which, prompted by true delicacy, she held as forfeited in the circle of dissipation, although rarely seen within their vortex; and when the sledge (for winter was then in its deepest horrors) stopped in the court-yard of the voluntary exile, she felt as if about to recover her long-lost liberty, and sighed only for the fate of those who still possessed her warmest interest.

Sigismunda had seen in the bold and haughty manner of Ulrica a false assumption of majesty; in Christian she had beheld its noble traits sullied by ferocity, dissimulation, and distrust. But it was only in the form and features of the graceful Blanch that it really triumphed; and though a sort of horror, blended with grief, struggled on her countenance as she rejected Sigismunda's attempt to kneel before her, nothing could destroy the impression her dignity created; for the youth of Sigismunda, in her former attendance upon this lady, permitted not the power of discrimination. Allowing for the feelings of a Queen, reduced to the humiliating necessity of resigning her station to an infamous rival, her new guest beheld with pity the emotions of a sensible heart; and modestly withdrawing to a distant part of the room, waited in respectful silence the result of this awful reception. But how was she amazed when Blanch, rising, and followed by several damsels, hastily quitted that apartment, veiling her eyes while she passed Sigismunda, as if dreading to encounter an object of abhorrence, while the attendants discovered the strongest tokens of disgust and affright as they withdrew.

"I see," cried that hapless young creature, in a mental agony, "I now see and deplore the fatal consequence my residence with Ulrica has produced. How could I think of rendering myself acceptable to this exalted soul after such a degradation? Oh my father! *you* would not reject the poor unfortunate for an involuntary defalcation, which has neither sullied my person, nor corrupted my principles. To *you* then I shall now be allowed to fly. Perhaps the beloved Catherine waits for the arrival of her long-lost friend; perhaps too——" Here a half-expressed hope arose, but it soon sunk; for it was connected with the success of Gustavus, and of that success who could tell the consequence?

Impelled now by an indefinable motive, she ventured to enter an antiroom adjoining the deserted one, under an impression that, from some of the domestics, whose voices she plainly distinguished, some decided explanation of Blanch's repulsive manner might be obtained; and gently opening the thickly-lined door, was advancing towards the stove, round which they stood: but this overture to a discovery only added to her perplexity, for, in imitation of their royal mistress, they left the room, observing a mysterious silence.

Grown almost desperate at such inhospitable treatment, she would have sought the sledge drivers, by whose assistance it was possible she might reach her long wished-for home; and had actually replaced herself on the vehicle which yet remained in the court, when a servant, who hastily approached, presented her with a paper, and at the same time briefly informed her the drivers were departed, but would return on the following morning, as also that it was expected she would obey the orders contained in that paper. He then retired, leaving the horror-struck Sigismunda insensible to every outward inconvenience, and almost unable to comprehend the contents of a mandate, whose characters imported destruction!—Descending, however, from the machine, she slowly re-entered the house, while her eyes, tearless and wild, were fixed on the paper, and seemed as though they would devour its contents, till raising her clasped hands to heaven, she appeared as if deprecating a sentence that suddenly explained itself to her affrighted sense, and which ran as follows:—

To Sigismunda Marienburg.

"We, the Members of the Secret Tribunal, provoked by repeated enormities, and disgraced by the offence meditated against our sacred order, do, in this citation, not only declare our hatred of such unparalleled wickedness, but charge thee to appear before us at our Tribunal of Munster, in Westphalia, immediately after the breaking up of the frost; and we do hereby charge, upon peril of equal consequence, every one whom it may concern, as amenable to us, to avoid all correspondence with Sigismunda Marienburg, as they shall answer to the numerous invisibles who compose our holy judicature. Signed by the

Free Judges."

On the envelope which contained this shocking summons, were the following words:

"Insulted and endangered by those who envy the purity they cannot imitate, and the tranquillity they can never possess, Blanch, Queen of Sweden, Denmark, and Norway, despises the impotence of that malice which sent hither a proscribed criminal to receive an order which ranks her with the vilest of the creation, and who, from the just detestation all ranks of people conceive against a person amenable to the holy Tribunal, must remain here till able to quit Stockholm."

"Sigismunda Marienburg is no criminal," exclaimed the unhappy girl, as she again glanced upon the paper, which in her innocent transport she had held up to heaven; "this is a subtile device of my cruel enemies to deprive me of the protection of the virtuous. Here in this peaceful retirement I thought to have recovered my consequence with the good and amiable.—My friend," she cried, interrupting herself, and addressing a servant who just shewed himself at the door, "say to the royal Blanch a guiltless victim waits her doom; nay, fear me not," for the man, who was no stranger to her awful situation, seemed impatient to be gone, "no harm can accrue from the delivery of such a message. Oh barbarous!" she continued, while the long-restrained tears faintly expressed the anguish of her soul, on seeing him reluctantly withdraw, "am I deprived of even the consolation of a fellow-creature's pity? Alas!" looking around, "what *is* to be my wretched lot?—Oh Blanch, dear injured mistress, how *am* I to obey the decree of injustice?—Taught and supported by you, even this evil might be lessened."

The entrance of another domestic with refreshments, and fuel for the stove, convinced Sigismunda she was not wholly deserted; and from this favourable circumstance, she began to deduce a hope of obtaining the Queen's future attention, purposing to unfold the whole of that contradictory treatment which she had met with at the Court of Christian, should she be indulged with an audience; and thinking the best proof of gratitude she could shew for the present indulgence, would be by a thankful acceptance of the Queen's liberality, she attempted to partake of what was set before her, stifling as much as possible the sighs and tears which such a calamity as she was threatened with would naturally excite, nor once offering to terrify the damsel, who waited till she had done, by any teazing and fruitless applications, although she fancied there was more of pity and grief in her gentle countenance than was consistent with the dread her presence, as a person cited by the tremendous Judges, induced, with whom all intercourse, while amenable to their power, was interdicted.

The solitude to which Sigismunda was now condemned, would have been preferable to the riot of a luxurious Court, had it arisen from common causes; but the agitation of her spirits prevented the advantages of a quiet repose, and the lonely chamber in which she was expected to remain, appeared but as a solitary prison: for even the comforts of conversation were withheld, and she saw the daily entrance and departure of a single domestic, with the bitter reflection that she alone under that hospitable roof was debarred the blessing of reciprocal communication: and this, even this indulgence she thought must soon terminate; "for it *is* an indulgence," said the devoted innocent, "when compared with what lies before me—a long, lonely, and dangerous journey—forbidden to seek or make a friend—obliged to shun the haunts of my fellow-creatures—prevented, by this horrid mandate, from visiting a dear participating father—and, to complete the climax, condemned perhaps, should I safely reach Munster, condemned (do I live to fear it?) to suffer an undeserved death! Christian, Ulrica, persecutors of the innocent, a dreadful retribution awaits your crimes—Sigismunda *shall* be avenged!"

While thus mournfully employed in lamenting the present moments, yet fearing all beyond them, the daughter of Marienburg saw with increasing anguish those days approach which must put an end to her comparative security. Already the snow began to melt on the valley that spread before Blanch's residence, while plants of the liveliest verdure were discovered peeping from beneath their soft and spongy covering—already a foaming torrent was seen to descend from the height beyond, gleaming amidst the stately firs, or overturning, in its hasty progress, those of a slighter texture, whose tender fibres could not resist the rushing waters; and she contemplated with terror the far distant path, whose traces, as it wound among the furze bushes, or crept along the rugged steeps, marked out those mazy recesses she was so soon to tread.

END OF VOLUME I.

Swedish Mysteries

Volume II

SWEDISH MYSTERIES.

CHAPTER I.

"For here, forlorn and lost, I tread
With fainting steps and slow;
Those wilds, immeasurably spread,
Seem length'ning as I go."
Goldsmith.

In ascribing to Christian and Ulrica the diabolical mischief which threatened our heroine with such various calamity, she had in one sense been guilty of premature judgment. Convinced, from repeated proofs, that her virtue was incorruptible, the Monarch ceased to torment where he could not triumph, and the gloom of disgust succeeded to the ardour of offensive admiration: but there he stopped; for though an object of concealed resentment, she had not absolutely been one of cruel revenge. Far otherwise was her situation with her vile principled detainer, who, fearful that a continuance of the severe restraint imposed upon Sigismunda, might, when the season would admit, induce her to practise some successful method of escape, chose to relax, even to a degree that would lull her into a peaceful security, till the schemes she was then agitating should be ripe for execution.

The effect of this conduct has already been seen, and the betrayed victim lamented, when too late, her mistaken confidence. To render her an object of attention to the Tribunal, she had been previously accused by Ulrica of such crimes as she judged atrocious enough to excite its cognizance: and as the placard, denouncing her accusation, arrived on the evening previous to her departure from Stockholm, her cruel betrayer availed herself of Sigismunda's request to visit the Queen, from a wish to shun that conflict which she foresaw would be the consequence of her amazement and terror when the summons should be presented. Accordingly, it was placed on the wall of Blanch's dwelling, and discovered by that lady's domestics several hours prior to Sigismunda's arrival.

Impressed with an idea of that beauty, innocence, and elegance, which, during Madame Marienburg's attendance at Court, she had often delighted to admire, Blanch beheld the horrible mandate with indescribable grief, while she trembled for the consequence in receiving a subject of the most terrible vengeance, and whom, although she was obliged to assume a conduct her heart disdained, that heart pronounced as injured by her bitterest enemy. Although aware of the cruel necessity of shunning Sigismunda, and obliged to acquaint every servant with her awful situation, the Queen secretly determined to preserve her from every insult or hardship while her stay could be safely prolonged; keeping, at the same time, a distance strict enough to authorize her own justification, should Ulrica's machinations extend even to *her* injury. But now a fresh source of disquiet arose to plunge the youthful wanderer in new affliction; and this originated in the blooming season and amended roads, which made Sigismunda's longer stay as dangerous to the Queen as to herself; and on the eve of a brilliant day, which was succeeded by a few hours' frost, the daughter of Marienburg received a note of three lines, importing a sort of command from Blanch to quit her house on the following morning; and this notice was accompanied by several little delicacies, which, with a tenderness almost maternal, the sympathizing lady prepared for the traveller's use in her intended journey.

Struck with this proof of a confidence in her innocence, our grateful heroine wept her thanks for the acknowledgments she meditated could be no otherwise expressed, so deeply was her heart impressed by this goodness; and she consoled herself with the sweet assurance that a certainty of her rectitude existed in one friendly bosom, while the idea that this certainty extended no farther than ineffectual pity could reach, damped the pleasure it created.

Unable to rest for the few hours which remained, Sigismunda prepared, as well as she was able, for her inauspicious pilgrimage, while tears, extorted by her helpless condition, added bitterness to the passing moments; nor could a lovely night and cloudless moon engage that attention, which, in happier circumstances, she would have been delighted to bestow.

As the business of packing was soon completed, and no means presented of cheating the intermediate hours that remained, she gave an entire loose to the anguish of her soul; when a low but sudden noise in the anti-room checked that torrent of grief which cruel reflections produced, till it occurred that her late attendant might possibly be returned with another commission from her royal mistress; and she waited in almost breathless suspense the approach of one, whose step she distinctly heard, and whose caution, as she gently advanced, was no new proof of her own sad situation.

"I thought," cried Sigismunda, "to have seen you no more. Has the noble Blanch again condescended to send to the poor Sigismunda? Did you give language to the gratitude which overpowered utterance?"

"Hapless young creature!" exclaimed a voice that spoke wonders to the astonished maid, "even Blanch herself ventures to defy the dangers of discovery, and appears before you, in the hope of gathering from lips that used to be the seat of truth, farther motives for believing you innocent."

"I am innocent, gracious lady!" cried the impetuous maid as she sunk upon her knees, "innocent of every fault which can possibly render me an object of criminality!"

"Alas, unhappy child! I see," cried the pitying Queen, "the real source of all this treachery. Lovely, youthful, and accomplished, would Ulrica have suffered you so near her but for some infernal purpose? Is it unknown to you that Gustavus has been the boasted subject of that bad woman's intemperate passion? And is Sigismunda ignorant of an attachment to which Christian only, of all his numerous Court, is blinded?"

"*Gustavus and Ulrica!*" repeated the half-fainting listener; "are *their* names united in a cause so infamous?—Now then welcome, most welcome will be the sentence that shall give Sigismunda everlasting freedom!"

"I perceive, indeed," observed Blanch, "you knew not of this long existing connection—a connection big with danger to the deluded Christian, who suspects not that Ulrica has heartily embarked in his adversary's interest, and waits but for an answer to some terms she recently dispatched to Gustavus, which, if accepted, will involve my wretched consort in a ruinous contention. And you, poor Sigismunda! you are one of her victims. She is doubtless acquainted with your virtuous friendship for Ericson, and carries her ideas of it to a height of conviction; for so corrupt are those ideas as to suppose the purest flame that ever glowed, must be founded in criminal sensuality! Admitting this to be her belief, is there any thing uncommon in her fears of a rival so formidable, or that, unrestrained by a sense of justice, she should hazard every thing to remove that rival? These are the considerations which, upon deliberate reflection, have pleaded with me in your behalf, and urged this stolen visit. Now, indeed, that I have heard your laconic but impressive declaration, my heart decides without an objection in your favour. Adieu, then, thou persecuted offspring of one I truly respected! may the fate we dread never be realized by Marienburg's daughter! may an honourable acquittal succeed your first appearance before that august Tribunal! and may this fervent embrace be the prelude to many future ones!"

Overwhelmed with feelings too poignant for expression, and too various for description, Sigismunda tremblingly returned the sweet embrace of condescending majesty, while her tears flowed to the recollection of Ericson's supposed attachment; and turning her humid eyes to the rising sun, which faintly touched the mountain tops—

"See, gracious Madam," she cried, "my time expires! Adieu, thou most revered of human beings! This consolation will beguile the tedious way; and when Ulrica's baseness presses upon my loaded heart, I will think of the royal Blanch, and be patient."

"Depart not, dearest girl, till you have breakfasted," said the sympathizing Queen; and with these words she reluctantly quitted the grateful maid, who ventured to imprint an affectionate salute upon the hand her benign companion extended.

"Alas!" thought Sigismunda, when she beheld her white garments floating in the distance, "could I have imagined an event so unexpected, almost so unhoped, as this benevolent visit, should produce the keenest torment my soul has ever experienced? What is the sentence of death compared to this stroke! Supported by an idea of a constancy unequalled, resisting all opposition, proof against all temptations even the most powerful ambition itself might offer, how light has every predicted evil appeared when illumined by a hope, now, alas, totally extinct!"

This melancholy apostrophe was interrupted by her usual attendant, who pressed her with a tenderness of manner, that Sigismunda readily ascribed to the Queen's visit, to partake of the comfortable viands sent her by her royal mistress; which were accompanied with a description of the nearest and safest roads to Munster, with an exact geography of the towns and villages she was to pass; and this paper particularly pointed out the best places of accommodation for a female traveller.

Gratefully alive to the value of this information, which Blanch had employed the preceding day in collecting, but which, in her interview, she had omitted to deliver, Sigismunda returned her warmest acknowledgments both for that and a small case of rich cordials and confectionaries that the beneficent lady had also sent.

Thus supplied with every possible remedy against the inconveniences of such a journey, our poor pilgrim quitted the lone but secure asylum her misfortunes deprived her of; and upon gaining the eminence opposite her chamber window, she sat down to indulge a burst of grief, the most painful she had ever endured. From this spot the palace and city of Stockholm were plainly perceptible, as the tempered ray glanced upon the more prominent buildings; even the faint hum of a busy world stole on the attentive ear; and imagination, ever awake to the most tender impressions, marked the very site of Marienburg's house to his weeping daughter, as she impatiently dashed away the starting tears, while anxious to ascertain the happy residence of her youth.

"There," she cried, "in those pleasant fields, the gay Catherine and once honoured Gustavus gilded the hours of Sigismunda Marienburg, and there too she first met harsh disappointment in the parental command to avoid the gratification of her chastest wishes! How often have I gazed on these lofty eminences, with those of greater magnitude beyond, and fancied, when separated from Ericson, that he was wandering, deserted and afflicted, among wilds still more desolate; now, driven by power uncontroulable, I am destined to prove the fate I once deprecated for him! My father! where art thou, Oh my father!"

She then hastily arose, as if impressed with some encouraging presentiment.

"I will visit him," she continued; "perhaps, returned once more to Stockholm, he seeks in vain his lost child!"—But again sinking upon the ground—"Shall I carry destruction to his declining age? Can I present to him a hitherto guiltless child an object of such terrible wrath? I am complying with the awful dictate that calls me from my native land; but should I slight the dread placard, such disobedience would involve a tender parent in its horrid consequences. No hope then—no appeal lies but from above; 'tis there my innocence is registered; from thence alone can any permanent comfort be deduced. Sustained by thee, O mighty Lord! the pathless desert, the rugged forest, the foaming cataract shall present no insurmountable difficulties to my wandering steps! Adieu, then, sweet scenes of blissful childhood! Adieu, all prospect of renewed peace, till the imputation of guilt be removed from thy servant's character!"

So saying, she cast a last reluctant look upon the supposed busy environs before her, and slowly descended towards the road that led to the frontiers, while her heart trembled to contemplate the immense distance she had to go; but again reverting to that most noble source of comfort to the innocent—a dependance upon a First Cause, she quietly took the path leading to the nearest hamlet her map delineated, and approached a small cottage, where, as evening was hastily advancing, she proposed to sleep.

To one who had so long considered herself as an object of terror, envy, or hatred to almost every human being among whom she had lately been thrown, the frank and good-humoured manner of her new hostess was a subject of delight; no cold restraint, implying a fearful caution, no curious and half-abhorrent aspect met the weary pilgrim as her foot rested on the threshold she dared not cross; but, emboldened by the cheering words of "Welcome, stranger!" Sigismunda applied with a tolerable grace for the lodging she eagerly hoped would not be refused, and accepted with a grateful tear the offering of common hospitality.

Cheered by the prospect of a glowing summer, the inhabitants of this secluded hamlet were engaged in various sports, presenting to our reflecting heroine a scene of gaiety sanctioned by innocence, where the want of luxurious stimulatives was supplied by Nature's unvitiated advantages; and she contemplated with pleasure the healthy hue of those faces which owed their comeliness to wholesome toil and peaceful hearts.

From a reverie induced by the cheerful scene before her, Sigismunda suddenly awoke to a painful comparison between her own case and those of the laughing villagers, whose labours, ending with the day, gave vigour to the body and strength to the mind, and whose slumbers no dread of danger interrupted, nor any anxiety for future events imbittered.

While thus employed, with her eyes fixed upon the road she had passed, a sudden apprehension crossed her imagination on beholding several men on horseback, accompanied by a small carriage, descending the heights through a path diverging from that usually taken by travellers, and apparently directing their steps towards the lively group.

Shocked at an appearance which she plainly saw had already excited among the peasants much curious enquiry, and conceiving herself, from some indefinable motive, to be the object of their pursuit, Sigismunda left her station, and almost without a determinate purpose, quitted the house; and hastily entering a wood of stately pines, which clothed a broad and swelling eminence that rose abruptly from the back of the cottage, she soon found herself far from the retreat it sheltered, and embosomed in the dreary wilds of a northern forest.

Satisfied as to her present safety, from the obscurity which enveloped her, she now indulged a moment's reflection; and the possibility of mistaking the object of her fears, wrung her heart with regret. She was in her duty—had commenced the task assigned by her imperious judges—of whom, then, should she be afraid? Doubtless both Christian and Ulrica were well acquainted with her situation—to them, then, she need not attribute any further designs upon her liberty.

With this conclusion she tried to be satisfied, and was preparing to leave her awful shelter, in the hope of regaining her comfortable cot before her absence should be noticed. In this attempt she was tolerably successful, till, turning into a broader path, which the dun obscurity that minutely increased, gave to her deceived eye as the one by which she ascended, Sigismunda saw, when too late, her precipitate error, for it soon ended in a small circular plat, from which no other outlet was visible.

Hastily, then, she endeavoured to retrace her steps; but, bewildered by the growing darkness, presently became involved in deeper and unknown intricacies. Not a sound which could indicate the proximity of a human being, occurred either to terrify or revive her fainting spirit; and she almost dreaded to glance a fearful eye upon the nearest objects, lest her raised imagination should people the wild gloom of evening with fancied forms.

While thus giving way to terrors of a *new* description, for our prudent heroine had constantly till that melancholy moment rejected the weak suggestions of superstitious folly, she beheld between the boles of some trees by which she swiftly passed, a figure, whose dimly discovered appearance promised no diminution to her distress, and hastened with all the speed her fears permitted, from the path it seemed to occupy; when, in addition to this alarm, several voices were heard to issue from the very track she was about to pursue.

In most other circumstances this interruption to a solitude so unpleasant, would have been doubly welcome; but again the idea of substantial enemies surmounted that of aerial visitants; for a sense of self-preservation awakening recollection, the daughter of Marienburg cautiously retreated from a discovery she dreaded, without exactly appropriating its cause: and to the very event that had threatened much mischief, she soon perceived herself indebted for an unexpected deliverance from present apprehension, as the path she precipitately took to avoid the objects of that apprehension, led her to the forest boundaries, and the cot she so unwarily quitted, with its hospitable owner, appeared almost at her feet.

Speechless from excessive joy, which soon became overclouded, Sigismunda could only listen to her landlady's description of several strangers, who, she said, were in pursuit of a young female, describing in tolerably exact terms her terrified lodger, who trembled to find herself implicated in Mary's suspicions.

"But indeed," cried the honest creature, "though I thought they certainly meant you, yet I did not like their looks well enough to humour them by telling any thing about you; but my Peter, ill fare the foolish boy! told them there was a pilgrim up stairs, who had lately arrived:—'Perhaps,' cried the simple knave, 'she can tell you about the damsel.'"

"Oh then," cried Sigismunda, gasping for utterance, "they will return, and I shall——that is——they will——"

"Give me patience, pilgrim!" cried the loquacious hostess; "how white you look! What marvel is it if they do come back?—Such a poor young thing as you can't have offended them. Let them come as soon as they will,—there's Godfred, and Stanislaus, and Charles, and Haslar: see, pilgrim, they all dwell in those two huts on the left of them peaks, don't you see, yonder? Well, I warrant they'll give them as much as they can carry away if you desire it; though as to Haslar, not but he's kind enough, but hang the lad, I say, he must needs tell them he saw you go up the forest, and off they ran. 'The devil take the hindmost!' says I, 'that poor damsel will have a hard matter to escape if it should be her they want;'—and yet, cheer up, damsel, as I said before, what can they expect of you? But there, there comes one of them, I protest! Yet he seems so old and so lame, that I think we can manage him if—— Marry! he seems in great affliction; I think, pilgrim, you need not be afraid of him however. Suppose I ask him to sit down, damsel? Poor old soul, he cannot hurt us!"

Very little of this harangue obtained Sigismunda's attention, which had been fixed upon the aged stranger, as he slowly and painfully advanced to the door, whose air and figure struck her, as belonging to one with whom she had been in habits of friendship.

"Perhaps you may know this poor damsel," said the incautious cottager, as he stopped to rest upon a stone near the entrance; "but mark, old man, she must not be offended. If you have a mind to speak to her, you may. So, now the others are coming down upon us, I'll go and call Godfred, and——"

"No," interrupted Sigismunda, laying her cold hand on Mary's arm, while her head sunk on her friendly bosom, "hide me from that dear but dreaded object!"

"Hide you! for what, indeed? Let me see the best among them dare to put a finger upon you! Keep off, old fellow! What now! Here Haslar! Charles!—why, what in the name of——"

"Silence, good peasant; this dear creature knows me well. My child! my Sigismunda! look upon your happy father! Support her, friend; this torrent of delight has overpowered her weakened spirits. But see, she revives! Speak not, my angel! I know all, my beloved—all your cruel sufferings! But they are at an end. Who shall dare to separate a daughter from her tender parent again! Alas, how thy sweet face is altered! but under my protecting roof this fading flower shall revive with additional beauty."

"Tell me, pilgrim," cried the incredulous Mary, "is this old man your father, and will you indeed go with him?"

"Oh yes!" answered the feeble and enraptured maid, "he is indeed my father!" But suddenly shrinking from the paternal embrace—"I cannot—no, I cannot go with him. Marienburg, my parent," and she attempted to rise, "adieu! If you know all my sufferings, you also know my present destination—you know I dare not visit Stockholm again."

"What means my love?" cried Marienburg; "art thou banished Stockholm?—If so, that city shall no more receive the aged Marienburg."

"Banished!" she repeated; "Oh worse—far worse! Leave me, Sir; my presence carries destruction with it. Alas! this meeting has deranged my plan—destroyed the little consolations I had encouraged!"

"Heaven preserve her!" said the agonized veteran; "it is indeed so—her charming faculties are sacrificed to the pleasure of those infernals. See, Von Hemert," he went on, addressing that worthy man, who had accompanied him upon this expedition, and just entered with two respectable Swedes, from their search for her in the forest—"see the effect of their inhuman cruelty! I have recovered my child—but how recovered her! She is no longer the cool, discriminating daughter in whom I gloried; her senses are gone—she refuses to accompany her protector, and half reproaches me for thus endeavouring to restore her long-lost tranquillity."

"For mercy's sake," entreated the wretched maid, "detain me not! Would to Heaven I was indeed insane!—Christian and Ulrica, how have I become an object of such implacable wrath? My father," and she clasped his trembling knees, "if you wish to preserve your own existence—if you would not utterly destroy your unhappy child, leave her to the care of this kind-hearted friend, return to Stockholm, seek not to develop the horrid mystery that darkens my prospects,—observe this, and there is a possibility of our meeting again. Sir," and she turned to Von Hemert, "you are my father's friend,—be mine also. I cannot, I dare not in these trying moments declare the awful, I may say the horrible, motives for what must appear to all present as an effect of contumelious obstinacy: but should life be spared, not many days shall be suffered to elapse before my father shall bless the caution he now condemns. Be then an advocate for my free election; accompany him from hence, and plead the cause of her who never will disgrace your interference."

Struck by the energy of these assurances, Von Hemert was inclined to accept the office of mediator in a case of so much importance, and stipulated for that night's indulgence, at least, to the poor pleader's request; but, silenced by Marienburg's positive negative, he could only attempt to sooth the half-frantic girl, as she again urged the necessity, the justice, and the consequence of her motives.

"And art thou indeed, my daughter, so lost to the filial and social duties," urged the tearful Marienburg, in a low but empassioned tone, "as to dare the perils of a wild excursion through pathless forests and lonely heaths, with all the train of dangers so peculiarly the lot of an unprotected, defenceless woman, for the mere romantic purpose (for such I now conceive it to be) of paying your vows to some helpless Saint, which superstition may have pointed out as your deliverer from recent calamities? Alas! is not this a species of insanity at best? for what can be that piety which urges such a defection from all that is beautiful in the natural and moral world? But I see my arguments are without effect: this night, however—this night, at least——"

"This night, my father, I consent to return with you; but Oh!" and she heaved a deep and agonizing sigh, "what may not to-morrow produce to those I best love!"

CHAPTER II.

"How thro' her tears, with pale and trembling radiance,
The eye of Beauty shines, and lights her sorrows—
As rises o'er the storm some silver star,
The seaman's hope, and promise of his safety!"

Francis.

With a heart somewhat lightened of its late oppressive load, the feeble Marienburg bade farewel to Mary, who, silenced by the important scene before her, yet convinced of her fair guest's reluctance to quit the cottage, dared not apply to the auxiliaries she had threatened to produce; and after whispering her wishes to Sigismunda for her return on the following day, returned her blunt but grateful thanks for the unexpected donation her ancient visitor had dispensed.

A sort of carriage was now produced, which conveyed the agitated parent and child to an asylum, which he fervently prayed might be considered as the dearest hope of poor Sigismunda's heart, because, though different in point of grandeur to that he once occupied, it was the abode of a parent.

It was long past midnight when the little cavalcade arrived at the destined habitation; then Von Hemert, with his friends, who had bid them adieu a few minutes before, but lingered near the carriage till it stopped, immediately set off for their respective dwellings.

Aroused by the clattering of horses' hoofs, the anxious Catherine, alarmed for the safety of her beloved guardian, followed the servant, whose business it was to attend his master, to the side of the vehicle, when the appearance of a female pilgrim, for Sigismunda had assumed that disguise as a protection on her journey, gave a momentary alarm to her astonished friend; but when Marienburg, on their entrance, pronounced his daughter's name, the happy Catherine, wild with excessive joy, caught this long-lamented friend to her throbbing bosom; nor marked, in the delirium of unexpected felicity, the repulsive yet feeling reception given to her caresses, till having exhausted every mode of unfeigned welcome, she had leisure to observe in the cold demeanour, the frigid silence, and tearful eye, an indication of some fatal change.

"She no longer loves me!" cried Catherine to her aged friend; "the Court of Christian has perverted my Sigismunda."

"Not love the companion of my early years!" exclaimed she, lifting up her pallid countenance, and fixing on the surprised Sleswie a look so tender, so soft, and so much like the angelic expression which once adorned her graceful features, at the same instant with a shudder of horror from her offered embrace, that Catherine felt half inclined to adopt Marienburg's scarcely rejected opinion of his daughter's insanity, and timidly avoided every enquiry or observation that might tend to draw forth stronger proofs of a malady so dreadful; and contented herself with quietly administering to the supposed maniac whatever she imagined necessary to her repose and comfort.

In vain could the unhappy lady avail herself of the comforts which an excellent bed under the roof of her natural protector held out. Obliged by the most cruel circumstance to shun the society which claimed her deepest veneration and sincere affection, she mourned the necessity of opposing indifference to love, and of quitting those who governed the softest feelings of her soul.

"Alas!" she thought, "how little are they aware of the miseries my detention must inflict! How would my father and the generous Sleswie execrate those who thus pursue with undeserved malice a devoted creature! Can I tell them that I am now subject to the power of those invisibles, who, at this instant, may be preparing the usual punishment for such as neglect their awful summons? Would it not completely terminate an existence, which requires a much slighter shock than that of a child's destruction, to snap the vital cord? Yet surely to Catherine I might confide the melancholy truth; her tenderness, her invention might supply or soften the tale she would fabricate."

These melancholy meditations were interrupted by the last-named object, who, equally restless as her afflicted friend, passed a few sleepless hours in painful and erroneous guesses respecting her once happy companion; till unable to follow up the rapid ideas that whirled through her brain, she arose, and, stimulated by the generous concern she took in Sigismunda's situation, resolved to gain, if possible, some certain information of her motives for a conduct so perplexing, and silently entering, beheld with sorrow, but without surprise, in her once beautiful countenance, the same united expression of grief, horror, and fatigue, which, upon her arrival, created a suspicion of insanity, while the tear that escaped from her half-closed lids indicated a sense of agonizing recollection.

Perceiving her presence unnoticed by her friend, Catherine would have quitted the room; but faintly rising, and motioning her to stay, the daughter of Marienburg attempted to give a solution to her extraordinary behaviour.

"I see," she cried, "in your affectionate attention, the nature of that opinion my Catherine has taken up. She supposes it totally incompatible with the duty of a child, so long deprived of an adored parent's society, to wish, nay to determine to avoid what has hitherto been a source of protection and consolation. Nothing, then, you argue, but delirium can countenance such a solecism against Nature's sweetest propensities. But, Catherine," and her features which, as she spoke, had softened into placid melancholy, again reassumed the wildest cast of terror, "you know not the source of all this misery; you are not acquainted with the strong necessity of such an impulse. Oh! did my father know that his fondly indulged child, bred under his eye, and taught by him the purest maxims of virtue—that she, who promised to be a solacer of his declining days, should, in the dark hour of infuriate malice, be doomed to a fate which the highest powers of Germany would shudder to incur! Yes, Catherine, even to you the curse extends, should I linger here another day!"

"What fate, what curse are these my friend denounces! Does Christian, does Ulrica point the cruel shaft which destroys the peace of a once happy family?"

"Catherine, they are agents only in the tremendous business. Perhaps I could——but no more of this. Time wastes. Between Stockholm and the spot where my weary pilgrimage must terminate, lie rocks and deserts (for I dare not take my passage by sea), the dreary mountain and dangerous morass; and my time is limited. Are you yet prepared, dear Catherine, for a still greater shock? I see you are;—why then, let me now own myself amenable to the

Secret Tribunal, an object of its resentment—summoned to appear before the free judges at Munster in Westphalia. No power, public or private, can shield me from its vengeance—no possible method of escaping the punishment of contumacy, but that of surrendering my person and cause into their hands. See here, Catherine," and she drew forth the fatal placard, "you suspected me of insanity; but will not this do away the sad suspicion? Thus criminated, thus fatally involving all who love me," she sighed—an idea of Gustavus fled through her mind, and tinted her pallid cheek, "all who love me in danger and disgrace, what is left for me but to depart immediately? Prepare then my beloved father, I entreat you, for the necessity of my absence. Say any thing which may tend to calm his mind; but if nothing else will avail, own that the Secret Tribunal——"

"The Tribunal!" cried her trembling companion, on whose working features sat the hue of death, "impossible! Who ever dared combine the imputation of criminality with all that is sweet, innocent, and lovely? But be comforted, my beloved; here you are safe."

"And are you yet to learn," cried Sigismunda, in a tone solemnly impressive, "that all who open even a door of friendship to the *condemned*, for such already may be my lot—all who lend the smallest assistance to their wants, or are seen in company with them, are open to the accusation of their numerous spies?"

"And will you really go? Merciful Heaven! is there no alternative? Half the fair season will be passed before you can arrive at Munster. Oh that Gustavus were present! He would prevent——"

"Name him not, Catherine, if you value my tranquillity!" Then lowering her voice—"He—he—is the primary—he is the—he—cruel—false—has heaped this load of shame and sorrow on the poor Sigismunda! But see, the sun already warns me to begone! To you, dearest Sleswie, I depute an office which once was my pride and pleasure. Administer to my father's wants, sooth his anguish, encourage his hopes, and be to him the daughter he has long lamented."

So saying, she took up the parcel containing her travelling apparatus, and almost unopposed by Catherine (who sat nearly unconscious of her parting words, so much was she shocked by the foregoing communication, as well as that which seemed to traduce the object of her dearest affection), the weeping exile quitted a roof she never thought to revisit, while every expected difficulty was magnified by the grief she felt for what her father would experience when acquainted with her departure, and its real cause.

Revived in some degree from the stupor of terror to a sense of Sigismunda's hazardous expedition, Catherine ran to the gate, prepossessed by a vain hope that she was yet within call, but had only time to catch a slight view of her pilgrim's garment as she turned into the path diverging from Stockholm. The first impulse of her mind was to urge Marienburg to send after her; but recollecting how unavailing his entreaties, expostulations, and commands had proved, as also her own forcible reasonings against a measure to which she would, in any less important circumstances, most gladly have acceded, she conceived the friendly purpose of preparing her ancient friend for a shock, to which no determinate comparison could be made: but while trembling to open a subject that threatened to curtail a life so essential to her comfort and safety, Catherine forgot to estimate that fortitude, which, in an event so unavoidable, was most likely to exert its highest energies; for no sooner had she explained the seeming obstinacy which thus snatched from his feeble grasp the prime blessing of his existence, than every exclamation of impatient grief appeared for ever silent; and after sitting for some minutes in the torpor of surprise, he wiped off a tear, and taking Catherine's hand—

"Weep not, my child," he cried; "*this* is a dispensation to which we *must* submit. To your prudence I am indebted for a discovery her mistaken tenderness would have protracted. I wish it had been made before she departed, as some mitigation of her long and toilsome journey might have been thought of. Were health and strength allowed, I would accompany my child through the doubtful pilgrimage; but there is nothing left for a feeble old man, excepting prayers and supplications for her welfare, and those shall not be wanting. This, then, was the intelligence Iwan was to communicate. Royal Gustavus, how must thy fond heart bleed for the innocence thou canst not succour!—But you weep afresh—there is no new calamity attached to that name?"

"Dear Sir," returned Catherine, "needs there any greater affliction than the present to supply the source of our tears?" evading an explanation for which no necessity appeared; "must not Sigismunda's loss be severely felt by——"

Marienburg gave an erroneous application to this break in her answer, as well as the renewal of her tears, and shuddered at the idea that no obstacle now remained to the intention he had formed respecting that hero's union with Catherine.

"And thus," thought the tried veteran, "are our wishes so often productive of the calamity we dream not of. Gustavus and this affectionate virgin may now be united; but how keenly will the indulged purpose of my heart be imbittered, when I consider it will most probably be attained by the loss of my excellent daughter!"

This was a subject of all others most likely to shake the fortitude of his soul; instead, therefore, of listening to the consolation Catherine attempted to offer, he took upon himself the office of comforter, referring to the solitary hour of retirement the indulgence of that anguish human nature cannot totally and at all seasons repress.

It was really a truth that Mr. Plesban became acquainted with the leading facts we have stated, and had entrusted them to Von Hemert's knowledge; but that Sigismunda had already commenced her journey, was a circumstance accidentally discovered by this friendly man in a conversation with the Queen of Sweden's Chamberlain, who, pitying the sufferer he yet believed innocent, made her the subject of his conference with Von Hemert.

Not wholly aware of the power he yet dreaded, the first use he made of this information was to hasten to Marienburg, who, he doubted not, would attempt to recover his child, and luckily, as he imagined, encountered upon the road the very object he was seeking, accompanied by several gentlemen well known to Von Hemert.

With his usual caution Conan avoided any particulars respecting his daughter's inducement for leaving the Royal Blanch, as that was a subject improper for present discussion; nor did he chuse, when solicited by the devoted maid to confess any knowledge of her awful inducement, to oppose those commands she had never before disputed; but anxious to know the exact situation of this unhappy family, he arrived at Marienburg's in time to witness his noble resignation to this afflicting stroke.

After much serious conversation upon the extraordinary destination of his deplored daughter, Marienburg determined that every means of elucidating it should be sedulously pursued, though he sighed to consider the improbability there was of counteracting schemes which the secret machinations of Ulrica (to whom he justly appropriated the flagitious business, without defining her real motives) had doubtless planned with as much art, as they were apparently executing with vigour.

In the warmth of her affectionate attachment, Catherine proposed, as it was extremely easy to follow, nay to overtake Sigismunda, that some one should be deputed to keep her in view while pursuing her journey, as also to stop for the night at whatever resting-place she herself might chuse.

The suggestion merited consideration; but who would undertake a pilgrimage, as it might be called, against which so many objections arose? for to mention no other, that of being suspected to favour an implied subject of a Free Judge's vengeance, carried strength sufficient to render the plan abortive.

"It is true," cried Von Hemert, who had given it several minutes' reflection, "this proposal bears much danger on the face of it; but for the child of Marienburg much ought to be hazarded. Her situation calls for the comfort of a guardian friend; half her difficulties would vanish, could she know herself within reach of certain assistance."—Then pausing, he seemed revolving the probable and possible consequences of such an undertaking, while Catherine, who venerated his character, sat eagerly impatient for the result of this important reverie. At length resuming the discourse, he went on to observe that—"*he* would not think of an action which could threaten the honour, peace, or safety of Christian. But to Ulrica," said the indignant Conan, "I owe no obligation; or if I did, this baseness to an injured woman invalidates every title to respect or esteem. To supersede her designs would be meritorious, and I will lend a helping hand to blast them. Yes, Marienburg, business relative to the mines calls me from hence, so that my absence will be unnoticed. I then will be the protector of that wandering innocent; she shall know me for her friend, but we will not converse. Opportunities may occur to do her a service, but they shall be cautiously observed. Doubtless those who have thus barbarously sported with the character, and even existence of so much innocence, have taken pretty good care to establish her imputed guilt with the Free Judges; consequently, her steps will be watched, as also the movements of any friend who may exert himself in her behalf. But fear not for Conan Von Hemert; that caution which has hitherto impeded the warm ebullition of a natural tendency to philanthropy (pardon the vain ascription), will check every rash and perhaps fatal impulse respecting the guardianship of Sigismunda!"

This generous and unexpected declaration was received by Catherine with tears of the truest gratitude, while Marienburg, unable to govern the emotions of his almost bursting heart, could only offer up a mental ejaculation for the success of this daring project; till the power of speech returning, he mixed his ardent thanks with a sincere representation of the infinite dangers attending such an expedition.

Struck with a disinterestedness that seemed to make Sigismunda's protection a secondary consideration, Von Hemert would hear of no objection to his journey, which he proposed to commence immediately, nothing doubting but he should overtake her on the following day; and full of the most benevolent hopes, Conan found himself on the succeeding morning, many miles from Stockholm. When confident, from the face of the country, that Sigismunda could not have gained much ground of him, he sunk into a sort of dell, where several cottages lay scattered among the thickets, in one of which he hoped to find her; but was somewhat alarmed by the appearance of two men, who suddenly rising near his horse's head, occasioned the animal to plunge with dangerous violence. However, he kept his seat, and was turning towards a path that terminated at the door of a pretty cottage, when one of them seizing the bridle, advised him to return, if he valued the safety of himself or *any one dear* to him—a mysterious expression, the import of which was significantly terrible; but the apparent solution was at hand, for at the moment of this address, Conan caught the glimpse of a female, whose exterior corresponded so entirely with that of Sigismunda, that he trembled lest his poor young friend should be exposed to the mercy of his ill-looking interrupters. Yet dreading the consequence of incurring a suspicion that might be fatal to the cause he had taken up, he dared not resent the palpable affront, but quietly withdrew, determined, however, to hover near a spot which he thought dangerous to the poor wanderer: for the warning given him spoke volumes to Von Hemert's apprehensive mind;—it announced the presence of people deputed by the Tribunal to watch her conduct, and that of those who might feel inclined to lend any assistance, independent of a limited supply to her necessities.

Perfectly instructed as to the nature and extent of their commission, the men beheld and understood those emotions which Conan vainly attempted to conceal; and with a dark expression of malignant triumph, one of them cautioned him against lingering in a valley which was known to be the resort of banditti.

Conan turned an eye of pointed meaning upon the speaker, and deprived of any alternative, began to ascend the hill with a heart full of pity for the innocent he was thus forced to abandon.

CHAPTER III.

"Jealousy of love,
Greater than fame—thou eldest of all passions,
Or rather all in one, I here invoke thee!
Where'er thou'rt thron'd, in air, or earth, or hell,
Bring me to my revenge!"

DUKE OF GUISE.

To the attentive reader, who cannot reconcile impossibilities, we shall now attempt to give an explanation of the true circumstances that induced Sigismunda's responsibility for her appearance before the Supreme Judges at their Chief Tribunal in Westphalia;—a place immensely distant, if we consider the delicacy of her who imagined herself destined to accomplish a task so fatiguing, that not her most vigorous resolution, or patient resignation, could be supposed equal to it; and these were circumstances which originated in the vilest passion of the most ruthless female bosom then existing.

Indeed it cannot be credited that the Invisible Judges, let the magnitude of the delinquent's crimes be ever so atrocious, could think of summoning her to a Court so distant, when doubtless there were places of judicature so much nearer; or that they could depend upon the resolution of a young creature, who, not fully competent to the task awarded, would naturally claim, and receive, in the protection of her friends, a temporary exemption from their decrees. It required, likewise, all the faith of Marienburg in that Tribunal's decisive power, to trust his child, upon the strength of a written order, to a fate so awful; but as he had previously been an object of their notice, that power was pretty well known to him: and let those decrees be ever so extravagant, he was aware that from them laid no appeal. But although conscious that to Ulrica Landen he owed his present unhappiness, he had never given credit to the depth of a capacity, which, in the execution of such a nefarious scheme, could make even (without their knowledge) the terrors of the Free Judges subservient to her bold design, and depending upon the excessive awe in which they were held, dared venture to sentence a helpless woman to such a dreadful fate. It is certain that, by her undisguised proceeding, much danger might arise to herself whenever the deception should be elucidated; but goaded by two of the most malevolent passions that ever arose from contrary causes, she despised the warnings of caution, and rushed rapidly on to destruction.

It is now necessary to mention, that among those who, struck by the glare of outward appearance, had unequivocally explained their intentions to rival the credulous Christian, was a rich Burgher of Hamburgh, who, detained at the Court of Sweden on a secret negotiation, found no desire to quit a magnet so powerful.

Caught by a commanding exterior, and fascinated with the wild and alluring glances he daily encountered, Hunsdorf would have obtained Ulrica's notice by a conduct exactly consonant to High Dutch delicacy, trusting to the splendour of those riches which constituted his chief importance, for the consent of her he could so powerfully bribe. But the thesis he tried to establish was erroneous, and the cunning of Ulrica proved an overmatch for German dulness; for tempering her refusal with a gleam of hope, she contrived to enjoy the brilliant advantages offered to her acceptance, without the disgraceful submission proposed as a necessary preliminary.

About this period the unfortunate Sigismunda became a resident with Madam Landen, whose motives for detesting the innocent girl have been fully related; and while she was forming and rejecting different plots for her ruin, Baron Hunsdorf helped her to establish one, which, though often glanced at, was beyond her single strength to execute.

Accustomed to frequent inebriation, that generally produced an afternoon's nap, the Baron chanced, during a disturbed repose, to drop some unconnected hints, which gave Ulrica room to suppose he held a distinguished post in the Free Tribunal. Of this incoherent intelligence she immediately availed herself, and challenged him upon the words he had thrown out. Shocked at the blunder he had committed, and feeling himself too much in her power to retract, he confessed his claim to the office, by consenting to a scheme, which, besotted by her arts, he was made to believe would secure his undivided and exclusive title to her affections.

The growing evil of excessive drinking, which rendered him extremely unfit for the important duties he had, till of late, discharged with tolerable accuracy, was, of all others, the failing most suitable to Ulrica's purpose; and she procured the placard for Sigismunda at a moment when its consequences could not be properly considered. Yet there were minutes when he shuddered at the disgraceful concessions; for he could not be blind to the malice which laboured to convince him that her life had, more than once, been endangered by young Marienburg's arts—nay, that she once actually administered a slow poison, which nothing but the purity of Madam Landen's constitution could have withstood.

Of this diabolical invention she made so light, and seemed to mix so much pity, more than resentment in her accusation, that while Hunsdorf execrated the sorceress, as he styled Sigismunda, he admired and adored that softness of disposition which sought no other mode of revenge than confining her enemy in a Convent, for that *was* to be the end of this pretended accusation, the authority of which she thought would totally prevent any exertion to be made in her favour. But as we have just observed, it was in the moment of sober discrimination only that Hunsdorf detected a latent malice in Ulrica's conduct; yet that moment occurred so seldom, that she oftener received a compliment on her sweet forbearance, than any strictures upon her cruel persecution of a blameless soul.

When this pretended mandate was made out for Munster, it was utterly inimical to Madam Landen's design that her enemy should make such a journey, when so many places of total seclusion offered themselves at a very small distance from Stockholm.

The monastery chosen by her on this occasion, was situated near Telga; a place of too little consequence to attract observation, but whose order, remarkable for its severity, and the strict confinement of its votaries, promised a high gratification to that wicked spirit, which knew no pleasure superior to the one of punishing the excellence it could not imitate. With her hands thus strengthened, she began her plan of operations, and, depending on the authority so falsely usurped, permitted Sigismunda to rest in tolerable safety till the time prescribed for her departure.—But now another subject for mortification occurred. No longer blinded by the arts that had armed him to the commission of an act dangerous to his character, and wounding to his feelings, Baron Hunsdorf, in an ecstacy of passion, created by the protraction of Ulrica's engagement, threatened to place her in the real situation to which he had made Sigismunda believe herself subject, as also to inform Marienburg of his daughter's intended destiny.

The dislike she had long conceived against this tool of her horrid designs, was strengthened into the most diabolical hatred by a denunciation so dreadful; and the alternative Hunsdorf proposed, seemed only less fearful than that she shrunk from.

It was true that Christian had no reason to boast of a passionate preference; but when compared with this terrible Free Judge, he appeared comparatively faultless. Of Hunsdorf then she would immediately have complained to him, but many reasons made any appeal clearly impossible; and driven from every other subterfuge, she could only plead for a few days' forbearance, urging as a motive, that the King was preparing to meet Gustavus in the field, and upon his departure she would accompany him to Hamburgh, a step he had repeatedly solicited her to take. With this assurance the Baron was induced to appear contented, and Ulrica meditated how to involve herself in yet deeper guilt—the sure and sad consequence of a first deviation, when stimulated by a proud and erring heart.

As yet no certain means presented for her own security. To accuse the Baron in his own Court would be but to criminate herself; and to irritate him to the performance of his threatened vengeance, would end in her sure destruction.

During a variety of perplexing cogitations, she was interrupted by one, whose mind was equally capable with her own of any daring exertion. With a perspicuity not unusual to souls similar to herself in low cunning, she had, heretofore, traced in the character of Fitzer's countenance, qualities of a nature similar to her own; nor was she a total stranger to the duplicity of his conduct.—Reports, created by recent events, had reached her ear, and strengthened the opinion she wished to confirm, respecting his treachery towards Marienburg.

The treatment of that noble veteran, provoked by no plausible motive, gave indication of a corrupted mind; and Ulrica had only to forge some feasible accusation against Hunsdorf, which should be spoken of as involving Fitzer in the subject of it, to engage *him* in her plan of methodical villany.

Need we observe that, in the very moment she was wishing for such a coadjutor, the arch traitor ventured to appear before her, with the intention of trying the most refined flattery to engage her in the ostensible business, which hitherto had produced to him the keenest mortifications; and improbable as it may sound, he actually unfolded so much of his design to Madam Landen, as threw him entirely into her power. His claim to Royalty she secretly ridiculed, but apparently listened with inward satisfaction to his declaration, "that in case of his success, he would immediately give her a legal title to Queen of Sweden."

"Heavens!" mentally ejaculated the infatuated woman, "that Gustavus were but the offerer of these charming terms!—Gustavus to Fitzer, what a comparison!" Then calmly turning to the vile claimant, she assured him "that on the exact performance of certain stipulations, she *might* be induced to consider his proposals in a favourable light."

This was a great point gained; and many hours had not elapsed when the destiny of Sigismunda, and the very agent of her present misfortune was settled by these miscreants in a way that threatened the existence of both. Agitated beyond bearing with the dread of becoming amenable, through her angry lover, to the Secret Tribunal, and well knowing the Baron must soon depart from Stockholm, she urged the necessity of being beforehand in her plan of revenge, and in less than a week from the infernal arrangement, Fitzer solemnly assured her *she had nothing to apprehend from Baron Hunsdorf.*

Ulrica gazed with a frightful earnestness upon the partner of her guilt,—her lips trembled,—her eyes, no longer fascinatingly wild, or tenderly languishing, assumed the horror of madness,—her hands shook as she clasped them in an unconscious way,—and her voice sounded like that of a terrified demoniac, while she faltered out—"He is dead then—and—and I am safe! Sigismunda too?"

"Both, Madam, are for ever beyond the power of giving uneasiness to the angelic Ulrica!"

"Say rather, Fitzer, they are now in the very situation——But no matter!" and she laughed convulsively, "no matter, Gustavus shall——"

"Be the next victim, lady!"

"Victim! Oh preserve him, every saint above, save him," cried the frantic woman, "from the hand of assassination! *He* a victim! Adored Gustavus! for thee I have imbrued these hands in blood—for thee the innocent have suffered—for thee I have leagued with a villain—a remorseless villain, who would not scruple to murder even *thee!* But beware, Fitzer—I counsel you, beware! The successor of Christian—the possessor of Ulrica's dearest affections, has no access to the Court of Stockholm; he winds not, with a crafty vileness, into the unsuspecting heart; his deeds, his noble, daring, his just pretensions are open to the world—open as the manly countenance of the darling hero. Think not then to prosecute *your* paltry scheme. When great revenge demands the murderer's aid, then boldly stand forth unrivalled in the sanguine trade.—I see your vast astonishment—resentment too sits on your contracted brow; but Ulrica laughs at the threatened vengeance. The blow that touches *her* will crush the foolish Fitzer, and send him to Hunsdorf, and *my* rival.—Go then, be prudent; drop thy ridiculous claim to Royalty, shrink into your original nothingness, and leave Ulrica to—to triumph—ha, triumph!——"

The sudden entrance of Christian, who came to report the absence of Hunsdorf, on the very day which was to have concluded his negotiations at Stockholm, gave a check to these violent effusions of a perturbed spirit; while it recalled to some sense of recollection the astonished and guilty Fitzer, who hastily turned from the Monarch as he advanced towards them. But his fears of discovery were needless; for, too much absorbed by internal conflict, Christian scarcely noticed the shifting crimson of Ulrica's cheek, the tear which hung upon it, or the awkward neglect of her companion, which, in a state of keener disquisition, would have excited a passionate curiosity; but attributed their causes to some trifling contradiction given to his mistress by the new favourite—a circumstance that never failed to inflame her irritable temper: and he not only overlooked Fitzer's deficiency in point of ceremony, but saluted him in a way that not only relieved his visible agitation, but calmed the trembling Ulrica; and she was enabled to receive Christian's intelligence of Hunsdorf's unaccountable defection in common etiquette, with a guarded steadiness. When, however, he added the information of a person being found in the moat of the Castle, so disfigured by ill treatment as not to be recognised, and that some suspicions had obtained of the Baron's being assassinated, she could hardly conceal her interest in the horrible business; but in the King's estimation this concern was natural, and he placed it to the account of friendship—a friendship which had not always met with Christian's concurrence: but, awed by the uncontroulable temper of Madam Landen, he gave but few testimonies of his dislike, although he now inwardly triumphed in her supposed mortification; and quitting the room with Fitzer, he left her under the dominion of every tormenting sensation that fear, love, remorse, and even hatred could induce; for the dreadful certainty that Fitzer had obeyed her commands in their fullest horror, removed, as is extremely common, the weight of her detestation against the sacrificed objects, to their destroyer.

It is true she was (at least she hoped she was) freed, by Hunsdorf's death, from every dread of the terrible Tribunal. There was too, she thought, no obstacle to her union with Gustavus, admitting his former scruples could be overcome, and that his grief for Sigismunda's loss was not insurmountable. But, had she not committed an incurable error in her recent discoveries to Fitzer? Would *he*, who stopped not at murder, to obtain his ambitious ends, tamely consider himself as an agent in her hands, to effect what we may justly style *her* diabolical purposes only, and submit, after all he had hazarded, to threats, reproaches, and insults? Might he not, at that very instant, be unfolding to Christian the true situation of Sigismunda and Hunsdorf, ascribing, at the same instant, their cruel fate to the real contriver of it, and by this confession secure to himself that arbitrary Monarch's forgiveness, while the full weight of his accusation would fall upon *her*?—What then would become of her scheme of ascending the throne with Gustavus, and how would the present Monarch approve an arrangement that struck at his love, his kingdom, his life!

"Yes," she cried, "my sun of glory sets in blood, while scarcely above its horizon—even in that of comparative innocents: and, Oh horror! the blood of the guilty—Ulrica's blood——What then have I gained by a series of deceit and cruelty? the practice of a life odious to others, perhaps not less so to myself?—Hunsdorf and Sigismunda! were ye yet alive, how vast a weight would that assurance remove!"

A noise at the door, as of people entering, pointed every fear; and agonizing under the idea of immediate apprehension, she met Christian, who had again returned, accompanied by Fitzer, with the look, and in the attitude of a maniac.

"It is false!" cried she, seizing the Monarch's hand, "believe him not! It was himself, *he* executed the base design—*he*, Christian,—the vile Fitzer!"

"Powers of mercy!" exclaimed her terrified agent, "what means this direful change? Be calm, gracious lady; your imagination, possessed with an idea of murder, paints every rising image with its gloomy tints."

"Ah, hypocrite! this will not do! *My* life must be the sacrifice, but *I* will not fall alone! *I* did not kill him! *I* did not kill——"

"Can it be" said Christian, "that a bare suspicion of the Baron's death has thus deranged her mind? There must be more meaning in these expressions than I can develop. She accuses *you*—she criminates herself. If Hunsdorf *be* murdered, you, Fitzer, are glanced at as the assassin. Some other crime too seems to press upon her feelings. Speak, Ulrica—say, wherefore this agony of spirit?"

With a wildness that countenanced Fitzer's hint of madness, Madam Landen now darted an eye of doubtful astonishment on him—now on the wondering Monarch,—her mind still harbouring a suspicion of her anxious coadjutor, yet unable to reconcile the questions of Christian with those suspicions, till Fitzer, comprehending the extent of her fears, and dreading the consequence of them, affected to pity and sooth her dreadful wanderings, as he artfully styled them, which he as artfully attributed to her foreboding doubts of Hunsdorf's fate.

"It would be well, my Lord, to leave this dear sufferer in the hands of her attendants:—recollection may act in her favour; perhaps, in the fervour of a disturbed fancy, she may have fixed upon my Lord as arbitrator of the Baron's destiny—if so, to friendship may be ascribed this sudden derangement."

"What would the traitor infer?" cried Ulrica, who fully understood the scope of these words. "What have I said to countenance an assertion of insanity?"—But hastily checking the rising passion, "My Liege, we are under some painful mistakes; I am willing to acknowledge myself highly displeased with your favourite, and perhaps went lengths—that is—exceeded—indeed I hardly know how to explain——"

"Enough, Madam," interrupted the King; "I enter not into the cause of your displeasure against my friend, and trust *he* also is mistaken in ascribing to Ulrica, the darling of his Monarch, any improper preference for Baron Hunsdorf."

Fitzer, eagerly catching at this credulous declaration, and tracing in Madam Landen's manner a desire to conciliate, dropped on his knee before her, entreating her pardon for his unguarded and groundless hints, which he confessed she had nobly resented, expressing at the same time his concern for exciting emotions to which the dignity of her resentment had given the colour of insanity.

"Enough, Sir; you have experienced the violent effects of a spirit wounded by unjust surmises;—be warned then in future not to irritate a mind which cannot stoop to illiberal sarcasms, without exhibiting alarming proofs of its delicacy. And now, if you please, attend in the antiroom;—my head is disturbed, my heart still experiences a painful sensation. Rest and solitude," here she sighed, "are necessary to recover the faculties I have so foolishly injured."

"We will both retire, my Ulrica; Fitzer's advice in this case is good. I will only say that my present business was to acquaint you with a report just now circulated relative to the arch traitor, Ericson, which gives reason to suppose him within a few days' march of Stockholm. It will, therefore, be necessary for me to retire to Denmark, for the purpose of collecting the opinion of the Danes on this perilous business, and from whence I mean to delegate my commands to the Governors and Officers of Sweden, for the purpose of quelling this most unnatural rebellion. It will be equally proper for my beloved Ulrica to leave Sweden; the bustle and hazard of war suit not a tender female: suspect me not of cowardice in flying from a besieged city. Christian knows not fear!" cried the vaunting Dane; "but my presence at Copenhagen must precede this intelligence, if possible: I leave you, therefore, in the hope that by to-morrow you will be enabled to begin the journey."

"And *for ever quit the idea of being united to Gustavus*," thought Madam Landen; "but I will *not* go with Christian!"

To this resolution she gave no utterance, but silently waved her head as the infatuated man retired, and again held a council of the passions in her disturbed bosom, in which the suggestions of remorse, fear, and hatred gave way to the all-powerful one of love, assisted by transient hope. In this arrangement she forgot to include the possibility of being forced to quit Stockholm, as a decided enemy to Ericson's cause, should that Prince succeed in the suspected siege; or that a heart, which had long defied her utmost powers of fascination, should yield to temptations still less interesting; but in the frenzy of despair she grounded new projects.

It was not with a ready will that Fitzer left the apartment at Madam Landen's command; for he greatly feared the consequence of a conference between her and the King, whose implicit submission to her requests he had often witnessed, and regretted. Of the promise she had made to give him her interest, and even share the crown with him, he now thought but little.

Her late extravagant insolence, her bold acknowledgment of the power Ericson held over her affections, and the ravings of what he understood to be remorse, held out such inconsistencies of temper and disposition, as allowed not the smallest ground for a dependance on her stability.

On himself, therefore, had he only to rely for a furtherance of his projects; and bitterly did he repent the facility with which he had fallen into her guilty measures. Those which referred to a royal establishment, he never meant to realize; for without knowing Marienburg's intentions respecting Catherine, upon her his choice had decidedly fixed for a partner of the throne he yet hoped to acquire, and felt excessive obligation to Christian for his intention to remove such bars to his own ambition, as himself and Ulrica,—a circumstance he quickly understood from the unsuspecting King.

CHAPTER IV.

"Fly! begone!
And hide thee where bright virtue never shone!
The day will shun thee! Nay, the stars that view
Mischiefs and murders—deeds to thee not new,
Will start at this!"

LEE'S ALEXANDER.

THE intelligence communicated by Christian to his mistress was by no means premature. Gustavus *had* succeeded beyond his utmost expectations in his late triumphs over those who persisted in their attachment to the Dane; and continued to march through the heart of Sweden with a firm determination to leave no step untrod that might lead to conquest.

Already had he defeated a body of Danes at Westeraas, and sent persons to the different provinces of Nericia, Sudermania, &c. gaining in each a number of friends. The Archbishop of Upsal, indeed, opposed his designs, and was very near defeating our hero before that city, but dearly repented the rash attempt, being repulsed, not only unexpectedly, but with infinite loss.

With Marienburg, Ericson kept a constant communication,

whose heart, cheered by such brilliant successes, and dreading to damp the Prince's courage, shrunk from sending any intelligence respecting the mournful destiny of his Sigismunda, at least till the report he daily expected from Von Hemert should make an account of her welfare desirable; but a circumstance took place about this time which rendered the tender caution useless, and totally destroyed the madly-conceived hopes of Madam Landen, eventually proving that wretched creature's destruction, while it created new sources of sorrow in the bosom of Gustavus.

We have already noticed his intention of laying siege to Stockholm, in a plain, near which he formed a strong encampment, on the fifth day of Christian's departure for Copenhagen; and, after the conclusion of a council of war, which our hero held at the head-quarters, he repaired to a magnificent tent prepared for him, on the brow of a small eminence that commanded a view of Stockholm, with the adjacent environs—a prospect considered in almost every respect, as peculiarly pleasing to Ericson, who hoped shortly to possess the whole of those extensive domains. It was such a scene as Claude Lorraine, had he been present, would have been delighted to paint, as every object was tinted with the rich glow of early evening; and the deep green verdure of the earth contrasted by the finest azure sky, received additional charms from its quick succession to a frozen landscape; yet, amidst the calm of sober evening, as it stole upon the brilliant views, Gustavus sighed, while he contemplated a city just rising to notice, and emerging from obscurity, now, perhaps, devoted by him (who, in the defence of patrimonial rights, must either conquer or die) to a fate he deprecated; nor was the prospect at his feet devoid of an inducement to serious reflection.

The bustle of pitching tents, arranging waggons, settling baggage, and scouring their arms, had ceased; and nothing was to be heard but that soothing *hum*, which Shakespeare so nervously describes. On the one hand, the pomp of war appeared in terrible magnificence—on the other, several flocks of sheep, delighted with the rarity of exuberant pasture, were eagerly making amends for the wretched fare of a tedious winter, while the stately reindeer, now turned loose to seek the tender sprouts and juicy leaf of those trees they best loved, enlivened that part of the scene by frequent boundings among their equally timid partners of the plain.

It was to be presumed by Ericson, that his enemies were preparing for a strong resistance, as he could faintly discern several horsemen issuing from the city gates, as if to reconnoitre the foes,—a liberty Gustavus quietly permitted, in the hope of deterring them from an obstinate resistance against such hosts of Swedes.

As the twilight at this season quickly closes, our hero soon lost all traces of the scene he thoughtfully enjoyed—a scene the rising moon but faintly restored. Often had he, on that very spot, listened to the sprightly Catherine and her charming friend, with sensations that now lent poignancy to their recollection. The meditations, induced by his grand designs, presently gave way to those of a softer, and yet more melancholy tendency.

The studied silence of Marienburg on the subject of his child, now struck Gustavus as predictive of some new calamity,—and yet there was a cheerfulness in his communications that encouraged no motive for these forebodings. But he had experienced the courage, the prudence, the fortitude of this mysterious father:—he *knew* that whatever *might* be his intention as to Sigismunda's future establishment, he was decidedly against her sharing the throne of Sweden with him, and even in that assurance saw numberless obstacles to his hopes, although it restored a degree of comfort in the idea, that her father's silence sprung from a reluctance to keep alive the unpropitious flame by any officious remembrances.

From these reveries the hero's attention was suddenly called to a subject of remarkable import.—The hangings of his tent were still thrown back to admit the refreshing evening breeze which gently agitated the splendid drapery, when every idea a rapturous hope could suggest, received a momentary confirmation by the appearance of two females, who, swiftly advancing, begged his protection from two Swedish soldiers, who attempted to prevent their reaching Stockholm, the ready way to which ran along that eminence where they now stood. Surprised at the temerity which enabled these young women to venture at such an hour into this great part of an enemy's camp, he could only attribute their arrival at that critical moment, to the possibility that his protection was required against foes of more consequence than those they would be thought to shun;—nor was the idea so unreasonable, when we recollect the notion Gustavus had long maintained, that his Sigismunda was either a professed Nun, or, if escaped from the Convent, might be subjected to a fate still more perilous;—and, in the person of her who spoke not, he attempted to trace the figure of his lost love; for, to strengthen this notion, she wore a sort of veil, which, while it concealed her features, shewed the whole of her majestic form. Impressed, then, with a sentiment of doubtful joy, he assured them, in the most solemn manner, of his countenance and assistance.

"Not the united force of the Romish Clergy," cried the ardent lover, "shall deprive me again of her whose image has never left my bosom! Be of good courage, lady!"

"No Convent, no Convent—it is from soldiers, my Lord," said the first speaker, "that we are flying! It is for protection against the besiegers of our city we ask your help."

Confused at the strength of his own expressions, and certain that the delicate Sigismunda, however circumstances might have thrown her into this awkward situation, would be keenly shocked to find herself recognised by him before several officers that now pressed forward to take a view of such unusual visitors, Gustavus was about to lead them from the tent to a part of his camp, designed solely for those females who were sufficiently attached to their husbands to brave every danger that threatened *them*, when one of the before-mentioned officers, Bernard Milan, from Lubec, who once had given a transient pang to the Prince's heart by toasting his lovely maid, stepped hastily forward, attracted by the figure of the supposed young Marienburg, on which the light of several lamps that blazed above her head fell strongly. The disguised lady perceived his intent, and would have eluded it; but although Ericson, with a frowning aspect, checked the forward intruder as he closely followed them, it produced not the effect he hoped for.—At length—"You are rude, Sir Bernard," cried the angry Prince; "*my* presence is sufficient to protect these damsels!"

"*Protect!*" repeated Sir Bernard in a peculiar tone; "*I* cannot be deceived, my Prince, in the person of this lady. You know her not!—at least you ought not to give your suffrage to——"

"To *what*, presumptuous Knight! Dare but to utter the slightest reflection against one who claims my tenderest affections, and I will defy you to the death.—Take courage, sweetest of human beings!" pressing the trembling hand which grasped his arm; "on the life of Gustavus depends the safety of his love once more!" and he haughtily turned to the interrupting Sir Bernard. "I counsel thee to retire, nor farther provoke the man, for whose cause you profess to draw your sword against his enemies!"

"And is it for *this* woman," said the enraged Sir Bernard, "you defy a powerful ally! for *her*—Oh mistaken man!—for *her*, to whom is owing the loss of that ornament to her sex, the fair Sigismunda!—for *her*, who, in conjunction with another infernal has robbed me of my noble kinsman, Baron Hunsdorf!—insulted the August Tribunal by forging its decrees, and even hoped, by her detestable arts, to deceive the noble Gustavus into a belief of her attachment!—Yes, murderous Ulrica! the tragedy must finish with thy existence!—Already the Free Judges have cognizance of thy crimes; and the destiny thou preparedst for innocence, will redound on thine own head!"

"Ulrica!" repeated Ericson, with an agonizing sigh as he drew the veil from her deathlike countenance:—"have I for *her* offered sacrilege to the person of my love, in mistaking the form of a devil for one so pure and hallowed?—Forgive me, Sir Bernard; or, if you cannot, the means of amends are in your power. But——" and his aspect betrayed rage, fear, and terror, "did you not accuse this woman of deeds that must sink her polluted soul beyond the hope of pardon?—Say, monster!" and he grasped her arm with a violence excited by the most excruciating apprehensions—"where is Sigismunda Marienburg?—in what dungeon hast thou condemned that fair excellence to waste her melancholy days? or who knows——Speak, Sir Knight! Perhaps she is——"

"Oh spare me!" cried the almost distracted criminal, whose dread of the Tribunal surmounted even her astonishment at these overwhelming charges, as well as her mortification at being so unexpectedly betrayed to the man, who, but a minute before, she had looked upon as her own,—"let me not be amenable to that tremendous power!—I am innocent of any violence offered to Sigismunda Marienburg—I know nought of Baron Hunsdorf!—Protect me, then, Lord Gustavus, Oh protect me from the consequence of these erroneous accusations!"

"My Lord," added her companion, "have pity on my poor friend!—far different was the errand which brought her to your tent!"

"Guard her as you value your honour," said Ericson to those who, drawn from the tent by this unusual scene, had witnessed most of what had passed, "guard her to the gates of Stockholm: it is not for Gustavus Ericson to revenge injuries become cognizable by the Great Tribunal. If you, Sir Bernard, can establish the shocking charge against her, what earthly punishment can equal such crimes?—Till then she must be protected."

"The gates of Stockholm, Prince, at this moment present a proof of my words. This night is the citation ordered: of what avail, then, is intended clemency?"

"Oh take me not thither, noble Swedes! pity a wretched woman who has now lost every hope! Cruel Knight! to *you*—to *you* is owing this horrid calamity!"

"There is no alternative," said Gustavus in a cold accent: "my friends, obey your leader."

Inflamed to a temporary madness, somewhat similar to that which Fitzer had caused, she tore off her veil, and with it the flowing tresses that had fallen from their confinement;—then dashing them on the ground, and stamping on them,—"Thus perish," she vociferated, "the beauties which have robbed Ulrica of the only one she ever loved!—Barbarous Ericson! thy triumph is short; yet have a care—it is not Sigismunda that shall share the throne of Sweden!—Sigismunda—ah glorious victim of disappointed love! *I* know the fate of that idolized woman!—But here—here, Gustavus, it rests:—tortures, even superior to all imagination may surmise, shall never wrest it from Ulrica Landen! Adieu, proud Lord! I go transported with the idea, that my absence will yield more torment than the presence of her you deem your enemy, since I carry the fate of her you love in this neglected bosom!"

Not the keenest invention of demoniac cruelty could have touched a dart with more poisonous venom than that which flowed from this artful address upon Ericson's heart:—it was calculated to impress the most dreadful ideas; and nothing but the respect he owed his own character, as a claimant of a regal crown, could have prevented him at that moment from humiliating himself even to this hateful object, in the hope of ascertaining the real truth of Sigismunda's situation. But Sir Bernard, who saw the involuntary emotion, and feared for its consequences, drew him aside till the enraged Madam Landen was conveyed, agreeably to his request, from the tent—a task that needed all the resolution of her conductors, on whom she employed her whole powers of rhetoric, to which her uncontroulable fears and passions gave the wildest energy; but the hint that she was a subject of Tribunal vengeance steeled their hearts, and in somewhat more than an hour, Madam Landen beheld the fatal scroll which effectually confirmed her most awful apprehensions.

To leave her unguarded, in a moment when the bustle, occasioned by Ericson's arrival, not only forbade the ceremony of a proper reception, but might possibly produce some insult to the woman, (who, as an usurper of Blanch's rights, had ever been odious to the nation), would have been both impolitic and improper; but Caroline, her attendant, assuring them all fear upon that head was needless, they beheld her enter the city gates, and then withdrew, not much concerned for the fate of a female who had taught them to despise her.

In the unequivocal behaviour of Gustavus, when Ulrica's threats and taunts wrung the secret from his soul, Sir Bernard Milan beheld the confirmation of his attachment to Sigismunda; and, although feeling as a man for sufferings that could not be openly pitied, he determined to communicate to the noble lover every circumstance, the knowledge of which had induced his accusation of Madam Landen. From this resolution Gustavus felt some relief: Ulrica was charged by the Knight as guilty of murder!—nay, it extended even to the daughter of Marienburg; and, while his manly heart shrunk from the dreaded recital, he urged Sir Bernard to satisfy his doubts.

The sentinels were now placed for the night; the officers were withdrawn to their respective tents, after receiving particular orders for the conduct of the next day's siege; and Ericson, when he had ordered his armour to be placed ready for the morning, discharged his attendants, and apologizing to the Knight for depriving him of his needful rest, prepared for the gratification of a painful curiosity.

"You will easily credit, my Lord," said Sir Bernard, "the truth of my assertions, when you are informed that the agent Ulrica has employed in her detestable schemes, is that Fitzer to whom the aged Marienburg is indebted for much sorrow."

"Fitzer!" exclaimed Gustavus; "is that monster again let loose to torment human nature?"

"Yes, to Peterson he holds obligations for his freedom; and he makes use of it to employ every means a criminally ambitious spirit can contrive, to obtain the crown you fight for. It has been the practice of this artful Pretender to sound every one whose power and authority he thinks may add to his own:—*me* he recently singled out at Lubec, as one, who, if properly managed, might bring many of the Lubeckers to his purpose.

"Aware of his intentions, and determined to detect the traitor, I listened without any mark of disapprobation to his plan; in the development of which some hints appeared that seemed to involve Madam Landen in his views.

"Astonished to imagine the mistress of Christian an agent in his enemy's cause, and conceiving some suspicions that my kinsman, Baron Hunsdorf, (of whose attachment to that woman I have certain intelligence), might be drawn into a dangerous combination, I quitted my troops, whom I left on their march to join your forces, and sought out the Baron. He had been some time resident at Stockholm, and I expected, from Fitzer's information, to find him there, when the disappointment I received made me doubt *his* existence.

"It was reported, on the day preceding my arrival, that he had, unexpectedly, withdrawn himself, without announcing his intention to Christian, who, you know, has occasionally made that city his temporary residence. Puzzled to account for this behaviour, I hastened to his abode, and found great reason for the cruellest suspicions, in an account given by his confidential servant, importing, that in consequence of a private interview with several strange men, who were evidently disguised, the Baron left his house, in their company, at a most unseasonable hour; and in a state which, I am concerned to say, must render, in case of violence, any opposition on his part feeble, nay useless.

"Sweyn would have interposed when he beheld his master led,

as it were, from home at such an hour; but receiving no answer to his question as to giving his personal attendance, he dreaded to incur the Baron's displeasure, and could only follow at a distance, till one of the ruffians, turning about, swore, if he did not immediately go back, his life should pay for his insolence. Hunsdorf, who heard the threat, bade him begone, for he wanted no other assistance.

"Sweyn then slowly retired, and, from that instant, saw the Baron no more;—'But,' added the poor fellow, 'I picked up a paper in the hall—here it is, which none of us can make out:—it seems to be in the Danish language; but neither Thomason, Peter, nor myself can decipher it;—therefore I meant to carry it to the King:—but perhaps you, Sir Bernard, may understand it.'

"Here, my Lord," said Sir Bernard, "read these horrid contents!"

Gustavus caught the paper from his friend, and read as follows, while every mark of astonishment and detestation was evident on his expressive features.

"Blood cries for vengeance! Thus argues the timid soul; but F—— is *not* timid!—Strike then deep!—and the hand of a Monarch's favourite shall reward the daring deed! Hunsdorf is a dangerous enemy! The Tribunal protects him!—*I* laugh at the Tribunal!—Ulrica has another enemy; let the Tribunal, or rather the dagger of a friend, extirpate that enemy!"

"I see your apprehension, my Prince," cried Sir Bernard as Gustavus returned the bloody mandate, "and fear it is justly founded; but to proceed:—It is evident to me that Madam Landen was the fabricator of this fatal business; and my next step was, if possible, to detect the primary cause.

'He is assassinated, Sweyn!' said I; 'the monsters who enticed him away, have murdered him!—Think you, if confronted with either of them——'

'I know what you would say,' cried Sweyn:—'the harsh tone of him who spoke I can well recollect; his form too——'

"At that moment entered Fitzer; a report had reached him, he hoped, without foundation.

"I looked at Sweyn;—his eyes almost flashed fire; he seemed to tremble, yet tried to speak, and unconsciously drew the bolt of the door.—This was enough for me; and, making a sign to the old man not to interfere, I resolutely charged Fitzer as an accomplice in the suspected murder! Sweyn could not keep silence.

'I saw him, Sir Bernard!' exclaimed this faithful servant: 'he wore a mask, but it dropped as he went out: it is the same voice, too, that bade me not follow my dear master!'

"Poor honest creature!—his accusation was fatal to himself; for, inspired with the malice of a fiend, the horrid Fitzer aimed a short dagger at *my* bosom, which, through Sweyn's sudden motion, I discovered time enough to evade the instrument, but only to transfer it to that valuable veteran, who received it through his heart, as a reward for virtue that deserved a kinder fate.

"Thrown off his guard by this action, Fitzer was easily conquered; and the door being forced, he was properly secured, and searched, when another paper was found on him, which not only fully criminated Ulrica, but contained a duplicate of her order for seizing Sigismunda Marienburg, and conveying her to some unfrequented spot, where her body (this was the equivocal expression) might be secreted beyond discovery!"

"Fool! infatuated fool!" vociferated Gustavus; "and have *I* let this fiend escape!—Sweet, suffering angel, art thou *indeed* the sacrifice?"

"My Lord," interrupted the Knight, "reproach not thyself;—Ulrica *cannot* escape; *I* know that the Supreme Court is preparing a terrible punishment for that fiend. I repeat—*she cannot escape*."

"Sir Bernard, your words are—pardon the suspicion if it *be* erroneous—but your words are those of a Member."

"Peace, Gustavus! I am *your* friend, the supporter of innocence, the punisher of guilt; but be not too curious,—Fitzer is properly secured; his crimes are—— But I can only say that, after the expected contest, you shall see him; for, aware of the uncertainty attending a siege, I had him removed to the little fortress of North

Malm, where he is under strict confinement; to which place his vile coadjutor should also have gone, but she was not then sufficiently within my power.—You, doubtless, wondered at my knowledge of that woman to-night, but *I* was the soldier she pretended to fly from; and, although uncertain, till the rays of the lamp fell strongly on her figure, of her identity, I had every reason, as I followed her across the hill, to believe that the voice I heard, and the furious attitudes I witnessed, belonged to Madam Landen.

"From her discourse I gathered her intention to solicit your protection, which, if it were denied, she vowed, with many violent indications of resentment, that the bitterest vengeance should follow your refusal; and I little doubted, from the subject of this declaration, and her confusion when she discovered us (for Lieutenant Holtzer was with me), that she apprehended we overheard her.—But no more of this! Our friends are in motion;—and now, my Prince, DEATH OR VICTORY!

CHAPTER V.

"Shift not thy colour at the sound of death!
— — — — — — —
It is to me perfection—glory—happiness!"

SOPHONISBE.

"Hark!—heard ye not yon footstep dread
That shook the earth with thund'ring tread?
Twas death—in haste!
The warrior past!"

MASON.

THE ardent heart of our noble hero, which, during Sir Bernard's tale, had floated in sorrow while contemplating the probable fate of his lost love, regained its glorious energy as he listened to the sonorous blast of trumpets, the rolling drum, and other signals of intended battle; when stepping without his tent, armed *cap-a-piè*, he vaulted upon his favourite charger, whose fiery vehemence could scarcely be restrained by the patting hand and soothing voice of its beloved rider.

Through the grey mists of a brightening dawn Gustavus perceived his faithful adherents already drawn up, and waiting his command. Their several officers, advancing from the different tents, now gathered about him, and gave their King elect a cheerful welcome; and then drawing off, they repaired to their different stations agreeably to the instructions of the preceding night. Ericson descended with them, and was received with the loudest applause.

Sir Bernard, who commanded a large body of Lubeckers, was designed to begin the onset, in a part of the suburbs deemed not so well fortified as the principal gates, while Gustavus chose to cover with the flower of his army, the attacks of those appointed to scale the walls;—but notwithstanding these unequivocal marks of a desperate attack, no signs of defence or actual resistance appeared on the part of the besieged.

Silent as death, the citizens seemed to wait a destiny which once before they had successfully parried. Not a soldier appeared on the walls, and the allies began to exult in the expectation of a bloodless victory; but apprehensive of some treachery in a conduct so unusual, Gustavus advanced to the very walls of Stockholm, and summoned the inhabitants to surrender, taking care to keep such a distance as should not endanger their safety by the springing of a mine—an incident he much suspected, although he was assured it must eventually prove the ruin of the besieged, and yet would possibly produce dangerous consequences to his army.

In answer to this demand, several substantial citizens appeared to ask a parley—but this ended in nothing; and the Prince, in a short consultation with his officers, determined to begin his plan of operations, still doubtful that more was meant by the Governor's delay, than merely a wish to evade the suspended attack. In this opinion his usual foresight supported him, and the event did it credit; for in the moment previous to the grand assault, a distant sound of drums and trumpets was distinctly heard, which was followed by loud shouts from the city, while the ramparts, hitherto deserted, were filled with a mixture of Danes and Swedes, who repulsed with great force the adventurous besiegers, as they boldly attempted to mount their walls.

Somewhat dismayed, though not confounded, Ericson continued the attack;—but in a few minutes beheld his *corps de reserve* engaged by some disciplined troops,—the same, doubtless, whose instruments he had so recently heard, while another body of forces had driven back Sir Bernard from his appointed post; and after several brave, but ineffectual attempts, Gustavus was obliged to turn the siege into a blockade, leaving a considerable part of his army upon that spot, while he endeavoured to contrive other means for the accomplishment of his purpose.

Thus disappointed in his darling scheme, and tormented by internal conflict, Ericson seemed to continue the sport of Fortune; but his great soul still rose superior to adversity: and although urged by the tenderest passion to discover the extent of Ulrica's menaces, he neglected not the noble cause of legal government.—No time was to be lost; more assistance was indispensable, and he immediately left the neighbourhood of Stockholm for the purpose of gaining it.

As this was a work not speedily accomplished, we shall again leave our valiant warrior to that important business, and return to the investigation of some of those events which he so imperfectly understood.

The hope that Marienburg conceived in favour of Von Hemert, the protector of his child, bore him up for some weeks against anxious tenderness, and the imbecility of almost exhausted nature:—it even furnished motives for consolation to Catherine, who could not so readily admit the probability of his success; but summer had already passed its meridian, and more than two months elapsed without hearing from the friendly Conan, in which time, had he been successful, some intelligence must have been received; when, no longer able to contend against the fears that succeeded, he sunk into a state of debility, the sure forerunner of dissolution.

Catherine saw and understood this terrible change; her heart bled for the protector of her youth and innocence:—she saw herself in danger of losing this beloved friend, and often wiped from his furrowed cheek the tears she shed, while supporting on her throbbing bosom his languid head.

In this sweet display of that exalted female virtue, she was one day discovered by Von Hemert.—Marienburg heard him enter, and turning a feeble eye towards him, faintly pronounced his child's name. Von Hemert had before this trying moment been the announcer of afflicting news; and this was, of all other, the least calculated for his benevolent disposition. What he had *now* to say, the appearance before him rendered almost incommunicable. With a fearful glance, as if dreading his errand, Catherine expressed her wish for his silence;—Conan understood its implication, and was happy to protract the hour of explanation.

"My guardian is extremely ill," said the apprehensive girl: "to-morrow, perhaps, he will be better able to receive a friend."

"No, no, not to-morrow—now, Von Hemert, tell me the worst—I can bear it!—We shall soon meet—Catherine—my only child—*you* know—Von Hemert!"

The contest between nature and a still vigorous soul became too powerful. Marienburg fainted.

"He is gone," cried Catherine, "my parent, my guardian, my benefactor! But no, he revives! Withdraw, good Sir, unless—unless—your presence forebodes comfort."

Von Hemert had no comfort to give, and silently obeyed his lovely young friend, who beheld, with additional distress, the altered countenance of this afflicted father, whose struggles to speak evidently announced a strong desire to communicate some matter of import, while his beamless eye appeared to seek some absent object; and with much difficulty he pronounced the name of Von Hemert. Catherine immediately sent a female attendant for the good man, who tenderly taking Marienburg's hand, attempted to sooth and console him. A smile of resignation sat on his shrunk features, which, upon looking towards his weeping ward, changed to a convulsive agitation.

"Is there any thing upon your mind, Sir," asked Conan, "respecting this dear child's welfare?"

"*You* will protect her," articulated the dying man;—"and, Catherine, rely upon this worthy being: he is acquainted with my wishes and *your's*. Remember, however, should—— But it is too late!—Yet, Oh Magnus! am I not avenged?—Remember, should a more powerful guardian be necessary, apply to Saxe Lunenburgh!"

The conflict now ceased, and there remained to the visible eye nothing but the motionless form of that truly great man.

Speechless from excessive sorrow, Catherine permitted the

pitying Von Hemert to lead her from the solemn scene; and several days elapsed before she could acquire fortitude enough either to listen to Conan's account of his fruitless journey, or what the venerable deceased could mean by recommending her to Duke Magnus.

On the latter subject she received no satisfactory intelligence.—To her questions, (which did not take place till after Marienburg's funeral,) relative to his late travels, she received the following account.

In consequence, he said, of his tracing Sigismunda to the before-mentioned cottage, he had rendered himself an object of suspicion to those who he now conjectured were appointed to watch her; and was obliged not only to quit sight of the house, but even the very road that led to it;—but as a dark and rainy night succeeded, he yet hoped to accomplish his purpose of returning undiscovered.—This hope was hardly established, when the cries of a female came on the air, apparently advancing from the dale; and shortly after several horsemen passed him, but not swiftly enough to prevent his perceiving a woman behind the foremost. To follow would have been madness, even though it were Sigismunda herself, and he could only pursue his first intention, guided by a distant light that streamed upon the lower branches of a laurel which overhung the cot. From its only inhabitant, a surly old Dane, he gained a tardy admittance, but to his interrogatories she remained obstinately silent.

"I *saw* a young pilgrim," said the anxious Conan, "but an hour since; she cannot be far from hence: say but that she is safe, and I will instantly depart!"

"A voice at the door prevented any answer to this question; and I was rather alarmed at the appearance of those very men who had so authoritatively forbid my entrance. They seemed to wonder at my temerity; and with a meaning glance at the other, one of them told me I might stay till morning, for every impediment to my stopping there was removed. Indeed I truly guessed it, but dared not hint my fears, till the surly old woman, in a grumbling accent, told them the stranger had been plaguing *her* about a young pilgrim.

'And did he not also tell you she was a cited subject of the Secret Tribunal?'

'No, by my truly that he did not!' answered she to the first speaker.

"This confirmed my fears that these men were appointed to watch Miss Marienburg, and I tried to wave the subject by an observation upon the midnight storm.

'Yes, by St. Mary,' rejoined my crabbed hostess, 'it is but a roughish night, and I suppose Johanson will come home, and then there will be no room for *you.*'

'Foul hag, be silent!' cried he whom they called the owner of the cottage; 'fetch some brandy and biscuits, and learn obedience!'

"Surely," said Catherine, "our sweet Sigismunda has not suffered by these terrible beings?"

Conan shook his head, and proceeded.

"I did not like my situation. Your friend certainly was not under that roof, but exposed to the horrors of a tempest, which I thought trifling when compared to a residence among those ill-looking people; however, I refused not their proffered refreshments, and determined to quit them at daybreak, when other voices hallooing among the trees, convinced me that Johanson was returned, and not unaccompanied.

"The door being opened by Matha, who again muttered her dislike to my stay, several people entered, their boots and jackets covered with mud, and from their appearance, I conjectured they had arrived on horseback. The foremost bestowed several horrible execrations upon Yiour for sending him in such weather upon a woman's errand.

'Woman,' cried another, taking up the subject before Yiour could stop them, 'yes, Johanson, you may hold your peace; methinks *I* had the worst of it, for in her struggles to——'

'Drink, sots!' said Yiour, holding a cup of brandy to each, 'and cease your foolish babble!'

"Alas, Catherine, I had heard enough! Miss Marienburg was the woman they hinted at, and these men were employed in carrying her to some place more remote from discovery, when those piercing shrieks appalled my soul.

"I have no doubt but Yiour noticed my agitation at these shocking observations; for he gathered his scowling brows into a frown so formidable, and cast on me such suspicious looks, as convinced his accursed agents they had been too unguarded. At length remarking how wet they were, and that a ride from Upsal in such a storm demanded rest, he quickly got rid of them, and then turning to me, said I might share *his* bed for the few hours that remained.—This I civilly refused, observing that, as the tempest was abated, I would set out for Stockholm, where I had urgent business.

'Why, yes, I can readily believe that,' said the taunting Yiour, 'but we cannot part yet;—you must mend your draught, and then a little sleep may be agreeable.'

'Sweet Sigismunda!' said my foreboding heart, 'what must *thy* fate be, when the least endeavour to do you service is thus rewarded! for I doubted not but *my* life would be sacrificed to the attempt I had made to preserve her's.'

"Perceiving his offer of the liquor was refused, Yiour took up a lamp, and after securing the door beyond *my* power to force it, and glancing at the only window, which was too small to admit even my head, he left the old woman and myself to entertain each other.—At first she appeared desirous that I should follow her master; but finding her request unheeded, she grumbled out a sort of threat, and quitted the room, leaving me to meditations that were not of the pleasantest nature; however, they were of no long continuance, for Yiour, who had not been absent above an hour, re-entered, and placing himself upon an opposite bench, told me that my rude curiosity had brought me into a deservedly dangerous situation.

'To make any resistance,' said the villain, 'would but accelerate a terrible punishment. You suspect that Sigismunda Marienburg, who is under the censure of the August Tribunal, arrived here last night on her way to Munster; and in consequence of that suspicion you chose, in defiance of a prudent warning, to come hither in search of her.—All this was immediately known to those who are bound to protect her on the road, although officious friendship supposes otherwise. Thus, then, you have forced her from a safe retreat, and incurred, by your obstinacy, great inconvenience to yourself, for, be assured, until *her* destiny is known, you remain a prisoner here;—nor can there be a possibility of escape, since you will be constantly guarded, and that in a place of total darkness.'

"To remonstrate, to accuse, or even to entreat I knew would be vain, as also to enquire the particular situation of my prison, for in that little habitation it could not be; however, they left me not long in ignorance, for after a breakfast, which was imbittered by cruel apprehension, I was conducted by Yiour and him they called Johanson, well armed, into the thickest part of a surrounding wood, where I beheld an ancient ruin, which I have since imagined was the remains of a state prison erected by Egill, in which he confined his Treasurer Thunno for life, and that afterwards served several Swedish Princes for similar purposes.

"The side on which we approached the nodding structure was partly covered with ivy, which, if there were any windows, completely hid them, and partly overhung a low door by which we entered; then descending several steps, I lost the cheerful light of a brilliant morning. Yiour then kindled a lamp which he bore in his hand, and holding it up, I discovered a melancholy apartment, devoid of every comfort, excepting a tolerable mattress, supported by a sort of frame to keep it from the damp ground. Without any further comment on this cruel violation of a fellow-creature's happiness, the wretches left me; and I am not ashamed to own that a situation so barbarous, extorted from my oppressed heart not only the bitterest groans, but tears also."

"Powers of mercy!" cried Catherine, "is it possible that the sweetest principle of the human bosom should be thus rewarded! Dear Von Hemert, how keen must be your sufferings!"

"Too much so, my dear Miss Sleswie, to dwell upon; for, added to all this, I soon grew certain that the wretched abode contained another being not less persecuted than myself: for I frequently heard the most mournful sighs, with now and then expressions denoting pain and extreme feebleness.

"To the man who regularly attended with a light while I took my meals, which were served both plentifully and regularly, I ventured a question upon these repeated sounds, but it was of no use; he frowned and left me in sullen silence. I dared not repeat my enquiries, but passed several weeks in hopeless misery, when I was, after a few hours passed in sleepless anxiety, alarmed by a glimmering light, more like that of early dawn than my gaoler's lamp;—and starting up, I perceived a figure standing at a half-opened door! It slowly advanced, and discovered features so sunk, a countenance and form so emaciated, that I hardly dared pronounce it mortal, till in a languid tone it said—'The moment of deliverance is at hand; our persecutors are absconded! Come then, dear fellow-prisoner, and view the face of day!'—Almost frantic at this blessed intelligence, I flew to the opened door, and inhaled such sweets as are not to be described.

"The glow of summer was passed, the hoar-frost began to fringe the hedges, but the air so refined possesses every power of renovation.—I felt it invigorate my frame; I knelt; my heart and eyes paid the tribute of gratitude to Heaven. I then turned to the stranger; he viewed me with anxious delight. I embraced the fragile form, which appeared as if melting into air, while I firmly clasped it to my bosom.—'Come,' said this dear deliverer, 'we must go; this morning I found my prison-door wide open, and Matha entered.—'Fly!' she cried, 'we are all undone! In the dungeon beneath this lies another prisoner; set him free, and depart together!'

"Yes, we will depart," I exclaimed, "and thou shalt be my brother and my friend."

"On our way to Stockholm, he informed me his name was Hunsdorf. I had heard of him as a professed admirer of the worst of women; but *you* know Ulrica!"

Catherine sighed at the odious recollection. *She* also had heard of the unfortunate Baron—nay, *she* had *seen* him, had noticed his ardent admiration of that Syren, and pitied the weakness that could not discriminate a character so full of criminal duplicity.

Von Hemert proceeded.

"From this victim to her arts I learned that she had sent him a verbal assignation, appointing him to meet her precisely at twelve, in the wood which commences near the north gate, when she would inform him of her plan for leaving Christian. Delighted with the arrangement, he drank several bumpers of brandy to its success, and then with the guides who brought this request, joyfully quitted Stockholm, walking cheerfully forwards, till Yiour (for *he* was Ulrica's confidant) stopped near the entrance of that ominous ruin; and blowing a horn which still remained attached to the half-dismantled wall, a gate opened at the east end of it, and several men appeared, bearing torches. Yiour then told him resistance was useless, for that tower was intended for the grave of a monster who dared to insult the modest Ulrica with his criminal passion.

'*Modest!*' repeated the amazed Baron, and was going on in a style of ridicule which even the dread of his infernal companions could not check, when he was seized, gagged, and thrown into the room appointed for his prison, after receiving several cruel blows, which occasioned such an effusion of blood, as reduced him to the lowest state of existence. Here he was occasionally visited by Matha, who administered the remedies common to the Swedish peasants, which barely preserved life; but that was a favour he had scarcely thanked her for, since he never expected to regain his liberty. He then proposed to return immediately to Hamburgh, and summon the agents of this inhuman proceeding to appear before the Tribunal, of which he frankly owned himself a Member."

"And will he not," cried Catherine, "exert himself to free my beloved Sigismunda from its power?"

"Alas, Miss Sleswie, would to Heaven our poor young friend was under no greater danger than that! The placard was false, invented by that imbecile man to gratify the unjustifiable hatred of Madam Landen, who barbarously accused the innocent maid of an attempt to poison her, though she artfully refused to suffer her to become a real object of their investigation, upon the suggestion that the life of a fellow-creature was too precious to be sacrificed, when a salutary confinement in some rigid Convent might afford opportunity for repentance. But ah, my dear Madam, no Convent affords *her* an asylum; she was certainly assassinated by those villains: indeed, I do recollect seeing some marks of blood upon the jacket of one of them."

"Yes, she is gone!" cried Catherine, wringing her hands, "my Sigismunda is no more!"—And turning a look of entreating anguish upon her visitor—'Will *you*, dear Mr. Von Hemert, will *you* be the protector of a helpless orphan?—My revered guardian spoke of Duke Magnus, but I know him only by report, and that speaks nothing in his favour;—he persecuted the dear deceased, and yet, strange to say, he is recommended to me as a proper guardian; but to *you* only I will look up for a father's attention. You *will* grant it, Sir, won't you?"

This artless appeal spoke to the heart of Von Hemert;—he kissed her cheek, and cheerfully accepted the trust.

"But Duke Magnus, Sir—know you of Mr. Marienburg's motives for——"

"Suspend your curiosity, my child—Mr. Marienburg had his secrets, but I know not their full implication, yet have reason to believe they comprise an important mystery, which, perhaps, may never be developed. He once referred me to an old inhabitant of Saxe Lunenburgh, who, if living, could explain the whole, but it was under a solemn engagement not to seek him while your guardian lived:—that impediment is now done away, and I mean to make a journey thither, in the hope of finding the aged German.—We will go together, for never will I give up the sacred trust till your true claims are established."

CHAPTER VI.

"Oh, thou hast search'd too deep!
There, there I bleed!—There pull the horrid cords
That strain my cracking nerves!—Engines and wheels
That piecemeal grind, are beds of down, and balm
To that soul-racking thought!"

CONGREVE.

HOWEVER the feelings of Catherine might be interested in the fate of those so dear to her, the mystery of her own situation occasioned much painful curiosity, plunged, as it too probably was, by Marienburg's death, into irretrievable obscurity; for she promised herself very little satisfaction in a journey undertaken upon such a precarious foundation; but willing to grasp at the slightest hope, she readily consented to accompany her kind friend on this uncertain expedition, and they arrived about the commencement of October at Saxe Lunenburgh, where Von Hemert proposed to pass the winter, unless the successes of Gustavus should encourage him to return, or the Baltic should be frozen before he could complete the business which had induced him to leave Sweden. Following the direction formerly given by Marienburg, Conan repaired to Wismar, in a village near which he was instructed to enquire for Mary Skelm, an aged Swede, who had left that country when first married, to attend Madam Marienburg during her husband's residence in the Dutchy; and pleased with the comparative mildness of the climate, she refused to return to Stockholm with the family,—at least this was her ostensible reason for giving up her national residence.

To his great satisfaction, Von Hemert soon discovered this important clue to Marienburg's mysterious conduct; and presenting her with a Ducal seal, formerly in the possession of the then reigning Duke, she gazed in trembling surprise upon a token which authenticated any enquiry Conan might think proper to make.

"Ah me!" cried the old woman, "this is indeed a precious token from my dear master! But, pray now tell me, is he yet alive? Could he not come himself? But no, he could not come to Lunenburgh.—Hush, hush! not a word—Wrangel is at hand! I see him coming just as usual! Mercy on the poor Mary! Would I was in my quiet grave!"

Von Hemert pitied the feeble woman, and easily understood she wished him to avoid her husband, in whose countenance, as Wrangel advanced, he fancied the characteristic of an evil mind; nor did his behaviour contradict that opinion, for fixing a stupid but malignant gaze upon Conan, at the same time he thus addressed his wife,—"And pray how came you to let this trim spark over my threshold? and what may be his business?—Speak, hussy!"

"Patience, Wrangel! He comes—— he comes from——"

"From whence, sorceress, and for what?"

"Upon no bad account, friend," answered Von Hemert, who comprehended Mary's reluctance to inform him of the token she had received, and wished to visit her when this surly wretch could not interrupt them; "I came but to ask a question; perhaps *you* can better inform me?"

"No, no, no!" said the eager Mary, "that he cannot indeed; he knows nothing of——"

"What, not of the safest road to Wismar?"

"Oh, if that be all," muttered the half-convinced Wrangel, "you have but to turn to the left of yonder wood, and there it is!"

Happy to escape any further interrogation, Conan immediately quitted the inhospitable cottager, and resolved to take his chance for a more successful opportunity of again speaking to his wife.

The following morning proving favourable for a little excursion, Catherine and her guardian wandered towards the proscribed cottage, for she was desirous to see a woman who retained such a faithful remembrance of her late protector, and glancing towards the opened door, beheld poor Mary alone, busied in her little household arrangements.

Conan stopped a moment, and caught her eye.

"Dear master," she cried, "you may come in; Wrangel is gone to Lunenburgh, but I fear upon a cruel errand.—The seal, that very seal you trusted to my hands last night, is missing. I was looking at it after my husband went to bed, thinking he was asleep, and indeed I was crying over it, when he called me to let him see that *bauble*—yes, he said it was a bauble.—I dared not refuse; and he looked at it so eagerly, and asked me so sternly where I got it from, that, in troth, I could not answer him; and so he said he was sure it was our Duke's arms on it, and that *you* had stole it! Oh dear, how I wished to undeceive him!—— But, holy saints! who is that sweet young damsel? The very eyes—the very countenance of my dear—— Do sit down, lady. Why now, if my treacherous memory deceive me not, she must be—— stay, let me look again—my old eyes are so dim:—why, good master, this precious creature puts me in mind of one most dear to our noble master, Marienburg;—but you have not told me any thing about that worthy gentleman."

"I came to hear, not to talk, good Skelm! My business," said Conan, "is to ascertain this fair maid's birth. Our worthy friend informed me you would, on my giving you that unlucky seal, explain the particulars of it. Wrangel may return, and then, you know, we shall be turned out with disgrace."

"Oh no, far worse than that! for he will bring the soldiers to bear you to the Castle, or else, mayhap, to the fortress of Calo, under both which places there are dungeons so terrible, and so deep, that——"

"Once more, Mary, comply with my impatience—you certainly can tell who are the parents of this young lady:—she has hitherto borne the name of Sleswie, and was educated by my friend Marienburg. You have already hinted that her features remind you of some one most precious to your revered master."

"Inform us, then," cried Catherine, whose anxiety urged her to speak,—"inform us whether I have a mother now in being?"

"It is her voice!—it is her voice!" said the frantic woman; "blessed moment!—Precious lady, let me kneel at your feet! Wrangel, I fear thee not!—the daughter of my adored mistress will protect her poor Mary!"

"But the name—the connection—the origin!" said the impatient Conan.

"Oh you ask too many questions at once, my worthy master!"

"Yet answer them, dear Mary, I entreat you!"

"I will, my sweet mistress—my adored lady!—First, then, as to your *real* name, (for that I suppose is most wanted as that of Sleswie is a counterfeit,) and yet who would have thought that the noble Master Marienburg could ever have counterfeited any thing? But what shall we say to these matters?—Well then, as I was observing—— Defend me, good St. Peter! here *is* Wrangel, and two soldiers with him!"

"And why do you object to Wrangel's being acquainted with my business?"

"Oh, because he never knew Madame Catherina—old Madam Catherina, I mean:—besides, the Duke is so jealous, and little thinks——"

"Was Magnus acquainted with the mother of this lady?"

"*He!* why it was about *her* that——"

At this moment Wrangel entered with the two soldiers, as Dame Skelm styled them; but instead of betraying any marks of his usual surliness, he attempted to be civil, even to Mary.

There was a fawning distinction in his manner while addressing Miss Sleswie that alarmed the cautious Conan; and he would have retired with her, but perceived, when too late, that Mary's fears were not without foundation; for upon a faint exclamation from the terrified woman, he looked up, and saw the cottage filling with strangers, the most distinguished of whom threw severe and penetrating glances upon Von Hemert and his fair companion;—when making a motion to his attendants, which they obeyed as a signal for retiring to a respectful distance, he ordered Wrangel and Mary to accompany them, and then closing the door, sat down in a state of evident confusion.

Incompetent to judge of such mysterious behaviour, and truly suspecting the quality of this august visitor, Catherine sat in trembling suspense, scarcely able to support the awful scrutiny of his looks, and Conan repented his hasty resignation of the important seal, while Duke Magnus (for him it really was) produced the valuable deposit, and demanded, in hesitating but angry terms, for what reason a gem so rich had been left in the hands of an ignorant peasant, and how *he* became possessed of it?

With an intrepid modesty, the result of conscious rectitude, Von Hemert said he was justified in the propriety of this action by the ardent request of a deceased friend, who had sent it as a token to Mary Skelm, as a means which would lead to the discovery of that young maid's parents; one of whom he had reason to think was, or had been, well known to the aged woman.

While Conan was speaking, the features of Magnus gradually lost their proud severity;—his eye reverted again to Catherine, and a melancholy tenderness softened its haughty beam—nay, it was dimmed by a tear; when hastily addressing the now silent Conan—"But you have not named the *friend* who took so great an interest in this fair young creature, nor by what way he became possessed of Saxe Lunenburgh's seal?"

"On this head I apprehend Mary Skelm can give your Highness the clearest information."

"Possibly; I will examine her."

Obedient to his call, the terrified woman appeared before him,—and, palsied with fear, prostrated herself at the Prince's feet, for Wrangel had disclosed his title to her. He bade her rise, which, assisted by Catherine, she did, who placed her on a chair, as the poor woman was utterly unable to stand, and equally so to answer the Duke's hasty interrogations, for something more powerful than his dignity seemed to withhold the confession her auditors so earnestly wished to hear.

"She cannot speak, my Lord," cried the pitying Catherine, "a sense of your Highness's presence doubtless awes her.—Give *me* leave to question her apart;—*I* am as much interested in this business, since it concerns the fame of my parents, and my own peace and honour!"

"How like the voice," said Magnus in a low tone—"the same sweet, persuasive manner!—Be it so, Lady," added he in a higher accent; "meanwhile *you* will oblige me," turning to Conan, "with all *you* know of the subject; for I will be frank enough to own, that when one of my equerries, through Wrangel's means, presented to me a jewel that once was a pledge of ill-treated affection, I naturally conceived a bad opinion of him who first left it in Mary's hands, and ordered a guard to attend me to Wismar, where I understood you resided;—there I was informed of your morning's excursion, which Wrangel assured me would be to his cottage. It is true, some of my suspicions are removed, but it remains with you to give me complete satisfaction, by particularly informing me of that prepossessing young woman's connections, and who consigned her into your power?"

Conan was conscious that the name of Marienburg would do his cause no good, and even feared that his helpless charge, when known to have been the ward of a man so unaccountably obnoxious to Magnus, might be the innocent victim of unworthy passions and prejudices.

"Your silence is offensive," observed the Duke, his tone reassuming its unpleasant sternness; "I cannot be put off with evasions!"

At that moment Catherine re-entered, her lips quivering with repressed agony, her face devoid of colour, and her whole frame trembling and feeble. Conan beheld her distress, and attributed it to some unwelcome discovery; but, alarmed for the consequence of his evident reluctance to disclose the dreaded name, for rising anger crimsoned the noble questioner's cheek, he pronounced, in an under tone, that of——*Marienburg.*

"Marienburg of Stockholm," repeated the eager Duke; "Ericson's tutor?"

"The same, my Lord Duke!—He fostered Miss Sleswie, gave her a proper education, protected her, and designed her the highest honours:—his whole conduct regarding her tended to that point, preferring *her* interest to that of his own blameless daughter's. *He* recommended her to my care, bade me endeavour to discover the peasant, Skelm, who, on sight of that seal, would give the most satisfactory information respecting this dear creature's origin:—indeed, her agitation convinces me some discovery has been made, the nature of which, I fear, has occasioned such painful emotion!"

During this explanation the face of Saxe Lunenburgh, now flushed with the deepest tint, now changing to the hue of death, betrayed internal rage!—and he twice repeated the name of Marienburg, while half-formed execrations through his shut teeth declared his abhorrence of it;—when suddenly, in a voice armed with the sharpest contempt, he demanded of Catherine the result of *her* intelligence, since it was necessary, in a case of such importance, to be possessed of every document that might illustrate her birth. Catherine had pride; and since Mary's communication, she felt it more properly founded.

This cutting speech acted, therefore, as a stimulus to her flagging spirits; and looking earnestly at the Duke—"If *you*, my Prince, are acquainted with the circumstance which rendered me a ward to the best of men, you also know how far he was justified in acting towards a deserted helpless," here her eyes filled with tears, "but not dishonoured sister, in the manner he has done!"

"Then you would insinuate that *you* are the offspring of that sister, and that—— But where is the wretch who dared avow such a base falsehood?" meaning Mary Skelm.

"My Lord!"

"Yes, Madam, your *reputable* informer!—she who was in the confidence of my treacherous, dark-designing enemy, Marienburg!"

"And why *your* enemy, my gracious Prince?" cried Catherine in a more conciliating tone, for she began to apprehend some fatal consequence to the poor Mary, and determined to conceal the full extent of her information. "In the present instance your Highness can have no charge either against him, or the faithful servant, who assures me that I am the child of his unfortunate sister, who disappeared in an unaccountable manner after my birth.—She likewise says that my descent is illustrious, and that the seal which was sent as a token, was——was——reserved by—that is——"

With a wild and furious eagerness Saxe Lunenburgh grasped her hand; and bringing his face almost in contact with her's, occasioned her to falter in the account, which was not exactly true.

"You dare not," he exclaimed, "you cannot know—— But I interrupt this pretty fabrication. Go on, young lady."

"I have nearly done," she cried, "nor should have intruded *my* private concerns upon your Lordship, had you not commanded it."

"Your's, are they your's only?—Confirm that, and I am satisfied!"

"Alas!" said she, weeping excessively, "what inducement should a helpless orphan have to impose her sorrows on a foreign Prince?"

"Oh then you believe yourself an orphan; and all the intelligence you have been so anxious to acquire, relates only to the establishment of a claim upon your *mother!*"

"Would to Heaven," she cried, "that I had a *father* that would own me!—but it is only *here*," throwing herself upon Von Hemert's friendly bosom,—"it is only *here* I can enjoy that blessing!"

"I pity your situation, Madam," answered the Duke, evidently pleased with this tacit confession, "and could almost ask pardon for a violence which shocking suspicions certainly justified!—but something yet remains to be understood which the old woman can possibly explain."

"The circumstance of the seal I presume your Highness means?—All then that can be known from her is, that my beloved guardian, when he quitted this Dutchy, where he long resided, told her never to relate the particulars of my birth to any but the person who could produce that seal, as the affecting situation of my dear lost mother rendered an absolute secrecy necessary."

"But I would ask if she can inform us how Mr. Marienburg," and he pronounced the name with rageful reluctance, "became possessed of that token; for I lost it, in a very mysterious way, long since!"

"Of that I believe your Highness cannot be satisfied, for the poor woman seems utterly ignorant of that circumstance, nor is she capable, at present, of any farther interrogation."

It was indeed a truth, that the fright she had received by the Duke's unexpected appearance and impetuosity, had so far deranged her intellects, as to afford to Catherine a very imperfect knowledge of her real descent, although enough was said to encourage hopes which she meant to confine within her *own* bosom, till some favourable occurrence should render Conan's interference necessary:—at present, any communication on her side would only perplex without informing; and she wished the enquiry to stop at the discovery of her connection to Marienburg's family.

"I remember," said the Duke, after a moment's reverie, "once giving this jewel in exchange for another; but certain incidents occasioned its restoration, and I soon after lost sight of it till this morning!"

He then sat silent, deeply musing, his features composed, but touched with melancholy, when, addressing Conan with a solemn air—

"There is yet a mystery attending your friend's conduct," said he, "which our present endeavours cannot elucidate. I once regarded that man as my dearest companion!—How the tie was dissolved, is now of no consequence; it is enough to say, that my deepest resentments even death itself cannot extinguish!—The stupid wretch he confided in, might, were she capable, confirm my dreadful suspicions, or remove them!—In the latter case, Saxe Lunenburgh's protection, in the most liberal sense, shall be extended to this unhappy young woman!—all that ambition itself can desire shall be her's! In the former, she must indeed continue in the deepest obscurity, the sport of Fortune, and a dependant upon casual kindness for subsistence!"

"Not while Conan Von Hemert retains a sense of his promise to the good Marienburg!—not while his heart remains in possession of one spark of affection for a suffering fellow-mortal!—not while this sweet neglected young creature will claim the love and paternal tenderness of her honoured friend, shall she prove the truth of your illiberal prophecy!—My Lord, adieu!—we trouble you no longer. The mystery of the seal time, perchance, may develop; and then, I trust, nay, am *assured*, Oh injured Marienburg! that thy fame shall be cleared, and this noble Duke be happily, and not too late, convinced of his erroneous suspicions!"

There was an energy, a pathos in this address and apostrophe that went to the soul of Catherine; even Saxe Lunenburgh felt rather checked by this unusual effusion of a spirit thus soaring beyond its natural quiet bounds.

Great and inexplicable were his motives for endeavouring to

come at the real truth of Miss Sleswie's pretensions, but with her discovery of a maternal connection the elucidation seemed to close; yet unwilling to lose the slightest clue to a solution of his doubts, the Prince not only waved any resentful notice of Conan's animated speech, but mildly expressed his wish that they would remain at Wismar till it was seen whether the old peasant would recover those powers of recollection necessary to throw a farther light upon the strange subject. To this request Conan had not a dissenting wish; but not so Catherine: what the Duke most eagerly desired, she as eagerly dreaded, unless every further communication could be kept from *him*; and desiring to conceal her reluctance on this head, she arose with a pretence to enquire after her old friend, who was attended by Wrangel in an adjoining shed, when she found every fear respecting the Duke's hope nearly done away, as the poor creature had totally lost not only her recollection of the recent events, but even of her husband, on whom she gazed with a wild and vacant stare. Catherine felt something more than pity for this victim to her cause, and gave up all hope of further intelligence respecting *that* cause.

The pride of dignity and situation now struggled in the bosom of Magnus, while reflecting on his late eccentric behaviour before obscure and foreign strangers, which Catherine's representation of Mary's indisposition very much strengthened; and concluding, as she had done, that all prospect of any further satisfaction was at an end, he arose, and reassuming his usual haughty reserve, (in which the awkwardness of mortified consciousness too plainly appeared), paced the room with an unsteady, but proud step; while Conan and his ward rising also, waited, in a sort of impatient doubt, the result of this extraordinary scene.—At length breaking a long uneasy silence—"It is apparent," said he, "that nothing further can be made at present of this untoward business. Should any discovery arise from your attempts to investigate it, I depend upon receiving the earliest intelligence!—a request which ought to be complied with, as made by a sovereign Prince, and which involves so much the fate of Catherine—Sleswie, as I think she is called."

To this Conan readily assented, with a mental reservation however; and then calling that Nobleman's attendants, who were scattered on the green before the cottage, he saw Saxe Lunenburgh depart with a joyful sensation, mixed with regret for the loss of that token, of which he hoped to have made a further use.

The illness of poor Mary rapidly increasing, gave Catherine considerable pain; and she assisted in conveying her to her homely bed, while Wrangel, whose ferocious ill humour had returned with accumulated force, accused his unwelcome visitors as the sole cause of her complaint; nor could they deny the charge, although to his officious representation in bringing the Duke thither, it might undoubtedly be imputed. Catherine hoped that rest and quiet might renew her exhausted strength, and restore recollection; but the deed was done!—and before Conan, with his adopted child, left Wismar, they had the mortification to lose, in the deceased Mary, all visible traces of a further development; and after respectfully announcing their departure to the Duke, lost no time in preparing for their return to Stockholm, which some recent information concerning the state of that city, made very hazardous, as war had set up its standard almost through Sweden with all its dreadful concomitants.

Catherine's latent inclinations would have carried her to the capital, but Upsal was Conan's choice, and to his prudent determination she quietly submitted; but when he naturally enquired into the meaning of her evasions, when questioned by Magnus, she found some difficulty in concealing her own suspicions of Mary's hints, and replied with a restrained and timid air. Conan, who was integrity itself, observed not the confusion which flushed her cheek while giving the following account, in which she observed the strictest truth, but omitted those circumstances which were yet involved in mystery, and could give no satisfaction in their recital to Von Hemert.—From what he could gather in this representation, it appeared, "that Mr. Marienburg had a sister many years younger than himself, whose person, from its extreme loveliness, had attracted the notice of John, King of Sweden, prior to Steen Sture, which alarmed Marienburg so deeply for the honour of his family, that in consequence of some knowledge of Magnus, and other motives concurring, he removed to Lunenburgh, where he resided till called upon to take the charge of the young Gustavus; that during the interval of his stay in Saxony, this favourite sister became the mother of a female infant, whose birth, notwithstanding Miss Marienburg's most solemn protestations to the contrary, was ascribed to the aforesaid John."

The distress of her brother on this occasion, though expressed in the most fraternal manner, could not draw from the young lady any farther confession than this:—"That she was honourably married—her child the heir of an illustrious house—and her own family unblemished by the connection!"

As nothing more satisfactory could be obtained, Marienburg was grounded in his first opinion, and determined to apply to John, in the hope of seeing his sister's character restored to its original purity, and he prepared to quit Saxony, under the plea of attending Gustavus.

When his sister was made acquainted with his real intention, she became almost frantic, calling upon all the Saints to witness that he was wrong in his conjecture—protestations which her absence from Stockholm would have fully justified, had she not been permitted to make a long visit to a relation who resided on the borders of Sweden, not a twelvemonth preceding this mortifying event. In vain then she entreated her brother to protract his intention, as all she could urge only served to increase his impatience; and the day was appointed for their removal, when the sudden absence of his sister gave him the utmost disquiet, nor could his most diligent researches after her prove effectual: when finding every effort vain, he took the child with him; and leaving Mary on the spot with proper directions, should she ever hear any tidings of the poor wanderer, exacting a solemn oath from her to discover nothing of what she knew to any but the bearer of the seal, which he privately shewed her, the disconsolate Marienburg quitted Saxony with his family, in the deepest dejection.

CHAPTER VII.

"Thou speak'st
As if there were some monster in thy thoughts
Too hideous to be seen!"

OTHELLO.

To the account given by Catherine, Von Hemert paid an undivided attention, and saw nothing in it that could contradict Marienburg's opinion, that she derived her descent from the Kings of Sweden, which clearly justified *his* attempt to bring about a match between *her* and his favourite Gustavus. Thus persuaded, he could only suppose that Magnus was acquainted with the intended arrangement; and the violence he expressed against Marienburg must originate in a detestation of his ambitious views, in seeking to aggrandize his comparatively obscure family, which might, he thought, (though Conan had no plausible reason for the suggestion), glance at some diminution of Saxe Lunenburgh's dignity, perhaps as a distant competitor to the Crown of Sweden.—But the hints Miss Sleswie had omitted to mention, threw a different shade upon *her* sentiments, and she once more revisited Upsal with hopes and sensations far different to those that filled her bosom when last she quitted that ancient city. There she proposed (if the tumult of war would permit,) to remain till the rights of Gustavus should be ascertained, or wholly destroyed;—nor was the hope of knowing her hapless cousin Sigismunda's fate, left out of the catalogue of reasons which induced her residence there: for Conan (who had entirely given up his Dalecarlian establishment, and the interest of a Monarch he was now ashamed to side with) determined, if possible, to find out Hunsdorf, with an intent to solicit that gentleman's assistance in a search after Sigismunda, although the season rendered such an adventure inconvenient, if not perilous.

Leaving, therefore, his fair companion in a situation as eligible as the distraction of the country would permit, he quitted Upsal, and was fortunate enough to find the Baron in a small village near Stockholm, where he had been detained by ill health, but was then sufficiently restored to enter with a hearty zeal into the cause of oppressed innocence. From him Von Hemert was informed of the various successes and disappointments Gustavus had endured during his visit to Saxony; and concluded his communication with some particulars respecting Ulrica and Fitzer, which Von Hemert, though shocked at the fate of an abandoned woman, could not help calling a just retribution.

The relationship, if we may style it such, that exists in different degrees between every Member of the Secret Tribunal, had brought together Hunsdorf and Sir Bernard Milan, who, without hearing his kinsman's name, was told by one of their secret spies, that a member lay sick at the before-mentioned village. Sir Bernard had given up the Baron, whose life he doubted not was fallen a sacrifice to the barbarous design of his enemies, and consequently felt highly pleased at seeing him once more in safety; nor was Hunsdorf much less gratified with his cousin's description of their present situation. From Sir Bernard he learned the whole process of their iniquitous plans, adding, to what we have before related, the following particulars, which his station as a Free Judge very easily procured him, through the means of the various emissaries commissioned to take cognizance of all persons amenable to their Tribunal.

It has been already observed that Ulrica was permitted to re-enter the city unmolested, nor did any one impede her safe arrival at the stately mansion appointed by Christian for her town residence; when, harassed, disappointed, and inflamed with tenfold rage against the authors of her disgrace, she threw herself on a superb couch, and endeavoured to procure a short respite from the torture of unrequited love and mortified ambition. Scarcely had this guilty woman availed herself of a transient oblivion, when she was suddenly awakened by the entrance of several attendants, accompanied by Caroline, who, in weeping accents, conjured her to arise and save herself. Confused and frightened at this sudden interruption, Madam Landen at first supposed that Gustavus had succeeded in storming the city; but she was soon undeceived by Caroline's expression of sorrow at being obliged to leave the unhappy woman to her dreadful destiny!

"Ungrateful wretch!" cried Ulrica, "art thou already weary of my company? Is it thus my generosity, in raising thee to a station so undeserved, is rewarded?"

"Alas, no!" answered her terrified companion, "the Tribunal, the awful Tribunal command us to depart!—On the door of your antichamber the summons is fixed!"

Ulrica was stunned. The evil so long dreaded, and so vainly deprecated, was fallen upon her; and the recent ridicule which ungoverned rage and maddening revenge extorted from her lips, was now changed to helpless appeals for that pity so often denied to others!—But in vain were her applications to Caroline for her company during the period of her present trial. The damsel shuddered, and with her fellows slowly withdrew from the entreaties they were obliged to refuse. Nothing then remained for the wretched creature but a submission to her destiny; and well knowing that a contumacious defiance of her Judges must prove her sure and speedy destruction, she surrendered herself in the way and manner commanded in the citation, and being accused as an instigator of Hunsdorf's murder, and Sigismunda's suspected assassination, without one witness to prove her innocence, she was finally condemned to suffer the consequence of accumulated crimes, while Fitzer, accused of high treason, was doomed to remain under the strictest confinement till Christian's pleasure should be known concerning him.

Von Hemert, when the Baron had concluded, could not help sighing out the word *retribution!*—and *her*, whom he could neither justify nor pity as a criminal of the lowest order, he yet felt inclined to lament as a creature devoted, perhaps by an indulgence of the passions, to eternal misery! Hunsdorf, who had been so great a sufferer by her arts, could scarcely rejoice at the decree which would for ever destroy them; and dismissing the shocking subject, resumed that of the intended search—a scheme Von Hemert chose not to communicate to Gustavus, who was at that time employed in a variety of military operations near Stockholm; and although daily expected in that very quarter, was thought an improper confidant in a business which might damp his military ardour.

Indeed, that noble warrior needed no additional vexations at the period of which we are speaking, for he was disappointed in his choicest dependance. Sir Bernard Milan, who, till then, had evinced the warmest attachment to Gustavus, suddenly receded in the very bosom of victory; for in consequence of a strong force from Lubec arriving at Sundercoping in behalf of Ericson, that nobleman sent Sir Bernard to conduct them forward: but these auxiliaries positively refused to march under their countryman's command, and insisted upon seeing Gustavus, whose fame had drawn them hither to fight under his banners. To gainsay a request made with such ardour, would have been highly impolitic; and the Prince immediately journied to Sundercoping, when, charmed by his affability, figure, and address, the Lubeckers attached themselves to his cause with an earnestness becoming his own subjects.

Thus evidently slighted for a comparative stranger, and one in whose private concerns he had deeply interested himself, no wonder Sir Bernard, whose disposition was somewhat tinctured with selfishness, should feel resentment against the supplanter of his power; and in a succeeding engagement it is asserted that he sounded a retreat when victory was within Ericson's grasp, whose earnest entreaties were insufficient to recal him to the charge; and the distressed General beheld his Danish enemies retiring unopposed by a single Lubecker, while he dared not express the honest rage which fired his bosom at such unexpected treachery, lest they should withdraw their whole force, and leave the weight of this furious war upon himself and his Swedish allies.—Thus disagreeably situated between fluctuating auxiliaries and professed enemies, the Prince and his adherents found no small difficulty in keeping up the spirit of his attempt. Stockholm was the principal object to which his operations pointed; and notwithstanding winter was again advancing, he contrived, by the vigilance of his staunch friends, to keep that city closely blockaded.

In an interview which took place before the departure of Conan and the Baron, Gustavus could not help reverting to the situation of Marienburg's family, but suffered not the name of Sigismunda to pass his lips, although he gave the tribute of a heart-rending sigh to the memory of that dear deceased, as his foreboding fancy named her.

To Von Hemert's prolix detail of Catherine's treatment by Magnus, and her probable descent from John of Sweden, Gustavus listened with increasing wonder. The account was feasible, and he gave it ready credence; but that this discovery should affect the Duke even to unmanly insult, both perplexed and offended him.

"If," said the generous hero, "that injured maiden, or *we* for her, can establish this extraordinary claim, Saxe Lunenburgh shall put no violence upon himself in holding out protection to the niece of *my* dearest friend. At any rate, should success attend Gustavus Ericson, it will be his pride and pleasure to defend the rights of those he so much loved!" Another sigh escaped to Sigismunda.

Von Hemert pitied, while he admired the great forbearance of his favourite, but had no hope to give, therefore listened in sympathizing silence.

"As a descendant from the Kings of Sweden," continued Gustavus, "I know not but this young lady has rights inferior only to mine! and it shall be my business when peace is restored, to trace them, if possible, to their source. *I* shall never take another partner in my affections!"

Conan trembled at this assertion, which was made in a low and melancholy tone.

"But," said the despairing lover, "the descendant of John shall share my throne!"

Baron Hunsdorf smiled at this distinction, and thought it incompatible with true policy or his own sense of those sort of combinations.

"But where," resumed Ericson in a more cheerful accent, "where *is* my valuable young friend? I hope not in Stockholm?"

"No, my Lord, Catherine is waiting at Upsal the result of your Highness's operations."

"Then I shall soon meet her, and trust also I shall soon be enabled to make good what I have now committed to your keeping."

He then congratulated Hunsdorf upon his wonderful escape, but without mentioning Ulrica,—that subject was too harsh for present discussion; and after regaling them both with Swedish hospitality, of which the Baron partook not with his usual indiscretion, the two friends retired to pursue their intended plan, and were deeply impressed with the fondest veneration of a man, who, in the midst of accumulated sorrows, and in the pursuit of such ardent enterprises, could preserve the coolness of a philosopher, the patience of an anchorite, and the fortitude of a hero!—But falsely, in the first degree, did they appretiate his coolness,—for while outwardly proof against an improper weakness, his very soul was tortured by the sad remembrance which Conan's visit and intelligence produced! Sigismunda lost, perhaps murdered, tinted the gayest colours of his fate! The gratification of his ambitious pursuit, with all its train of consequences, faded into nothing in this hour of bitter recollection!—and he experienced in that trying moment how weak was the hero while deducing strength from mere temporal causes:—but Gustavus was *more* than a hero; he was a *Christian* on the purest principle, and had already meditated the establishment of Luther's doctrines as soon as he should be authorized by regal power to support and mildly enforce them. Nor did the feelings of a generous heart revolt against any one of the tenets he professed, since his resentment was curbed by sober reflection, and his love sublimed into virtue by its purity and constancy:—even the grand propellant of his present designs was justified by its laudable tendency, and the legality of its claims! If rage or revenge maintained a momentary sway in his bosom, the natural rectitude of his principles soon assigned them their proper bounds; and in the very moment of victory he sighed over the carnage it created!

It was likewise an usual trait in his disposition to turn aside from the contemplation of decided evils, to fabricate plans for the prevention of those that were yet avoidable; and in so doing, he blunted the arrow of indulged retrospection. In the practice, therefore, of this latter virtue, he reverted to the strange conduct of Marienburg, Magnus, and King John, respecting Catherine and her lost mother; but he could make little of it, since every motive for Saxe Lunenburgh's unaccountable interference was hidden in clouds of the deepest mystery!—And after revolving the whole of what he had heard, Gustavus was forced to drop the investigation where he had taken it up, till a more favourable leisure; and, rising from his meditative posture, he prepared for a little expedition against some marauding Danes, who had recently committed the most cruel excesses in several undefended villages, inhabited by peasants of the poorest and most helpless description; and in his march against the lawless spoilers, Ericson found sufficient cause for the exercise of his various virtues—Cottages converted to smoking ruins! barns, lately filled with forage and corn for the ensuing season, robbed of their valuable contents! decrepid women, aged men, and helpless children, lingering about the destruction of their hopes, or fleeing, with all the speed debility or infancy would admit, from the approach of troops sent, as they supposed, to conclude the horrid mischief! For these unhappy victims Gustavus indulged the highest pity, but he stopped not there; all the assistance they could receive, or his troops communicate, was readily given; and the curses their barbarous visitors had justly incurred, were exchanged for blessings on their noble deliverer.

While thus benevolently engaged, the eye of Ericson was attracted by a small and apparently deserted monastery, till an infernal shout from within convinced him it was not devoid of some sort of inhabitants. An aged peasant, who observed his surprise at the uncommon noise, with a shake of the head, informed Gustavus, 'that the Danes had not yet quitted the country, since some of them, he feared, were robbing the miserable Nuns of St. Frances!'

The intimation was sufficient:—the General, calling some of his troops, and putting himself at their head, gallopped over the heath to their assistance; when, just as he reached the roofless portal, two officers in the Danish uniform issued from thence, with each a wretched female, who shrieked, and endeavoured to elude their savage grasp! Gustavus beheld, with thc highest indignation, this cruel attempt to drag two poor peaceful individuals from a station to which it was likely its locality had given a charm; and who, from long seclusion, might be wholly unfitted for a re-entrance into that world, of whose present inhabitants and transactions they possibly now knew nothing: and lightly dismounting, seized one of the culprits, as Iwan, who accompanied him closely, did the other. In this scuffle one of the women, dropping her veil, discovered a countenance which the horror of her present situation could not rob of its touching graces!—She was apparently of the middle age, majestically formed, but, faint and wild, every feature bore a painful testimony to the terrors she endured!—The other, who appeared much older, sunk under the shock her spirits had received; and when the soldier loosed his hold, fell senseless into the arms of Iwan as they were extended to receive her! It was with no small difficulty they were preserved from further violence from the tumultuous crew that now poured into the court, where

Gustavus was busied in giving necessary orders for the protection of his helpless charge, whom Iwan conveyed from the scene of action to a small ruined fort within sight; when, leaving them to the care of several grateful peasants, he again returned to assist his Prince.

Enraged against the unfeeling Danes for their unprovoked inhumanity, the Swedes shewed them no quarter, and they mostly fell a sacrifice to their vicious rapacity—a measure which all the lenity of Gustavus could not wholly condemn. The skirmish concluded, he immediately penetrated the interior of this gloomy recess, and inwardly commented on the melancholy bent of those ideas, which could render a situation, so truly desolate, in any degree tolerable, since what remained of the structure, seemed damaged to its foundation; and what might have been barely decent previous to the arrival of their Danish visitors, was then reduced to a footing with the rest!—It was with some surprise that Gustavus, as he ranged the obscure passages and darkened cloisters, (for the evening began to render objects indistinct,) could meet with no vestiges of the inhabitants, till suddenly turning into a sort of refectory, he trod over something, which, upon inspection, offered a terrible reason for the solemn desolation; for it was a lifeless body! and appeared to be that of a Monk. Ericson shuddered, but continued his researches, when he was again shocked by observing several more scattered about the pavement, whose order, and unarmed state, declared them to be the objects of unprovoked brutality!

"Poor fellows!" cried one of his followers, "we have pretty well revenged your cause!—But where are the Nuns I wonder?—Sure they are not all murdered!"

"Hark!" said another, "I hear a noise."

The Prince stepped towards a door from whence the sound issued, which was that of low restrained groans and sighs, and attempted to unclose it, but something within prevented his success, when a Swedish officer striking against it with his foot, the door gave way; and as Gustavus entered, he was struck by the most terrible shrieks, while several women appealed, in the humblest posture, for his mercy! Happy to find these helpless creatures had escaped their ferocious enemies, he readily undeceived them, when they poured forth the most unfeigned thanks for this wonderful deliverance. Lights were then procured, and the names of the whole community called over, when Sister St. Alexa and the Abbess were found missing; but the uneasiness this discovery caused was soon removed by Ericson, who explained the circumstance which occurred upon his first arrival; and after promising the assistance of his troops to repair as much as they could the mischief done by their foes, and remove the dead bodies, over which the Nuns lamented with sincere regret, he departed to send back the Abbess and her companion.

Recovered by the friendly peasants to a state of recollection, Mother St. Frances expressed a decent gratitude to her deliverer for the services he had conferred, and then requested the favour of a guard to conduct them to the monastery, which was immediately appointed, when taking the arm of St. Alexa, she was preparing to depart, saying, "the harassing they had endured required repose!"

"Repose!" repeated St. Alexa, "repose! and in the house of St. Frances!"

"And where else!" answered the Abbess in a haughty tone; "where else should its professed Nuns seek it?"

"Any where—Oh in the obscurest hut—any where is preferable to that house of perdition!"

"Holy Saints! what mean this impious refusal, this blasphemous language? My Lord, I call upon you, in the name of the Church, to force this profane mortal to that calm asylum, where she has passed years of useless penitence!"

"And *I* call upon *you*, Lord Gustavus, to search that den of serpents!—Leave no part unexplored, and *there* you may learn my reasons for this resistance!"

"What, would the wretch encourage a second profanation of those holy walls? Seize her, soldiers, and bear her back again to a place where she shall dearly rue her flagitious conduct!"

"Not as you know of, old dame!" said a gigantic Swede.—"Perhaps she has good reasons for being tired of *your* company! and now, let me see the stoutest of my companions but lift up a hand against this pretty damsel, and I will try whose scull is hardest!"

"Peace, soldier!" cried the frowning Gustavus; "if this lady can venture with *me* to St. Frances, and explain her motives for thus acting, *I* will pledge my honour for her safety in all respects!"

"Oh you are indeed," cried St. Alexa, dropping on her knees, and kissing his hand, "you are indeed the Gustavus I have heard so renowned for the champion of our sex!—Yes, I will go in *your* company, for you will not leave me a subject of this woman's illegal tyranny!—Much as *I* have suffered in a course of eighteen years, there is—— But I will not anticipate."

"Come, Madam!" and she arose, "we will depart; my heart tells me that out of evil arises good!"

The furious Abbess cast a vindictive look at her offending daughter; nor did she express any satisfaction in the company of the General, who was too deeply touched with the aversion shewn by St. Alexa to refuse her request; and giving her his hand, he left Mother St. Frances to the care of his veterans, two of whom attended her in silent disgust!

By the time of their arrival, the soldiers, who had made quick work in disposing of the poor slaughtered Monks, had also removed the remains of their murderers, and were busied in restoring some of the dilapidated furniture to a more tolerable state. The Abbess burst into tears on beholding the vestiges of rapine as they every where met her eye, nor once hinted her thanks for the endeavours of the generous soldiers to restore some of her former comforts. Without speaking, she hastened to that apartment where the Nuns, who still continued there, were discovered by the Swedes; and whispering to one of them, she disappeared in a moment, but not unobserved by St. Alexa. She trembled for the consequence of her assertions, and doubted not but this woman had received a commission to defeat her hopes and wishes.

Gustavus had just quitted her to speak to one of his men, when hastily returning, he missed St. Alexa!—This occasioned no surprise, as he conceived she would quickly reappear. He went on to point out what part of the interior of the edifice was reparable; still St. Alexa was absent, and the Abbess preserved an inflexible silence to his questions respecting the poor Nun, every one of whose suggestions now arose to his mind as fully confirmed by the behaviour of Mother St. Frances.

"I will see St. Alexa immediately!" said the determined Prince;

"produce her instantly, or a worse fate awaits this house and its inhabitants, than that so lately experienced!"

"I know not of her, my Lord. It well becomes a Prince who is fighting for the Crown of Sweden, to begin his career with a violation of the Church duties!"

"*Produce the Nun*, Madam!" cried Ericson, who disregarded the pompous declaration and stern look which were assumed to cover the tremor his threats occasioned. "She would not have absented herself willingly at this time, I am well assured."

"It is likely," said a lay-sister, "that she has repaired to the chapel, to return thanks for her wonderful escape."

"Or rather, daughter," interrupted Mother St. Frances with a sarcastical sneer, "or rather availed herself of this opportunity to seek another and less sacred protection."

Gustavus, weary of useless altercation, abruptly quitted the room; and giving a signal to some veterans, immediately began a strict examination of the cells and chambers of the upper floor; the dreary silence and emptiness of which convinced him no light was to be obtained from their dismal recesses! Disappointed, but not hopeless, he continued the search, preserving, however, a strict decency in whatever related to the Nuns' apartments; where, finding no communicating doors concealed in the mouldering wainscots, no sliding panels, or convenient trap-doors, he reluctantly descended the narrow stone steps, and crossing a small hall, whose broken pavement shewed its long disuse, he examined a mouldering arch that overhung a half door cased with iron, and defended by thick but rusty spikes, which rose high to prevent any one getting over. Of a lay-sister, who just then passed, he asked its designation. She looked round with an air of wild affright, and would have retreated.

"This door is locked," said the Prince, while he earnestly watched her changing countenance; "I must have the key!"

"That door, my Lord—that door leads to—to——nothing, I believe! but I will ask the Lady Abbess."

"No trifling, woman!" and he half drew his sword: "*you* know the secrets of this diabolical prison!—Lead then to the dungeons, which, I doubt not, lie beyond this entrance. Force that door, my friends!"

The soldiers obeyed him with alacrity, when the appearance of St. Alexa speeding towards him, suspended for a moment, any further operations, who, dreading the vengeance of St. Frances, had concealed herself in a small recess, till, convinced by the indignation Gustavus expressed against the Abbess, of his intention to protest all she had injured, and fearful he might not discover the object of his present care and fears, she ventured from her retreat, to confirm any doubt that might arise in their researches.

"You are safe then, Madam; I congratulate you!—But tell us,—is it not in *this* woman's power to corroborate your testimony?"

"Most assuredly, my noble Lord, but leave me not to further danger!—and yet I cannot explore the shocking prisons of——"

"No need, St. Alexa; my soldiers will protect you."

She looked her gratitude, and catching the arm of her gigantic defender, declared herself free from apprehension in his presence. Gustavus then, turning to the trembling lay sister, and giving her a lamp, ordered her to descend the steps that sunk beyond the dismal entrance. Silent from excessive terror, she faintly obeyed him, while the glittering sword, officiously displayed, procured a prompt compliance; and she glided, with an unsteady step, across vaults and through passages, guarded by small loopholes from the pernicious effects of confined air, when, perceiving she was leading towards a flight of steps that ascended on the contrary side to that by which he had entered, Gustavus felt dissatisfied, and suddenly stopping her—

"Swear," he said, "on this good sword, and by your patron Saint, that we have visited every place beneath the monastery, and that no creature exists in these dreary regions!—Swear, also, that no object of Catholic vengeance, no wretched Nun obnoxious to *your* Lady Abbess, has ever yielded up a persecuted life within these cells.—Speak, or——"

"My Lord, my Lord, have pity! *I* am only an agent. *My* heart has bled for sufferings I was made to inflict! Oh tell me the consequences of a free confession!"

"Pardon—absolute pardon! A deliverance from monastical power, and sufficient means for the prolongation of your existence!"

"Then follow me, my Lord:—and Oh, how happy shall I be to

make some amends for the sorrows, of which I have been a secondary instrument."

So saying, she ascended several steps of the flight before them, when coming to a small landing, upon which a low door opened, a sudden faintness apparently pervaded her, and she sunk upon a rising stone that crossed the entrance.

"Thus," said she, in feeble accents, "have I been lately punished when about to enter this abode of despair!"

"Give *me* the key!" exclaimed Gustavus, observing one in her hand;—"my heart forebodes a terrible scene!"

"Pardon me, great Prince! but some caution is necessary. I will not deceive you—only let me enter first."

She then regained her feet with difficulty; and drawing several bolts, whose fastenings were assisted by a stout lock, the Sister entered, and Gustavus heard her speak; but no answer was returned. Fearful of committing some error, he stood still as death; but the appearance of his guide rendered silence no longer necessary.

"Too late, too late!" vociferated the unhappy woman, "too late is this visit made! Death has conquered!—Wretch! barbarous wretch!—What agonies have I witnessed! what entreaties for pity have I withstood!—How taunting were the Abbess's reproaches! how unavailing the meek sufferer's quiet resignation! But she is gone!—gone to bear witness to the most atrocious wickedness that ever the earth concealed! Ah, go not there, my Lord!—Tortures, racks, death itself would be a blessing in exchange for the horror that sight affords! Yes, sheath thy sword within this flinty bosom!"

"Begone, serpent!" cried the distressed General; and throwing her against the step, he entered—entered to behold, amidst the glooms which a single lamp could scarcely dissipate, (for the Sister had left her's on a bench in the dungeon,) a sight calculated to rouse the feeling soul to madness!

Close to the door, insensible, apparently dead, the hands clasped, the head reclined against the wall, as if receding from a kneeling posture, emaciated, every feature shrunk, her complexion touched with the hue of death, breathless, cold, and clad in the coarsest garment, Gustavus entered to behold his *Sigismunda Marienburg!*

CHAPTER VIII.

"What is this world?—Thy school, Oh misery
Our only lesson is to learn to suffer:
And he who knows not that, was born for nought!"
YOUNG.

"Revenge is laudable
When resentment's just."
WANDESFORD.

IN every scene of difficulty and distress, (and Gustavus had experienced a variety of such scenes), the fortitude of our hero was tempered with the resignation of a Christian. A duteous son, an affectionate friend, a sincere and loyal subject, were his usual characteristics, and well he deserved the eulogium; but although he had witnessed the violent death of a martyred father, had suffered the excruciating loss of a mother and sisters through the same nefarious wickedness that deprived him of paternal affection,—and endured every hardship the attempt to establish his claims to Royalty could create, something still was wanting to subdue the courageous soul; but *that* something was now supplied by the tremendous scene before him: and while he gazed, a film came over his terror-struck eyes, his senses failed, and the great Gustavus sunk helpless by the side of his lost, his murdered love!

The exclamations of his guide when she first discovered Sigismunda's situation, were not unheard by Iwan; who, closely following Ericson, beheld him bending in agony insupportable over the motionless prisoner, while the lay-sister was vainly attempting to raise him.

Shocked at the distress of his beloved master, the faithful soldier first strove to recover him by such means as his anxiety, or the dismal cavern, would permit, by placing him upon a stone bench, and sprinkling some water, which he found in an earthen jug, on his face.

Recovered from the temporary suspension of his faculties, Gustavus caught up the affecting object of his misery, and bore her through the passages to an apartment where Mother St. Frances sat trembling for the consequences of a discovery she dreaded. St. Alexa, who had continued under the Swede's care, perceiving her deliverer as he passed, bearing his helpless charge along the hall, rushed after him, exclaiming,—

"My friend, my sister, my dearest Sigismunda! art thou indeed gone? Precious sacrifice to diabolical cruelty! I was then too late in my information!"

"Yes, dear Alexa," said the agonized hero, as he gently deposited the fragile frame on a couch, "she is, I fear, beyond the effort of friendship to recover.

"Monster!" he cried, addressing the Abbess who was gliding towards the door, thinkest thou to escape *thy* share of punishment for this most atrocious cruelty practised upon the sweetest, the most injured of all created beings? Look at that pallid countenance, behold that emaciated form, and triumph in the vilest act of barbarity that ever devils rejoiced in! Murderess, look there!—Even devils themselves would tremble at the sacrilege!"

So saying, he dragged her to the couch, where St. Alexa, assisted by several Nuns, were busied in exerting their earnest, though hopeless, endeavours to restore the animating spirit of existence.

"No," he continued, while tears of anguish forced a passage, and dropped upon the beloved features, "no, sweet St. Alexa, thy cares are vain!—the sainted soul is fled! In that cavern of destruction, fit only for such criminals as her murderers, the persecuted spirit winged its flight; needless is all this care—this tenderness is too late bestowed!—Sweet faded blossom! no effort can invigorate thy pure spirit! no art restore the tints of health to that sunken cheek!—What then remains but vengeance?—And here again," seizing the Abbess, "it shall be inflicted! Ulrica, Fitzer, Christian, retribution awaits ye all! Here, Iwan, to you and my veterans the task of punishment belongs! That serpent too, who introduced me to my murdered love!—but no, she is safe!—*My* promise shields her from deserved resentment!"

Happy to express their detestation of a wretch who, they found reason to suppose, had too often made use of the subterranean abodes they had so recently examined, as prisons for the poor Nuns, the soldiers advanced to seize her; when shrinking from Iwan's grasp, and tearing from another the hand he had caught, she threw herself upon the cold pavement before Ericson, her fingers clasped in all the agony of fearful expectation, while she implored his interference. But, with such an instance of her savage brutality before him, the General knew no pity; and, could he have relented, it might have been dangerous to hazard his authority in repealing a command his soldiers were delighted to execute. Pointing, therefore, expressively to the poor Sigismunda as a motive for his non-compliance, he suffered military justice to be inflicted, and the Abbess met her deserved fate. With a hopeless attention, Ericson again reverted to St. Alexa's unintermitted attempts to revive her lamented friend.

"She is *not* dead, my Lord," said the worthy creature, in reply to his eager questions, "and I would recommend your Highness's absence till her recovery is either ascertained, or——"

"Her recovery—is it possible then," interrupted he, "that she still breathes?"

"She does, my Lord; but the prospect of her restoration is gloomy. We will remove her to my chamber:—in the meantime, let me entreat that the wretched victim to her own crimes may be interred, if she is, indeed, no more."

Gustavus immediately withdrew to the portal to obey this humane request, and gazed for a moment in silent horror upon the corpse of her he so justly detested, when he ordered Iwan to see her decently deposited in the adjoining cemetery.

While this ceremony was performing, he continued in the court, which was sheltered from a piercing north wind by the mouldering walls, when the abrupt appearance of a courier, who entered in breathless haste, recalled his ideas to their wonted object, which a faint hope of Sigismunda's recovery brightened into their usual radiance.

The business of this soldier was to inform his General that, in consequence of Christian's cruel and impolitic behaviour in Denmark, particularly to the Clergy, who encouraged the nation to take up arms against him, there was every probability, if Gustavus availed himself of this fortunate event, Admiral Norby, who, with his fleet, was deputed to relieve Stockholm, might be wrought upon to renounce his intention, and leave that city to the mercy of its besiegers.

This intelligence, which was brought by some deserters from the Danish fleet, would, in any other situation, have been received by Ericson with the most eager delight; as it was, it lost some of its value, in the consideration that he must immediately depart from Telga, if he meant to make a proper use of it.

There was no time for internal debate. Bidding, therefore, the courier to summon his soldiers from the cemetery, and commanding those, who were holding themselves in readiness for marching, to draw up without the walls, he once more sought St. Alexa, in whose countenance he saw no support to the hope she first held out.

"She *is* alive, my Lord," cried the Nun, "but totally insensible; nor do I think she can ever recover, her constitution is so debilitated. To *my* care you may trust the gentle maid. All that can be done, I will do for a dear creature so barbarously treated!"

"I know it, St. Alexa, good, considerate, and tender!—But may I not once more behold the unconscious sufferer?—May I not *once* more contemplate in that exhausted frame the overthrow of my sweetest domestic prospects?"

To this request St. Alexa gave a reluctant consent; and Gustavus pressed the almost lifeless hand, under a certain presentiment that it would be for the last time. He then arranged every matter necessary to the security and comfort of the remaining Nuns, leaving a guard sufficient to protect them, and repair, to the best of their power, the mischief done by their late ferocious visitants, and under the strictest regulations with respect to their conduct; ordering, likewise, that a courier should bring to the camp, or wherever he might be, daily accounts, if possible, of Sigismunda's situation. He then quitted the Monastery of St. Frances with the prayers and blessings of its preserved inhabitants, who jointly conjured St. Alexa to supply the place and dignity of their late wretched Superior; a request, however, she chose not to comply with, as her conscience inclined to the Reformation, and her profession, as a Nun, had been the effect of fraud and force.

Unwilling to omit the slightest opportunity of gratifying his Sigismunda, should she be ever restored to the consolations of friendship, her anxious lover applied to the worthy Conan, who had made one successless attempt to discover the daughter of the deceased Marienburg, and was returning, by the way of Stockholm, to Upsal, as the increasing severity of the weather prevented any hope he might entertain of meeting her, should she have escaped the fury of Ulrica; and he arrived at the camp of Gustavus but a few hours before that Prince had reached it.

To the account which Gustavus gave of Sigismunda's sufferings, Von Hemert listened with undissembled pity and abhorrence, and immediately offered to procure the company of Catherine for her poor insensible friend,—a proposal so agreeable to Gustavus, that he could not avoid an expression of the sincerest gratitude for such an acceptable favour; and as Conan seemed rather apprehensive of Catherine's safety in travelling, unattended, through a part of Sweden, the most subject in that perilous time to the Danish marauders, the General deputed a select party of veterans to conduct her to Telga, the spot where St. Frances was situated, under the direction of Von Hemert, and once more felt that secret hope so often rejected, so frequently encouraged, and so falsely founded.

The distance from Stockholm to Upsal being little more than forty miles, Catherine was soon gratified by the sight of her preserver, and eagerly enquired for Sigismunda.

Von Hemert seemed as if chosen to communicate irksome intelligence, and there was little in what he had in charge to deliver of a pleasant nature, since even the wished-for recovery of Miss Marienburg could only gratify friendship, while it must prove the destruction of *love!*

"I see my dear guardian has not succeeded?" cried Catherine, who read in that faithful index, his melancholy countenance, her disappointment.

"Not exactly in the way my Catherine would wish. Your cousin is found, but I know not if she be living. Her cruel sufferings, it is to be feared, have shortened a life so precious to all who could justly appretiate her worth."

"Sweet Sigismunda, beloved of my heart, who could betray such superior worth? But where is she, my dear Sir? Can I not see her? Did *you* discover her? Oh, whoever has done that blessed deed, may they be rewarded with the grant of their heart's choicest wishes!—But is she at liberty?"

"She is, my child, and was delivered from the most barbarous persecution that ever followed a helpless maid, but *not* by *me*."

"Whoever did, I repeat, may his fate be that he most desires!—may he be gratified with the society of her he best loves!"

"My Catherine," said Conan, "your warmth is commendable; but is it permanent? I have not yet told you by *whom* this happy event is brought about."

"Name him!—Were he even my bitterest enemy, I could not retract!"

"No, dear daughter! Gustavus Ericson is *not* the enemy of Catherine Sleswie, yet *he* is the deliverer of Sigismunda Marienburg!"

"No matter!" cried she in low and trembling accents, while the deepest confusion glowed on her changing cheek, "no matter, Sir; he has procured me an exquisite pleasure!—But let us depart: you say she is in danger!—Let us hasten to the friend of my youth, the child of my revered uncle!"

Conan saw, in the hurry she affected, the perturbation of a harmless soul; he pitied her, but he could not alter the decrees of Fate, and thought it better to comply with her request, than continue a conversation which could produce no good purpose. As he had journied all night, not stopping till he had reached Upsal, there was yet daylight enough to last them to Telga; and by the close of the following evening, Catherine beheld upon a barren heath, the half-ruined vestiges of the monastery of St. Frances. Her heart misgave her as she entered the portal, and crossed the lonely hall; when meeting a lay-sister, she faintly requested to be led to Sigismunda Marienburg. The Sister, on whose pale features the rays of the lamp she carried feebly beamed, looked earnestly at the stranger, and conducted her in silence to a gloomy parlour within the grate, which parted her from Conan, who was averse to this separation; but the soldiers, then resident at the monastery, joining their companions, conducted all of them to a sort of kitchen, where his doubts respecting Catherine's safety were fully removed by the friendly guard, and his want of refreshment freely supplied.

While the lay-sister went to announce the arrival of Miss Sleswie to St. Alexa, she endeavoured to arm herself with fortitude for the expected scene, hardly daring to trust herself with an examination of her own heart on this trying occasion; but the appearance of St. Alexa, to whom she had not been announced, changed the course of her ideas, and she tremulously enquired if her friend was yet in existence, and whether she might be admitted.

"She is yet living," answered the Nun, "but extremely low.—Who shall I say requests to see her?" curious to know the name of a visitor so unexpected, and painfully surprised by a circumstance which occurred in a delivery of the lay-sister's message.

"I think," said the now cautious Catherine, "it might be better to avoid the mention of a name, which, however pleasing, may operate too powerfully on her wasted spirits."

"You are right," cried the Nun; "but against my knowing it there can certainly be no objection."

"Doubtless, Madam, nor have I any reason to conceal that of Catherine Sleswie."

"Catherine!" repeated St. Alexa, with a heavy sigh, "I think that name has occurred more than once in our poor friend's incoherent ramblings. Oh, she has suffered," continued the affectionate Nun, melting into tears, "beyond imagination to surmise! Dear girl, when she was first trepanned to this den of vice,"—(Catherine started)—"I tried to sooth the unhappy maid; but lenient treatment was not the plan her enemies had marked out. St. Frances, the wretched Superior of this place, checked me severely for my attention to a creature, whose crimes, she infamously asserted, had brought her under the censure of the Supreme Tribunal; to avoid the condemnation of which, her *friends* (Oh prostituted word!) rather chose to subject her to the Church's wholesome discipline: therefore any attempt to meliorate her salutary punishment, would be attended by severe consequences to those who should dare to offer it, and most certainly end in her own condemnation by the Tribunal. Bold in a cause which I conceived to be that of my sex and situation, I defied the anathemas fulminated against me by the Confessors who attended the monastery, and continued, when opportunity served, to supply her with wholesome provisions; and even conveyed a small stove into the miserable cell, where she was then confined, visiting her as often as possible, and striving to cheer the patient sufferer with a hope of better days.—Alas! I fear my officious tenderness only precipitated her shocking fate! In those hours of leisure, when sleep protracted the powers and inclinations of her, I should say, *our* persecutors to torment, I learned that she had been accused of some crime (but what she could not perfectly tell) to the Tribunal, and was on her journey to Munster, when she was taken by several men from a cottage, where she proposed to pass the night, and brought hither;—that in consequence of her resistance, one of them struck her on the face, which produced an effusion of blood from her forehead. This excited fresh rage in him behind whom she rode, as it stained his clothes.—'It is evident,' concluded the sweet complainer, 'that my destruction is determined upon. I have only, therefore, to pray that it may be speedy; and Oh Gustavus!' she cried, weeping bitterly, 'may the woman for whom you have neglected me, by her kind attentions teach you to forget the means by which——' Here she fell into such an agony of grief, that she could say no more, nor could I ever induce her to renew the sad subject.

"In a few days after this conversation, I was summoned before the Abbess, her Nuns, and the Confessors, to answer a charge of contumacy in relieving, comforting, and consorting with a culprit who was under spiritual censure. Ah dear Miss Sleswie, I knew too feelingly the pains of that situation, for I had experienced them. To this accusation I made no answer, and this fresh instance of impious obstinacy procured me ten days' confinement in the upper dungeon—a place not quite so dark and damp as those designed for more atrocious offenders, but sufficiently so to fix a hoarseness on my lungs, which it is likely will never be removed. What then must be the case of those who incurred still greater punishment? Ah, lady, my heart suggested the worst of evils, when, on my emancipation, I could no where discover the dear Sister Martha, for so she was called; nor could I ever learn her true name, excepting her Christian one of Sigismunda, during our little intimacy.

'Ask me not, good St. Alexa,' she would say; 'my name imports suffering. It was entailed upon the parent, and descends to his child.'

"Notwithstanding the taste I had received of monastical vengeance, I still persisted in my enquiry for Sister Martha, when a lay-sister, to whom I was rather attached, because she seemed not to possess that hypocritical sanctity which distinguished many of the Sisterhood, hinted to me the shocking truth, that on the fourth day of my confinement, a Swedish gentleman held a long conference with the Lady Abbess, whose gaiety of dress and demeanour gave Ursula a curiosity to know his business; and slipping into a grated confessional, made use of by the Nuns who might be too much indisposed to attend chapel, and which joined the parlour, she there heard this deep villain urging the necessity of destroying the innocent Martha, and engaging, when the matter was certainly accomplished, to endow the monastery with a pension, that should enable the Abbess either completely to repair it, or build an entire new one. St. Frances made some cunning objections, but they were overruled; and the next morning the sweet devoted victim was conveyed to a place called the Nun's torment, where she was stripped of her decent clothing, and clad in a coarse spare garment; the devil Ursula, whose character I so falsely estimated, being commissioned to attend with subsistence barely sufficient to preserve life;—'and this portion,' said the diabolical monster, 'is to be daily lessened till——'

'Till when,' I cried, maddening with resentment against the wretches who could so coolly carry on and execute such nefarious acts.

'Only till she will cease to live!'

"This answer, pronounced in a way so cold and decisive, was given me but the day preceding the Danish visit, which seemed to me as if necessary to effect a signal retribution; for among the Priests who suffered, were several, I am well assured, deeply concerned, though not primary agents, in our friend's sufferings—nay, it is possible that I, on the contrary, may owe my life to their interference, since the vehemence of my expressions, and the bitterness with which I accused Mother St. Frances on the active part she took in this dreadful business, would doubtless have brought on me a punishment as terrible."

"Oh no more—no more!" exclaimed Catherine, in an agony of tears. "What punishment can be found adequate to guilt so atrocious? Dear, sympathizing lady, I entreat you detain me no longer from my sweet Sigismunda! Revered guardian of my early years!" and she lifted up her surcharged eyes, "happy art thou to be spared the knowledge of thy child's tortures!"

"You knew her father then?"

"Knew him—yes, lady, I well knew that best of men—the generous Marienburg!"

Catherine stopped to wipe away the officious drops, when, again looking, she beheld St. Alexa leaning against the wainscot; a cold perspiration bedewed her forehead, her eyes were closed; but when the compassionate Miss Sleswie addressed her in the most soothing terms, she lifted up the heavy lids, and gazing mournfully at her, seemed as if incapable of speech.

Catherine rang a table-bell for assistance; the sound alarmed St. Alexa.

"No, no," she cried, "I am better—do not be afraid. My spirits are weak—the subject has affected us both! Come, we will go to Sister Martha; but you say her name is Marienburg, and that her father was your guardian—the guardian of Catherine—Sleswie, I think you said?"

"Yes, Madam, that is the name I—"

"Well, well, I do not ask for particulars. Excuse this weakness. I have resided here till the gloomy desolation of the place, and the recent terrible events I have witnessed, have affected my spirits."

She then took her visitor's hand, and after looking stedfastly on her, again sighed out the word *Catherine*; then passing on in silence, led her to Sigismunda's apartment, where that poor young creature lay totally unconscious of a visit that would have cheered her fainting heart.

"You see," cried St. Alexa, stepping softly to the bedside, "I have not exaggerated the danger of our friend's situation. She is now in a state of insensibility; those sweet features now so shrunk—that faded complexion once so radiant, must have excited a criminal degree of Envy; for nothing but that malevolent harpy could have blighted so fair a flower."

"Yes," said the sobbing Catherine, "my beloved Sigismunda has long been its distinguished object."

"Was she not supposed to resemble her father?" asked St. Alexa. "Were not his eyes peculiarly brilliant? His form too, was it not majestic?"

"Madam, what said you? His eyes—his form—wherefore these questions? They imply a foreknowledge of his person."

"And yet they are but natural—the result of innocent curiosity."

With a groan, that contradicted the import of her words, St. Alexa dropped the incoherent observation, and continued for some minutes in a reverie, that appeared to exclude every visible being from her attention. Catherine now attributed the irregularity of her conversation to some derangement, which required the most cautious treatment; and, affecting to turn her regards to the insensible Sigismunda, gave St. Alexa time to recover herself. This she presently did, and joined Catherine in the tender offices which pure friendship dictated for the benefit of the forlorn sufferer, not forgetting to press upon her new assistant the refreshment she stood in need of; but in vain did Catherine attempt to benefit by this thoughtful kindness. The vacant eye, the motionless form, the dreadfully weak state of her she loved, destroyed every incitement to eating, and she could only weep her refusal of the offered viands.

It soon became her fixed resolution to relieve St. Alexa in her affectionate office of attending on Sigismunda, whose sad situation promised no favourable change. In consequence, she sent the result of her determination to Von Hemert, and requested his permission to be left at Telga. Satisfied with the propriety of her conduct, and the security of the place, he expressed a ready acquiescence, and bade her adieu at the grate, whither she went to meet him; when he promised to return to Gustavus with a more particular account of his Sigismunda, than he could receive by the means of a courier.

For several days succeeding her arrival at the monastery, Catherine continued in a state of hopeless anxiety, witnessing the distressing changes of her friend's disorder, unattended as they were by any consolatory symptoms; and as occasions frequently occurred, wondering at St. Alexa's unsteady manner and extravagant expressions, when under the influence of some secret malady, which appeared to be deeply seated in the soul. It was true, she had related Sigismunda's affecting tale, as far as she knew of it, with tolerable precision; but the perturbation she could not hide, expressed something more than affection for the sufferer; and Catherine waited in a sort of uneasy suspense for its elucidation, since there was no visible cause for those marked wanderings which daily became more frequent, and felt increasing surprise upon being once questioned by St. Alexa upon Miss Marienburg's real origin, asking if she were sure it might be traced from the Marienburg family; and then suddenly flying from the subject, said—"It was no matter—time would discover all."

Thus tediously passed the first four days of Miss Sleswie's residence in Telga, when the lamented invalid, in the thick low accents of exhausted existence, expressed a wish to be raised in her bed. Catherine, who, till that moment, had not understood a word of what she had unknowingly uttered, flew to obey her, gently pressing the drooping form to her beating bosom, and fondly kissing the yet lovely features, over which her tears fell fast, as she tenderly drew her from her recumbent posture. Sensible of this soft expression of sisterly solicitude, Sigismunda threw a languid, but alarmed, look upon St. Alexa (as she stood at the foot of the bed), as the only person from whom she could expect a treatment so kind; and then wildly turned towards her new attendant, at the same instant feebly whispering—"No—it is all a dream—Ulrica has destroyed her too!"

"Destroyed whom, sweetest Sigismunda? Look up, and tell me who you suspect she has destroyed!"

"See!" said the poor wanderer, "I told you so—she left her in the dungeon where I died; it was very cruel, but she took me for her rival,—it was a bitter revenge."

"Think not of that monster, my beloved creature—she can do no more mischief. Gustavus will protect his Sigismunda and her Catherine."

"Gustavus!—hush!—talk not of Gustavus! Ulrica will hear you, and then—ah me—the Tribunal——But surely," and she turned her beamless eyes upon her friend, "No—it is an angel—it is not my Catherine!"

"It is your Catherine; she will never leave her long-lamented companion—she comes to serve her! But here is the angel," and she drew St. Alexa nearer, "here is the saviour who was delegated by Omnipotence to restore my Sigismunda."

A ray of recollection now burst upon the wearied sense. St. Alexa came forward, and in impassioned tones expressed her delight, while she convinced the trembling, still doubting, maid that she was in perfect safety, and under the protection of Gustavus, who had sent Miss Sleswie to her assistance. Sigismunda listened in wondering ecstacy, but, unable to articulate another sentence, she could only lift up a feeble hand in gratitude to Heaven for its mercies; and then sinking again upon her pillow, fixed a look of love and tenderness on those to whom she was so much indebted for their humane and affectionate offices.

In the performance of these important duties, Catherine rejected as much as possible every idea that led to Marienburg's design of uniting her to Gustavus. It was true that time did nothing more for Sigismunda than to restore her intellects; she was still a prey to devouring illness, nor was there any room to hope that her constitution, though once healthy even to firmness, could resist the united shocks of famine, cold, and internal distress: yet it was extremely improbable that he, whose soul itself had imbibed a tenderness, which even her supposed death could not lessen, should, even if that event took place, think of her, in whose favour there would be none to plead. It was a situation that called for greater self-denial than Catherine formerly possessed, to be borne with fortitude; but Catherine had acquired a more generous way of thinking—even reason did a great deal in conquering the habits she had perhaps indulged with a blameable facility; and she could now look upon this fragile flower without a wish to combat her rights, or look to her demise as an object of aught but the sincerest regret.

To St. Alexa she communicated the whole of Marienburg's intentions respecting herself, his rejection of Ericson's love for his child, and that hero's strong and unconquerable attachment to Sigismunda. St. Alexa listened as usual—now wildly inquisitive, now totally inattentive—at one moment ready to clasp the interesting relater to her bosom, at another shewing a marked neglect. Catherine saw this behaviour in a light which made her repent the too ready confidence, and determined in future to lead to no subject important enough to excite such disagreeable symptoms.

CHAPTER IX.

"The hero shakes in vain the wizzing spear,
Boasts the rich trophies, and the pomp of war.
Tho' captive Princes sweat beneath his chains,
A greater foe unconquer'd yet remains;
Love feels, with rival's pride and envious shame,
His growing honours and aspiring fame."

BECKINGHAM.

DURING several weeks of watchful attendance, and painful uncertainty, Catherine gathered from her languid friend at different intervals the particulars of Ulrica's savage treatment, with her reception from the noble Blanch, even while under Tribunal cognizance; and [Sigismunda] received in return a full account of what had transpired respecting Gustavus, Baron Hunsdorf, Fitzer, and the strange discovery [Catherine] had made of her own origin, not forgetting Ulrica's dreadful doom, which she supposed must be decided, or nearly so.

Sigismunda wept at the description of Ericson's sufferings; but when she was told of her father's demise, attributable as it was to her own disastrous fate, she lay pale, silent, almost immoveable, and once more Catherine found reason to blame her want of caution. To the consolations she would have offered, deep convulsive sighs only were opposed; and St. Alexa, who was absent till the mischief was done, suggested patience and silence till she should be inclined to notice those about her. The advice was judicious, and exactly observed. The two friends waited till her deep affecting sorrow should admit of speech. At length, struggling as it were for utterance—

"I see," she cried, "the extent of my destiny—it points to death! In its gloomy shades comfort reposes. My father, once an example of patient fortitude, couldst thou not have lingered a little longer? But his sufferings are ended!—Ah, St. Alexa! why did you, with more than common humanity, bring back a soul that had ceased to be miserable? When cold, faint, and hungry, I called upon the name of Ursula, she came not to assist me! Oh, that was a time of anguish!—I thought of Gustavus—thought of him as Ulrica's consort; and once the cruel Abbess told me (for she could visit me to add to my afflictions)—she told me that their nuptials were preparing, that Christian had quitted his claim to Sweden, and that Stockholm hailed them as worthy of each other. This was another addition to my affliction, but yet there was one earthly consolation left—I had a father! Now that is denied me! Bear with me, my Catherine—nay, do not weep! Oh, had you seen me when torn from my little cell, and the valuable comforts that good Sister procured me! Then I was not resigned, but clung to every thing my grasping hands could catch at, to stop the progress of the horrid Monks, four of whom were employed to force me along the dim and narrow passages."

As this was a subject she had never before touched upon, and it seemed to divert the channel of her grief, the two friends attempted not to check her, but waited till she could resume a recital that wrung their feeling hearts.

"Yes," she added, after a long and solemn pause, "I now remember the dark and damp dungeon, as it appeared to me when they threw back the large iron door, and placed me by an old table furnished only with a pitcher, a lamp, and a basket with some black bread. Oh, I was not then the courageous Sigismunda—I could not see even those miscreants depart without a pang. It seemed as if the world had shut me from all its endearing privileges; and the sight of Ursula, who came not, as I imagine, for many hours, brought no consolation, for she was the chosen confidant of Ulrica. I knew her well, but had never seen her in the Monastery, nor knew she had disgraced a sacred community by her crimes."

"You remind me," cried St. Alexa, wiping her eyes, "of her first coming hither, which I heard was in consequence of that very Ulrica's recommendation."

"Yes, doubtless she was fixed upon as equal to the task of tormenting a poor creature, who once incurred her displeasure by a friendly remonstrance while in Madam Landen's household; but, alas! I knew not how lightly that woman estimated an observance of virtuous duties."

St. Alexa could not reconcile the intelligence she had received from Ursula with this account of her attachment to Ulrica; and observing Sigismunda's inclination to continue the subject, she ventured to relate what the lay-sister overheard.

"This is all very possible, my dear friend," said Miss Marienburg. "She was chosen as an inferior agent, nor could there be any necessity for admitting her to any further confidence. Who was the cruel instigator of my imprisonment I know not; but he must have a hard heart to join in the destruction of a wretched maid, who could not have injured him. As to Ursula's communication, it might originate in revenge for being left out of the pernicious plot, or employed only as an emissary. Is she now in the Monastery?"

"No, my dear, she left us immediately, and we saw no more of her. Her life was spared by your Gustavus."

"My Gustavus!" said Sigismunda, turning her head to conceal a trickling tear.

Catherine noticed not the tender effusion, but continued—

"He spared it in consequence of a sacred promise made to her, if she would lead to the abodes of misery. Her behaviour when she supposed you to be no more, gave us reason to imagine compunction has touched her soul, and she was permitted to depart unmolested."

"Thank Heaven!" said the angelic forgiver, "I would have it so. Even Ulrica's restoration I ardently wish; and the Abbess, tell her, my Alexa, how freely I forgive her! May she too have time for repentance!"

Fatigued beyond the power of further conversation, Sigismunda again sunk silent, nor noticed the confusion her last words had created. When abandoned to cruel contemplation, she betrayed the anguish of her heart by feeble groans and stealing tears.

"Is it possible," asked St. Alexa when they were alone, "that a creature so pure, so gentle, so affectionate, could ever have given cause to the wickedest of human hearts to imagine the evils that have overwhelmed that charming innocent?"

"It is plain," said Catherine, "that she stood in the way of some iniquitous plan, most probably induced by the monstrous hope of supplanting her in Ericson's affection."

The sudden appearance of that gallant warrior at the grate of the parlour in which they were conversing, crimsoned Miss Sleswie's cheek; it was a trial for which she was by no means prepared, any more than for the request he came to prefer, as that was nothing less than to be introduced by her to Sigismunda, whose extreme danger he well knew; and, stimulated by his fears, he had quitted his camp before Stockholm, to convince himself of her real situation. It was a perilous attempt, that situation considered; but he could take no denial. It was of consequence to his future peace to know her sentiments, should there be a possibility of her recovery. There was now no father to raise visionary obstacles. The prospect of undisputed sovereignty cleared every moment. The citizens of Stockholm, attacked by war, famine, and disease, began to relax in their vigorous defence; and, willing to preserve some plea to the claim of their long-abused rights, talked of capitulating upon terms honourable to themselves, and gratifying to the noble besieger.

"What then remains," thought Gustavus, "to complete my happiness, but to behold the chosen of my soul saluted as the adored partner of Sweden's lawful King?"

Thus glorying in visionary bliss, he felt somewhat impatient of controul, when informed that Sigismunda's precarious existence depended upon circumstances rather to be hoped than expected; that her grief for her father's death had already caused much mischief; "and the presence of one so dear," said the hesitating Catherine, "may produce the defeat of all our wishes."

"You are my friends—I know it!" cried the empassioned lover, "and can allow for an affection which has been confirmed by time, stimulated by opposition, and increased by absence and misfortune. Say then if, persuaded by your entreaties, I leave the sweet sufferer once more, will you prepare her for the acceptance of a heart which can never know another love?"

What a denunciation and what a request for Catherine, whose sorrow had the distress of the moment for its ostensible object, and passed unheeded! She could only bow to the petition, which St. Alexa verbally complied with; and Ericson, rising, left the grate with a reluctance that nothing but the necessity there was for his immediate presence in his army, could in any degree subdue.

As if the calamities under which Sigismunda so deeply suffered, had reached their climax with the demise of her much-loved parent, she seemed to throw off every encumbering idea, and might be considered as divested of the most troublesome appendages to mortality. Silent, meditating, and resigned, she exhibited no more tokens of excessive grief. Her intellects were clear, nor did her strength decrease. Calm and collected, but averse to conversation, she appeared to have conquered those feelings so often exercised, and so properly regulated.

Her friends were astonished at the change, but dreaded to hazard the discovery of Ericson's sentiments, lest it should disturb the tranquillity of her soul.

Gustavus grew uneasy at the protraction of his wishes; but although the courier carried almost daily accounts of returning convalescence, for she visibly amended, and could sit up for several hours in the day, yet her extreme weakness made the utmost caution necessary, and they were careful to avoid every hint that might shake the composure of her spirits, till a peremptory message from the Prince, amounting almost to a command, determined Catherine to begin the arduous task. It was at the conclusion of a day unusually lenient for the frosty season, when, cheered by Sigismunda's serene manner, and her attempt to speak upon some subject, which her friendly companions were good-naturedly discussing, that she prepared to obey the ardent Gustavus by pronouncing his name, as a prelude to further communication. Sigismunda started, evidently discomposed by the abrupt beginning; a faint tint flew across her pallid cheek, and she trembled excessively. Sensible of her error, the poor girl would have retracted; but she had touched a string too delicate, and how to prevent the powerful vibration she knew not. To abandon the subject would not restore peace to her cousin—to continue it might destroy the fabric her generous hopes had erected. While thus employed, she perceived the lovely invalid turn a wild and suspicious eye to the door of their apartment, where a loud whispering bespoke some rude intruders.

"Catherine," said the terrified Sigismunda, "you have betrayed me!"

Catherine understood not the abrupt charge, but St. Alexa comprehended it better. She went to the door, which instantly opened; and—Gustavus Ericson was at the feet of his adored! He looked up at her pale expressive countenance with an emotion of fond delight, while her motionless hand was clasped to his beating bosom; and in a voice, to which love had given the sweetest melody, entreated her to forgive the presumption of him who could no longer submit his cause to the procrastinating pleadings of cold friendship. He would intrude no longer than to tell her that all his expectation of mortal bliss rested upon her acknowledgment of reciprocal affection, and a solemn assurance that she would share with him a regal crown.

"Promise but this, my gentle, my persecuted love, and I will see you no more till, authorized by the establishment of my just pretensions, I can remove you from this obscurity to the splendour you were born to inherit. Nay, speak not, my Sigismunda, but to confirm my hopes!" (for he observed that she struggled with her fluttered spirits, and strove to articulate a few words.)—"Hear your Gustavus, and then determine."

Catherine and St. Alexa shuddered at the effect which they saw this interview had upon their terror-struck friend, while the Prince continued—

"Ulrica—" (again Sigismunda expressed marks of distress)—"Ulrica can no longer hurt you. She is in daily expectation of suffering by a severe but just sentence. Blanch, the amiable but neglected consort of a worthless Prince, would not return with him to Copenhagen, but has promised to join her tenderest cares with those of these kind companions, to comfort and restore her estimable friend. Look up, then, to a happier destiny—give way to hope, nor permit one gloomy thought to shade the brightening prospect. Waste not your weakened spirits by an attempt to answer me. Adieu, most worshipped of women! I ask only permission to love, and that no denial to my ardent suit may pass those trembling lips. The assurance I look for may be expressed by a single word—that sweet affirmative which will nerve the arm of War, is all Gustavus seeks for; but even that condescension he could wave, if you forbid not his speedy return. No, Catherine, she will not give sorrow to Ericson by checking his hope! Once more adieu, then, Sigismunda! When next we meet——"

"Ah, Gustavus, *when next we meet!*"

She could say no more; her accents failed, and her head sunk helpless against the hero's bosom. He supported her in silent anguish, nor would either of the weeping witnesses to this solemn scene, offer services, perhaps just then wholly unacceptable. They guessed her mind on this sad occasion; they saw the symptoms of convalescence shaken, if not destroyed, by him who would have died to save her; but all appeals to reason, even humanity, were vain. The mischief was done, and they could only pity what could not be retrieved.

At length raising herself, she made an effort to disclose the conflict of her soul; but Gustavus, perceiving her intention, arose also, and conjured her to take a future opportunity for the discovery of her sentiments, which he would hope were in favour of his claims.

"In a few days," he added, "the gates of Stockholm will open to their deliverer; nor shall one inhabitant of that city view me in any other light. Contrasted with the enormities of Christian, even common clemency will obtain the reward of gratitude and obedience. Then shall Sigismunda enjoy, and share the glory of her Gustavus! The palace, once defiled by Ulrica's impurities, shall receive its former mistress, the noble Blanch, who will accommodate us till further arrangements can be made."

"My Lord," cried the daughter of Marienburg, evidently exerting herself to speak, "you are under a pleasing delusion. Sigismunda never can be your's—her fate is decided——and—Death—demands his victim!"

Gustavus would not appropriate this affecting denunciation to any other cause than extreme dejection; and in the most soothing terms endeavoured to soften it. She saw his error, and looking upwards—"Sainted parent!" apostrophized the lovely invalid, "why didst thou exact the rigid promise?—Alas! there was a reason! Hear me, Gustavus," addressing the alarmed Prince, "I repeat, Sigismunda *never* can be your's!—Lord of my earliest choice! dear and only possessor of a heart that, while it beats, can beat but for thee—this person never can be your's! It is forbidden by the dead!—From the cold, still tomb, a voice pronounces the fatal sentence—nay, it does more—it points to another, as the sharer of those honours that—— But go, my beloved Prince!—The path of glory never boasted a greater hero!"

"Nor a man more wretched, if Sigismunda be denied him! Is it for this my steps were guided to this place of desolation—for this reception I came on the wings of Love to claim my betrothed?—What power—what rights—what promise hold you from me? Exert yourself, my Sigismunda! Conquer the fantasies of a mind enervated by unexampled cruelties, and obey the dictates of a heart that sides with Ericson. Only say you will consider—say you will receive me once again! The glory of Gustavus depends upon the important but flying minutes; even now he is missed by his eager allies. They defy the inclemencies of the season, and ask to be led on to victory. Encourage then, by your smile, the emanation of an impetuous soul, and give him an additional stimulus to deeds of noble daring!"

"Depart, my Lord; I can no longer contend."

"Then you give me hope?"

"To what purpose? Death would rob you of it."

"Lord Gustavus," cried St. Alexa, who saw the effect of his earnest pleading on her changing countenance, and could no longer witness the acute distress, "this is downright persecution—the dear creature will sink under it. Leave her at present; your cause will sustain no injury in our hands, but she must be spared this impetuosity."

Alarmed at the consequence to which his eyes were now opened, the passionate lover ceased his importunity; and after strenuously recommending the idol of his soul to their tenderest care, he departed with a reluctance which partook of the most horrid forebodings, accusing himself of a precipitation that nothing but his situation could excuse; for this was the eve of a day designed to witness, if possible, the conclusion of a long and tedious siege: and as the event, however flattering, might be attended with fatal effects even to himself, he could not resist the impulse that pointed to one interview, as gratifying to his long-suffering love.

Catherine, who beheld the strong ungovernable attachment of this generous lover, without a hope, almost without a wish, to find such exalted affection transferrable, wiped away the fast flowing tear, and united with St. Alexa to comfort and calm the agitated mind of this child of disappointment and misfortune. She saw their endeavours, and would have rewarded them by appearing composed; but Sigismunda's constitution would have been more than mortal to have triumphed over such repeated shocks: and this was one so violent, so unsuspected, given when reviving nature was making a last effort to recover from a state of overwhelming debility, yet not less liable to the danger of a relapse, that, sensible of its force, she seemed to summon her decaying powers, for the purpose of giving that consolation they would have bestowed; but it evaporated in sighs, and feeble attempts to speak, till the following morning, when, in answer to Catherine's affectionate enquiry, she languidly replied—"The blow is precipitated, my Catherine, by the hand which I know would sooner have destroyed——" She stopped—then resumed—"But this is a subject I ought not to touch upon. It seems to breathe a reflection upon the purest love that ever honoured an obscure maiden. Tell him that the death of Sigismunda Marienburg deprives him of no expected happiness; for when induced to believe that Ulrica Landen had won his noble heart, I repeated to *him*, who has ratified the oath, a promise once most solemnly given to my father, never to pledge my faith to Gustavus Ericson, whose glory, claims, and future establishment depended upon another choice,—that the crown he aspired to, belonged not to the daughter, but the *niece* of Marienburg."

"What do I hear?" cried St. Alexa. "The *niece* of Marienburg!—and who is that niece? Can *you* tell, Catherine? Oh let me not be deceived! my brain would madden at the thought!"

"Peace, dear Alexa! we will talk of this hereafter. Disturb her not—she has more to say."

"No, nothing more," said the departing excellence; "only farewel, my friends! Gustavus, adieu till—Oh, who can say when? But Ulrica, dearest Catherine, tell him to pardon Ulrica!"

The symptoms of approaching dissolution now prevented any articulate utterance; and St. Alexa, roused from the alarm given by the mystic words of Sigismunda, attended only to her dying friend, while Catherine hastened for an officiating priest, to perform the sacred offices usual on such solemn occasions.

Sigismunda beheld the holy emblems with meek and pious gratitude. Speech was denied, but the glow of pure devotion spoke in the palest tint on her cheek with a momentary but celestial radiance. Her sweet eyes recovered their brilliancy; her trembling hands pressed to her palpitating bosom the worshipped cross; and when the priest talked of forgiving all her enemies, as a prelude to the absolution he was about to bestow, she made a feeble motion with her head, kissed the cross, and faintly, though eagerly, pronounced the word "All!" when a soft quick sigh announced the inefficacy of any further holy ceremony, and the pure spirit ceased to animate its lovely frame.

* * * * *

Superadded to the poignant distress which this sudden and regretted demise occasioned to her sorrowing friends, was that arising from an idea of the agonies Gustavus would experience when the cruel intelligence should be transmitted to him; nor was either of them composed enough to frame a message adequate to the dreadful business, till St. Alexa proposed to send for the good Von Hemert, who had withdrawn to Upsal as a place of safety, and whose well-known discretion and softness made him the most proper announcer of evil tidings.

Conan received the terrible information with sincere concern; he sympathized in idea with the wretched Gustavus, and greatly pitied his dear ward, whose feelings were so deeply exercised.

"And am I always," thought the reflecting Von Hemert, "to be chosen from among mankind to carry sorrow to the worthy heart? But be it so; perhaps the temper which can accommodate itself to the impetuous grief of a wounded heart, may—nay, I know it does—receive its reward, if by one well-chosen expression, one tender hint, one consoling idea, it can allay the sharpness of that poison its possessor has been obliged to communicate."

Thus satisfied with the rectitude of his own conclusion, this good man set out to announce the heaviest intelligence his noble favourite could now dread: but upon his arrival before Stockholm, his ears were every where assailed with sounds of the most joyous confusion; shouts, acclamations, prayers for Ericson's welfare, congratulations, praises, all arose in one undistinguished medley. The city gates were thrown open, from whence issued people of all descriptions, Burghers, artisans, Noblemen, and those of the lowest order, forming one grand mass of matter, which gradually separating, afforded Von Hemert room for contemplation and pity, since the countenances of many exhibited the ravages of famine and disease. From this appearance he justly concluded that the citizens, reduced by severe necessity, had capitulated to Gustavus, whose name, as deliverer and guardian angel, resounded from all quarters.

While meditating in what way to conduct his painful negotiation, he found himself before the warrior's tent, which was surrounded by another happy party, who were impatiently waiting for a sight of this glorious hero, among whom he discovered Iwan speaking, with apparent energy, to the eager crowd that jostled him on every side. It was with infinite difficulty Von Hemert could obtain a situation in which he might be seen by Iwan; but no sooner did the faithful fellow notice his royal master's well-known friend, than he applied his utmost endeavours to join him: and after assuring the disappointed Swedes that their new Monarch was not returned from Stregna, whither he went for the purpose of being duly elected, Iwan conducted Von Hemert into the tent, where refreshments of every kind the season would afford, were assiduously offered, and as thankfully accepted.

As Ericson's arrival was extremely uncertain, Conan, who felt a trifling relief from the transient respite, took directions for the late Queen of Sweden's residence, where he was received with a polite attention, and genuine dignity, that reflected the deepest disgrace upon her unworthy consort, who could prefer to such excellence the meretricious charms of an unprincipled wanton. Of Sigismunda's cruel persecutions she had been informed by Gustavus, and had wept at the sad recital; but when Conan related their shocking consequences, Blanch's grief was unbounded: she wept for that sweet victim's undeserved sufferings, and freely accused herself of pusillanimity in submitting to a cruel deception, which a cool investigation might have detected. Conan exerted all his powers of honest oratory to set her mind at ease in this respect, by placing her surrender of that unfortunate angel to the implicit obedience which a Court, so tenacious of its self-acquired rights, and so remarkable for its severity and despotism, ever exacted.

"Yet," cried the candid accuser, "I ought to have estimated the irrespectability of Ulrica, her deep cunning, and malevolent disposition, with the motives she had to induce her barbarous hatred of this patient goodness, according to my knowledge of her wickedness; and then, where so much preponderated on the side of malice, I should have drawn a more favourable conclusion, and adopted more cautious methods. Sigismunda Marienburg had probably been spared, and her aged father lived to see his objections to her union with Gustavus completely done away; but now I fear the royal Prince will never look up to a female partner of his glory."

Von Hemert confirmed this but too probable opinion, for it was his own; and they both united in lamenting the grief and disappointment of that gallant hero, when informed of his almost irreparable loss; and the Queen expressed a generous, though hopeless, wish that Catherine might hereafter be invited to ascend the throne, which Ericson so earnestly desired to share with her cousin.

Disturbed by those various expressions of the people's joy, as they arose from the different parties of citizens who lined the roads, which, however grateful to hearts sincerely impressed by similar feelings, struck them as being repugnant to their royal master's real situation, the two friends separated—Conan to revisit the camp where he expected to meet Gustavus, and Blanch to seek retirement in an apartment that overhung the river, by which the city was partly surrounded. Here the sounds of congratulation, although more distinct, were agreeably softened; and she meditated without interruption, but with solemn composure, upon the sublunary state of events. Herself she considered as the sharer (and not long since) of a triple Crown—Denmark, Sweden, and Norway being alike subjugated to her consort's tyrannic sway; soon after supplanted in that changeable Monarch's affection, and preserving only the shadow of Royalty, while a cunning, unprincipled wanton usurped her most sacred privileges, and drove her from the once honourable shelter of a royal husband's roof, the sweet indulgence of maternal tenderness, and the society of her natural friends, to that comparatively humble retirement in which she received the sainted Sigismunda.

From these sad changes the thoughts of Blanch descended to her present situation and that of Christian, in which last she perceived that retribution such a conduct as he so brutally persevered in, must naturally bring about—deserted by the woman for whom he had forfeited every claim to the pure and sacred attachment of conjugal love,—rejected as a Monarch by the nation he had oppressed with every species of cruelty, even for the man whose relatives and friends the remorseless tyrant extirpated from the earth,—and obliged to the forbearance of those he had injured, for the life his vices rendered detestable!—To what seemed humiliating in her own case, the patient Queen gave no such gloomy representations. Contented to enjoy the love of the good, she calmly gave up every appendage of troublesome grandeur, and coolly settled with herself to support and promote, when opportunity should occur, the interests of Catherine with Gustavus—a plan which at present afforded no likelihood of success; but she considered the character of the new King, and though there was much to fear from his noble principles, yet a faint hope would spring from that very foundation.

END OF VOLUME II.

Swedish Mysteries

Volume III

SWEDISH MYSTERIES.

CHAPTER I.

> "We know
> There oft is found an avarice in grief;
> And the wan eye of sorrow loves to gaze
> Upon its secret hoard of treasur'd woes
> In pining solitude."
>
> MASON.

WHILE Conan was arranging in his friendly mind the various modes of consolation which his benevolent heart suggested for the use of Gustavus, that Prince had anticipated his own unhappiness by visiting Telga before his return to Stockholm; where, in an interview with St. Alexa, he learned the excruciating tidings of Sigismunda's demise, and this in the very moment when he came to offer wealth, dignity, and the possession of his hand, which would be accompanied by a heart that had never known another love. As if certain of attaining his highest wishes, that of Sigismunda's convalescence, and its own concomitant effects, he approached St. Alexa with that confidence which certainty inspires, nor noticed, while making his eager enquiries, the extreme melancholy of her air and countenance.

"Go," said this enraptured lover, "prepare the gentle maid for the reception of her faithful Gustavus. Does she not wonder at my unexpected absence? Are her remarks upon it dictated by a fond and affectionate heart? Is she not ready to accompany me to Stockholm, where a grateful people would be impatient to express their veneration for her virtues? But, dearest St. Alexa, lead me to her; at least go and announce my arrival to the lovely creature."

The entrance of Catherine, pale, confused, and unhappy, now caught his attention.

"My friend," he cried, "the friend of my adored Sigismunda is in tears! Wherefore this sadness? Far, very far be every motive for sorrow from those whose tender cares have contributed to the revival of that drooping excellence! It shall be the business of my life to procure peace and joy to those by whose means I am primarily indebted for my more than hope!"

"*Hope!*" said St. Alexa, for Catherine could only weep.

The tone in which this monosyllable was uttered, awoke Gustavus from his dream of bliss.

"And why not *hope*, St. Alexa? Surely she is well enough to authorize the sweet expression?"

Ericson almost trembled to whisper to his throbbing heart the fatal presentiment which succeeded his recent expectations; and catching a look of horrid import, as it passed from Catherine to her friend, he could no longer bear the torment of a suspense which his own impetuosity created.

"There is a dreadful meaning, Catherine," said he, "in this joint reluctance to answer my questions. I am distracted with uncertainty; relieve my unutterable apprehensions, and conduct me to Sigismunda!"

He was then advancing to the door; when St. Alexa, who, although severely distressed, felt not that complicated grief which nearly suffocated the sobbing Catherine, respectfully caught his hand, and shutting the door, asked him for Mr. Von Hemert.

"I have not seen him," was the laconic reply.

"Nor any one deputed by him to inform my honoured Lord of——"

"Of what, St. Alexa?—Speak while I have life to hear!"

"Ah, noble Prince!" and she dropped on one knee, "forgive this seeming inattention to your questions; but it is *you* who should be prepared for the events I dread to announce—she is——"

"What? Torture me no longer with the monastic jargon of cold-hearted sophistry!"

"Ah, my Lord! there needs no sophistry to prove that Sigismunda Marienburg is—*no more!*"

"Dead, Catherine! Do *you* too say she is dead?"

Catherine bowed over his extended hand, while a convulsive sigh corroborated St. Alexa's testimony; and a deep chill silence followed this sad confirmation. No groan, no tear, no impatient expression marked the lover's grief, in whose horror-struck view the pomp of war, the sweets of peace, the hope of domestic tranquillity, and the possession of regal honours, with which he was just invested, appeared without one charm to recommend them; but drawing the warlike helmet over his forehead, he suffered its sable plumes to shade his eyes, and sat as if deprived of sense and motion.

Desirous of awakening him from such a stupor of sorrow, Catherine recovered fortitude enough to join with St. Alexa in an attempt at consolation. Gustavus threw back the helmet, and gazed steadily on them with a wild and frigid look, somewhat approaching to anger. They were awed into silence. He saw the effect of this conduct, and inwardly accused himself of unkindness to the friends of his deceased love;—addressing them, therefore, in the gentlest terms—"Forgive," he said, "the waywardness of a distress which mocks the pageantry of politeness, and loves to dwell upon its cruel cause without a witness.—Adieu then for ever the dear companions of my lost Sigismunda! We shall meet no more till the rites of burial are performed, and that will be, perhaps, for the *last time!*"

"They are already performed, my gracious Prince."

"Already, St. Alexa!" said the Prince, abruptly, "and *I* not present! Shew me at least the turf that covers her precious remains. The obsequies of a Sigismunda, a Monarch's betrothed, should have been graced with royal pomp—but no matter."

He then followed St. Alexa to the cemetery, leaving the poor Catherine in a state not more enviable than his own, excepting that she could lament her sad disappointments in some sacred retirement, unchecked, and uncontrouled; while he, lifted by the circumstances and pomp of Royalty, must stifle the ebullition of hopeless sorrow.

When directed to the humble receptacle of her for whom his fond heart had assigned the choicest appendages of grandeur, Gustavus indeed felt himself a mortal. St. Alexa respected the anguish she could not sooth, and retired till the effusion of it had partly ceased: when looking round, and perceiving her at a distance, he made a farewel motion, and quitted the ill-fated monastery, with a firm intention never more to approach its gloomy walls.

As Iwan could give no probable reason for his Lord's stay at Stregnez, where the ceremony of Ericson's election he knew had already passed, Conan easily guessed the *true* motive for an absence which his new subjects began to cavil at; and those who dared not betray their rebellious principles, silently congratulated themselves upon the apparent neglect: but the King's arrival, while it confirmed Conan's suspicions, removed every hope of future disturbance in the breasts of the insurgents.

No sooner was our unhappy hero known to be in the camp, than every testimonial of welcome was renewed; and Gustavus found himself obliged, while his heart floated in anguish, to put on the semblance of cheerfulness and peace. Von Hemert saw the internal struggle—he saw, and returned the glance of sympathetic sorrow; but when a moment of leisure was given to the friends, he admired that fortitude which suffered no complaint to pass his lips. True, Ericson's features insensibly caught a melancholy cast, and a silent dejection succeeded the enthusiasm of gratitude which attended his reception of the Governor's Ambassadors, who were deputed to offer terms of amity; but, as if conscious of the growing weakness, and determined to deserve the character he had just heard ascribed to himself, that of an invincible, patriotic, and disinterested father of his people, he welcomed Von Hemert as the congratulator of his high fortunes, not the consoler of a dear and hoarded grief: nay, he even proposed the removal of Catherine to Stockholm, where, with the abdicated Queen, she would be accommodated agreeably to the lustre of her supposed origin. Nor was St. Alexa neglected, whose dislike to monastic institutions would make her solitude insupportable without her friend; an apartment, therefore, in the same Palace assigned to Blanch, was to be ordered for the compassionate Nun.

"And can it be," thought Von Hemert, "that one so formed to fill every station, whether public or private, with such brilliant success, should suffer one irremediable disappointment to cloud his future glories? No, Gustavus will be all himself, and the wish of Marienburg in time be established: Catherine will share his throne, and Sigismunda be soon forgotten."

This conclusion was injurious to the character of our hero; it was inimical to his principles, contrary to his sentiments, and wholly repugnant to the constancy of his disposition. But Conan had never been in love: when his pity has been excited, his reason has been unconvinced; and though he affectionately regretted Sigismunda's hapless fate, he regretted it as a friend only, and could see no inducement in that fate powerful enough to prevent in future a happier attachment.

Pleased, therefore, with that prudence which suppressed the starts of passion, and every expression of despair in his admired hero, Conan ventured to leave him, for the purpose of conveying to his favourite Catherine the intentions of her still adored Ericson:—indeed it required a cordial as stimulating to support her sunken spirits.

Telga, since the catastrophe they deplored, was become more desolate, more melancholy than before. The inequality of St. Alexa's manners grew yet more unpleasant; and her sudden fits of fondness for Catherine was equally a subject for disgust, with those of repulsive horror and cold dislike which she occasionally displayed.

To change a scene that every day rendered increasingly painful, was an object extremely interesting to Catherine; while St. Alexa beheld its advantages with less sanguine expectations, although she expressed a desultory kind of eagerness for an interview with Blanch.

"I knew her once, Catherine," said the poor Nun, "I knew her when but at intervals I could recognise a friend!—Ah, that was indeed a period of sorrow—of madness! It was not she who forced me hither—it was not Blanch who shut me up in this dreary abode—it was *you*—*you*, Catherine, who tore me from all I loved!—Go then—leave me!—Go with that fascinating look—that meek appeal for pity!—Begone—lest, in my great revenge, I perform an act of terrible justice!—Go!—keep your tears for him who pleads for pity in every line of that insidious countenance!"

Catherine needed not the addition of these mysterious hints to send her from St. Alexa's presence;—her malignant glances, her vehement tones, her menacing actions were not to be disregarded; and as she fled, she silently prayed that some occurrence might separate her from a woman whom yet she loved and pitied.

This flight of passion concluded, as the others had done, in bitter tears and apologies when next they met for the inconsistencies which St. Alexa attributed to bodily indisposition, and the shock her intellects had received in her early days. As every effort made by Catherine for the development of this extraordinary conduct had hitherto been unsuccessful, she had so far vanquished her curiosity as to cease every attempt to investigate it; but the hint respecting Blanch again awakened it, and she hoped, through that lady's means, to have it explained. Patiently then she awaited the wished-for summons to quit St. Frances; and, with some faint emotion of joy, she beheld for the last time its dilapidated walls illumined by a morning sun.

Von Hemert again arrived with intelligence that Blanch was settled at Stockholm in the Palace she formerly occupied, and that the King resided at that used by the Governor before he surrendered, where Gustavus proposed to remain till a more superb building could be prepared for himself, which, in compliment to his friends, who wished to see him appointed, in all respects, as their chosen Sovereign, he determined to execute in the highest style of elegance and usefulness.

In answer to Catherine's half-expressed question regarding his mental situation, Conan praised him to a degree of enthusiasm.—"That he has moments of painful reflection, or that he does sometimes indulge a blameable luxury of grief, I have no doubt; but all this is laudably restrained, even to the glance of his penetrating eye, which, while it enters, as it were, the very heart of his auditor, sparkles with cheerful intelligence, or conveys the sober reproof and indignant reprehension. In his Cabinet (for even there I have been admitted to this wonderful man), his counsels are unerring, his decisions just, his conception clear and rapid. In his Secretary's department I am told his dispatch is incredible, his diction florid, copious, yet unaffected, and, when occasion allows, very brief; for, although the composition is his own, he has transcripts made of them all. As a General, for there is still a necessity to keep an army together, he maintains his usual consequence, reviews his troops as a soldier, commands them as a Monarch, and loves them as a father. Can such a man then give way to irremediable misfortune, or suffer the dignity of his spirit to sink in imbecility? No, Catherine, Sweden may rejoice in the first of Monarchs, whose greatness will not be disgraced by a puerile weakness; and Catherine, the descendant from Princes, will, at some future period, assist this noble Sovereign in the toils of government."

This conclusion to an eulogium so justly fancied, covered Von Hemert's favourite with the deepest blushes; and she ran to hasten St. Alexa, from a consciousness of betraying a hope she had long suppressed. With a mixture of pain and pleasure, Catherine found the Nun utterly unprepared for her journey; her eyes were heavy, and seemed ready to overflow—her pulse rapid, and indicating disorder. To Catherine's enquiries she gave but little answer, till, being fully pressed upon the subject of her departure, she fixed a penetrating look upon her, sighed deeply, and—"No," she cried, "the presence of St. Alexa shall never check the flow of joy which, doubtless, is still resounding through an emancipated nation. Here it disturbs not the gloom of an unhappy soul. I once thought to quit this sad abode in search of comfort; but, disappointed in the dearest wish of my heart, it matters not where that heart shall lose its tumults, nor how soon its painful pulsations shall cease for ever. A shocking mystery, at last, is on the point of being solved, the leading events to which concern my friend—yes *you*, Catherine: and I am preparing a brief recapitulation of them for *your* perusal, that the thunder may not vent its dreadful influence without some antidote to its effects. I once harboured a suspicion that sometimes vented itself in irrepressible effusions, which might be naturally attributed to a wandering imagination; but reason, reflection, and the improbability of their foundation induce me to reject them entirely. Certainly I do not prefer this monastery, where I have witnessed such various distresses; but the liberty I have enjoyed since our wretched mother's decease, renders its inconveniences more tolerable. Cease then these persuasions, which are totally useless; and leave me to the task of arranging incidents that pain me but to think of."

There was little necessity for this concluding injunction, for Catherine was so employed in revolving the hints which St. Alexa had thrown out, as to disregard every thing she uttered, but what related to *the shocking mystery in which* SHE *was concerned*.

"Then there *were* motives," she thought, "for those starts of passion which I once imagined the mere impulse of temporary madness; yet what can have rendered *me* an object of them? Why am *I* to dread the thunder she threatens me with? What connection can there be in *our* fates, to involve *me* in its destructive influence?"

"You are offended, Catherine," resumed the Nun, observing her melancholy silence, "at my steady refusal, or, perhaps, are canvassing the hints I have thrown out; but suspend every thought to my disadvantage till you have seen the royal Blanch. She—and yet it is not from her—no, you must wait; ask her no questions, since her answers may perplex, but they can never convince. Endeavour to secure her friendship; she is all that is noble, affectionate, and pious: she loved *me* once, and would have loved me still; but she knows not that I now exist, nor could that knowledge afford her any pleasure, since there yet lies a stigma on the name of—— But why detain you any longer? Yet if the peace of a poor victim to a remorseless enemy be of any consequence, speak not of St. Alexa.—I would extort a promise, but extorted promises are not binding: and thus situated, how can it be freely given?"

Of her compliance with this request Catherine felt the impossibility, and even grew eager to anticipate the discovery of a secret she supposed to be in the late Queen of Sweden's possession. St. Alexa saw her reluctance, and suddenly assuming a more satisfied air, said—"The affair was of no avail; her friend was free to act as curiosity should suggest, since restraint in any particular too often acted as a stimulus."

The reproof, couched under this observation, brought a blush into the cheek of our conscious self-accuser; but, too sincere to enter into a hazardous engagement, she pursued not the subject, and interdicted from any further entreaty, she tenderly bade the mysterious Nun adieu, for whom, notwithstanding her inconsistencies, she felt a sincere and affectionate friendship.

The appearance of Stockholm, which Catherine had not visited since the revolution it had undergone, produced in her bosom the united sensations of joy and concern. Reduced by famine, and dilapidated in many parts, it exhibited to a feeling soul, unaccustomed to the ravages of war, scenes of melancholy import; and although new and more magnificent edifices were already rising, like the Phœnix, from the ruins of those which had been rudely formed by the late founders of that city, yet she could not help giving a sigh to the sufferings of those who once possessed what was now no more, and saw, in imagination, the emaciated countenance, the weeping eye, and trembling hands of aged matrons and helpless children as they gazed upon the destruction of their hopes, their property, and their peace,—she saw those hands lifted up to deprecate a milder fate, and wept at the thought that, in some degree, the half-starved infant and debilitated veteran had probably execrated her glorious Gustavus, as the principal agent in their undeserved punishment.

Conan, who guessed the cause of that conflict which agitated her speaking countenance, accompanied her in silence through the busy streets, knowing that her feelings were but the effects of a compassionate heart, and trusted to succeeding scenes for the cure of this suddenly excited grief:—nor was he mistaken in his conjecture, for the interior of the city, which lay beyond the operation of death-dealing engines, exhibited a very contrary appearance. But Catherine could not just then give any attention to Von Hemert, who now exerted himself to point out the spot Gustavus had chosen for the site of his new palace. It was a rising ground, and crowded by workmen of every description necessary to the vast undertaking; but as she cast her eye over the motley tribe collected on the higher part of the little eminence, it rested upon a commanding figure literally exalted above its fellows. She soon got near enough to discover the interesting person of the new Sovereign, who was clothed in solemn black. A composed gravity sat on his fine features; his looks were directed to a spot, about which he seemed to be conversing with an architect, apparently of no mean order: his brilliant eyes, softened by a thoughtful cast, appeared, in Catherine's estimation, to possess a more superior degree of interest than when blazing with all the fire of a just resentment, or darting their ardent glances towards the dear-lost object of his affections. While thus sweetly, though painfully, engaged, she found by his abruptly leaving the place, that he had seen them.

Ashamed of being detected in her pointed admiration of our gallant hero, she would instantly have retreated; but this the observant Conan forbade, for Gustavus was already before them: and, as if he had totally forgotten his resolution to avoid the kind companion of his Sigismunda, saluted the new comers with a graceful serenity; and though no smile played about his lips, there was an easy familiarity in his manner that convinced her his coming to meet them was a matter of choice.

After expressing a friendly regret for the absence of St. Alexa, he accompanied them to the palace, where Blanch received her timid visitor with so much gentleness and true dignity, as to convince Catherine how very compatible those qualities were, and how much they both owed to each other's exertion.

CHAPTER II.

> "Fair peace, how lovely, how delightful thou!
> Blest be the man divine who gives us thee,
> Who bids the trumpet hush his horrid clang,
> Who sheaths the murd'rous blade!—
> Of him the shepherd in the peaceful dale
> Chants———
> And the full city warm, from street to street,
> And shop to shop, responsive rings of him."
>
> Thomson's Britannia.

If Catherine found in the vestiges which war had left of its ravages a theme for pity, she was amply repaid for the commiserating tear by the heart-exhilarating scenes which a nearer view of Stockholm's rising glories afforded. The palace in which she and her lamented friend had experienced the bitterest insults, and been disgusted with exhibitions of criminal luxuries, now assumed a far different appearance; and in the modest, yet cheerful regalings that took place under the auspices of its noble mistress, she found subjects for the most striking comparisons, when the contrast, as she drew them, gratified her ardent spirits.

With Conan she visited the streets once polluted by Christian's massacres, and echoing the shrieks and groans of unhappy senators and their mourning relatives,—now resounding with songs of peace, and the eulogium of *him* by whom it was obtained. Encouraged by their great deliverer, trade already reared its drooping head, and the different sciences, so lately disregarded by a barbarous nation, ventured to produce their beautiful effects, protected by the gracious Gustavus; while pure and sacred piety, divested of meretricious ornaments, looked to this guardian of its rights for his generous countenance.

Disgusted with the foppery, glare, and superstition of the Romish Church, Gustavus listened to the pleadings and arguments of unadorned religion; and Catherine beheld the churches, once distinguished for their superfluous ornaments, unessential ceremonies, and the thunder of anathemas occasionally hurled against those who could not afford to pay for sinning—now converted into the abodes of true religious worship. Even the environs of Stockholm presented fresh sources of congratulation to the exulting pair—those, however, which had escaped the late devastation, where a joyous confidence reigned in every face they saw; and as the busy season was fully commenced, the peasants appeared with that sort of independence which bespoke them subjects, not slaves; a happy security gave labour its truest relish, and the field they cultivated was owned by no haughty taskmaster, but held out the rewards of industry to its humble possessor.

While Catherine was thus delightfully employed, she softly articulated her hope, that the earthly dispenser of these desirable blessings might enjoy the fruits of his own goodness.—"Alas!" she thought, "when that afflicted bosom was torn by pangs of disappointed love, he suffered not *his* private sorrow to mar the noblest plans that mortal ever conceived. Disinterested patriot! not the wounds of thy bleeding heart—not the crush of thy sweetest expectations, gained from a beloved and suffering people one atom of that tender attention thou hast ever shewn to their dearest concerns; even now, while the wounds still rankle, no signs of their existence appear. O Gustavus! may *I* learn fortitude from *thee!*"

To Catherine's warm and animated praises of this gallant hero, or rather this patriotic King, and her description of the pleasures she had enjoyed in her excursion, Blanch listened with evident satisfaction; and, entirely pleased with her new companion, she endeavoured to give variety to her entertainment of the gentle Catherine, who, grateful for the distinction, conquered as much as possible the anxiety which St. Alexa's tremendous hints had left upon her mind; till roused by the Queen's questions respecting the poor Sigismunda's death, and her own then existing circumstances, she felt her curiosity no longer repressible; but in the course of her information, mentioned St. Alexa's name in a way that she thought must excite her royal hearer's attention.

Amazed to find no effect from what *she* thought would have occasioned an interesting enquiry, she went into the particulars of that Nun's behaviour—her flights of passion, her contradictory behaviour, her hints, in which Catherine was so mysteriously implicated,—in short, every thing so far as memory would permit, that had passed between them, except what immediately respected Blanch; and on this head she feared to commit herself, as not knowing in what light the Queen might consider a liberty which the eager narrator began to think was only the consequence of St. Alexa's violent emotions.

How little did Catherine suspect the true cause of this inattention! and yet how easy it was to suppose that the *name*, not the *person*, was unknown to her august protector, as the only one she knew, was that given to the Nun upon taking the veil; and it appeared extremely feasible that Blanch's knowledge of her's, had terminated prior to this change. Thus then was Catherine again left to those tormenting doubts and surmises which no probable incident promised to elucidate, unless the narrative preparing by St. Alexa should tend that way. But now another event occurred to add its perplexities to those our heroine experienced. The privacy, in which her noble entertainer had passed her days from the period of her deserting Christian's licentious Court, was now at an end. Her character, in every stage of exaltation, suffering, and patient resignation, was established even to the German dominions; and the illustrious exile, no longer induced to shun the tribute paid to such brilliant merits, received at her palace the numerous Nobles who came to congratulate Gustavus on his accession.

With a friendly partiality she insisted upon Catherine's sharing the honour of these visits, and introduced her upon those occasions with a gracious distinction, where her youth, beauty, and modest deportment gained the esteem of many, the admiration of all.

On a day set apart for the reception of several Princes and Ambassadors from different Courts, Blanch entreated her young friend to abandon the mournful style of dress she had worn for her beloved Sigismunda; and, without adopting in her change the heavy ornaments of those times, to appear in the sweet simplicity of a fancied habit, to which the decoration of her person was to be suited.

Ever desirous to oblige where even the merit of compliance was lost in being the result of inclination, she immediately obeyed her royal patroness, whose taste, unvitiated by a love of gorgeous splendour, exemplified itself in the choice of Catherine's habiliments, where a plain but happy elegance corresponded with that of the figure which embellished it.

Pleased with the effect of her own refined taste, the Queen viewed this interesting young woman with a secret wish that she might supplant Sigismunda in the affections of a Monarch, who, from all she could gather in the account given by Conan, (which was as much as he knew himself,) would not be disgraced by such an union. While thus sanguinely encouraging hopes which Miss Sleswie dared not even whisper to her own heart, she was pleased and gratified by the presence of him to whom she would have given her new friend. He was accompanied by a Nobleman, who yielded only to Gustavus in the majesty and dignity of a person, from which time had stole but little. The kind-hearted Blanch glanced a look of intelligent import at Catherine as the King approached to present his august visitant; when, observing her to be excessively agitated, it confirmed her opinion of a latent predilection in favour of the people's idol.

As there were more ladies present, and the ceremony of announcing the stranger confined only to the Queen, Catherine's confusion passed unnoticed by any one else, till Blanch found in the fierce and ardent looks with which she was regarded by Ericson's companion, a fresh motive for the agonies she pitied, and that Gustavus himself was equally occupied in reading the countenances of them both; till, almost senseless from the strength of her emotions, Miss Sleswie tottered out of the room by a door near which she sat, while the formality of etiquette detained the Queen from attending her poor friend, the cause of whose uneasiness she was anxious to understand;—but to her great relief, the Court soon after broke up at the instigation of Gustavus, whose penetration discovered the real inducement for Catherine's quitting the circle; and Blanch, impatient to learn that inducement, followed to the garden, where she supposed to find her, as the folding doors by which Catherine made her escape, opened only to that, and a wilderness then in its utmost beauty.

Here on the base of an antique statue sat the object of her search, whose eye indicated terror and affright, while she seemed eager to fly from the Queen.—"Whither would you go, my love? Of what are you afraid? Whom do you dread?"

"Ah, Madam, detain me not! I cannot see him! Oh, what brought him hither? Pray do not insist upon my stay—his presence is dreadful!"

"Sit down, Catherine; the circle is broken; our visitors are departed."

"*All*, gracious Queen—is it possible?"

"Certainly; Gustavus was concerned for your indisposition, and kindly led the way, inviting those who chose it, to sup with him; you may believe, therefore, I was soon deserted. And now tell me——"

"Tell you! ah, my royal mistress, the mystery of your servant's fate hangs yet in a painful suspense."

"But why is our good King an object of abhorrence to my young friend?"

"The King did your Highness say? He an object of abhorrence! Oh Lady, accuse not the grateful Catherine of such a horrid crime! Oh no, revered Lady, *he* is entitled to my veneration—my—my—but *he* did you say? No, not the great, the glorious King of Sweden—it was not from him I flew—it was from the awful Duke of Saxe Lunenburgh."

"I guessed as much, my dear; forgive me then for a wilful mistake; perhaps I had reasons for it, which may be hereafter explained. I once saw him in a terrible light, but succeeding events have changed disgust to pity. *Your* aversion has been fully accounted for by the good Von Hemert, but do not condemn Saxe Lunenburgh; suspend your censure till I can obtain a private audience of him. Fear nothing, my child! Protected by Gustavus, and under *my* roof, you are safe from every species of fraud or violence."

Blanch smiled at the ardency of Catherine's gratitude, who imprinted on the royal hand a fervent kiss, while she declared the consequence this assurance was to her present and future peace;—even St. Alexa's threats lost their terrors, and she determined to wait with patience the issue of her present situation. This eclaircissement produced some very pleasant effects to Catherine; she felt a respectful confidence in the Queen, which almost encouraged her to trust St. Alexa's hints to that noble dame.

Of Saxe Lunenburgh she saw but little; and as he expressed no sort of anxiety to speak to her, she almost disregarded his piercing glances; even the dislike his former behaviour had created seemed to lose its object, for her situation was so much amended in many other respects, that his presence gave her no great disquiet.

No longer neglected by the distinguished of her own sex, the confessed companion of an illustrious matron, noticed with a testimony of high esteem by the only man she had ever entertained a favourable presentiment of, it appeared as if her path in future pointed to a safe and honourable establishment, over which no dreaded cloud extended its influence, if we except her expectations from St. Alexa, and a sort of apprehension that sometimes shaded the pleasing prospect when the Duke's former unprovoked rudeness obtained a momentary influence. But, while indulging the modest hope of peaceful enjoyments, her gentle heart received a severe shock by an application from Ulrica, who, contrary to the custom of the Free Tribunal, had been permitted to languish in a severe and solitary confinement on the borders of Westphalia, from whence she was suffered to escape, owing, as was supposed, to some uncertainty in her case, which occasioned a repeal of the sentence denounced against her. But the real fact was, that Baron Hunsdorf, who possessed considerable influence as a Free Judge, and whose bold forgery had never come before that Tribunal, which had been wholly attributed to Ulrica, infatuated by his unextinguished passion for that bad woman, had, on his reappearance in the mystic Court, given such a turn to the accusation, as produced a suspension of the punishment they had decreed; and, determined still further to serve a creature who merited nothing but evil at *his* hands, the Baron successfully contrived a plan, by which her enlargement might be secured. And here we may note the fallibility of a Court that defied deception; since even to Sir Bernard Milan, who was also a member, the true fabricator of Sigismunda's relation was totally unknown, and Hunsdorf preserved his consequence among them. But with her emancipation from the fortress where she was imprisoned, his power to assist her concluded; for, although restored in some measure to a tolerable degree of health, his constitution became so debilitated as to give way to every exertion, and the journies he had lately performed, produced a long and lingering disorder; so that Ulrica quitted Germany without the smallest cognizance of her deliverer; for, on this head, her guard was enjoined the strictest secrecy.

To her, who, till her recent sufferings, was insensible to every species of fatigue or poverty, the distress she endured on the road to Stockholm, was excruciating in the highest degree; but it was preferable to remaining where she was, or going to Copenhagen. The triumphs of Gustavus, and deposition of Christian had met her ear: to visit, therefore, the Monarch she had so treacherously deceived, and whose disposition, revengeful and unforgiving, she could not trust, was a task she dreaded.

That her crimes were equally, if not more fully, understood by the new King, she was not ignorant, or that *he* had been a still greater sufferer by them than Christian; but his character for clemency, generosity, and the magnificence of his spirit, held out an encouragement to throw herself at his feet, confess her atrocious wickedness, and entreat forgiveness. Thus determined, she commenced a journey of more than three hundred miles, part of which was performed with tolerable ease, as the ice was just broken up, and the Baltic on which she embarked free for navigation.

To follow this unhappy creature through the various difficulties she encountered previous to her arrival at Stockholm, would be productive neither of pleasure nor necessary information. Suffice it to say that, in a miserable cabin, in the suburbs of that city, this once vain, luxurious woman was sheltered by the executor of her wicked will, who had been justly described as the unfeeling, abandoned Ursula, to whom she was known through all her tattered disguise, and amidst the melancholy disadvantages of an emaciated form, a deathlike countenance, and a drooping feeble gait.

No sooner had Ulrica recovered the power of utterance which this unexpected interview had interrupted, than she looked in Ursula's face, and piteously pronounced the name of Sigismunda

Marienburg. The lay-sister started at the mention of her innocent victim.—She was not then unfeeling:—repentance had fixed its fangs deep in her remorseless bosom, had extracted the poisonous qualities of a barbarous heart, and she was become humane, even tender!

To the miserable appearance before her she could justly ascribe much of her vicious propensity, and its awful consequences; but she saw her deserted, humbled, and reduced by her vileness to a situation that asked the helping hand of pity.

To be indebted to a menial, and one to whom much of her vile character had formerly been displayed, was a mortifying circumstance to the yet unsubdued Ulrica, who (however induced by the sudden impulse to mention a name she still detested) preserved a haughty sense of her own superiority over this former dependant on her greatness. But to claim any tokens of respect in her terrible situation would have been impolitic; she affected, therefore, to be grateful for the unhappy woman's attendance, and learning from her that Catherine resided at Stockholm, she formed the wild project of soliciting the presence of one to whom her crimes had rendered her so obnoxious, and this with a view of prevailing upon her to obtain not only the King's entire forgiveness for so basely stepping between him and his hope of domestic felicity, but to grant her a pension for her future support.

The ignorance of Ursula saw no impropriety in the bold request; and certain that her person was entirely unknown to that young lady, she gave into her own hands a letter prepared by this astonishing woman, containing a petition to the above purpose.

Catherine read the presumptuous letter in Blanch's presence, who, alarmed by her changing countenance and evident disorder, imagined it to be some manœuvre of Saxe Lunenburgh, or it might be the packet from St. Alexa; but observing the increasing agitation of her young friend, she ventured to question her on the subject.

Catherine was no stranger to that lady's fortitude, but trembled to inform her that Ulrica was at liberty.

The Queen saw her reluctance to communicate the strange contents, and rising, with a smile, said she would not press her to disclose what might be improper for her to know.

"Dearest Lady, forgive my seeming want of confidence in your goodness: take this paper—it will be a sufficient apology for me."

The Queen read; and returning it without the smallest emotion, said—

"There *was* a time, Catherine, when such a letter would have created some confusion *here*," pressing her bosom; "*then* I might have blamed, *now* I can only pity.—But what can be done in this case? It is plain she is wholly liberated from the Tribunal; but that her liberty originates in an acquittal of the charges laid against her, I cannot believe, although she dwells so much upon that circumstance:—at any rate, Gustavus must not know of her arrival; it will add to the mortification he endures from what has transpired respecting Fitzer."

"Ah! what of him, my royal mistress?"

"Only this, that in consequence of his diabolical contrivance, by which you know he fled from Stockholm when the siege was raised, with the Danish soldiers appointed to guard him, he has safely reached Dalecarlia, where, supported by a few worthless insurgents, the plotting monster has set up a claim to the throne prior to that of our gracious Sovereign;—and this is done under the ridiculous plea of a royal descent—nay, I am informed the infatuated Dalecarlians believe him to be the son of Steen Sture, who, when he was a mere youth, received him at Court, and treated him more like a child than a subject. Judge then what the noble Gustavus must feel to find his and the poor Sigismunda's cruel enemies not only at liberty, but enabled to form fresh plots against his reviving peace!"

After lamenting with Blanch the probability of seeing their beloved Monarch again a prey to recollections which Ulrica's presence, and Fitzer's active treachery would produce, Catherine proposed to offer that dangerous woman a sufficiency to support her in one of the distant provinces, on condition she quitted Stockholm for ever.

To this the Queen not only assented, but named the sum *she* would employ on that occasion; and commissioned her young companion to visit Ulrica, and acquaint her with the result of her application.

However loth Catherine might be even to look upon the efficient cause of so many sorrows, she permitted not any selfish consideration to withhold her from an act which might essentially benefit her revered Gustavus; and on the succeeding morning, attended by one of the Queen's women, set out to execute her project.

Ursula's cottage stood at the extremity of an obscure street in the suburbs, which opened to a wild forest not yet deprived of its stately trees, which almost sheltered the rude dwelling. They had nearly reached the door, when, alarmed by several faint groans, the attendant urged her mistress to hasten back. Catherine stopped for a minute, looking fearfully towards the wood from whence the appalling sounds issued; she then turned towards the cottage door. It stood open.—"There can be no danger," she cried, "*here*; perhaps we shall find some one who will enquire into the meaning of those melancholy exclamations." She then entered, but nobody appeared:—to return seemed equally dangerous as to stay, since they must of necessity cross an angle of the forest opposite to the place from whence they imagined the sounds proceeded:—therefore Catherine determined to wait till somebody should appear, and sat down near the entrance, though not without some degree of trepidation. But she had not long to wait, as the sounds of grief not only continued, but seemed to approach; and she presently beheld a woman coming slowly from the trees, whom she immediately recollected to be the bearer of Ulrica's letter. She was weeping violently, and wringing her hands in all the extravagance of unrestrained sorrow—sometimes stopping, and looking behind her; when seeing the strangers, whom she directly recognised, she gave way to a fresh gush of passion, exclaiming—"Oh Lady! the Tribunal! the cursed Tribunal! Dear Lady, step with me!"

"Oh dear, not for worlds!" said the terrified attendant; "my mistress has nothing to do with the Holy Tribunal!" making an obedience at the formidable name. "Come home, my sweet mistress—do not speak to her! She blasphemes that just Court! Somebody will hear her, I doubt not, for they used to say at Dortmund that the very birds were informers."

"Alas! no; *I* have nothing to do with it, damsel, but——"

"Lead on," interrupted Catherine, inspired with a terrible presentiment, which however involved not her own safety, "lead on, Ursula!"

"I will, Lady, it is but just by:" and then bursting into an agony of tears—"You know me, Lady, I perceive?"

"Yes."

"You know me for an accomplice with—"

"What is that yonder?" exclaimed the attendant who closely followed her mistress.

"Merciful Heaven! what do I see?" cried Catherine, shuddering, and suddenly retreating.

"She cannot hurt you now, Lady, she is dead and cold!—See," taking a sword which was stuck in a tree, under which lay the lifeless body of the once-dreaded Ulrica—"see this terrible signal of cruel vengeance! Alas! I understood they had no further power over her! Wretched woman! it was but last night that she called me to the door, and pointing towards a noble Lubecker as he passed near my cabin,—'There,' she cried, 'there goes one of my former persecutors!—I know him well—he was my chief accuser—by proxy indeed, but it was sufficient to criminate your poor mistress! Now I can laugh at his menaces, and defy his proud looks! What a wrathful frown gathered on his brow as he gazed on me! what threats, poor and impotent as they are, did that frown seem to impart!—But I am no longer in Germany; he cannot usurp any further authority; they may accuse, they may seize any one obnoxious to them, but they cannot execute a sentence once repealed. Ulrica is now doubly secured; she is beyond their jurisdiction by their own decision, and the power of Gustavus.'—Alas! I thought she was right, and rejoiced with her while she exulted in the protection of the new King, upon which she depended."

"But how," said Catherine, who examined with horror the mangled spectacle before her, "how came she here? You say the body is cold; therefore some hours must have elapsed since this dreadful murder was committed."

"I will tell you, Lady. It was near the dawn of day before we either of us thought of rest; for she was so much revived by my attentions to her, and the result of your message, that I believe she thought herself equal to any thing;—and perceiving the sun rising with that splendour so common to us in our short summer, she went to the door. 'I cannot sleep, Ursula,' said she; 'the morning is beautiful; I shall step into the forest for a few minutes, and yet,' faintly smiling, 'any one would suppose a bed more agreeable to my enfeebled limbs; but rest seems quite departed from me.'

"She had not been gone two minutes, when the Lubecker I mentioned rushed past the cottage. I directly recollected her defiance of him, his stern glances, and his awful occupation;—my heart trembled within me, but I ventured among the trees, and soon discovered my unhappy mistress struggling with the base assassin!

'Keep off!' he said, holding his sword against my breast; 'interfere not with our immutable decrees!'

"Oh, how sick I turned, as I sunk on my knees before him, while he buried the dreadful weapon thrice into the heart of my shrieking mistress! Her death was almost instantaneous; she was not permitted to call for mercy—that mercy we have both so much abused; but I think she called upon Sigismunda Marienburg and the name of Hunsdorf."

"And have you staid ever since by this poor corpse?"

"Oh no, Madam, for I expected *my* turn would come next, the murderer looked at me so maliciously; but after sticking the sword where you see it, and looking down upon her yet writhing form—'Thus perish,' said he, 'all who defy our power, or protect the subjects of our wrath.'—I never shall forget his words, for was it not as much as to say he would kill me for giving her protection?"

"You are certainly in danger, Ursula; but I think if he had intended your destruction, he would have done it immediately."

"Why so I think, Lady, but he only bade me depart, and make no noise; and yet I could not help grieving after he was gone, though I went home first, and staid till I supposed the cruel wretch was far enough out of hearing. To be sure, when I came back, the sight seemed more sad than ever; and though I smothered, as much as possible, my heavy complaints, yet they would burst forth.—But you look very pale, Lady; let us go to the cottage."

"I will, Ursula; for the sight of this mangled object, so suddenly cut off without any previous preparation, shocks my soul."

She then fixed a long last look upon the insensible remains, and bitterly weeping, suffered her attendant, who gladly quitted the sanguinary spot, to lead her from it.

Before Catherine left the miserable Ursula, she counselled her to let the body continue where it was till disposed of by proper authority. Ursula reluctantly agreed; but she dared make no objection, and tried to be satisfied with the assurance that no time should be lost in representing the shocking case to Gustavus.

When the Queen was told of this awful catastrophe, she felt every trace of resentment subside, and wept for the enemy to whom she had wished the benefits of true repentance. Averse to taking any steps in this affair without the King's sanction, Blanch dispatched a trusty messenger to his Majesty with a concise account of the whole transaction. Gustavus heard it in silent sorrow; for the death of Ulrica excited afresh that poignant feeling which strong fortitude had concealed from public observation;—nay, he turned aside to dash off a tear, but still desirous of supporting a character which cost him so dear to maintain, he calmly issued orders for the interment of the murdered criminal, whose assassination he very properly imputed to Sir Bernard Milan: and this was the very utmost limits to which the King chose to carry his attention to the deceased, as the case before him admitted not the cognizance of a Civil Court.

Ursula felt as much satisfaction at this arrangement, as a mind, torn by guilty recollections, and concern for a woman she really grieved for, could enjoy; and though reduced to a state of extreme poverty, endeavoured to consider it as a just consequence of her atrocious treatment of the sainted Sigismunda. But as this state could not be wholly hidden from the exalted Blanch, she generously assigned to Ursula a competent share of that sum designed to relieve her wretched mistress; and had the pleasure to find, from Catherine's representation, who occasionally visited her, that gratitude and repentance went hand in hand in fully possessing a bosom, once hardened to the extent of unfeminine cruelty.

CHAPTER III.

"The painted clouds, which bore my hope aloft,
Alas! are vanished now to yielding air,
And I am fall'n indeed!——
How weak is reason when affection pleads!
How hard to turn the soft deluded heart
From flatt'ring toys, which sooth'd its vanity!"

EARL OF ESSEX.

RESTORED to a degree of temporary quiet, Catherine had leisure to examine a heart which had preserved, through a series of terrible events, its sacred attachment to the only man who had ever endangered its peace; but with pain she discovered that the interests of that heart were not forwarded, in the least, by the melancholy circumstances of the past months. Esteem, respect, and friendship marked the words and actions of him she still continued to love with an enthusiasm that nothing but his glorious virtues could excuse.

From esteem, respect, and friendship she could deduce no hope; yet there was a consolation in knowing that her alliance was not rejected in consequence of any preference for another, since Gustavus had refused several splendid offers.—"But in what instance," she thought, "do these rejections advance my wishes? Guarded as my secret predilection has ever been from him at least, I am equally certain that no consideration for *me* induced those refusals. True, he has even proposed *me*, if descended, as I am taught to believe, from a royal stock, to be a sharer of his throne, but there the magnificent design stops; for, ah! how undesirable would be an elevation which has the recommendation of high advantages without those that sweeten the toils of royalty!"

There was nothing in this estimate of hopes and fears that pointed to any decision; and Catherine was obliged to fly from a subject which was utterly beyond her abilities to settle with any happy certainty: since, added to the determined silence of Ericson on every theme leading to his conjugal arrangements, was the mystery of Saxe Lunenburgh's former hints, and St. Alexa's dreaded explanation, who still pleaded indisposition for the protraction of her promise; nor would she in the course of several months, admit her anxious young friend to her presence, although both Catherine and the Royal Blanch had several times visited the Monastery, and earnestly solicited an audience.

Particularly interested in what related to her favourite, that amiable Queen set herself to discover, if possible, the Duke's motive for his extraordinary behaviour at Wrangel's cottage; and relying on the esteem he professed, she scrupled not to question him freely on that head. Perplexed and irresolute, he continued silent and confused. He knew Blanch was acquainted with some remarkable instances of his early youth, and between those incidents and that conduct there was an awful connection. This he confessed, at length, in a manner which fired his auditor's curiosity to a high degree; but without making any comments, she carried the result of this interview to Catherine, who felt more impatient than before for St. Alexa's communication, although she could not account for this renewed ardour in her cause;—however, she no longer hesitated to detail the unconnected hints St. Alexa had dropped of her former knowledge of the Queen.

Blanch listened with an attention that absorbed every faculty of her soul. Catherine observed the effect of her information, and began to think the crisis of her fate very near.—"I *must* see this woman, my child; the elucidation of some dark transactions is at hand. Alexa is not her name; it was doubtless assumed when she took the veil; no wonder then that, upon recollection, she should withdraw her objections to your mention of her.—Were I to explain the various tumults that agitate my mind, you would be no gainer by them, since I can neither account for, nor tranquillize them till I have seen this Nun. Should my suspicions be well grounded—— But I would neither flatter nor deceive; to-morrow we will visit her, nor leave the place till my doubts are ended."

Catherine thought she should be much happier had the Queen been more explicit; but, accustomed to the deepest veneration of her virtues, and respect for her commands, she dropped the subject, but passed a sleepless night in fruitless conjectures, and in the formation of hopes which soon evaporated in gloomy fears.

Ever alive to the demands of friendship, and the interest this amiable young creature had obtained over a susceptible heart, Blanch had quitted Stockholm, and was on her way to Telga before Catherine supposed her to be stirring; when a new disappointment awaited the Queen, for in reply to her eager enquiries at the monastery, she was answered that St. Alexa had been missing since the foregoing evening, and no one could tell what was become of her. It likewise appeared, on questioning some of the Nuns, that, tempted by a serene afternoon, she had wandered among the woods surrounding their residence, and this, as they were led to believe, with a view to recruit her spirits, which had suffered extremely by her unremitting attention to the transcribing of many loose papers,—a task she finished on the preceding morning.

The Abbess, who was recently chosen from their small community, proceeded to say—"she thought Sister Alexa betrayed of late some extraordinary symptoms of a mind laden with guilt or distress; that her fear of the former supposition prevented any attempt to calm that agitation, lest it should increase, without removing the cause."

"*I* have reason," interrupted an ancient sister, "to imagine our unhappy companion's absence is owing to a conference which I saw her holding with a Knight of a martial appearance."

"Indeed," cried Blanch, who expressed much surprise at this circumstance; "pray can you describe his person?"

"But slightly, lady; he seemed tall, and wore the insignia of some illustrious order. I happened to be passing the great beech near Halden's Cross, when I discovered our sister on her knees, and counting her beads with great devotion. Unwilling to disturb her, I stepped forward, and scarcely lost sight of her, when a sudden scream induced me to turn back; but, holy saints! how astonished was I to see her struggling in the arms of a noble Knight!—Well, I knew not what to do! Sister Alexa is pretty violent, and I was afraid to interfere; for he did not look like one who would injure a woman, so I stood still where neither of them could see me, till at last St. Alexa broke from the gentleman, and came towards me so suddenly, that I could not slip away. Her beautiful face was as white as my veil; but when she saw me, it turned to crimson. I expected to be finely lectured for standing there; however she spoke not a word, and I came in directly, and saw no more of her."

"We waited," resumed the Abbess, "in expectation of her joining us at vespers; but as her absence was not unusual, I concluded she was in one of her gloomy fits, for Sister Mary had not told me of what you have now heard; and as she did not appear at the refectory, I ordered her supper to be sent to her cell. It was plain she *had* been there since her meeting with the Knight, as her Nun's dress lay upon the bed. Her box, which contained some of the garments she formerly wore, was emptied of its contents, and this packet, neatly folded and directed as you see, was found upon the lid."

Blanch took the parcel with a trembling hand, and read upon the envelope as follows:—"This packet to be delivered to Catherine Sleswie, or any one deputed by her."

"Mysterious Providence!" said the Queen, "do I see aright? This writing—this seal speaks wonders! it reveals tidings from the dead. Ill-fated friend! hast thou indeed fled the only means left to clear thy fame, and restore thy lost happiness?

"Surely, Madam, she cannot be far from hence; but I am losing time. Adieu, holy Abbess! should the dear wanderer return hither before you again hear from us, send intelligence to the palace immediately:—tell her also that love, joy, friendship await her arrival at Stockholm: unfortunate was the interview, which properly managed, might have prevented this ill-timed absence!"

Blanch was eager to depart, but her hospitable entertainer had already ordered some little delicacies to be produced for her refreshment; nor would she suffer the agitated Queen to leave Telga till she and her attendants were plentifully served. It now required some little management to check her young friend's curiosity in this business without alarming her sensibility; but this proved no very difficult matter, for Catherine had become so habituated to implicit obedience to the amiable Queen, that when she was briefly told of St. Alexa's absence, she restrained her natural desire of information, and seemed more attentive to alleviate Blanch's fatigues, than thoughtful of her own gratification. But the following morning presented an interesting scene to her feelings; for when she entered the royal chamber, her tender heart was affectionately alarmed at her benefactor's appearance, whose languid eye betrayed a want of rest, while the traces of many a tear evinced some latent cause for unhappiness.

She smiled faintly upon Catherine as she advanced; and taking her hand—"You are surprised, my child, at seeing me thus, and will be more so to know that I have not been in bed the whole night; but *there* is my excuse," pointing to some papers that lay near her, "there is the packet for which we have so long waited! Forgive my silence on this subject last night; I knew not the nature of its contents, nor how far they might affect my gentle girl; perhaps, if you could suppress what even *I* found irrepressible, it were better you should trust to me for a brief repetition of them: but I see my error in those enquiring eyes. Take the papers, my love, and exert your fortitude while reading what may eventually concern your future interest, and excite pity founded upon just and relative claims."

"Now then," thought Catherine, as she took the packet from her noble benefactress, "now is the hour arrived which St. Alexa had foretold, as replete with horror to an unoffending innocent!"

"Doubtless you wish to retire, my love," said the Queen; "go, then; and when you have read the awful contents, return to her who regards your welfare with a mother's affection."

Pleased with the permission, Catherine went to her own chamber, when, tearing open the parcel which was slightly folded, she discovered the following loose disjointed sentences, evidently written with a tremor that rendered them scarcely legible.

"I have seen him! Tremendous Providence! I have seen the author of all my wretchedness!—How cruel to destroy the repose of her who loved thee with a sacred fondness!—Murderer—yes!—If to destroy domestic confidence—if to betray innocence—if to confine, and bring to the verge of the grave, by various species of barbarous treatment, a creature who had the claims of humanity to guard her, be murder, then art *thou* a murderer! Yes—I have seen him, but I will behold him *no more!*"

We will pass by the pitiable emotions which marked our poor heroine's comments on the contents of the whole, as she now laid them down to wipe off the flowing tear—now took them up to furnish herself with fresh sources of anguish; and proceed in the style and manner of the unhappy St. Alexa, who seemed, by the desultory order of her communications, to be influenced occasionally by those flights of a disordered imagination, to which Catherine had often been a melancholy witness.

ST. ALEXA'S NARRATIVE.

Cold was the north wind, cold the hail,
    And cold the falling snow,
But colder still the frozen heart
    Of him who works my woe!

These nodding towers that overhang
    The silver stream beneath—
These nodding towers must be my tomb
    When I shall sleep in death!"

"Often, when strolling about this pile of ruins, have I applied the above simple lines to my own sad fate; and the woes of poor mad Margaret of Arensburg was an excuse for the tears which my own sorrows have continued.—Alas! alas! for wretched Catherina, whose early youth was distinguished by such felicity as deepens with a darker tint the sombre shade of twenty succeeding years,—is it possible that the sufferings of a miserable maniac, which I once thought of as evils entirely shut out from the sphere I then moved in, should now be considered (in an inferior degree) similar to what I have encountered?—Oh my great, my gallant brother! tenacious of thine honour, jealous of a hapless sister's purity, what a stain has that sister's equivocal conduct thrown upon a character bright as the radiant sun! and how cruelly was I circumstanced, when the pleading tears, the kneeling attitude, the affecting adjurations, and sometimes the vehement threats and expostulations of this noble brother were alternately exerted in vain to bring me to confession!—I have a long and melancholy story to detail, Catherine Sleswie. Oh my sweet girl! how often have I foolishly encouraged wishes which that name and your interesting features created, and have as often discarded them! You are not to expect an accurate and well-digested history of St. Alexa's sufferings;—alas! that name befits me best: it implies imprisonment, coercion, monastic rigour—the very sound shuts out hope, and a cheerful expectation of untried good. But as I was saying—thou must expect to meet with strange incongruities, eccentric observations, and irregular remarks in this sad history of abused affection; and even now I can picture thy disappointment in my forbearing to mention the names and titles of those who were actors in the sad tragedy; but should any of them be personally known to thee——No matter, Catherine, *I* have reasons—thou hast curiosity;—let it sleep—awake it not; it is perchance a serpent that may sting thy tender heart;—enough may be found in these pages to wring it!

"I have already hinted that my early youth bloomed with the promise of a lovely harvest. The loss of my excellent parents took place before I could appretiate their virtues, or indulge the propensities of an affectionate nature to a degree that might imbitter the sad deprivation; and in the household of Stanislaus, my noble brother, I passed fourteen years of calm, rational felicity!—Alas! I ought not to have expected its permanency—I was exactly in that sort of situation, which precludes a moderate enjoyment of life.—Will my Catherine believe that St. Alexa was once famed for superior beauty and its corresponding advantages? Will she credit that this cadaverous countenance—this drooping figure, once caught the attention of Royalty, or that the modest dignity of her manners failed to repress licentious attentions?—Yes—this was the era of my misfortunes, and I was snatched by a too vigilant brother from a deprecated evil to——Ah! how erroneously do our immature judgments estimate the mysterious decrees of Heaven!—Weak mortal! to shun a pass that was strongly defended by feminine virtue and masculine honour!—Protected by this noble brother, what was there to fear? Unfortunate is the lot of those whose beauty is of a description that attracts with irresistible energy, that seizes upon the passions without a consent of the judgment, and overpowers prudence, caution, and every barrier which true wisdom opposes to its influence.—Such once was mine; and think not, dear Catherine, that vanity obtains any share in this acknowledgment.—Vanity!—that folly so powerful with the weak and misjudging—had *I* ever sacrificed to thy shrine, how truant-like have I been to thy precepts!—How dead is this poor bosom to thy instigation! Were all thy votaries dragged to the altar of superstition, had they experienced the pangs which a cold and lonely confinement has often raised in my conflicting mind, how much of thy powers would be lost, and its suggestions disregarded!

"As the place, to which Stanislaus thought fit to convey his sister, was far—far from the cause of his groundless suspicions, his confidence in me returned; and I was permitted some months after to visit a relation who resided on the frontiers.

* * * * *

"It is now, Catherine, that I must commence my self-accusation. Hitherto the spotless leaf is clear and unsullied;—no blame attached to actions, pure and open as those of immortal spirits,—nor could that brother, so jealous of the honour of his house, refuse his justification of a sister's name: and yet my crime was merely the tenaciousness of a soul resembling his own. Do not ask me for the name of him to whom I pledged my sacred vows—the betrayer of my person, and destroyer of all my happiness!

"At the Court of N—— I was presented by Stanislaus, and heard, with conscious pride, the whispered praises of all around me; but who, in all that noble circle, possessed the irresistible power which is ascribed to Cæsar—*to come—to see—to overcome*—but the unspeakably graceful N——? His address—his attention—his politeness, so rare in Princes whose will is law, were so many stimulatives to my admiration.

"Pleased with the notice of this amiable Sovereign, my brother renewed a friendship with him that had long been interrupted by absence and intervening incidents; nor once, in a long course of interrogations, persecutions, entreaties, and suppositions, glanced at his confidential friend.

"What an error in human nature was this deplorable oversight!

Cool, prudent, and penetrating in other instances, is it not wonderful that Stanislaus should be blind to an attachment which began to be suspected at Court?—Here I must (to save the character you perhaps already condemn) relate the circumstances that led to my ruin. At a tournament given in honour of the Prince's sister, your poor namesake made a conspicuous figure: her dress was green and gold—the ornaments suited to that style of beauty I then possessed—my countenance illumined with the smiles of hope, love, and self-congratulation, for in every person present I beheld a future subject. Oh vanity unexampled! Oh weak and erring dependance upon mortal integrity! When shall I be sufficiently punished for indulging the fatal propensity? Do you not understand, my Catherine, by this time, that I had listened to the passionate addresses of N——, that he had, by dint of specious argument, induced me to confine them to my fond believing bosom? Yes, prior to my visit to the frontiers, I knew my influence over the Prince.

'It is the torment of my soul,' said this studied deceiver, 'that I cannot yet place the idol of my affections on a throne to which she would lend the highest lustre; but thou knowest the business of the Ambassadors from Saxe Gotha is to offer, with every advantage, such an alliance as can bring the hand of the eldest Princess, whose colours I am expected to wear at all future tournaments. Oh, how little do they know of thy betrothed to make such a proposal! and yet I must temporize for the present, at least till I am in a situation to reject their suit; for the friendship of Saxe Gotha is necessary to a plan I am forming for the security of my dominions!—Canst thou then, beloved lady of my affections—canst thou deign to confine the important secret of thy N——'s adoration to that charming bosom?'—

"It is unnecessary to repeat the various lights in which he placed my compliance with a request, whose essence was a degradation to the purity of feminine delicacy and the dignity of his future consort, since they proved decisive; and at the before-mentioned tournament, which took place prior to my excursion, I received a sweet, endearing, but in his situation I thought dangerous, proof of his preference.

"My noble brother was then absent on a visit to his wife, whose ill health induced her to reside at some distance from Court. I was seated near the Princess. Several lances were broken in honour of that illustrious lady, when a Herald at Arms announced a cessation of the sports till the following day; and, in consequence of her royal brother's absence, who was summoned upon some important business, another lady was deputed to bestow the prize which he produced, namely an embroidered scarf, and this lady's name was that of thy unhappy friend.

"Alas! Catherine, sinking with confusion, I wished to retire, for all eyes were upon me, and a loud shout declared the highest approbation of this arrangement; but the Prince detained me as I arose to go, and presenting me to his sister, put my hand into her's, which she graciously accepted, while I gently pressed it in speechless joy. She seemed pleased that her brother chose to be present when the Knights were to finish the tournament given in honour of her beauty, and promised to support me on the following day while appearing as Queen of the sports; but I sighed to think that he, whose love absorbed every faculty of the soul, could not be present.

"How beautifully the sun arose on that important morning—how brilliantly the Knights and their Squires were appointed, who entered the lists soon after we were seated; but he who could have given lustre to the blackest night, had withdrawn his influence, and all this splendour faded before my prejudiced eyes!

"Thou seest, Catherine, I am giving the history of a too susceptible heart; but however my confessions may offend delicacy, they are consonant to the strictest truth, and I am too sincere to varnish over faults which have produced such bitter consequences.

"Dost thou remember when, in all the ardour of enthusiastic youth, whose light and rapid finger traces its happy expectations on every portrait drawn by fancy, but obliterated by cooler judgment—dost thou, I repeat, remember thy sweet earnestness to draw me from this dismal retreat, and how frantic my denunciations were against thy peace—the peace of unoffending innocence? Forgive me, gentle creature, for the frenzied ebullitions!—alas! I thought at times that—— Be not terrified, Catherine, for I now am certain my hopes and fears were alike erroneous—No, thou art *not* the child of—Catherina——But the name—the whimsical idea of thy features resembling his whose form and face still haunt my bosom, and some other circumstances equally groundless, did, as occasions arose, impel the strange infatuation. Now the sad deception is too clear to be any longer encouraged:——I must proceed.

"There was one Knight among the noble train, whose matchless prowess bespoke the undoubted possessor of the trifling trophy; and I was instructed by my royal companion in the ceremony attending its bestowal. The sports were stopped; the judges came forward to declare their approbation of the claimant, who, lifting his beaver as he approached, discovered a face I had often seen, but never without disgust. Even his smiles seemed the result of malignancy, and his fierce scowling brow gave additional gloom to his dark complexion. The Princess glanced a look of pity on my countenance, which exhibited marks of affright and dislike; but startled at the sound of a trumpet at the barrier, he turned wrathfully to the judges, and asked them if they meant to admit another candidate for the prize he had so dearly earned.

"Disdaining the pride that dictated this haughty remonstrance, the veterans spoke not; but, re-entering the lists, advanced to a Knight who, with his Squire, had been instantly admitted. Relieved by a hope that the ferocious Sir Gormund must break a lance with the new comer, I answered the Knight's courtesy as he rode round the lists with unusual complacency, while his black competitor, for he wore sable armour, darted such looks of vengeance upon his gallant challenger, as communicated their venom to my trembling heart. The contrast of persons, address, and decorations of these cavaliers struck all present; and in spite of Sir Gormund's rudely expressed claims to the honours of the field, it was determined that he should try his fortune against the unknown. The decision was unfair, yet I could not but rejoice in the hope of escaping a persecution that promised a thousand ill consequences; for it was too evident that my hateful champion meant not to stop at empty admiration; indeed I had previously been informed by Stanislaus of his intention to solicit my hand.

"All eyes were now turned to the spirited combatants; when, perceiving his antagonist's superiority, Sir Gormund threw away his lance, and drawing a tremendous weapon, aimed it at the heart of his opponent. Alas, Catherine! I saw no more till, revived by the Princess's attentions, she presented the conquering Knight, (who had escaped unhurt) to receive my hearty congratulations.

"No wonder Sir Gormund's rancour was excited, or that his jealousy should extend to the life of a competitor, whose figure and elegance of manners threw all others into the shade of obscurity. His dress too, or rather his armour, as I then considered, was exactly suited to the occasion. How refulgent shone the burnished steel, which, striped like the zebra with the brightest green, gave a new and fanciful appearance to the whole! A magnificent plume of green and white feathers waved over the rich helmet, and his shield was surrounded by a laurel coloured agreeably to nature. His motto—ah, Catherine! that motto discovered to my penetrating eye the person of him who bore it; but I should first have told my friend that the device was a mid-day sun peeping from a dark retiring cloud—and the motto—'*No longer obscured!*'

"Oh what volumes of sweet hope did that motto disclose!—'The time is at hand,' said my believing heart, 'when *my* sun of glory shall be *no longer obscured*;—it is already breaking through the cloud of mystery, and through the means of this dear, this much-loved defender!'—for need I say that my beloved N—— stood before me!

"Thus were his excuses to be absent accounted for, and in this way did he chuse to celebrate those charms which influenced—but Oh! for how short a season!—the impetuous N——. Catherine, that eventful moment sealed my destiny; the echoing space resounded my unknown Knight's praises; his forbearance of revenge—(for Sir Gormund was permitted to escape any farther punishment, and was carried off with a flesh-wound in the sword-arm, and one of greater consequence above the hip, gnashing his teeth, and muttering execrations against his own ill fortune)—N——'s forbearance of revenge, I repeat, his gallantry, his mysterious concealment excited alternate astonishment and admiration; and the grace, added to those above described, with which he received from my trembling hand the well-earned scarf, impressed upon his Catherina's delighted heart the strongest sense of her expected happiness; since in this description was compressed those dazzling but unsolid advantages which seized my youthful affections.

"Here I must repose a while: it requires more fortitude than I can at present boast to enter upon scenes of treachery, opposition, violence, and distress of almost every description. I will therefore give you but the leading feature of those combined evils, which was that of my marriage with N——, which took place the following morning.

CHAPTER IV.

"No, there is none—no ruler of the heavens
Regardful of my miseries! What crime
Has drawn these fortunes on me?—I have been
Too insolent perhaps in youth's proud joy,
And felt not as I ought for others' sorrows;
Thence came this tempest of affliction o'er me."
Hill.

It is true that, intoxicated by the accomplishment of a purpose which led, as I had the strongest reason to suppose, to scenes of grandeur, wealth, and power, I thought little of the injuries my character might sustain till it could be honourably re-established; and it was with real reluctance I undertook that journey to the frontiers which the cautious affection (as I then thought it) of my N—— suggested as a means to prevent any suspicions his frequent, though private, visits might occasion; and to this I was the more readily induced to consent, because he proposed to follow me thither *incognito*. But—can I write with steadiness!—I never beheld him afterwards! No heart-soothing line to excuse his breach of promise—no motive could my sick soul invent to account for the long delay!

"It was then glowing summer, but it was hastening to a close. Winter, in that northern situation, would soon render the roads impassable, until the plains, vallies, and rivers were hardened by frost. I trembled at the idea that N—— had deserted me, and I watched from day to day the swift declining sun as it shortened its diurnal course. To the friends who tried every method to allay my fears, I had entrusted the hoarded secret of my love, but without naming its object;—indeed the precaution was necessary, and they tried to detain me, till I was in a situation to appear before Stanislaus, without alarming his jealous honour. But the mountain-tops began to whiten with a frosty dew, a thin ice was seen to creep over the standing pool, and there was nothing offered but immediate flight to save me from spending a tedious winter in all the horrors of despair; and I bade adieu to those worthy relations with an unequal mixture of hope and fear, feeling a degree of comfort from an actual effort to know the worst.

"Five melancholy months had elapsed since I had parted from my excellent brother, who received me with the sincerest tokens of fraternal affection; and putting on a cheerful smile—'You are almost too late, Catherina,' he cried:—'one week longer, and the gay Court, which is preparing for a brilliant festival, would have missed its fairest ornament; yes, my beauteous sister will now shine most conspicuous among the ladies of ———, and I shall witness those honours which my absence from the last tournament deprived me of enjoying.'

'A tournament,' whispered my wretched heart, 'gracious Heaven! of what cruel evils was the last productive?'

'I have heard,' continued this unsuspecting brother, 'of your Green Knight, and how mysteriously he absented himself after the sports were closed; I have heard also of Sir Gormund Gottsler, and am concerned to say he charges my sister with levity: but I made him retract his assertion in open Court, which pleased the Sovereign exceedingly.'

'He,' cried I, while indignation burned on my cheek, 'the cowardly assassin—he dare to give Stanislaus occasion to defend his sister!'

'Peace, Catherina,' said this generous brother, 'he is a coward, and as such I treated him; but you are quite incurious about the subject of these intended rejoicings?'

"Alas! I was indeed alive to nothing but my own wretched, desolate, cruel situation. My brother proceeded.

'Well, as you seem attentive at least—'

"Before he could proceed, a sudden presentiment darted on my harassed mind, and I abruptly said—'Brother, where is the Princess? Where is——' I was just upon the point of asking for my faithless, my still dear husband.

'The Princess,' replied he, 'is with N——. They are at Saxe Gotha's Court, whose daughter is by this time espoused to our good Prince.'

"Catherine, I did not faint at this soul-distressing intelligence—I did not shriek, groan, or even sigh:—no invocation to Heaven followed the fatal stroke, nor did the secret, now more deplored than ever, escape my trembling lips. Pale, silent, and convulsed, my appearance terrified this dear, affectionate brother.

'I knew she was unwell,' said the still unsuspicious Stanislaus, to those his cries for assistance had brought together, 'or our conversation must have pleased her. What can have happened, my dear child, to affect you thus?'

'Her journey possibly,' answered a cousin, who had accompanied me from her northern home, and was to pass the winter with us in Germany.—Alas! she had discovered a part of the tremendous truth. My brother was satisfied with the excuse, and I was permitted to retire with this kind companion, who watched in silence, till, relieved by a burst of tears, she found my senses returning.—But why should I dwell on a subject so hateful, or one still more so?——Sir Gormund Gottsler, in defiance of my brother's positive refusal, still dared to persecute me with his nauseous overtures through other hands; and when, enraged by his detestable perseverance, I sent him the most contemptuous answer, he openly declared I should either marry him or no one—nay, he cautioned me to be sparing of my proud invectives, for they would only enhance the weight of my punishment. Amazing effrontery!—Had not one vast, overwhelming calamity swallowed up lesser considerations, his insolence should not have passed unresented. But two months had elapsed since my return—*two months*, Catherine, added their dangerous increase to those already burthened with my shame, and the barbarous destroyer of my conjugal hopes still remained at Saxe Gotha, where it was reported he should continue, till the young Princess was recovered of an indisposition that threatened her existence.—I pitied the gentle virgin for the shock her sweetest hopes must endure, when told her claims were superseded; for it was the determined purpose of my heart to disclose my real situation when N—— returned. Yes, Catherine, I meant to present the dear child of sorrow to the unnatural author of its lamented existence—I meant to declare, without subterfuge or reservation, my legal right to that exalted station, for which I had sacrificed the temporary loss of character, and the sure, sad, and perpetual one of peace.

"It could afford no pleasure to thy susceptible feelings to describe the distress of my soul, when concealment was no longer possible, or the feelings of a brother, whose honour, confidence in a once blameless sister, and the high sense he entertained of virgin delicacy, were so deeply wounded by the birth of my hapless, desolate, almost abandoned offspring!—Sweet and spotless innocent! I still feel thy balmy breathings on this poor pale cheek—still see the unconscious gaze of infant helplessness, as it pursued the retiring light, or closed its little orbs to exclude the stronger glare.—I marked the graces of an aspect, once so idolized, faintly blooming on the beauteous countenance; and while I held the precious gift to my fond conflicting bosom, vowed never to reveal the secret of its illustrious origin, till its mother's claims could be established beyond contravention or dispute.—Alas! the fortunate era is not yet arrived when such a discovery can be made to any advantage. My child is no more—my unworthy consort——Catherine, when I first arrived at this den of horrors, they told me that my smiling darling had fallen into the hands of its murderous parent, and that his——Oh God! his impious hands were imbrued in his offspring's blood!——

"There needed not this to unsettle my burning brain! No, it could scarcely stand against the trials I was exposed to from fraternal affection! Dear Stanislaus! how vain were thy pleadings, thy suggestions, thy threats!—I must change the subject.

"Could it, Catherine, be supposed that, in a situation which so greatly detracted from virgin dignity, Sir Gormund Gottsler could renew his detestable addresses, or that I could be made to tremble at the menaces he had used when informed of my repeated and scornful refusal? But my spirit was bent by misfortune, and the cruel doubts under which I continued to labour.

"Again the summer spread its rapid but short-lived beauties over the softened earth, and again the festive preparations were resumed at Court for the long-protracted marriage.—'Now then,' I cried to my infant darling, 'thy mother's fame shall be cleared, and thy rights established. Into thy neglectful father's hands will I deliver thy pleading softness; let him but own his child, and all her mother's wrongs shall be forgotten.'

"At this time my brother's unceasing importunities took another turn. He had even identified the object of my disgrace, and threatened to pursue him with unceasing vengeance, unless he would make an honourable reparation. Worn out with incessant interrogatories, I faintly, once for all, assured him he was mistaken in his conjectures; that the time was at hand when my sullied name should be restored to its original purity, and his infant niece rescued from the cloud which then obscured her innocence. But this assurance was ineffectual, and I quitted his presence with a sentiment of disgust.

"Refreshed by the cheering warmth of noon, I stepped into a garden that branched from my brother's house, among the banks of a sheltered lake. It was a spot I had frequently visited since the excessive cold had subsided, and usually walked under a high yew-hedge, which fenced off the chilling blast. The solemn stillness that reigned in this lonely place restored my tranquillity, and I wept with a secret complacency; till hearing several voices behind the hedge, among which I could distinguish that of my babe's nurse, I stood in anxious suspense, till the sound grew fainter, as if removed to a farther distance. The incident was trifling, yet I continued to listen; till, shocked beyond description by the piercing cries of an infant, I ran to a gate which opened to the road, and saw a man struggling to take my blessed darling from the arms of Christina, my confidential friend.

'Monster!' I cried, and darted forward with the utmost velocity, 'touch not my infant! spare, Oh spare my little blossom!'

"Tiger-hearted and unfeeling, the wretch obtained his horrid purpose, and Christina fell helpless and exhausted. I then made the neighbouring woods resound with my exclamations, still following, still raving: my strength and speed seemed supernatural. I thought not of Stanislaus—I thought not of my own danger in plunging into woods of so vast an extent, and so thickly planted, that they shut out the bright noon-day beams—I thought only of a tender, delicate, helpless creature, feebly struggling in the infernal gripe of some agent of hell!

"For some minutes he eluded my sight; but Oh, the transport when, turning an angle formed by a vast oak, I discovered my precious treasure in its rugged nurse's arms, and smiling sweetly on his hideous countenance! Nature was now exhausted; I held out my eager arms, and sunk insensible at the villain's feet!

"No wonder my exertions were suspended, since I have reason to think that part of the forest was twelve long miles from the garden, or that my senses were overpowered for more than four hours; as the first object I remember upon my revival, was a sloping sunbeam which, darting from beneath some tall firs, streamed upon my sleeping cherub's cheek. It was some minutes before I could arrange my ideas, or rise from the ground. My limbs felt sore and contracted, my feet smarted excessively, and an universal shivering seized my whole frame. However, I crept to my babe, and took it without resistance from the man who was sitting beneath the oak.

"Nature now demanded its rights. The little creature awoke; and, too much fluttered to dread the consequence, I gave it the sustenance it eagerly sought. While thus employed, I turned my heavy eyes to another quarter of the wood, when they encountered the tremendous figure of Sir Gormund Gottsler. Oh what an allay to maternal ecstacy was his appearance!—I clasped my infant still more strongly to my heaving bosom, as if I dreaded some fresh violence, and looked with a piteous expression towards the Knight. He was soon before me, and seemed astonished at the strange encounter, while my rough companion, rising suddenly, offered to escape; but the strong grasp of Sir Gormund prevented him, and addressing me—'Why, Lady,' he cried, 'do I find you so far from home, and thus accompanied? Who is this fellow? He cannot be a serving man!'

'He is equally unknown to me,' I faintly answered, 'and has drawn me to this distance in pursuit of my child, whom he took by force from its attendant.'

'Yes,' said the fierce German, 'I know his errand—aye, and his employer also!—But you are free, Lady, and this harmless infant too,' taking the happy innocent from my feeble arms; 'I will protect the offspring of the diabolical N——.'

"Catherine, this bold intruder understood my long concealed secret; he knew the origin of my sorrow, and yet he dared insult me with his nauseous love; and placing himself on the grass, began to renew his former detestable proposals.

"How could I preserve my senses amidst the horrors of that

moment? yet they did not forsake me; but I could not speak—I could only look my abhorrence of his conduct, and strive to take the little smiler. Oh, can I ever forget the terror of my soul, when, drawing back—'No, Lady,' said he, 'it is my turn now to make conditions:—enough has Sir Gormund Gottsler submitted to fantastic insolence, and there is only one method left of conciliating my revenge. Consent this night to accompany me to Gottsler Castle, and your child shall be, next to its still adored mother, my dearest concern:—nay, lay aside these frantic airs; behold those men in whose custody I have left the wretch you seem so much to dread—they are my attendants:—you have none, wretched Lady!'—(I had none indeed!)—'they shall be your's, if——'

"He might have said more, but I had ceased to hear; and the night was nearly closed before I again recovered to distracted recollection. The first words I heard were 'Bear her off—it is dangerous to continue any longer in the forest!'

'But my child, my child!' I exclaimed, 'where is the object of my hopes, my joys, my all?'

'She is safe, Lady; but we shall not be so in this resort of wolves and bears.'

"I looked wildly round—the strange man was lulling her again in his arms.

'Give her to her agonized mother!' I madly exclaimed; and was springing forward to take her when Sir Gormund interposed.

'You know my resolution:—this man is an agent of a cruel monster who seeks an innocent's life;—more still, he, the noble N——, understands you have deceived him—that the child is not his; but that, dazzled by the hope of enjoying splendour to which you have no right, you are waiting to throw this obstacle in the way of his marriage;—thus instructed, he means not to return till you and the poor infant are effectually removed. Now then the alternative is only this—whether you will become the envied bride of Sir Gormund Gottsler, and bring the little stranger forward with every advantage, or part with it now and for ever? No more of these pretended deliriums!'—for I had sunk at his knees, which shrunk from the eager grasp,—'consider well before you decide!'

"I then stretched my arms towards the child, who was immediately delivered to me; I gazed on its cold pale face, and again lifted my eyes to Sir Gormund, when a sudden exclamation of—'This way—I have found them!' put a final end to the contest.

'Will you consent?' cried my dreadful assailant.

'Never,' replied my indignant soul, which sprung to my convulsed lips. That *never* was the fiat not to be repealed; and my blessed babe was torn from its shrieking, helpless mother!

* * * * *

"They told me, on my arrival at this gloomy prison, that I had demanded my murdered child—that I had accused the Lady Abbess of detaining its little corse, and that I frequently fancied it was present, would talk to it, admire its beauties, and then lament its death. Alas! I knew nothing of all this:—it might be so; but from a computation of time, I guess three months must have passed, unknown and unacknowledged, by me; and when my feeble optics could bear a ray of light, I used to turn aside, melt into tears, and try to shrink from observation.—But even this comparative comfort was soon denied me, and my company was requested in the parlour.

"As the little room I so long occupied, was remarkable for nothing but its plain and cold appearance, I could not give the slightest guess at my situation; but, upon descending a narrow stone staircase, from the walls of which appeared yawning chasms that opened on one of the dilapidated rooms below, I discovered in the dismal recess several niches filled with rude effigies of saints, and other tokens of a monastical residence.

"My soul shrunk from the suspicion this appearance conveyed, and I entered the parlour a prey to fearful surmises and perplexing doubts; but there every certainty of my mournful fate was immediately established:—the grate—the church beyond—the veiled attendants—and their haughty Superior, who, lolling upon a couch, appeared not to notice my tottering steps and enfeebled frame, as I was supported through the room, gave my senses an inconceivable shock; and, casting a wild and helpless look at the portentous objects, they settled for a moment on the stately dame; till, unable to bear the images of despair and desolation which crowded on my weakened brain, I had my face in her hallowed robe, and relapsed into one of those gloomy fits, which had so recently been the consequence of my poignant sorrows.

"I was afterwards told that St. Frances, this holy Abbess, drew the sacred garment from my convulsed grasp, as if polluted by the touch of wretchedness, and rising suddenly, left my insensible form upon the floor. This was probably the case, as my face had received a violent bruise, which the poor Nuns said was owing to its striking against a stone bench, near which their Superior sat.

"A little revived by their civil attentions, I found myself enabled to listen to a pompous eulogium made by Mother St. Frances upon the happiness of those who had escaped the contagion of a wicked world, and what advantages might accrue even to the fallen sister, who had resolution to seek in the Holy Church protection and refuge from farther evils. I looked upon the surrounding auditors, nor saw one countenance on which the pious assertions were engraved: a cold formality, or listless inattention, served, as I truly imagined, as necessary substitutes for the marks of disgust and impatience, which they dared not exhibit.—Poor patient sufferers! I have since wondered at your quiet submission and uniform obedience to that child of the devil, and yet my sufferings exceeded your's! and yet I was forced to acknowledge her turbulent authority. Alas, Catherine! what were my sensations when the Abbess concluded her formal address with a more pointed reference to its devoted object!—Coarse were the flowers of rhetoric she culled to pervert the judgment; for, observing my extreme dejection, and evident dislike to her discourse, she threw into her forbidding aspect a haughty severity, and—'Here,' cried the unfeeling woman, 'here is a proof of the wickedness of human nature left to its own crooked bias! Bred up in the lap of luxury, and suffered to run wild in the garden of wantonness, is it to be wondered at if the sweet blossom of unsullied virtue should droop and perish before the glaring beams of shameless sensuality?'

'Woman!' I hastily said, 'is it me upon whom you bestow these horrid observations? Am I the subject of aspersions which reflect neither candour nor delicacy upon their gross inventor?'

"Oh Catherine! I have neither patience nor memory to repeat the furious aspirations of her provoked spirit; but as if she had discovered that vulnerable spot in the maternal heart which gangrenes at the slightest touch, she suddenly stopped in the midst of a bitter invective, and smiled—(Oh may I never see such a demoniac expression upon the human countenance again)!—yes, she smiled upon her trembling victim, and regulating the tones of her voice to that expression,—'You are offended, my poor child,' said this fiend of darkness, 'at my honest hints of your disorderly conduct, and style yourself a virtuous wife and tender mother. Now let us take a view of your claims to those sacred characters; but remember I will not be interrupted.'

"'Too much exhausted to oppose or even reply, I suffered her to proceed.

'It is now more than two months since a noble Knight arrived at Telga, and requested admission for a lady, who meant, when able, to become one of our order. I demanded her name and character; he refused both with an invidious smile, till finding me resolute, he mentioned you as a frail wanton, whose friends had delegated him to guard you hither; that your senseless situation was owing to the exertions you had made to preserve the life of an infant, whose birth——'

'The life said you, dearest Madam?' I cried, for this unexpected revival of my heart's deepest anguish created a power to reply which nothing else could have done; and throwing my helpless frame before her—'Say but that its precious life is safe, and I will worship the blessed creature that relieves my agonized heart!'

'Still weak, still attached to criminal pleasures, how can I answer a soul so immersed in sensual gratifications?'

'Holy Heaven!' answered I, 'is the indulgence of the purest, the chastest affection a mortal can encourage, subject to such a vile construction? But my child—speak, holy Abbess!—(Alas! how was my spirit humbled!)—Oh tell me if I shall again clasp its little frame—again whisper to its unconscious smiles a father's infidelity—a mother's sorrow!'

'Profane not these sacred walls with language such as this, nor ask impossibilities!'

'Tell her the truth, reverend Mother,' cried an artful Priest who stood near the horrid Abbess; 'she will then turn her thoughts to religious consolation.'

"Ah! what a groan burst from my tortured bosom at this request.

'My child is murdered—Ah wretch, my babe is murdered!' cried the maddening mother, 'and I am bid to seek for consolation.'

'Yes, earthly-minded woman! she is sacrificed by the royal N——, whom you sought to deceive. Provoked by your obstinacy, the noble Sir Gormund Gottsler gave into the hands of the emissary of an injured Prince the spurious darling, and——'

"To all I have hitherto written, my aching sense bears painful testimony; but this confirmation so horrible, so artfully detailed, mixed with the cruellest sarcasms and hypocritical pretences to our Church's honour, who could have borne it as I did? Alas! I remember no more! The little world of cruelty, hypocrisy, and defamation which then contained your ruined friend, sunk from her weakened sight, and weeks of peaceful insensibility succeeded the excruciating interview.

"As soon as reason again illumined the horrors of my situation, I felt them all consolidated in one terrible pang: betrayed and deserted by an unfaithful husband—a source of grief and shame to my noble brother—the declared object of a worthless Knight's ungenerous passion and furious revenge! Still one faint hope had sustained my drooping heart; but that soon sunk beyond retrieval. Even doubt, painful as it generally is, admits some ray of light to a creature benighted in the dark mazes of a dreadful uncertainty. This doubt, which at intervals became a cherished idea, was totally destroyed by the officious repetition of my darling's fate, and that fate involved, nay swallowed up, every other sorrow.

"I could not be blind to the doom intended me. I saw in every face the hated expectation that another victim was preparing for the altar of tyrannic superstition; but I made no opposition, nor yet did I join in their cold and tedious ceremonies. Listless, inattentive, and fearless of that storm of reproaches my conduct produced, a vacant look or bitter sigh was my only answer. The dress they gave me, which was grey for a Novitiate, the veil white, and the whole appearance somewhat more lively than that worn by the professed, were my constant habit. But my behaviour indicated nothing of the pious intentions of those who wear it. They styled me impious, because I confessed not crimes which I had ever abhorred; they accused me of heretical depravity in not paying adoration to the senseless wood, or polished stone: but they saw not the deep devotion of the worshipping heart; no merit was allowed to the still small voice that preferred its pious petition in continual mental exercises, nor limits its holy breathings to the dropping beads, and observance of ostentatious pageantry.

CHAPTER V.

"Pity, like a new-born babe,
Striding the blast, or Heaven's cherubim hors'd
Upon the sightless coursers of the air,
Shall blow the horrid deed in every eye,
Till tears shall drown the wind."

SHAKESPEARE.

"DOST thou not repent, dear Catherine, that wish thy lovely eye has oft confessed, to know the secret grief that gives such inconsistency of looks, expressions, and actions,—and art thou not wearied with the same dull tale of miseries? If so, close up the packet, my friend, for more remains than yet has met thine eye. But I see displeasure tinge thy youthful cheek at what the ardent spirit of friendship will term ungenerous.

"Hitherto thou hast beheld me too deeply struck to reflect upon my strange and dangerous situation; but respited by some artful policy from perpetual teazings, and suffered to think and act with tolerable freedom, I began to advert to the legality of my confinement. The motives of my being brought to the Convent, and the consequence of being immured for the remainder of a hated life, without one earthly source of consolation, and the spirit which once was irrepressible, again suggested a resentful investigation of this treatment. Was there a species of violence I could not complain of? An infant torn from the maternal bosom, and unequivocally doomed to death!—an infringement of all laws civil and religious, in forcing me to remain in a place to which I was carried helpless and insensible!—not permitted to offer the smallest objection to the future disposal of my person!—Surely, I argued, some nefarious enemy to my peace has followed a regular system of cruelty, of which this is to be the climax!

"It remained only, therefore, to give this ideal monster existing reality, nor was that long wanting; for in consequence of a request which, when made by Mother St. Frances, was in reality a command, to attend her in the parlour, I quietly descended, when, to my utter astonishment, I saw her in close conference with Sir Gormund Gottsler, who was seated on the other side of a large open grate, erected in the modern style, and which divided the room for the purpose.

"But why do I describe a prison to you so well known? How instantaneous did the idea of those sorrows he had forwarded, crowd to my soul!—Catherine, I saw him in the act of seizing my child, of tearing her from her supporter and protector!—I saw him even attempting to assassinate the guilty N——! His sight was detestable, but I was yet to endure it.

'Daughter,' cried my haughty jaileress, 'here is a friend!'—(A fiend, Catherine, she should have said)—'the valiant Knight who brought you hither. Approach, and give him welcome.'

"I did approach, but the calm indignation of conscious innocence was denied. A burning blush rushed into my pallid cheek; every pulse throbbed with excessive resentment, and in the Abbess's wondering eye I saw my own intemperate manner acknowledged. Alas! I could not speak, but dared to seat myself beside St. Frances. She reddened at the liberty; I was near the grate, and Sir Gormund, pressing his fingers between the bars, caught my hand, which he would have carried to his lips.

'Proud woman,' he cried, as I snatched it from him, 'art thou yet not humbled?'

'Humbled by thee, miscreant!' said I, in a weak fluttered accent, and again stopped. He glanced at the Abbess, who understood the deep signal.

'It is unnecessary, daughter,' cried the holy hypocrite, 'to make *me* a witness to the impious ebullitions of an untamed spirit. I had hoped that, mortified by the length and severity of a salutary punishment,'—(Wretch! she pitied not the miserable mother)—'you would have embraced a life of penitence and utter seclusion; but since your contumacious behaviour threatens the peace of our community, we must no longer suffer the contagion of example. The world and all its sinful allurements are again offered to your notice: to-morrow you may quit these holy abodes of piety, and renew the indulgence of those vicious propensities, that render your society so dangerous to the pious Sisterhood.'

"She ceased; but her permission to depart so sweetened the cruel language in which it was conveyed, that I forgot to resent where there was so much to rejoice at.

'But the terms, devout Mother,' observed Gottsler, 'they yet remain to be explained?'

'That task I leave in better hands. Farewel, Sir Knight! The bell is ringing for vespers. This erring child may well be spared from every sacred duty.'

"This said, she arose, and met four Nuns with lamps, which they bore before her to the chapel; while I continued seated in an agony superior to any I felt from uncertainty.

"At last Sir Gormund broke the ominous silence.—'Are you displeased, fair lady, with the prospect of re-entering that world, where beauty such as your's is so rarely to be met with?'

"He spoke as if he thought the vanity of happy youth had not received its rising blow. I noticed not the fulsome panegyric, but collecting all the fortitude my wasted spirits could produce, asked in a tone as cold, as haughty, and as severe as his absent partner in iniquity had assumed, what *she* meant by naming *terms*, intimating that there were none which involved *his* interest that could influence *me*. I added, there were terms indeed which, if necessary to my emancipation, would confine me for life at Telga—Oh how thankful I felt for being thus collected!

'The terms, Lady,' he quickly answered, 'are these—to depart with me this night, and become the bride of Sir Gormund Gottsler.'

"Vain man! how he drew up while pronouncing the mighty name! This was exactly what I expected, and it required no comment; but, rising hastily, I was leaving the room, when, raising his voice,—'What,' cried the torturer, 'have you no curiosity—no wish to hear the mysteries of the last six months elucidated? Is that haughty heart dead even to the memory of N——, and the once loved infant you so greatly mourned?'

"I sat down again; my blood rushed to my fluttered heart, which could hardly sustain the beating tide. Oh, what a string he touched!——But, my dear Catherine, in this part of my story I must be brief. There is no relating the horrid tale with the calmness necessary to give it perspicuity and probability.—A friendly Sister, to whom I have given the papers to arrange respecting this final explanation, has written what you will next read.

"Sir Gormund Gottsler acquainted my unfortunate companion that, instigated by her cruel husband, he made her the offers she so frequently refused, and that the scheme of enticing her to the wood in pursuit of her child, was planned by them both, in the hope that maternal tenderness would induce her to close with those proposals which would evidently have preserved its life. But, irritated by her obstinacy, he took advantage of the false alarm, and her helpless state, and witnessed the death of her innocent, who was strangled by the monster's hands that first bore it away; that he sent word immediately to its father, and putting her into a litter that waited at the edge of the forest, conveyed her by slow marches to Sweden, in all which time the unhappy lady seemed totally lost to recollection, or any sense of the miseries she had endured. He then unfeelingly told her it was the Prince's settled determination, if she came not from Telga as Sir Gormund's wife, to prevent her return to the world, by forcing her to accept the veil; and concluded by once more offering himself to her acceptance.

"Our poor Sister heard this cruel detail in perfect silence, nor gave any other tokens of attention than by frequent shudderings as he dwelt upon the massacre of a harmless babe, or the barbarous triumph of its merciless father; when, finding he could gain no answer to this last stroke of wickedness, he arose, saying—'The Prince should be informed of her impolitic rejection, which would only strengthen his aversion to one who vainly attempted to combat his interest and affection, since neither of them was then within the reach of her arts.—'And indeed,' added the horrid designer, 'if beauty even superior to that I now behold,' bowing with a sarcastic respect, 'can keep a heart which Queens have contended for, his happiness must be fully complete. I yesterday beheld the Royal pair, and was by my enraptured friend introduced to this blazing beauty, when N——, with conscious triumph, whispered—'Thinkest thou, Sir Gormund, thy Prince can envy thee the bride thou hast chosen?'—Alas, Lady! my heart was steeled, and that he knew.

"The dear sufferer could hear no more; but faintly crept to her mournful cell, nor ever saw him afterwards.

* * * * *

"No, Catherine, that horror has been spared me. Never have I since beheld the wretch who could so deliberately, so frigidly sport with feelings his unmanly bosom could not value. In all this inhuman representation, one improbability struck me, which was the strange confidence so suddenly placed in a wretch who had so recently attempted the life of N—— at the tournament; but who can answer for the coalitions formed by guilty creatures? Might not the forgiveness of that cowardly attempt be the pay of such atrocious services. Be all this as it may, I was the sacrifice.—Barbarous coalition! infernal demons! how have ye wantonly sported with the peace, the honour, the tenderest and purest gratifications of a harmless creature! Where could a female be found so competent to the completion of the wicked *trio* as she with whom so much of my wretched life has been wasted? And yet the utmost exertion of barbarous despotism has hitherto failed of the one great and proposed end, since, wonderful to say! I have so long outlived the galling sufferings they jointly imposed.

"Catherine the attempt was useless:—yes, my pen had traced scenes equal to that from which I shrunk.—My companion's trouble might have been spared, since the tragedy of my life, from its first inflictions, is replete with horrors; but somehow I wished to shun just then a repetition of the anguish my soul endured when told of——Oh bursting heart! thy wounds now bleed afresh!—Before me lie the papers on which I sketched the terrifying features of that deadly scene! Sister Mary has left them on my desk—that desk is my coffin! Thou knowest, good Catherine, one of the rules of our order is, to have the solemn receptacle placed at the foot of our mattress, its lid adorned with a scull, crucifix, and cross-bones.

"I must hasten to a period; but will first say that my kind transcriber had formerly been a painful witness to the cutting reproaches heaped upon me by St. Frances, and heard enough at those times to make what she saw of my unconnected story no secret to her.———

"And now what remains of this dismal proof of human endurance, but to say that my conflict with St. Frances, succeeding my contemptuous conduct to Sir Gormund, was dignified with a spirit on my side equal to her own. Alas! it was five days before I was sufficiently restored, to be thought capable of bearing further trials; for, like the diabolical inquisitors of the southern world, they suffered me to enjoy a respite from actual tortures. Alas! are not those of the mind equally galling with corporeal ones? and if not materially, do they not as truly exist, and produce consequences as terrible?

"But to avoid digression.—Insensible to present pain, I was permitted, like those sufferers, the indulgence of a sad interval, possibly to increase new pangs by the renewal of past torments.

"On the sixth day of my confinement, the Abbess entered the chamber. I had regained a calm and clear recollection, and found myself enabled to determine positively against either of the alternatives formerly proposed;—but I was soon too fatally convinced no choice was left; for, disappointed and enraged at my determined refusal of Sir Gormund's addresses, which, judging by my hatred of her house, she falsely supposed would be received with gratitude, her rage was boundless.—Worldly-minded woman! I well knew her motives for wishing to part with one whose loss, as a Sister of that order, would be doubly compensated by a private compact.

"To describe the violence of her soul when I absolutely refused to be professed, is beyond the power of my pen; and to explain the various means of punishment she used to complete her mercenary purposes, would only add to the pain this long and incoherent account has already inflicted on thy susceptible heart. Much as I had endured, it required still more mortification to bend my inflexible resolution; till, weakened and exhausted by monastic rigours, which extended even to merciless flagellations, I was dragged to the altar an unopposing, though unwilling, victim. No forms of sumptuous ceremonies gave the hated sacrifice a tempting appearance—nothing of the grandeur common to the professions I had several times attended, marked my forced resignation;

not a creature, excepting our own people, was seen in the church. No joyful anthem, or rapturous strain, burst from the pealing organ, or harmonious voice. When I advanced, or rather when I was dragged, to the sacred altar, one harsh, unvaried note sounded its deepest base from the swelling instrument, which was accompanied by the rough unmusical tones of discontented Monks, who terrified rather than supported my sinking spirits by the denunciations those tones seemed to convey to my fainting heart.

Soon the hated pall was thrown upon a creature, whose only hope was death and eternal peace; and in wrapping it about my prostrate form, I felt as if it shut out every endearing relative affection.

"From this period, Catherine, for fate had done its worst, I resigned myself to the most gloomy despair. Even the influences of religion in a house where I saw its purest essence profaned or mocked, were too faint to dispel that torpidity of the soul. No, the favourable smile of true piety irradiated not our gloomy cells;—often have I heard the choral anthem, which from the distant chapel swelled into ecstatic harmony—often have I heard it sink into the low repining tones of discontent, and sighs, perhaps groans, of anguish succeeded the lofty expression of assumed devotion.—Observe, that I never once sanctioned the violence committed upon free-will by joining the Nuns in any part of their worship.———

"Only one observation more.—You wished me to receive the royal Blanch. Catherine, accuse not the poor Alexa of obstinacy, but judge her candidly.

"There was a time when, favoured by that gracious Princess, I passed some happy months in her society, previous to her marriage with the hated Christian. She honoured me with a confidence I could not return; and after my cruel misfortunes commenced, I never saw her benign countenance.—At the first mention of her name, my delighted heart seemed to regain its long-lost powers of enjoyment, and the sight of a former friend I thought would restore some feeling to my frozen bosom; but thus criminated, thus deeply laden with censures I know not how to disprove, would it be prudent to renew a friendship that had virtue for its foundation? Oh no—no—no!—Let me and my misfortunes sink in peaceful oblivion, without exciting compassion that cannot heal, or raising remembrances calculated but to inflame!—And here thou mayst naturally ask, why, since liberty, and the powers of seeking evidence are granted to me, to prove, or rather disprove, the vile assertions of my enemies—why I do not permit some investigation to be made?—The reason follows:—from what I have the strongest motives to imagine, it appears that the perjured N—— has long since made another choice, whose interest I do not now even wish to supplant, therefore have made no enquiries into his situation.

"I have since heard that Sir Gormund has met with a retributive reward for his deliberate cruelty, in the very forest where he so unfeelingly witnessed my darling infant's sacrifice; for being on a journey from Stockholm to Hamburg, the season, which set in unusually severe, had operated so sharply on the half-famished wolves, that on his travels through that horrid forest, they seized upon the horse he rode, and happening, in the rage of famine, to tear his leg, were so gratified with the taste of human blood, that the wretched mortal, deserted by his attendants, who fled from the fierce assailants, fell an immediate prey to their devouring hunger.

"Deprived then of a witness so consequential, supposing he could have been wrought on, (and that supposition his own vile conduct forbids, for in attesting my innocence he must have criminated himself), how else could I have cleared my sullied fame?—deprived then, I repeat, of this evidence, where was I to seek redress?—My brother—No—his interference—ah Catherine! there is a mournful reason why his interference is useless. Had indeed the precious child survived—could I look on its innocent countenance pleading for the sacred rights of an injured heir to its father's glory—could I then have sat in silent apathy, nor stirred heaven and earth to defend its claims, what is there within the scope of human probability that should have prevented my endeavours to restore her virtuous title to honourable notice?—Yes, to the ends of the habitable globe should my search have been extended for champions in such a cause!

* * * * *

"Catherine, there is an image occasionally passing its faint traces over my desultory mind respecting *thee*—something of thy contributing to my sufferings!—Cruel suspicion! unworthy the gentle creature to whom I write! and yet if my eager fancy chose to form similitudes where none really existed, it was foolish, very foolish; but it accounts for my strange conduct. Even now I could almost weep at the precious idea that the eye, the lip, the brow——

"Another thing too I sometimes dwell on. Did I not in one of my painful reveries speak of the royal Blanch, as if she had visited me since my calamity? Alas! no, Catherine, believe it not—cast not away one thought upon my contradictory manner while at Telga—think no more of it, as thou valuest the poor Alexa——Oh that name! how it seems to draw my thoughts from a world which yet contains some valuable objects, and brings again to my disgusted view that tremendous moment when, shrouded with the spreading pall, I was called upon by that new title, and summoned to the awful consideration that, at the foot of the sacred altar, I must forswear the pomps, the vanities, the criminalities of a wicked world!——Hateful hypocrisy! under what various descriptions have I noticed thy subtile operations! The cowl, the courtier's dress, the veil, or helmet, all in turn have distinguished thy votaries!

* * * * *

"Only a few words more.—Dost thou remember when, urged by pity for my sad misfortunes, it was the wish of that tender heart to have St. Alexa mentioned to Queen Blanch, and that I suddenly overcame my reluctance to that step?—Ah, Catherine! she knew not the name of thy friend; for I recollected that none but my enemies, and the inmates of St. Frances acknowledged me by that title.—And now let me entreat that this unconnected history of my wrongs, my griefs, my injured affections may be confined to thy dear bosom; for although thou canst not be the *daughter*, I am sure thou art the friend, of St. Alexa.

* * * * *

"At length the tedious task is finished! Farewel, Oh most beloved!—and when a sigh shall issue to the remembrance of the sainted Sigismunda, let that of St. Alexa be united with it."

CHAPTER VI.

"Peace, child of Grief! nor task Almighty Power,
Lest you offend in your despair. The cloud
Which overwhelms you with its gloom, may break
In blessings."

MACKENZIE.

IN St. Alexa's statement of her motives for permitting Catherine to mention her to the Queen, she had forgot that she had more than once mentioned her real Christian name, or that in so frequently naming the Princess of Saxe Gotha, she had hazarded her secret; but the error was inconsequential, since there were events sufficiently striking in the former part of her history to ascertain her identity to Blanch, had that error been spared.

With a burst of anguish, superior to any Catherine had ever known, she fervently repeated—"The daughter of St. Alexa—yes, dear unhappy being, I am thy daughter:—in vain dost thou conceal the revered name of Marienburg, while that of Stanislaus is so unaccountably dwelt upon.—Dear blessed Lady!" addressing the weeping Queen, in whose presence she had concluded the melancholy manuscript, "relieve the pangs of filial tenderness! Say, for sure you know, is not this sweet complainer the parent of your wretched Catherine? Oh yes, I see it in that overflowing eye. Too justly indeed did she attribute to me much of the sufferings of twenty years: my birth produced accumulated sorrows,—my supposed death gave them their highest poignancy,—and now, at the very instant which offers a large amends for past miseries, she flies the child so vainly lamented! But who can be the author of her present as well as past agonies?—Can there exist a man so lost to every tender feeling of the heart?"

"No, dear Catherine," replied her pitying companion, "a dreadful mystery still hangs over some parts of her story. It is impossible that a husband so ardent—a person so accomplished, should all at once assume a character which barbarians would blush to bear. I, as well as you, am much puzzled to account for the motive which induced my poor friend to leave her residence, as well as astonished at the opinion she has taken up respecting your father."

"Father!" repeated the agitated girl, "Oh sweet and venerable sound!—Then the noble Blanch does confirm the presumptuous opinion I entertain?"

"I do, my dear, and, prior to my reception of these papers, had founded a suspicion even of the person of your mother's Prince, which, I am concerned to say, is utterly destroyed by an assertion contained——"

"Contained—on whom, Madam?" cried the gasping Catherine; "say, revered lady, on whom did that suspicion fall?"

Blanch shook her head; the answer which came prompt to her tongue, comprised volumes of intelligence, but prudence withheld it. She had indeed, from several circumstances, collected hopes which she earnestly wished St. Alexa's communication might strengthen: for the present, however, those hopes were overthrown; and, accustomed to the Queen's laconic manner of denial where acquiescence would be improper, Catherine submitted to the rejecting motion, and that part of their conversation was immediately dropped.

The next subject of discussion was to search for the unhappy fugitive, and the good, the friendly Conan was named by his trusting ward as extremely adequate to the undertaking. Happy to be of any use to his favourite, and flattered by the confidence of her royal friend, Von Hemert directly obeyed the summons, and received from Blanch every intelligence her own private idea of this business furnished. To him she scrupled not to name her former reasons for identifying Catherine's father, but Conan, as well as herself, rejected this notion, when told of that Prince's former situation; however, the grand object at present was to recover the wandering mother, when it was to be presumed every elucidation she could give would follow of course, since the character of herself, and establishment of her daughter, would undoubtedly be her highest consideration.

We have hinted, in Catherine's interview with Mary Skelm, that she had reason, from that communication, to suppose herself derived from a Prince illustrious as him so warmly suspected by the good Marienburg.

Nothing was wanting but the name of this Prince, whose dominions she was told formed a part of Germany; and at the very moment that his title hung on Mary's trembling lip, the awful voice of Magnus arrested its progress, and the old woman's consequent delirium preserved the secret. Now that her mother's narrative presented another clue to it, Catherine employed herself in comparing the different accounts she had heard, and nothing but her dread of offending Blanch prevented her disclosing her suspicions.

During events so important to the present peace and future situation of this child of mystery, she forgot not the sweet delusive hope which her admired Gustavus unknowingly strengthened by the suavity of his disposition, his gentle manners, and evident attention to Catherine, when suddenly that hope seemed to lose its entire foundation. A cold and melancholy demeanour marked the Monarch's succeeding interview; nay, she fancied a somewhat of disgust appeared in his notice of her. Heavy sighs, hesitating language, followed by an abrupt departure, filled her heart with anguish, and her eyes with tears. His visits, which had been frequent, and upon the most friendly footing, now seldom occurred, and when they did, were short and silent.

Blanch saw and regretted the mysterious change, although in Catherine's absence nothing of his former manner seemed wanting; but tenacious of the honour of her young companion, and anxious to discover a motive for this conduct in one, who was above the littleness of caprice, and the starts of passion, she took occasion to mention that poor child's present inquietude, caused by her uncertainty respecting her mother's fate and father's identity; and delicately observed, "that in such a state every seeming neglect was set down as real; it should, therefore, be her study to make up every relative deficiency by increasing tenderness."

Gustavus heard her in strict silence, when, suddenly starting, as if touched obliquely by this hint, he arose, took several turns along the hall, and then seated himself again. At last—"You are my well-wisher, noble lady," he cried; "you have wept the sorrows of poor Sigismunda, and I know any thing relative to her will pain your friendly soul: if any thing in my conduct to her cousin has favoured of coldness, let this be my excuse."

He then drew out a small packet from his bosom, and giving it to the Queen, who was astonished at the singular address—"Read this, royal Blanch," said he, "and you will be amazed at the contents."

Blanch received the paper with a trembling hand, while Gustavus softly withdrew. It was addressed to "Gustavus Ericson, the deliverer of Sweden," and exhibited the following contents.

"In obedience to the commands of a dear deceased parent, Sigismunda Marienburg resigned the choicest, nay, the only hope which sweetened existence. Those commands were given when sprightly youth, adoring love, and expectations of future grandeur made a compliance with them beyond measure difficult; but even then I did comply with them, and Gustavus censured the coldness of a heart that beat in unison with his own.

"Yes, dear possessor of my virgin affections, the first, last, and only conqueror of that heart which never, while pulsation lasts, can know another Lord—now, that approaching death destroys every objection false delicacy would urge against the free confession—now thy Sigismunda can declare without a blush her fond and faithful love.

"Much hast thou done—much suffered for the envied maiden of thy choice, and dearly hast thou proved it; yet, Gustavus, if her influence still continue over that noble soul—if yet you wish to lessen the agonies of a final adieu—if yet thou canst sacrifice a little more to the daughter of thy friend, and would enable her to close her eyes in all the serenity of peaceful submission to Heaven's high will, accede to her dying request:—it is but a little addition to the many obligations thy love has conferred!

"Gustavus! my noble, my inestimable Gustavus!—Oh how my heart responds the endearing title!—you cannot possess the crown of Sweden without a partner. Patriotic, an enthusiastic lover of his country, its glorious Monarch must ensure her privileges by providing for its future welfare, and give to posterity a race of beings, benign, gracious, and valiant as himself. Need I add, you must select a woman whose excellencies of life and manners shall be a surety for the conduct of her successors. If she be possessed of half your virtues, Sweden may glory in her present enjoyments, and equally brilliant prospects.

"It only remains then to identify the object I have chosen, to fill the vacancy Sigismunda Marienburg must soon create in that noble heart. Trust to me, Gustavus; jealous of your honour, proud of the distinction I have so long gloried in, and sensible of the consequences an erroneous choice would produce to the nation and its King, I have been extremely careful to select a proper substitute for your Sigismunda. It is true that superior advantages respecting the blaze of greatness, and the enlargement of power might attend a more splendid election; but if modest worth, an unpresuming sweetness of temper, noble principles, and refined sense are sufficient to constitute the happiness of a Gustavus, then is *Catherine Sleswie* deserving of your acceptance:—yes, my dear Lord, she alone is worthy of your hand; and although comparative obscurity attends her birth, the qualities of her soul give it a brilliance not always the concomitant of high descent. Possibly in this recommendation I may have infringed in some degree a father's wishes, which once extended to a niece of his; but no—recollection assures me that Catherine Sleswie was my father's choice.

"It is all over: this last shock—this unexpected interview severs the feeble bands of existence!—Adieu! I shall never receive the dear confirmation of my soul's last wish."

The Queen, who saw in her royal friend's manner towards Catherine a defeat of the hope she once had fostered, read this wonderful recommendation of that unfortunate maid with a mixture of pity, sorrow, and admiration. It threw a different hue upon the King's behaviour to her. To what both of them understood to be neglect, this paper gave the appearance of tender concern. His silence, thus interpreted, originated with a reluctance to mislead, where he could not encourage; for Gustavus wrongly imagined that Catherine knew of her cousin's request. But when in a conference which immediately followed, Blanch assured him of his mistake, it gave him equal cause for regret and satisfaction. Concerned for the suspicion he had entertained, and pleased to suppose she knew not of Sigismunda's wishes, he then said that this paper was delivered by a special courier from the new Abbess at Telga, who received it, torn and rumpled, from the hands of a boarder that succeeded Miss Marienburg in her apartment, and found it with several writing materials beneath her mattress.

The Queen listened with silent attention to his candid description of feelings still sacred to Sigismunda's memory.

"It would be an injury, Madam," said he, "to that lovely woman, to offer a heart which feels no pleasure equal to that of dwelling upon perfections for ever lost to me. In the hurry of business, in the duties of my station, I feel a temporary refuge from corroding remembrances; but in the hour of domestic retirement, that beloved image returns to memory so sweet, so amiable—Ah, royal Blanch! how can I do violence to the sacred attachment by attempting to introduce another?—Certainly, could I bear to give a moment's consideration to a fresh choice, that choice would fall upon the gentle Catherine, whose misfortunes demand every distinction; but the very idea——Pardon me, lady—I scarcely understand myself, and will only say that every thought, every affection of this wayward heart are still occupied by the cold and humble tomb at Telga."

There was something in this confession, declarative as it was of aversion to marriage, that encouraged a latent hope in the Queen's bosom; but it was too feeble, too transient to bear much comment, or to admit of a partner in it: and Blanch contrived to relieve her young friend's anxiety respecting the King's altered manner, without communicating any part of the contents of Sigismunda's paper, or the conversation to which they gave rise.

In this uncertain way, sometimes elated by a fond presentiment of happier times, sometimes deeply depressed by the dread of new calamity, Catherine passed the days of Von Hemert's absence, when the arrival of a visitor (whose long stay at Stockholm surprised those to whom his secret motives for lingering near that spot were unknown) gave another turn to her ideas; and she felt unusual perturbation when the title of Saxe Lunenburgh was announced.

There was a pensive languor in his countenance, a gentleness of demeanour while addressing her, so unlike his former manners, that she hardly felt more astonished than pleased at the grateful change, till quick-eyed delicacy gave a solution to this behaviour, that furnished her with suspicions of no very pleasant nature. Blanch read in her young friend's countenance the apprehensions she entertained, and almost smiled at her blushing repulse when the Duke would have taken her hand; and she addressed some trifling question to her august visitor, merely to relieve Catherine's fancied distress, which he answered with a sort of distracted inattention, again resuming his fond regards so ungrateful to the subject of them, till the Queen in her own mind acquitted Catherine from any imputation of prudery, while she herself took up an opinion, the very adopting of which crimsoned her own fair cheek with a flush of joy. After two hours passed in silent comments, rapturous attentions, and chilling reserve, a circumstance occurred which banished every sentiment from our heroine's mind that had so recently employed it; and caution, the cold ceremony of distant politeness, with every indication of displeasure, fled at the appearance of a damsel, who informed the Queen that Von Hemert was arrived.

Blanch saw in Catherine's varying cheek the effect of this intelligence, and was rising to receive him in another apartment, when, unacquainted with the exact etiquette of Courts, the good man presented himself at the door of the saloon, where the first object that caught his eye was Saxe Lunenburgh. Confused, and somewhat intimidated, he bent his knee, and would have withdrawn; but he had caught the already overflowing eye of Catherine. She flew towards him, caught his hand, and pressing it to her lips, exclaimed—"My friend, my father, have you succeeded? Is she found—is she safe? Shall I embrace a dear unfortunate——"

"Who found," interrupted the Duke, "Madam," to Blanch, "who has this fair young creature lost?"

"Retire, Catherine," cried the Queen, with a look of evident displeasure, "you are imprudent—I cannot allow of these ungovernable flights: retire with your friend."

"Oh pardon," cried the unhappy lady, "pardon my incautious behaviour! I feel I am wrong—but my heart, my heart will burst with its painful emotions, if not speedily relieved!—Come, dear

Sir, let us obey the Queen; in the next room we will speak of the dear St. Alexa."

"St. Alexa!" repeated Magnus, "who knows aught of St. Alexa? To whom are the repose and safety of St. Alexa dear? But——"

The tear, which rolled along his glowing cheek, the convulsion of his pallid lip, the tremulous motion of his fevered hand, as he pressed the arm of his royal friend, conveyed to that lady suspicions of high import; and after considering for a moment, she entreated the Duke's patience, while she explained a long and circumstantial story. They then reseated themselves, and Blanch was about to begin, when suddenly recollecting *St. Alexa's narrative*, and regardless of her injunctions respecting secrecy, she fetched the consequential deposit, and giving it to the Duke—"Here," she said, "your Highness's curiosity to know the fate of an unfortunate sufferer may be perfectly gratified. St. Alexa was my friend—she is now missing. Could she but be restored, I think almost every wish of her maternal heart may be gratified."

Saxe Lunenburgh, unmindful of the Queen's exordium, had broken the seal; and meeting with the words contained in the envelope, he started, threw his eyes upwards, and then thrusting the papers into his bosom, departed in visible uneasiness.

That there was a mysterious connection between the fates of Magnus and St. Alexa the Queen retained no doubt, but of its true import she was still ignorant. At one period of supposed discovery, she had named Saxe Lunenburgh as the father of Catherine, and husband to her unhappy mother; but this decision eventually disagreed with a circumstance in the manuscript, which pointed to the Princess of Saxe Gotha as the guiltless consort of N——, for under this feigned name St. Alexa chose to shield the real title of him she called her destroyer. Now as Magnus had not wedded another woman, but remained single, it defeated, in some measure, the hope she had formed; nor, although from Conan's information, she felt a detestation of the Duke's conduct to Catherine in Saxony, could the goodness of her disposition forbear to commiserate a man, who must have some great, if not just, reason for terrifying an innocent creature with undeserved threats and menaces.

From these perplexing thoughts she was roused by repeated

sobs from the next apartment; and hastily entering, beheld Catherine reclined on Von Hemert's shoulder.

"Oh madam!" cried the poor girl, "my mother—my beloved mother fled from the author of all her miseries, and that author is—Duke Magnus! He is the father of your honoured Catherine; and this dear mother will not live to clear her own fame, and that of her wretched daughter!—But I will go to her!" and she arose with a wild, impassioned air; "I will attend her with duteous reverence! On this bosom she shall repose her weary head; cheered by the attention of her poor child, she shall yet find some consolation in a world that has treated her so cruelly."

To Conan the Queen looked with mingled surprise and concern for an elucidation of this wonderful business; who perceiving his ward too much exhausted by her own unrestrained grief, gave Blanch a brief recital of the success he had met with, and its consequences.

From this it appeared that Von Hemert's first visit was to the Monastery St. Alexa had quitted, where he received a certain assurance that the object of his search was in a state of debility that rendered it impossible for her to travel far. He was likewise informed of a religious house several miles from Telga, in which there was a probability she might be secreted, as it was particularly adapted for the reception of pilgrims, &c.

Pleased with the prospect of recovering the distressed wanderer, Conan lost no time in fruitless enquiries, but hastened to St. Mary's, as directed by the Abbess of St. Frances. It was situated in a deep vale, enclosed by mountains of a stupendous height, which were clothed from their base, half way up the summits, with trees of the largest growth. The neatness of its aspect, the seclusion of its site, the view of a large and well-defended garden, that spread along the feet of the northern acclivities, formed a striking contrast to the desolated appearance at Telga. Von Hemert beheld it with a secret wish that in a place so well calculated for the repose of a broken spirit, he might meet with the object of his present anxiety.

To his questions respecting the arrival of St. Alexa, the portress gave a confused but rejecting answer; yet with this he could not be satisfied, and the aged sister, perceiving a Nun advancing towards the grate, referred him to her for more decided information. She heard his ardent representation with a sober, collected seriousness, and frankly assured him that no one bearing that name resided there.

"Possibly," said Conan; "but know you of no female stranger entering these walls within the last fortnight?"

"None to whom your presence can be of importance. We have a Nun, it is true, who, disgusted with her former residence, has thought proper to exchange it for our's; but she has no claims upon the world, or the world upon her—in fine, she comes here merely but to die!"

"No claims, Madam! Yes, there are claims which demand her presence! Go, good Sister—say that the dear relative she has never beheld since its infant state, languishes to be received by her; tell this poor mourner—(for I cannot be mistaken in my opinion respecting her)—that Conan Von Hemert brings the happiest tidings her fainting heart can wish. He does not ask her to quit this hallowed retreat—he even rejoices to find she has chosen such an asylum, and engages to keep the place of her seclusion a secret from all she may deem her enemies. Only ask her consent to this request, that she will permit that long-lost, that beloved fair-one to cheer her dreary moments!—You say she bears not the name of St. Alexa:—mention it in her presence—I will abide by the manner in which she hears it. If cold and unmoved, my labour is lost; but if confused and distressed, then I conjure you to plead my cause!"

There was too much apparent sincerity in this representation to fail of success. Simple and guileless herself, the good Nun could not refuse her belief of those qualities existing in another, and immediately departed to forward his petition; but soon returned with an air so awkward, shy, and repulsive, as convinced the disappointed Von Hemert of his mistake.

"I have informed our Sister," she said, "of the nature of your commission; I have even mentioned the name you spoke of, but she refuses to acknowledge any title to it, nor could hear with patience the strange account you charged me with; therefore any farther attempt to disturb the peace of a poor dying invalid will be useless and offensive."

She then motioned to leave the grate, adding—"It is now evening, and our gates will soon be closed. Farewel! May success attend your laudable researches!"

Conan sighed as he quitted the parlour, and thought himself particularly unfortunate in his best endeavours to benefit his fellow-creatures; and as she turned to shut the door, he hastily cried— "One word only!—remember to tell your friend that Conan Von Hemert, the guardian of——" He was going on, when a female figure, whose flowing drapery and fragile form indicated a supernatural appearance, glided towards the grate he was leaving; and sinking on a bench, discovered extreme agitation.

The Nun, by whom she had passed, followed in evident surprise, and silently waited the event of this unexpected scene; till observing her visible anguish, she addressed her by the title of Sister Ignatia, and began to sooth the disturbed Nun. Conan, on whose imagination the truth instantly flashed, caught her hand through the grate, and softly pronounced the name of Catherine. Ignatia started, threw back her veil, and lifting up her humid eyes, seemed as if ejaculating a mental prayer. Again the sweet sound of *Catherine* met her ear.

"Oh tell me," she wildly cried, "where is that lovely creature? My heart forebodes a discovery so rapturous! Tell me, Von Hemert, for I recollect that benevolent countenance—tell me, may I hope to embrace in that dear girl the precious child of misfortune?"

"You may, lady," said the happy Conan; "she waits impatiently to recognise the mother whom, as a stranger, she loved; not only so, but through this revered mother, she hopes to find a——"

"Father, my friend—yes, the painful secret is now no more, and the Duke of Saxe Lunenburgh shall acknowledge his virtuous child, born under the sanction of holy wedlock, and establish her real claims."

To the Sister who, not ten minutes before, had witnessed in that unaccountable stranger an aversion tinged with horror, when told of the enquiries made after her, this sudden change appeared mysterious—almost profane; but the elucidation which immediately followed, quieted the pious recluse's fears, and she silently wondered and adored.

"You know, my good Sister," said St. Alexa, "how desirous I was to be concealed from the notice of every one, and made it a condition of my residence here, to remain uninterrupted in the room set apart for my separate use. You also witnessed my recent terrors when but now informed of this kind friend's solicitations to see me—Alas! I had reason then for the terrors he raised.—'It is Saxe Lunenburgh,' said my affrighted soul, 'the destroyer of his blameless infant—the persecutor of her wretched mother, comes to plant another arrow in her wounded affections!'—Thus thinking, how could I brave the storm from which I had fled? But, impelled by some powerful motive, which seemed to urge me to fly even this asylum, I wildly descended the stairs, and glancing a fearful look towards the parlour, my steps were checked by a glimpse of a person just then turning from the grate; and at that moment the name of Von Hemert struck upon my charmed ear.—'This is no deception,' whispered maternal affection; and with a thousand nameless ideas rushing on my feeble brain, I entered."

Thus far the Duchess's (for so we now must style her) articulation was clear and rapid; but a wasted constitution, and exhausted spirits, made good their claims, and she was borne from her pitying friend, insensible to his good wishes for her recovery.

CHAPTER VII.

> "It cannot be! my senses all deceive me!
> And yet it is! Oh, let me gaze upon thee,
> Recal each trace that marks thee for my own,
> And gives me back the image of my heart!"
>
> WHITEFIELD.

FROM the representation given by Von Hemert of her mother's extreme debility, Catherine deduced a thousand unreasonable fears, and would have quitted Stockholm that very evening, if the Queen's consent could be obtained; but Blanch had meditated the discovery of another joyful event to the impatient maid, which rested on the effect her communication might have on the Duke, whose anxiety she expected would bring him immediately to her for further intelligence.

Catherine wept some passionate tears to this seemingly unreasonable protraction to her happiness, but sent by a courier, which the Queen directly dispatched, every tender and dutiful assurance of the fondest affection, with a promise of attending the Duchess on the following day; for so Blanch permitted her to word this important message.

While the Queen was using her strongest eloquence, and those reasoning powers for which she was peculiarly distinguished, in calming the agitation of her friend, she forgot not to give her opinion respecting Saxe Lunenburgh's supposed ill treatment of his suffering lady, his hatred to Marienburg, and incongruous behaviour to Catherine; and warmly defended his cause, upon the principle of giving credit for innocence, where there existed no actual proof of guilt.

The character of his only accuser was infamous to the last degree; not a movement in the whole machine, which was constructed of hypocrisy and every baleful passion, but what tended to render its every motion suspicious; and whoever calmly viewed the whole tissue of his plots and contrivances, as related in his poor victim's narrative, must, she was well assured, suspect him of still deeper designs than those of forcing her compliance with his base wishes.

Happy to catch at the slightest circumstance that might exonerate a father of such nefarious crimes, his weeping daughter allowed full credit to the Queen's ingenuous statement, and felt a sentiment of duty, if not so sweet and unmixed as that which warmed her heart towards the Duchess, yet it was new, and divested of much of its awe, towards a father whom she already wished to love; and waited impatiently for the moment when she hoped to hear his exculpation from crimes she shuddered to attribute to any one. It seemed as if this was the epocha of every discovery necessary to the restoration of the Duchess's peace, honour, and long-suppressed affections.

We have mentioned that lady's description of the terrible death of Sir Gormund Gottsler in the eventful forest, which prevented every chance of his repentance, or that amends which a consciousness of evil might wring from him, by a full and free confession. Of this misfortune the Duke was aware, who, with a heart enraged beyond the controul of reason, now uttered, as he dwelt upon the shocking pages, the most dreadful execrations against that monster of iniquity, as he styled the Knight—now burst into tears of anguish, as the affecting sufferings of his lawful Duchess met his eye, depicted in all the incoherent language of maddening grief, till at length arriving at the part where she mentions her indifference to promote her usurped claim, unless her child was miraculously to come forward, as the heir of her father's fortunes, he dashed the manuscript from him, clasped his hands in the deepest agonies, exclaiming, with a voice hoarsened by rage,—"Curse upon the villain, whose detestable politics have rooted from a bosom so pure, so tender, so faithful, that interest her wretched husband so long maintained! Cursed be the head that could plan, the heart that could permit, and the hand that could execute such determined cruelties! Why is not the wretch upon earth, to meet from an injured husband the punishment he so well deserved?—Abused Marienburg! soul of honour! how have I pursued thee almost to death!—Angelic Catherina! wife of my first, last, and sole affections! who shall plead my cause with thee?—Alas! will the sweet child——but Oh my distracted brain! where is she?—Lost, murdered—Ha!——"

He then, overcome by excessive mental anguish, darted from the couch on which he had thrown himself, and without attendants, divested too of the formalities of dress, and giving way to the impulse of despair, crossed the hall, determined to overcome every impediment in his way to Blanch's palace, where he rather dreaded, than hoped a still farther elucidation of these horrid events.

It was then nearly dusk;—a mild gloom overspread the cloisters of the great Church, under which he was passing; a holy calm enwrapped the solemn objects on which he cast a transient look, that settled on a dark and slowly moving figure emerging from a low door, leading to a side aisle of the Cathedral. Its height, although diminished by a bend of the shoulders, the groan it uttered as it closed the iron door, its black drapery, and musing melancholy attitude detained for a moment the Duke's haggard eye. It soon advanced, and Magnus discovered a Friar of one of the most rigid orders Stockholm contained. With the unsteadiness of a disturbed imagination, he caught the Friar's cowl as he was unconsciously proceeding.

"Thou art," he cried, "a messenger from God! To thee is given the power of dispensing comfort to the unhappy—say hast thou comfort for me?"

"Comfort!" repeated the Father, "I dispense comfort!"

He ceased, his trembling lips responding in the lowest accents Ave-Marias to the falling beads. There was a solemnity in this holy man's manner that impressed the Duke with a pious awe, and he waited till this little act of devotion was finished, when he resumed the conversation.

"Father," said the distressed Prince, "I am miserable; accused of crimes my soul disdains, suffering under the imputation even of murder—a false friend!"

"Friend," echoed the Priest, eagerly crossing himself, and uttering a deep groan, "I once had a friend!"

"But," interrogated Magnus, "was he false too? Did he rob thee of thy best beloved?"

"He did rob me of my best beloved!"

"And yet, holy Father, he did not murder thy harmless little one—he did not destroy thy faultless lady! None could do that but Sir Gormund Gottsler! He—detestable murderer——Oh farewel! That name awakens the fellest rage in my burning bosom! Say," and he seized the astonished Friar, "didst thou know that——"

"Peace, Magnus!"—The Duke started at this appellation—"thy wrath is useless. I knew that man perhaps——" but in struggling to free himself from the grasp of the Prince, his cowl slipped aside, which he hastily replaced, and with a voice impeded by the beatings of a fluttered heart, the priest thus continued, while he slowly retreated—"I knew that man—knew every motion of his corrupted heart—every action of his base, notorious life, and can explain the whole of those schemes, by which thou hast suffered so much. Nay, keep off!" and he drew an Italian stiletto from his bosom; "to-morrow thou shalt know all; to-night it is impossible!"

With these words this mysterious being suddenly vanished, leaving the Duke involved in an astonishment that swallowed up for a moment the dearest and most painful interests of his heart; and he found himself in the Queen's anti-room before a sense of his strange appearance suggested the impropriety of it. Stopping therefore near a door, from the other side of which he distinguished female voices, he was about to return, when, in a tone sweetened by affectionate duty, he heard Catherine exclaim—"Oh royal Madam! how my heart burns to acknowledge these dear and long unknown parents! Sweet is the hope you give me of beholding, freed from the imputation of guilt, or even of neglect, this venerated father, this awful Duke of Saxe Lunenburgh!"

"Then I am in possession of unexpected bliss!" exclaimed the agitated Prince, rushing forward, and clasping his sinking child as she dropped on her knee before him, while he dispensed the tearful blessing her grateful bosom panted to receive.—"Thou art my child, and thy father can own thee without a blush; for no guilt, no neglect attaches to the name of Magnus. Credulity indeed has urged me to deeds of injustice; perhaps—Oh sweet Catherine! daughter of my precious Duchess! credulity indeed has been our ruin. A confidence falsely placed—a combination of incidents favourable to the purpose of——But why dwell upon events no power can annihilate?—Felicitate me, Madam," said he to the Queen, "upon this blessed discovery! and would to Heaven thou couldst add to my happiness by speaking of——"

"My Lord," returned the Queen, whose tears would hardly permit articulation, "I anticipate your wishes—the Duchess is safe. She still lives, and is religiously protected. To-morrow we will accompany this dear girl to the asylum of her other parent. You can exculpate yourself, and the house of Saxe Lunenburgh will recover its pristine happiness and glories!"

Magnus could only evince his strong and overpowering rapture by pressing still closer to his beating bosom the sweet pledge of returning felicity; and several hours passed in the confused but exquisite enjoyment of filial love, duteous kindness, holy friendship, and grateful aspirations, which the heart silently but sincerely accords to the Dispenser of his gracious providences.

The Duke, when restored to that recollection which this scene had so happily stifled, recurred to his adventure in the cloisters, dwelling much upon the information he was promised by the mysterious Friar, whose manner of escaping from his researches savoured much of supernatural influence.

"Doubtless," cried Blanch, when he concluded, "this man was Confessor to Sir Gormund, who, I am told, was borne alive to the

Priory of St. Thomas, not far from the spot where he received his death-wounds."

"It must be so," returned Magnus, "and he is possibly arranging the subject of that confession which, in a case of such importance, renders the secrecy of that sort of communication improper to be observed."

Relieved from the anxiety his appearance and strange interruption had occasioned, the Duke apologized for his own abrupt behaviour, and added a wish to be excused for the negligence of his dress, to which he then adverted. Blanch allowed every indulgence to his request, and suggested the necessity of taking some repose previous to the intended visit.

With real surprise Saxe Lunenburgh observed the dawn rapidly advancing, and reluctantly quitted his precious new-found charge to prepare for the intended interview; and as he passed the gloomy cloisters, threw an apprehensive look upon the spot from whence his alarming companion had vanished. Here he was fated to encounter fresh wonders; his own name was distinctly pronounced, followed by a heavy sigh! He stopped irresolute: the sound, which was repeated, seemed to issue from a small tomb, which stood near the place, and apparently had received the Friar on the preceding evening. Acquiring new resolution, Magnus cautiously approached, when, to his utter amazement, the Friar again appeared from behind the tomb, and came forward, with his arms crossed, his head bent over his bosom, while his cowl just shaded his large dark eyes, that seemed as if they would pierce through the sacred pavement to the hallowed recesses beneath.

Possessed of the mystery so dear to his throbbing heart, Saxe Lunenburgh felt an eager desire to know in what way the execrable deception had been so successfully completed. The day was yet young; the idea of repose in that state of inquietude hardly tolerable; the importance of the promised communication so truly essential to the sweet reconciliation he meditated, all taken together, determined him to question the Priest, although he should again produce the dreaded stiletto.

Thus determined, he drew towards a column that sheltered him from immediate notice, and turning suddenly upon the Friar, as he leisurely passed, saluted him with a courteous benediction, while he cautiously eyed his hands as they were drawn from beneath his garment.

"Thou seest I am punctual, Father," observed the wary Duke, "and expect the performance of thy promise given last night. Say then, what knowest thou of Sir Gormund? If, as I shrewdly guess, thou didst shrive him in his dying hour, perchance he then entrusted to thee the history of my wrongs?"

"Weak Prince! and dost thou judge so lightly of the Church's servants, as to accuse an unworthy member of so heinous an offence as sacrilege."

"Pardon me, Friar, I will not suppose it. Relieve my anxiety, for too surely it is in thy power."

"Son," returned the Priest, in a solemn accent, "one condition must be the price of my compliance. Knowest thou not that the forgiveness of those we have injured, is of consequence to souls in purgatory?—The bitter denunciations of thy rageful heart follow the wretched spirit.—Say then, canst thou accord a full and free pardon to that miserable offender?—Nay, thou must do yet more. The discovery I am to make, implicates an abhorred living sinner. Say then, will thy forgiveness extend equally to the living as the deceased, and can it be so freely, so truly dispensed, as that no circumstance, however horrid, shall destroy the effect of such a pardon?"

Magnus hesitated. He saw the Priest equally upon his guard as himself, and without fearing the effects of a denial (his cautious eye following every movement of this interesting stranger), the Duke demurred as to the extent of his request. To pardon the dead, who could no longer offend, was no great exertion of pious charity; but extended to the living, did not this clause imply a dangerous accomplice in Sir Gormund's guilt?

"Is it too hard for Christian kindness to forgive injuries which cannot be recalled?" demanded the Friar; "and has curiosity no foundation in thy bosom—a curiosity that could be amply gratified by thy compliance? For assuredly it is in the power of him who now standeth before thee, to clear thy sullied fame, and that of her who suffered by the machinations of a remorseless enemy. Is it nothing to be told by what a train of dreadful events the miseries of many preceding years were employed in tearing up domestic peace?"

"Cool, sophistical villain!" said Magnus, "thou playest with my feelings! Will nothing content thee but the sacrifice of a great and just revenge?"

"Nothing!"

"The Duke struggled with his rising rage, till, certain he should lose but little in making the wished-for promise, he coldly answered—"Be it so, Priest! I agree to thy hard conditions."

"Swear then, Oh Prince! by all thy hopes of present and future felicity, that no danger shall arise to any one whom my information may criminate."

"None, except——"

"No exceptions, Duke; on that ground I rest my performance of the conditions. Freely and to all must thy grace extend."

"Torturer! no more! It shall extend to all!"

The Friar paused, muttered an Ave-Maria, and putting his hand to his bosom, slowly drew forth a bundle of papers. Magnus watched every motion; his heart beat with thrilling expectation.

"Now then, Oh Magnus! forget not thy awful engagements, for I am going to *try* thee. Behold these papers. In them thou shalt read the extent of Sir Gormund's crimes, the wrongs thou hast done to the noble Marienburg, the injuries thy virtuous Duchess has sustained, and the means by which thou mayst discover that lost treasure. And now dost thou repent thy sacred vow? Does it now remain in full force, and wilt thou never cancel it?"

"Oh never, worthy Father," said the delighted Duke, "with pleasure I confirm the willing oath."

"Then view this face!" said the Priest, dropping his cowl.

"Oh blasting sight!" exclaimed the horror-struck Prince, "do I not behold Sir Gormund Gottsler? To him have I pledged the honour of Saxe Lunenburgh!"

"No," said this once cruel enemy, "Sir Gormund is no more: his vices, his pursuits, his chimerical notions of greatness, all sunk with his claims to worldly grandeur. Incorporated with a society, the rules of which can only be observed by those whose repentance is deep as Father Anthony's, for so I am called, my nights are passed in tears, and watchings; my days, for the claims of nature are few, and ill attended to, are distinguished by various penances. Farewel, thou most abused!—If ever I can indulge an idea of consolation, it will be in the supposition that by this discovery I have made some small atonement for past transgressions."

The wretched Anthony again resuming his cowl, was retiring to the tomb, in which, as an act of self-inflicted mortification, he passed many miserable hours, when Saxe Lunenburgh almost pitying a fallen enemy, who now had offered what poor amends the consequence of his atrocious crimes permitted, bade him "go in peace! and if," said the penetrated Duke, "my pardon for what cannot be recalled, will, in any degree, promote thy comfort, claim it—it is thine in its fullest extent."

Father Anthony, in whom the cruel spirit of Sir Gormund was effectually destroyed, raised his eyes, obscured by repentant tears, to that Heaven he had so grossly offended, and fervently implored its blessings upon the charitable forgiver; and then silently resumed his station in the marble tomb, behind which he so suddenly disappeared on the preceding evening.

Thus wonderfully possessed of the clue which unravelled the cause of his own and the poor Duchess's sufferings, Duke Magnus hastened to prepare for the interview which, prior to all others, gave the most exquisite sensations to his soul; and desirous of doing public justice to the character of his beloved, so long shrouded by dark and cruel aspersions, set forward with a troop of horse richly caparisoned, and accompanied by several Knights distinguished for birth and gallant achievements. These surrounded two magnificent litters—one to convey his feeble consort, the other to accommodate Blanch and his new-found child.

Upon his arrival at the Queen's Palace, he experienced a new pleasure in the unexpected presence of Gustavus, who, confined to no rules of formal ceremony, was breakfasting with the happy Catherine and her royal friend.

"I congratulate you, my worthy cousin," said the good King, "upon your present prospects. I have already felicitated your amiable daughter, who has reason to glory in a discovery so honourable to herself and the mother she is prepared to venerate;—and I rejoice with this noble Princess on the accomplishment of her former predictions. But my friend is losing time. Farewel, Duke! I shall hope shortly to see you once again in love with martial deeds, and, armed at all points, charging the enemies with which your State is threatened!"

This remark brought a blush of self-accusation into the Duke's countenance, who had, by lingering so long at Stockholm (a place rendered precious to him by the confidential society of its heroic King), given too good an opportunity to his neighbouring foes for making several inroads upon the frontiers of Saxe Lunenburgh: but even a reproof from Gustavus did honour to its object; and, only determined to retrieve his character, he bowed in grateful conviction.

While this short scene was passing, Catherine was engaged in surveying from the window her father's gallant attendants, when, observing a carriage leaving the road to Stockholm, which rose about a quarter of a mile distant, and turning slowly into the avenue before the palace, she called the Queen's attention to a circumstance for which *she* could not account. It was covered with black, and guarded by several men habited in the same gloomy colour. This appearance struck terror to her apprehensive heart; every bright expectation faded before the idea that her mother was no more; and the second notion she indulged, was that of losing by a disappointment so cruel to his impetuous feelings, the father she had but just allowed herself to venerate.

"Doubtless you think as I do, Madam," she whispered to Blanch, who stood gazing in motionless suspense:—the surprise was too much for her gentle spirit. "She is gone!—My mother! I shall never see thy sainted form—never crave a maternal blessing!"

The alarm now became general; Saxe Lunenburgh caught her concluding sentence, and the same idea thrilled his bosom.

"You are too precipitate," said the Queen, while she supported the half-fainting Catherine; "that vehicle contains no deceased object:—observe its make—some forlorn widow approaches!—See, Catherine, it is a litter!"

Catherine hid her face in the Duke's bosom, who, eager to develop the mournful mystery, stood earnestly watching the progress of the carriage, while Conan, who waited to join the splendid cavalcade, stepped forward to gain some certain information. Solemn and slow it now wound among some lofty pines that crowded a space near the house, not yet cleared of the verdant encumbrance.

"Oh Lady!" said Magnus, "my child's fears are too well justified!—Von Hemert speaks to the driver, and he turns out of the avenue!—yes, that vehicle contains my soul's lost treasure!"

"Impetuous and ill-discerning man!" cried Blanch, "whither would you go?" for he was rushing towards the grand entrance in an agony of impatience. "Wait at least the return of our common friend. But see!—he comes with no harbinger of death in that faithful countenance!"

* * * * *

To describe the scene which succeeded Von Hemert's entrance (who supported a faint and speechless figure on his arm), would lessen the effect upon the reader's imagination, when he is informed that Catherine and the Duke beheld in the fair and drooping object, *her* whose supposed death had wrung their hearts with excruciating anguish! We shall omit, therefore, the fervent expressions of love, duty, and rapture strained almost to enthusiasm, and relate the cause and consequence of this unexpected arrival.

* * * * *

From all that the Duchess could gather in Von Hemert's information, it appeared that a fond, a long-lost, duteous daughter was impatient to acknowledge and revere her suffering parent; and that daughter had already, in the character of a friend, obtained an interest in her wounded bosom. Often had she admired (without defining the latent motive,) a form and face which imagination depicted as familiar to her sweetest yet most melancholy ideas! To see then, to fold to her enraptured heart this sweet author of revived felicity, was the chief and eager wish of her soul.

Possessed with a notion that her life was near its termination, and dreading to be disappointed in a matter so essential to present peace, she prevailed upon the Abbess, against that lady's better reason, to indulge her with the use of a commodious litter, which she reserved for special occasions, and which, in consequence of the strictness of that order in point of dress, was covered with the gloomy insignia of death!—its attendants wearing also the same sable appearance.

Anxious to realize the ecstatic idea with which her mind was filled, the Duchess immediately set forward on her journey. Von Hemert had informed her of the name of her daughter's protector; and a wish to renew her former friendship with the noble Queen, to whom she owed such an important obligation, warmed her grateful heart.

Overcome by the length of her journey, and the pathetic exertions of contending passions, she expressed an inclination to retire with her precious daughter. Saxe Lunenburgh (whose unexpected presence and strong effusions of long-suppressed love affected her weak and doubting spirit) forwarded the request; a compliance with which he thought might help his cause, as Catherine and the Queen would certainly attempt, by candid argument, to soften the aversion amounting to horror that seemed to influence her prejudiced mind, as she cast from time to time a look of terror upon the wrongly-aspersed Prince. It was true, one great accusation against him had fallen to the ground. He was *not* a murderer!—his child still lived to bless a doting mother with her presence! but it remained with Sir Gormund's confession to exonerate him from *all* blame; and till this was examined, some of her prejudices he knew would hold good. Leaving, therefore, any attempt to recover his claim to her affection till better qualified to make it, Magnus retired to his house at Stockholm, accompanied by Conan, and the noble train who had been assembled to do honour to the Duchess; and too much agitated to think of rest, employed most of the night in unravelling the arts of a nefarious villain, in doing which, he more than once condemned the lenity that had permitted crimes like his to escape condign punishment. In reading the Duchess's representation of her sorrows, every fibre of his heart was wrung with anguish. In delineating the arts of that monster by which they were inflicted, rage, almost demoniac fired his bosom!—but in tracing the deep and skilful subterfuges of a mind bent upon one decidedly cruel purpose, something more than rage—something softer than pity united to produce tears which his glowing cheek immediately absorbed!

CHAPTER VIII.

"Howe'er in private mischiefs are conceiv'd,
Torture and shame attend their open birth!
Like vipers, in the womb base treach'ry lies,
Still gnawing that whence first it did arise,
No sooner born, but the vile parent dies!"

CONGREVE.

As it will be necessary to blend with Sir Gormund's account of the cruel deceptions he practised, a description of the effects they produced on Saxe Lunenburgh, and the good but deluded Marienburg, which grounded in either bosom such a burning resentment and determined hatred, we shall select from the Duke's representation of his own conduct, and what may be gathered from Marienburg's hints, and several papers which he had entrusted to Conan, with a solemn injunction to keep them unopened till the birth of Catherine should be honourably elucidated, such circumstances as shall contribute to a full development of this eventful story. And to do this, we must advert to the era of the Duchess's fate, when she gave her first refusal to the impetuous Sir Gormund, who, enraged by the Duke's contending for the prize himself had lawfully obtained, and still more so by Catherina's (for this was the name she was so loth to acknowledge) haughty and repeated denials of his suit, became fully bent upon the most cruel revenge!—But this was a business not easily effected. It was at first necessary to regain Saxe Lunenburgh's countenance, which he had partially enjoyed, previous to the dishonourable attack made upon that Prince, whom he was supposed not to know, but who could not escape the cunning of Sir Gormund. In this he was so far successful as to be received upon the usual footing: and when defied and checked by Marienburg for daring to accuse his sister of levity, chose rather to submit to the disgrace, than hazard the overthrow of his deeply-concerted plan.

As it was impossible for Miss Marienburg to admit of the Duke's addresses without a confidant, she unfortunately pitched upon one who, although honourably allied, had sullied her character by a criminal intimacy with the Knight—a circumstance that escaped Catherina's detection. To her then she committed the secret of her pregnancy, always affirming her claim to the title of a wife, without betraying the name of him to whom she owed it; as the Prince, in all his visits to that unhappy lady, constantly appeared in a disguise which defeated the prying eye of the most curious observer. But, assisted by his vile agent, Sir Gormund contrived to make the discovery he meditated; and still more highly enraged at his total disappointment, he set himself to intercept every letter or message, which the unfortunate couple attempted to send, while he observed, with diabolical triumph, the Duke's dejection daily increase, whose ignorance of his lady's delicate situation made the trial Sir Gormund ventured upon his credulity, rather more effectual than it would otherwise have been.

It was during her residence on the frontiers that he opened his plan of operations, when the mind of Magnus, already poisoned by artful hints, and open declarations of his rival's attachment to Catherina, became fitted to receive still more decided proofs of her falsehood.—An event too, which happened near the time fixed for his visit to the retreat of his Duchess, greatly assisted Sir Gormund's design.

The Duke of Saxe Gotha, in consequence of some former, but private overtures made by Magnus to obtain the hand of his sister, and which, since his attachment to Catherina, he had impoliticly neglected, had threatened that Prince with a severe revenge, unless some means were immediately found to satisfy his injured honour, and the delicacy of the young lady, whose spirit was roused at the insult her love and dignity received from the unpardonable negligence. Unwilling to involve his subjects in a war, and conscious of Saxe Gotha's claim to an explanation of this unknightly treatment, Magnus, accompanied by his own sister, whose representation he hoped might be of use to his cause with the Princess, hastened to the Court of Saxe Gotha, after sending a courier to his Duchess with such an excuse as he trusted would appease the suspicions of that poor lady, while his own respecting her infidelity were daily gaining ground: but the evil genius which was let loose to persecute her prevailed, and the courier was corrupted.

During this visit of Saxe Lunenburgh, his artful rival was not idle. No intelligence came from Catherina for four months; all which time was employed by Magnus in evading what he could not absolutely refuse, and endeavouring to quiet the minds of the brother and sister by various excuses, which were founded on the present situation of his country, labouring, as it then happened, under an epidemic distemper; and the Duke of Saxe Gotha chose to have the marriage celebrated at Lunenburgh, whither he meant to accompany the noble couple previous to their union. But the motive for this protraction soon ceased, and the Duke could no longer find the shadow of an excuse, when the arrival of two letters, written by his beloved Catherina (for so it evidently appeared) put an immediate end to the perturbation of a cherished hope that she was still innocent, still faithful to her vows. The first accused him of inconstancy in visiting the Princess of Saxe Gotha, and at the same time declared her unalterable resolution never to see him again, protesting also that if he took any steps to establish his claim as a husband, that power should extend only to the corse of her he had so irreparably injured.

There was nothing in this effusion of a jealousy, apparently too well founded, that could justify his opinion of her defalcation; but from the courier who brought it, he learned that her character was already spoken of at Lunenburgh as devoid of the purity by which it was formerly distinguished, who then produced another letter, intended, as he said, for Sir Gormund Gottsler, in which she not only declared her preference of the Knight, and her aversion to Saxe Lunenburgh, but disclaimed, in the fullest sense, every title to the Duke's heart and hand.

Stunned by this unequivocal avowal of her baseness, Magnus wanted presence of mind either to detain or examine the courier, in whom he had placed a former confidence; but, in the height of ungoverned rage, sent a bitter renunciation of his passion in a few short lines to his deceived lady: and without further consideration, pressed Saxe Gotha and his sister to prepare for their journey to Lunenburgh. But before he had time to repent of his precipitate conduct, the Princess became so seriously indisposed, as to give birth to a secret hope, which again seized his heart, that he should for some weeks longer be permitted to indulge, without a crime, his reviving love for the suspected Catherina.

Although the pride of abused confidence forbade him either to offer excuses for his own conduct, or to search into the motives for her's, it was not till after the unhappy Duchess's confinement at Telga that Magnus returned to his Dukedom, which was, in consequence of a melancholy left by her illness upon the mind of the Princess, that induced her, against the will of her brother, to found a religious house, of which she was chosen Abbess, leaving Saxe Lunenburgh in the possession of that liberty the supposed perfidy of Catherina had also restored.

The plots of Sir Gormund, so far as related to this unfortunate couple's separation, had hitherto been attended with uncommon success; but his vengeance was still incomplete. An adept in the art of deciphering, he now prepared fresh anguish for the Duke, whose evident dejection carried pleasure to his hardened soul. The confidence of Marienburg in his friend was still reciprocal; but the name of Catherina, her absence, and misfortunes never passed the lips of either till the following alarming information laid the foundation of that deep hatred which mutually burnt in their bosoms. It was given to Magnus by means of an anonymous writer, and imported that, in consequence of the confession made to Marienburg by his sister, who mentioned the Duke as father to her infant (which in truth belonged to Sir Gormund Gottsler), her brother, after vowing eternal vengeance against the supposed seducer, had spirited away the unhappy Catherina, and threatened to destroy the innocent babe.

"Wretched lady!" cried the Duke, while a tear fell on the abominable forgery, "cruel as thou hast treated me, I feel for thy miseries. Detestable Sir Gormund! thus basely to step between my love and me, and corrupt a heart which once belonged to Saxe Lunenburgh exclusively!—And still more barbarous Stanislaus! to give up the fair offender!"

While he was thus encouraging fresh pity for Catherina, contempt for her brother, and glowing rage against the Knight, the appearance of Marienburg gave fresh pangs to his aching soul; and so much was he engaged with the mandate before him, as not immediately to notice the flaming countenance and abrupt entrance of this once esteemed friend, till his attention was diverted by Marienburg's evident agitation.

With so much cause for reprehension and the bitterest accusations, Magnus was astonished to behold in the subject of his resentment equal, if not superior, tokens of displeasure. True, he might have adverted to the paper in his hand for a ready explanation; but Marienburg's spirited demand for his lost, his ruined, perhaps murdered sister, deprived Saxe Lunenburgh of the prompt power of utterance.

"Her infant too," added the high-souled Stanislaus, "the heir to infamy, but the idol of that misguided creature's affections, is that too sacrificed to the base lawless invader of her innocence? But mark me, Duke! if thou hast completed my wretchedness in the dishonour of my house, and the destruction of those in whom it was partly vested, I will have vengeance. This good sword," and he half drew the glittering blade, "this good sword shall purify its master's sullied dignity in the blood of him who has brought it in question! Say then, Saxe Lunenburgh, I repeat, say, where is my sister? where is her unoffending offspring?"

The Duke had now recovered his haughty spirit; he had reflected upon the insult offered to his name by her to whom he had consigned it, and considered this violence in Marienburg as a mean and artful subterfuge to conceal his own villanous secretion of his unhappy sister. Unable, therefore, to controul his rising rage, he arose, and putting himself into a defensive posture, inarticulately urged his opponent to the contest; when the Princess of Lunenburgh, alarmed at the tones of defiance which reached the saloon in which she was sitting, darted into her brother's closet, in the moment when the combatants were aiming at each other's life, and shrieking with terror, gave a timely interruption to their sanguinary intentions. But Magnus, turning wrathfully upon his fair protector, commanded her to leave him, that he might chastise a villain.

"Villain!" exclaimed the exasperated Stanislaus, his eyes beaming unutterable vengeance, "perish the opprobrious utterer of the disgraceful epithet!—Lady, retire! this scene suits not thy gentleness!—Come on, Magnus! defend thy title to a barbarous seducer, an infringer on the rights of friendship, and a betrayer of virgin innocence."

Certain of his own detestation of crimes so heinous, and more than ever convinced of Marienburg's guilt, the Duke disregarded all entreaties to forbear, and these so late friends fought with a rancour which nothing but the death of one could destroy, till the cries of the half-distracted Princess reached the Chamberlains, who rushing to the scene of action, forcibly separated the vindictive parties, and more assistance coming in, Magnus whispered a bitter defiance in his opponent's ear, and reluctantly submitted to postpone for the present his thirst for revenge.

It may now be necessary to mention, by way of justification of the irritated Marienburg, that Sir Gormund Gottsler, by whom this complicated business had been wholly conducted, visited Marienburg previous to Catherina's mysterious departure; and by artful submissions, and well-timed hints, laid the foundation for future communication, leaving upon that good man's mind certain suspicions, which were soon after confirmed by the faithless courier already mentioned, who was the identical person employed to take the child from its treacherous attendant, Sir Gottsler's before-mentioned female confidant. Corrupted beyond the power of goodness to reform, he began to delight in vile fabrications, nor shrunk from the anguish his wicked suggestions created, insomuch that his base employer thought him equal to the task of poisoning Marienburg's mind, as successfully as he had done that of the Duke's: and it was in consequence of a cautious and well-managed accusation (which, without positively criminating Magnus by name, implicated him in the barbarous acts of seducing, and then confining, if not destroying his unhappy sister and her babe) that Marienburg, who till that instant had most unaccountably omitted Saxe Lunenburgh in his guesses at her real lover, seemed to feel the truth of this slily conducted information in all its horrors; and too much enraged to exert his general cautious discrimination to investigate or coolly relate what he had heard, prevented, by his impetuosity, which was rarely the characteristic of this good man, any satisfactory *éclaircissement*. Indeed had it happened even to the exposure of Sir Gormund's schemes, the Knight would not have repented the steps he had taken, since he inly determined never to revisit Lunenburgh, and he did not once suspect Marienburg's intention of returning to Sweden.

Disappointed in the dearest purpose of a resenting heart, Stanislaus waited to hear from his vindictive adversary; but a long and dispiriting illness, with which Magnus was seized, in consequence of the distraction of his mind, prevented the prosecution of his intention; and in some degree softened by the restoration of his little niece, whose life Sir Gormund wished not to destroy, he dropped the design resentment had cherished, and taking the woman, to whose care the child was committed on the night when it was torn from its insensible mother, he returned with his family to Stockholm; where, soon after his arrival, he lost an exemplary wife, and strove to derive consolation from the society of his daughter, niece, and the youthful Gustavus.

Doubtless it is already understood by our readers that the letters received by Magnus, while a resident in the Court of Saxe Gotha, were a forgery of Sir Gormund's, who had evinced, in a long course of successful villany, a hardihood of disposition that spurned detection. Indeed there was a concomitancy of different circumstances extremely favourable to his iniquitous designs throughout; but in the defeat of his darling project, that of obtaining the subject of his ungovernable passion, the completion of his schemes lost their end. He was miserable, even more so than those he so cruelly injured; and from his written confession, it appeared that he never knew one moment's tranquillity, while aiming to destroy that of his fellow-creatures; but wandered from clime to clime, a signal example of restless guilt, without the power of lessening his crimes by restoring peace to the victims he had made, till that dreadful accident, which befel him in the forest, threw him into a society, whose business it was to awaken, rather than sooth, the condemning conscience.

"I knew not," observes this once singularly wicked man, "to whom I was indebted for my removal, or rather rescue from my savage assailants, till three days after, when I revived to a sense of anguish so extreme as to make life a burthen, my groans and tears moved the pious woman, to whose house I understood a party of peasants conveyed me from the forest, where I was found apparently dead, lying near the remains of my horse, which two wolves were greedily devouring, perhaps at that instant a sweeter morsel to them than the body they had for the moment neglected. This good hostess, after attempting to comfort me with an assurance that my wounds were not mortal, spoke of a holy man that had promised to indemnify her for any expence attending my cure. She was interrupted by this good Father, who announced himself as member of an order severe in its penances, strict in its rules, sparing in diet, but mercifully indulgent in cases of distress.

"For many weeks I was indebted to this blessed Samaritan for chirurgical assistance, and to his skill I owe, through Heaven, my present advantages. There was a mildness in his manner, an irresistible persuasion about him, which soon drew from me, in that weak state, a full confession of the dark transactions of a guilty life; and without glossing over, or attempting to extenuate, the magnitude of my crimes, he spoke of pardon to be obtained, in consequence of my attempting to make retribution for those crimes. But it required a long residence in the society to which he belonged, to effect a purpose so humiliating; and it is only within these six months that a conviction of my lost state is become strong enough to surmount the pride of a wicked heart;—it is now, however, deeply humbled, and I have visited Telga in the hope of restoring one precious creature to her rank in society; but she is gone, and I have vowed till she be either restored, or her true character established with her injured husband, never to return to my peaceful, melancholy solitude. Marienburg has been made full amends ere this, if the masses which are said for his precious soul, are effective; my fortune, most of which is settled on our house, will be employed in similar methods to obtain mercy for myself and others. While resident with the pious brethren belonging to the great Church in Stockholm, I am permitted to perform my penances without interruption, one of which is to pass some hours of every night in a tomb, beneath which lie the remains of the once guilty Phedora. Alas! the wretched Jacob too, that wicked tool of a corrupted master, he has paid the debt of nature! How successfully, in the character of a courier, did he deceive the deluded Catherina and her affectionate Magnus! Blessed St. Mary and all Saints, plead for the once guilty Gormund, now the penitent Father Anthony."

* * * * *

Thus concluded Sir Gormund's narrative, written, it was presumed, while a resident in the Society of Grey Penitents, and which he bore about him as a dreadful memento of former vices. If the heart of Saxe Lunenburgh had glowed with vengeance against the author of so much evil, he certainly found, in the conclusion of this candid confession, an excuse for the pity his generous nature accorded; nor once attempted to seek again that conscience-stricken sinner, who he readily supposed would immediately return to his religious asylum.

In the loose papers Conan gave up on this occasion to the Duke, which were entrusted to him by Marienburg, that Prince discovered the following particulars among others already mentioned—that Stanislaus, confiding in the known sincerity of Mary Skelm, settled her near Lunenburgh, in the faint hope that his poor sister, should she escape from her unknown prison, would fly to that faithful woman for a present asylum; engaging her solemn promise never to discover what she knew of the infant Catherine's origin to any one but the possessor of that seal, about which Saxe Lunenburgh had been so deeply agitated.

"Ah how interesting," said the noble Stanislaus in his brief notes, "was that gem to my poor sister! It was the gift of her seducer; I had marked its beauty and elegance while in her possession, but how little did I suspect at what an enormous price she purchased it; or that she had restored the jewel, till on the morning of our last meeting, I perceived it thrown carelessly among other less valuable ornaments, upon a table in his closet. Methought its neglected situation reminded me of her's to whom it had belonged; and with a meanness I afterwards condemned, but which my attachment to every thing once dear to that sweet, lost creature, excepting her dark betrayer—I——blush, Marienburg, while thou ownest the disgraceful action!—I brought away the precious bauble, determined to preserve it as a means to identify my niece's birth."

On the back of this paper was mentioned his confidence in Conan's fidelity which he trusted would extend so far, as not even to hint to his niece that such a packet was in his possession. It is needless to add that this injunction was religiously performed by that worthy man.—"I have sworn," concluded Marienburg, "by the *manes* of my sister, to prefer the interest of her offspring to my own, and I will perform it in the event of her future establishment."

"Oh that beloved, that patient soul!" cried the Duke, as he concluded this little history of the seal, "how did I affront the integrity which scorned to deceive—how did my cruel taunts and ungenerous suspicions distress a heart so noble!—But, my dearest child," said the penitent Duke, in a conference he afterwards held with Catherine on that subject, "was it in nature to be calm in the presence of one, whose mother I then considered as the destroyer of my happiness, my fame, (should the secret ever transpire), and all my hopes of perpetuating an illustrious race?—'Perhaps,' said my haughty spirit, 'should this young creature be enabled to substantiate her guilty mother's claim as Duchess of Saxe Lunenburgh, I may be necessitated to acknowledge her spurious offspring, as the legal heir to my Dukedom.'—Thus thinking, no wonder my behaviour was so eccentric, so rudely inconsistent! Had I then known this supposed intruder was indeed the precious pledge of a true and ill-requited love, what contrary transports would have warmed my bosom!"

Catherine kissed the hand which was held out to draw her to a paternal embrace, and acknowledged the justice of his motives for a conduct she once thought so mysterious.

CHAPTER IX.

> "Who ever felt a joy unmix'd with care?
> This breast, while swelling with excessive bliss,
> Yet labours with such pangs, as sink the high-
> Rais'd ebullition of that joy."
>
> MACKENZIE.

THUS furnished with the most effectual supporters of his cause, and the justification of his character, as a husband and a parent, Saxe Lunenburgh impatiently looked forward to the moment when he should be allowed to plead his right to Catherina's long withheld love and confidence; and after an hour's disturbed repose, hastened to Gustavus, who rose with the dawn, to communicate to the generous Monarch his present situation.

Gustavus was materially affected by this discovery, which

rendered Catherine a match for Kings. The niece of Marienburg proved to be the very object of his Sigismunda's recommendation, royally allied, an heir to greatness, with the addition of those merits so sweetly expatiated upon by his sainted love.

"Is it not," said his reflecting mind, "decreed by an all-controuling Divinity, that this fair creature must share the throne of Sweden?"

Gustavus sighed. His heart, still aching with the remembrance of his idolized Sigismunda, rejected the plea reason would have brought forward in favour of the only woman he could bear to think of in that light, without horror; and the idea that this struggle had escaped the notice of his visitor, reconciled him, in a degree, to his own good opinion, which he had forfeited for a moment, in giving way even to a wish that he could forget Sigismunda.

Too much engaged with his own prospects, Lunenburgh saw nothing extraordinary in this great man's reception of the intelligence he brought; and as the hour was arrived when he might be admitted to his royal friend's palace, he quitted the King, who kindly congratulated the happy Duke upon his expected felicity, and condescendingly promised to visit his family as soon as the Duchess's indisposition would admit.

As the windows of Blanch's residence reflected the beams of a rising sun, they gave to Saxe Lunenburgh's ready fancy the representation of his vivid hopes, glowing with all the brilliancy a fervent expectation could give them. Already the gates of that hospitable mansion were thrown open, and in the vestibule he met his darling daughter. A sweet smile played on her expressive features, and passing her arm through that of her father's—"Oh my Lord!" cried the delighted girl, "we are all hope—my mother is serene and patient. She confesses her opinion respecting my revered father is greatly staggered—nay, in some instances entirely changed. She wishes and prays for a sight of that manuscript you mentioned to the Queen."

"Take it, my love; I will not ask to see your mother till she has read a husband's exculpation. Go—tell her though my heart agonizes for an interview, I will not appear even in a doubtful light. She shall have nothing to forgive in Magnus of Saxe Lunenburgh but a credulity founded on motives she can readily excuse."

Somewhat awed by this ebullition of a noble spirit, Catherine took the papers with silent reverence, and was hastily departing, when catching her hand, and gazing affectionately on her gentle countenance, he said, "Did not my Catherine remark a change in her father's demeanour a few days previous to these happy discoveries?"

Catherine blushed at the recollection, and her own simple suspicions.

"It was then, my love, that thy parent fancied he traced in that eye, that cheek a similarity to his own; perhaps thou knowest not that in the gardens of Telga I saw thy mother:—but hasten with the manuscript—I will wait thy return."

She flew to execute the commission, and as hastily re-entered her father's presence, who thus proceeded—"Yes, my child, that interview revived my confidence in one I had always loved. It could not be, I thought, that a dear creature, once so uniform in her attachment, so noble in her principles, so delicate in her conduct, could throw off so suddenly every sweet propensity to virtue. Oh that I had thus discriminated before passion threw its fatal veil, in conjunction with artful villany, over my better judgment! From the moment of that interview, as my prejudices respecting thy mother's purity rapidly declined, so did hope spring with a mixture of doubt respecting thy origin, and occasioned the alteration in my behaviour which thy tender delicacy falsely appropriated; but there were moments when that hope seemed totally extinct, for the perusal of thy mother's sufferings in the forest, left no room for aught but the cruellest apprehension."

* * * * *

As there was little prospect of realizing his ardent wishes to embrace, without one self-accusing reflection, his adored Duchess, till she had fully perused his exculpation, given as it was in the most decided manner, the Duke mentioned his intention to pass the irksome moments with the noble Gustavus, whose excellence in governing both his people and himself roused in Magnus a spirit of emulation.

At the mention of a name so truly dear, Catherine deeply

blushed, and appeared so visibly agitated, that Blanch, who had left the Duchess to an undisturbed perusal of the important manuscript, fearing she might betray the dearest secret of her heart, counselled her to look in upon her mother for an instant. She hastily obeyed the prudent request; but Magnus had observed the sudden tremor, and, addressing the Queen, while strange uneasy suspicions rested upon his mind, he anxiously demanded an explanation. It was then that amiable woman's turn to exhibit marks of confusion; but, superior to unnecessary disguise, she frankly owned that, in consequence of the King's hazarding his life to procure Catherine's deliverance from Fitzer, her gratitude had produced the usual effect on a heart like her's.

"Enough, Madam," cried the Duke; "some allay is necessary to felicity like mine; for Gustavus has no heart to give, and she who has loved a King, so good, so great, so perfect, can never descend to another choice. Sweet girl! how great will be thy disappointment if thou hast nourished hopes like these!"

"My Lord," said the friendly Blanch, "I apprehend you fear too much. Gustavus must marry, and I know that Catherine holds the first place in his esteem. I also am assured that the dear creature encourages no expectations of such felicity: she looks up to him in no other light but as her guardian, her Monarch, her deliverer; but yet I may be allowed to confess that, while in her parents she beholds the objects of love and duty, and in the good Von Hemert and myself those of the softest friendship, all those tender attributes are concentered in Gustavus, although devoid of the slightest hope."

"I will take comfort, lady," said Magnus, "from this assurance. Certainly such an alliance would gratify the highest ambition; but as that great Monarch must be left to the decisions of his own almost unerring wisdom, as no one can, with the smallest propriety, dictate in a matter of so tender a concern to a female mind, I see but little prospect of such a desirable event."

Blanch could have mentioned Sigismunda's dying request; but respecting the just dignity of Saxe Lunenburgh's spirit, she resolved with him to let the workings of a noble heart operate as its feelings should dictate.

Again the Duke was preparing to while away the tedious hours in his intended visit, when Catherine suddenly re-entered; her face overspread with tears, her voice choked with audible sobs, one hand eagerly held out to invite the wondering Duke, the other pointing towards her mother's apartment. Blanch understood the expressive motion; and, rising, told Magnus there was nothing to apprehend in this strong effusion of his daughter's joy.

"She invites my Lord to his Duchess's presence!" continued the Queen. "Come, Prince, I will lead the way."

Magnus, almost trembling for the event of this long-wished-for moment, supported his happy child, who acquired power to tell him that her mother was weeping in agony over the papers, as she entered the little saloon where that lady was seated, and upon seeing her approach, exclaimed,—"Where, my love—say where is thy dear injured father? Enough have I seen to convince me of his innocence and——"

They were now in the saloon, at the upper end of which sat the Duchess, who, on the sight of Saxe Lunenburgh, extended her emaciated arms, at the same moment dropping on her knee, as if to entreat his pardon for her terrible, though justifiable, suspicions.

"Faultless angel!" cried the Duke, gently raising, and placing her again on the couch, "why this posture to thy transported Magnus? Is he not equally culpable, supposing there were grounds for accusation? Did not he give way to the machinations of an infernal villain, and were we not alike dupes to his baseness?"

"Dupes indeed!" whispered the exhausted Duchess; "that shocking truth is established in every line I have yet seen. At present a perusal of this guilty scroll," giving it to her tearful child, "would sadden the sweet prospect of returning happiness. Take it, my love, and read the arts by which we all were nearly destroyed!"

"My adored Catherina then is convinced of her Lunenburgh's integrity?" said the Duke.

A fervent embrace, an eloquent look were his only answer, and Blanch beheld, with joy too sublime for utterance, the complete felicity of this long-tried couple.

For several weeks following this happy event, the Duke, who was impatient to put his government upon a footing, in point of skilful management, with that of Gustavus, as well as to check the incursions of his hostile neighbours, watched, with anxious perseverance, the slowly returning health of his drooping consort; till, encouraged by her amended looks, and eager assurances that she was equal to the fatigue of travelling, he ventured to announce his intention of quitting Stockholm in a few days, to Blanch and his daughter; and, unwilling to behold the emotions of friendship and disappointed love upon this occasion, he left them, to obtain an audience of Gustavus for the same purpose.

Continually in the habit of admiring the serene, steady, and thoughtful countenance of this wonderful man, the Duke felt surprise mixed with concern, upon seeing a deep glow of resentment overspread his fine features; but, upon observing several Danish Officers apparently engaged with the Monarch, Magnus would have retired.

"You are come in good time, my Lord Duke," said the Sovereign, "to witness the extraordinary intelligence brought by these kind friends to me and my cause. They would persuade me that Christian is in possession of an army sufficient to destroy my *pretensions*, as they are called, and that all Sweden wait only for his arrival to strengthen his claims by every means in their power. What thinks your Highness?" calmly smiling; "is the interest of Gustavus so poorly grounded in his subjects' hearts, or do you agree with our friend Von Hemert in his opinion, that, secure of my people's love, I may defy the Dane's utmost efforts."

"Von Hemert discriminates justly," said the ardent Duke; "I honour his opinion, and freely abide by it."

The officers looked exceedingly disconcerted, and were about to retire, when Gustavus, with a solemn aspect, bade them tell their Sovereign that no schemes, fabricated by foreign policy, could ever corrupt a loyal people; that, secure in their affection, he dreaded no change while their true interest was his glory.—Go," added this extraordinary politician, "sound them as to their confidence in my protection. Set before them the advantages you think may arise from a change of government, recapitulate the *blessings* they enjoyed in Christian's reign, and ask if they wish a repetition. Do this, and I will trust to their decision.—And now, Von Hemert, let those messengers of Christian's covert demand have honourable conduct from Stockholm."

Von Hemert, who had been recently preferred to a confidential post, immediately obeyed; and the departure of the Danes was succeeded by the entrance of Van Melen, the faithful miner from Dalecarlia.—Unused to the splendour of a Court, and beholding in the Monarch of Sweden the once humble Linden—a fellow-labourer in the northern mountain, Van Melen felt extremely abashed, and could hardly deliver his important credentials, which spoke of a powerful insurrection among the unsteady Dalecarlians, who, with Fitzer, the pretended son of Steen, were employing every means to corrupt the neighbouring provinces.

"Thou seest," cried Gustavus to Magnus, "that all my subjects are not faithful; but there are still enough left to establish what I have just mentioned to the Danes; and for the rest my northern troops are sufficiently powerful."

He then took a friendly notice of his newly arrived adherent, acknowledged his obligations to that good man for his zealous services, and conferred on him a reward equal to his own magnificent spirit, commissioning him to attend his northern Generals with instructions for quelling the fickle Dalecarlians, but despising the poor attempts of his unworthy competitor too sincerely, even to order any criminal process to be issued regarding him.

* * * * *

After a plain, but plentiful repast, to which the Duke was warmly invited, Gustavus spoke of the felicity his friend enjoyed, with a sincerity that glowed in his cheek, and sparkled in his penetrating eye, while a sigh would burst its way impelled by latent feeling; but when Magnus mentioned his intention of quitting Stockholm before the expiration of that week, a sort of uneasy expression shaded his features—the Monarch was for a moment subdued; friendship, with all its claims, dictated what he could not utter, for it would have suggested excuses for a further delay, which prudence and the title Saxe Lunenburgh's people had to his protection, had already made too long. This disorder of his soul was visible to the Duke, and a faint hope arose that, undetermined with respect to Catherine, he might yet wish to detain them in Sweden.

Of this truth Magnus was easily convinced by the King's asking if he meant to leave his family at Stockholm till peace was established in Lunenburgh. The Duke paused for an answer, which, while it gratified the illustrious questioner, would not detract from his own dignity, or the delicacy of his child.

"I should think," added Gustavus, as if fearing to trust to Lunenburgh's opinion, "that under the good Queen's protection, those amiable women will escape the inconvenience attending intestine feuds, for such I may call them; and by obliging Blanch with a continuance of such society, you will repay the obligations I have heard you confess to that noble dame."

To treat a character so generous with duplicity, the Duke abhorred—to confess the state of Catherine's affections was equally inimical to his sentiments; and yet some reply was necessary to be given, which Gustavus prevented, by resuming the subject.

"I see your reluctance, my Lord, nor can blame it. You will *all* depart, and——"

He could not proceed. The tender recommendation of Sigismunda—the necessity there was of giving a Queen to Sweden—the preference in that instance which his heart accorded to Catherine, whose unwearied gratitude a vainer mind might easily have construed—all rushed upon the hero's imagination, and so completely engrossed his thoughts, that, stimulated by his fears of losing the only chance of comfort his fate had left, every shadow of restraint or uncertainty fled, and grasping the hand of Magnus, he entreated his patience while disclosing the movements of a wayward heart.

The Duke was all attention; expectation, doubt, and hope spoke in his eye; and Gustavus was about to commit the workings of a generous soul to his friend, when suddenly recollecting the possibility there was of his addresses, however pleasing he knew they would be to the father, not being perfectly so to his child, and detesting every idea of giving pain to a gentle heart, he begged for a few hours' indulgence on the score of his intended communication.

"I will see you to-morrow, my Lord," he cried, "and explain my motives for this seeming rudeness. Believe me they are honourable both to you and myself."

Dissatisfied, yet certain the delay would be accounted for, the

Duke cheerfully accepted this apology, and retired to communicate to Blanch and the Duchess his hopes and fears. Blanch was profuse in her congratulations of the noble pair.—"Her sweet Catherine would now," she said, "reap the reward of her patient fortitude, for Gustavus could not deceive."

The Duchess, not quite so sanguine, put up a secret prayer for the success of her beloved child's wishes; and the day passed with this noble party in a state of anxiety, similar to some they had formerly experienced.

To Catherine, when the King's name was announced on the following morning, it occasioned only her usual sensations—a palpitating heart and rosy blush, which soon subsiding, she sat in silent tranquillity, indulging the pure and chastened delight of hearing him converse. Gustavus, who had arranged in his mind the line of conduct he meant to pursue, seeing her, after her mother had retired, reluctantly rise to follow her, gently detained the trembling virgin, while he requested the favour of her company to air in a new-constructed carriage, around the environs of Stockholm. Delighted at a distinction so grateful to her innocent heart, she cast a timid look towards the Duke, who gladly acceded his compliance, while Blanch shot an eyebeam of triumph on the countenance of Magnus.

* * * * *

The conversation which took place during this interesting ride, was too deeply impressed upon Catherine's mind to be consigned to oblivion; and, eager to make her beloved mother a sharer in the pure and exquisite delight she experienced, this tender, duteous daughter, upon alighting from the magnificent vehicle, hastened to Blanch's apartment, where the Duchess was indulging her own delicious sensations on this blissful occasion, expressing to that generous friend the fervent gratitude which filled her maternal heart, while detailing the high obligations she was under to the prime cause of so much bliss, and acknowledging her sense of Blanch's goodness to her dear child, when deprived of every other female support.

With all the genuine modesty of an uncorrupted heart, Catherine confessed to her sympathizing friends that Gustavus had, in the most unequivocal manner, confessed an attachment, which he candidly owned was the result of a cool and sober judgment, rather than the ebullition of romantic passion.

"I would not deceive you, Catherine," said this exalted soul; "my heart is truly your's. The amiable daughter of Saxe Lunenburgh possesses an entire and exclusive right to those affections which once belonged to another object; but I need not tell you that heart still pays a frequent, though silent, tribute to the excellent Sigismunda's memory."

"Oh my mother!" apostrophized Catherine, "how I wept at the mention of that beloved name!—'Precious tears,' said the King, 'sweetly do they embalm a remembrance so dear to both: greatly does this affectionate effusion raise my Catherine in the opinion of her honoured friend!'—How flattering was this approbation, when sanctioned and justified by principles so noble! and yet, my mother, a sort of humiliating sentiment mixed itself with the proud but latent congratulations of my throbbing heart. Gustavus beheld the effect, though he could not detect the cause of that confusion which scarcely permitted an oral acceptance of his addresses; for when he delicately reiterated his suit, I could only refer him to those whose suffrage was entirely necessary to sanction them. Satisfied with a reference from which he had nothing to fear, this noble lover contrived to obtain (before we parted) a—sort of——Dear Madam," continued the timid girl, "was I wrong in confessing an attachment which must redound to my future glory? Was it an infringement on delicacy to own a sense of gratitude for an offer which gives dignity even to a daughter of Saxe Lunenburgh's house?"

"Oh no, my lovely child!" said the weeping yet happy mother, "with Gustavus your character is safe, your consequence secured. Guarded by the principles, the virtues of that Monarch, how blessed will be the woman of his choice! for is not an alliance with him the summit of the highest ambition? Yes, my Catherine, the proudest maid may glory in such a lot! But, alas! how limited are our most perfect enjoyments—how much is wanting to the completion of mortal felicity! Not many hours are elapsed since the uncertainty of my daughter's establishment gave my heart a maternal pang;

now that suspense is no more—now that I contemplate her future glory, that heart has encouraged fresh disquiet. A tender apprehension clouds the brilliant prospect; and though the cause for anxiety has changed its ground, it exists in another shape; for—Oh selfish consideration! how shall I part with my Catherine? her so lately found, so truly beloved! Forgive me, revered Blanch!—forgive me, sweet Catherine, but how can I part to meet no more?"

"*Part* did my precious parent say?" and the tone of rapture—the look of exultation sunk to dejection and despondency—"what, part for ever with a blessing the most filial tenderness can scarcely appretiate! No, Madam, I cannot give up a treasure so recently discovered!" and she threw herself into the Duchess's extended arms, who wept in silence, while Blanch, in her usual friendly, but dignified manner, declared her disapprobation of this imbecility.

"You are wrong," she cried, "my friends, in thus rejecting, as I may say, so great a portion of felicity, and poisoning all its sweets by reverting to future contingencies. Look up, dear Catherine, and receive the congratulations of one who sincerely rejoices in the fulfilment of her most zealous wishes."

The Duchess felt all the force of this honest reproof, and candidly imputed to her own weakness the melancholy foreboding of her sorrowing daughter.

"We are indeed to blame, my sweet girl," she cried, "and are guilty of the highest injustice both to this revered lady and the matchless Gustavus, by thus saddening, with the most selfish ingratitude, an hour so replete with blessings."

Catherine blushed for this apparent deficiency in politeness and common generosity, and could have knelt for that forgiveness, which she was conscious her behaviour made necessary. Blanch smiled her pardon, and sealed it with a fervent embrace, at the same time cautioning her young friend against the indulgence of feelings which, she justly observed, were, while under proper restraint, the very essence of temporal felicity; but, if suffered to obtain an undue influence, would poison the cup of human enjoyments, how equally soever its other ingredients might be tempered.

To dwell longer upon scenes to which no description can do adequate justice, would be both useless and unnecessary. The Duke, during Catherine's conference with her mother, had received, with a delight his words, his actions, his countenance betrayed, the manly and open confession of his royal friend's predilection for his admired Catherine; and without offending the delicacy of a parent concerned for the honor of his child, he contrived to inform Magnus of his sufferings respecting Sigismunda, whose partiality to, and recommendation of, her cousin as a proper partner of his throne, he failed not to place in a light which, if ever that amiable victim's ardent application to him in Catherine's behalf, should transpire, would gratify rather than displease the noble Duke; and this laconic recital was given by Gustavus in a style equally free from undue pride and degrading servility.

Saxe Lunenburgh expressed his almost rapturous acquiescence with the Monarch's proposals with a readiness that carried sincere pleasure to the petitioner's heart; and he followed up his request with a wish for a speedy celebration of the nuptials, which would open, he doubted not, the fairest prospect of domestic peace.

CONCLUSION.

"Hail, wedded love! mysterious law!
By thee adult'rous lust was driven from men
Among the bestial herds to range: by thee,
Founded in reason, loyal, just, and pure,
Relations dear, and all the charities
Of father, son, and brother first were known."
MILTON.

IN the arrangement made by Gustavus for the establishment of his royal household, in which an union with Catherine would necessarily occasion considerable alteration, the Monarch gave every testimony of a magnificent spirit. The Palace he contemplated was scarcely founded, and the scale of his present residence much too small for the accommodation of his Queen, although the architects were forwarding, to their utmost power, the designs of their noble employer in raising the edifice, for the splendid finishing of which a grateful people were eager to contribute a willing and unlimited assistance. But in this calculation they considered not that noble pride which secretly scorned to owe an obligation of a nature so trivial; and while his ready acknowledgments soothed their consequence, his determined rejection of the liberal offer pained their feelings.

Dissatisfied with the comparative smallness of the late Governor's house, yet unable to make a better choice, Gustavus could only select and improve its richest apartments for the reception of Catherine, whose modest approbation of her Sovereign's endeavours to promote her ease and happiness, was not lost upon that discerning Monarch. Every word, every action of that timid maid gave her additional interest with her betrothed. Even the comparison his once refractory heart would sometimes bring forward in favour of Sigismunda, no longer preponderated with such decided sway; and the sigh of retrospection was soon suppressed by a cheerful certainty, that he was not only obeying the dictates of that regretted angel, in chusing the estimable daughter of Magnus, but was giving to himself the best chance for recovered peace in making a choice so eligible; and to add to Catherine's happiness, he lost no time in making proposals to Saxe Lunenburgh for detaining his Duchess at the Swedish Court, till his dominions should regain their former tranquillity.

In return for this goodness, or rather to gratify the benevolence of her own spirit, in contributing to what she imagined was the hoarded delight of Gustavus, the generous girl made Sigismunda's beauties, her tenderness, and self-denial the frequent subjects of conversation with her lover; and this totally independent of any illiberal sentiment, for she freely avowed her sense of the ravage disappointment must have made in his devoted heart, and by this conduct secured to herself the admiration, esteem, and affection of this generous man.

Willing, nay eager, to make his intended alliance with the Swedish hero as public as the shortness of his stay would permit, Duke Magnus expressed a wish for public tournaments, where he proposed to maintain the pre-eminence of his lady's charms over the frigid beauties of the north; but this the Duchess positively forbade: and Gustavus, to gratify the high chivalric spirit of his guest, proposed to take the lists in behalf of his affianced bride.

In consequence of this resolution, dispatches were sent to the several provinces, with courtly invitations to any Knight who might be inclined to break a lance with that renowned hero; while various improvements were making in the ornaments and interior appearance of the King's temporary abode—even to a degree of luxury till then unknown to that comparatively infant city, which, founded only in the preceding century, exhibited but few traits of polite civilization, or elegance of manners, till the reign preceding Christian's usurpation. This palace, which was built in the form of a pavilion, that opened on each side to apartments deigned for state, was situated on the Lake, where it was proposed to exhibit a nautical engagement, the season being favourable to such amusements; and before the grand entrance of the pavilion, a large space was cleared for the lists, while the back front opened to a wilderness, planted in the taste of ancient times, and furnished with several antique statues brought from Rome by John, who had visited that city to procure some immunities for his subjects.

Desirous of evincing his attachment to the Reformers, Gustavus engaged a Bishop, suspected of favouring Luther's principles, to give him the nuptial benediction, which ceremony was to take place at the closing of the sports; and Catherina felt happy in the idea that her child would be emancipated from the superstitious imposition of the Romish Church, by pledging her vows in the simple and pious manner of the Protestants.

Sensible of the honour done them by the royal challenger, all who could avail themselves of his gracious invitation, appeared at Stockholm within the time limited; and every arrangement being concluded, a trumpeter proclaimed the commencement of the military sports, which were to open with the following day. Catherine's heart trembled at the idea of being made a public spectacle, while her modesty predicted that mortification, which she feared her supposed vanity might incur, in appearing as a candidate for honours due only to superior beauty; and though she doubted not the skill and courage of her valorous Knight, she was fearful his dignity might suffer in the erroneous choice he had made, as viewed in the light only of the lady of his gallant devoirs. But this idea she ventured not to communicate; and her blushing reluctance to appear as Queen of the sports, was attributed by her encouraging friends to a natural timidity, which the Duchess tenderly exhorted her to conquer.

If ever Catherine's person could justly claim unbounded admiration, it was at that moment, in which she returned her grateful, but scarcely articulate, thanks for the thundering shouts of applause which met her delighted ear, when, seated beneath the superb canopy, she bowed to all around, and, placed between Blanch and her mother, exhibited, in her varying countenance, the mixed sensations of chastened rapture and diffident humility. The Duchess sighed at the recollection of a similar scene, when, proud in youthful beauty, she secretly gloried in her distinguished lot without an idea of its dreadful consequences, and mentally implored a happier fate for her child.

Saxe Lunenburgh, as he stood for a moment proudly surveying her still lovely features, observed in the passing cloud (which shaded their matronly sweetness) its real origin, and softly whispered—"There are no more Sir Gormunds to poison my Catherina's felicity!"—Then ardently pressing her hand, while he threw an exulting glance upon his smiling daughter, withdrew to attend her royal Knight in the capacity of his Esquire—a post which Gustavus found great difficulty in permitting the father of his intended bride to fill; but eager to express his delighted approbation of the hero who had so publicly honoured him, Magnus felt no degradation of character in the temporary inferiority of his station, and in a few minutes after appeared in the Monarch's train, bearing an extra lance, and habited in a style which, though extremely sumptuous, declared his situation for the day.

If Catherine, by her demeanour, person, and ornaments, had secured the attention, and excited the praise, of a surrounding multitude, the entrance of her illustrious Knight changed for a time the object of their clamours. His armour was far from gaudy, but extremely valuable, being an equal mixture of purple and gold, and tastefully fancied, without departing from the fashion of those times. The feathers, which bent gracefully over his golden helmet, were of the above-mentioned royal colour. His shield, surrounded with a twist of laurel and crown imperial, bore the expressive device of Venus crowning Mars with a wreath of the same kind as the border, whose foot rested upon the figure of a monster, with this motto enclosing the whole—"*Right overcomes might.*"—The grace, the animation, the fine proportion, and peerless skill of this noble challenger in the management of his fiery dappled charger, won all hearts, and engaged every eye; till, attracted by his elegant and tender notice of the confused but happy Catherine, they again admired her modest yet fascinating appearance, whose dress in some measure corresponded with the colours of her Knight.—A robe of light purple, richly decorated round the border with an intermixture of pearls and diamonds—a girdle of the same costly ornaments, and a coronet of gold lightly studded with similar jewels, were gifts of the noble Blanch; who, with the state and title of a Sovereign, threw off its troublesome appendages, and beheld her beloved Catherine in these splendid adornments, with a pleasure they never communicated when they made a part of her own personal decorations.

After the different Knights had successively paraded the lists, and again retired to their stations, one of whom, clad in black and white armour, and mounted on a black steed, wore the colours of Catherine as a sash girt upon his arm, and gave a sentiment of displeasure to all her noble friends, the tournament began, in which the motley dressed Knight was tolerably successful, till Gustavus approached to dispute the prize with him, when his dread of such an adversary appeared in his reluctance to engage. Gustavus pitied the raw challenger, and lightly disarming him, gave over the conquest.

"Another Sir Gormund!" whispered Blanch to the Duchess, smiling.

"But I trust," answered that lady, shuddering, "not mischievous."

Catherine beheld the disguised Knight's visible shame, and experienced a sort of horror at seeing him quit the lists with every mark of rage and indignation. Even Gustavus was concerned to find the stranger had absented himself from the grand banquet which succeeded this first day's sports; and ordered every enquiry to be made for him, but without effect.

Decked with the trophy of his easily acquired victory, Gustavus led his Catherine to the pavilion prepared for their numerous guests; and perceiving his illustrious Esquire had not resumed his proper dignity, humorously restored it, by knighting him upon the spot, and placing him on a seat next to that prepared for himself.

The magnificent scene which this apartment presented, produced a most brilliant effect. At the upper end, upon a temporary floor, which was covered with a sort of embroidered tapestry, and raised about two feet from the ground, was a table spread with every delicacy a northern climate could produce, for the accommodation of the royal party, who sat beneath a stately canopy of fawn-coloured velvet, lined with a pale blue satin, and ornamented with tassels, fringe, ropes, and lace of the purest silver. The curtains were tastefully drawn back, so as to admit a full view of the august company, while garlands and festoons of every blooming production Sweden could boast, mixed with the hardy laurel, hung gracefully pendant from the drapery above. The whole suite of apartments were furnished on the same scale of local grandeur, and excited much applause from the Knights and other guests, who were placed at tables to the right and left of the royal board.

In the evening of this festive day, a sort of mask, representing the state of Sweden in its more barbarous time, proved a high gratification to the admirers of Heathen Mythology, taken from the Edda of Saemund. The characters were properly dressed, and as well sustained. Rinda, Odin, Dager and Friga were skilfully personated; they performed the song of *"The Traveller, or Descent of Odin,"* with much critical knowledge; and the death of the Pagan Balder drew tears from some of their gentle auditors. As soon as the mask was concluded, dancing closed the joyous sports, which were on the morrow to be supplied by a nautical review.

When Catherine retired with her anxious mother, they both reverted to the mysterious Knight, whose sullen conduct indicated more than Gustavus would assign to it, who smiled at the fears of his bride when she ventured, in the course of the day, to mention her apprehension of some unknown enemy. The Duchess, prejudiced by fears founded on former events, was exceedingly dissatisfied with this incident, and began to fancy the designs of a Gottsler in the singular behaviour of the Knight.

While thus giving way to the suggestions of a foreboding heart, they were suddenly alarmed by repeated outcries from the city, and shortly after distinguished the words—"Treason!"—"Gustavus is in danger!"—"Seize the traitors!"—"Save the King!"—"To arms, citizens!"—Frantic with terror, the Duchess and her daughter rushed to Blanch's apartment, who, equally amazed, was leaving it to learn the cause of an uproar so shocking. The Duke was absent, for he had not quitted Gustavus. All was confusion—trumpets, drums, and shouts from different parts mixed their discordant notes, and produced a scene in the highest degree alarming, when Saxe Lunenburgh hastily entered the hall, where the Duchess and her friends were agonizing with horror. He calmed their fears by assuring them that the present disturbance originated in a false report; that the black and white Knight was indeed discovered in the anti-chamber leading to Gustavus's room in disguise, and that on being examined, a short sword was taken from beneath his cloke; but, eager to quiet the apprehensions of his Duchess, her child, and Blanch, he staid to hear no more.

"My father!" cried Catherine, throwing herself into his arms, "leave us not here, I entreat you. Dear Madam," cried she to the Queen, "and you, my mother, stay not here unprotected!"

"We will all go, my love," said the Duke; and unmindful of the tumult which still raged, he bore the trembling females safe to the temporary palace, when the first object which encountered Catherine's eyes as she entered the Council Chamber, was Gustavus calmly examining several people, whose business was to criminate her mysterious Knight. On him then her regards were next fixed, and with horror she recognised Fitzer's person. In his features guilt, fear, and shame seemed struggling; his frame was almost convulsed; and when called upon by his awful but serene judge to defend himself, he could scarcely deprecate the wrath he had justly incurred.

From all that could be gathered during this examination, it appeared that Fitzer's design was if possible to destroy Gustavus while engaged at the tournament. His motive for chusing Catherine's colours was to impress a sense of his attachment, sufficient to counteract any suspicion his presence might create; and, made desperate by his disappointment, the witnesses, who were people he had brought from Dalecarlia, declared he offered a high reward to them, if they would assassinate the King!

Catherine could scarcely support herself when this atrocious intention was asserted; but she expressed the greatest astonishment when Gustavus, turning to the culprit, with all the majesty of offended dignity, demanded his reasons for such base, unworthy conduct. Fitzer could not speak; and the Monarch, perceiving his incapability, slowly arose, and addressing his people—"You see," he cried, "how low guilt debases the human mind! Think you that a reptile like this can hurt the peace or safety of a Gustavus? No, my friends, by thus acting, he can only wound himself. It is therefore my pleasure, and it must not be disputed, that this man shall quit Stockholm, nay Sweden itself, in safety. Go, Von Hemert, inform the people of this determination, and by their obedience to my wishes, I shall judge of their future fealty."

Accustomed to obey this extraordinary Monarch, the multitude quietly dispersed, and, wonderful to say! the criminal escaped that punishment he so richly merited.

Dispirited by this disagreeable incident, neither Blanch, Catherine, nor the Duchess could attend the nautical amusements which took place on the following day; and even the nuptials were celebrated devoid of that pomp by which they were to have been distinguished: but this was a circumstance that affected not the happy party, who tasted more felicity in the calm retirement of domestic enjoyments, than all the pomp of grandeur could bestow.

Possessed of her highest and most rational wishes, Catherine set herself to study the duties of her twofold station:—as a Queen, she was cautious to avoid the extremes of pride and familiarity; and by the steadiness of her conduct, soon made herself a blessing to her royal consort, and all around her.

The Duke of Saxe Lunenburgh, before he departed from a family rendered still dearer by accumulated ties, was solicited by a charitable Priest of the Grey Friars Society, to send his free pardon, which that wretched mortal feared might be withdrawn since his perusal of the tremendous confession, to Father Anthony (late Sir Gormund Gottsler), who was supposed to be in extreme danger. This was freely given, and made doubly precious by being united to that of the Duchess.

"Tell him," said that generous woman, "all is as it should be—the aggressor is punished, the persecuted rewarded. May everlasting happiness await his entrance to another state! The faith I have of late adopted, rejects any belief in purgatory; therefore I am justified in hoping that his sufferings will terminate with this life. Doubtless, Father, my abjuration of the Pope's supremacy offends your principles, and an apostate Nun you think is herself an object of abhorrence; but remember that, in renouncing an erroneous belief, I have extended my charity, and that virtue is the first and greatest in the eye of that Being, who disregards the outward daubings of pompous nothingness."

Blanch, ever excellent and respectable, felt a pang for Christian's fate, whose death happened near the era of Catherine's nuptials: but in the converse of her estimable friends, she soon learned to pity, without regretting, that miserable victim to his vices.

Iwan, the faithful follower of his master's fortunes, rose, as much by merit as favour, to a dignified rank in the Army, and obtained high raise from his Sovereign for his behaviour in several succeeding campaigns.

"The friendship of a Monarch," observed Gustavus, when complimented on his firm attachment to those by whose assistance he had ascended the throne, "ought to be fervent, steady, and useful as the beams of yonder sun. Its power should penetrate the obscurest recesses of neglected worth—its influence extend to the happiness of all to whom it may be needful. No accident should injure it—no ill-founded suspicions destroy it; an individual lives for the benefit of his own little progeny—a King is accountable for the interest of a nation!"

Thus spoke the greatest Monarch that ever ruled a turbulent, unsteady people; and as he spoke, he acted. When depressed, poor, and even labouring for the morsel he shared with his fellow-miners, their interest, their security were the objects of his patriotic designs! when mourning the fate of parents, sisters, and an idolized fair-one, he was still Gustavus—his soul rose superior to misfortune! and when surrounded by the insignia of monarchical government, the same modest, steady demeanour distinguished that exalted man!—Patient in affliction, magnanimous in battle, merciful in conquest, moderate in prosperity—tender, affectionate, and lively in his domestic moments—such was GUSTAVUS ERICSON, the deliverer of his country, who died a Christian as he had lived a hero, on the 22d of September, 1560, aged 70 years!

FINIS.

NOTES

Title page: these lines appear on the title pages of all three volumes in the 1801 edition; mistakenly attributed to Fielding they are instead from Aaron Hill's *Merope: A Tragedy* (1749), Act V (Misquoted: ". . . / Dangers, and doubts, and toils, each moment seize, / . . .").

5 *epigraph*: John Milton (1608-1674), *Paradise Lost*, Book I (1667), lines 111-116.

5 *Dalecarlia*: Sw. Dalarna, province in central Sweden, to the north-west of Stockholm and Uppsala. In his *History of the Revolution in Sweden*, Vertot represents sixteenth-century Dalecarlia as a province of inaccessible mountains, ruled by a savage people defying government interference.

5 *the barbarous despotism . . . Norway*: Christian II sought to reinforce the Kalmar Union, a 1397 treaty according to which Denmark, Norway, and Sweden were to be united under one sovereign while retaining a certain degree of national self-government. Yet periodically from the 1430s onwards, the Swedes resisted Danish sovereignty and elected administrators (Sw. riksföreståndare, also translated as "regent") who opposed current union politics, and, from the early sixteenth century, the actual union itself.

5 *Sudermania, Westermania, and Nerecia*: Sw. Södermanland, Västmanland and Närke, provinces in central Sweden.

5 *His servant . . . was missing*: this incident is retold both by Gustavus Ericson's first chronicler, Peder Swart, and by Vertot.

6 *assassinating his father, and confining his mother and sisters*: the historical Gustavus Ericson's father was executed in the Stockholm Bloodbath in November 1520, and after the massacre his mother and two of his sisters were brought by king Christian as prisoners to Denmark, where they died.

6 *from which he had been recently delivered . . . disinterested Dane*: this refers to a historical incident in 1518, where the hostages, demanded by Christian II to ensure his own safety during a planned meeting with the Swedish administrator Sten Sture the Younger, were treacherously abducted to Denmark. Gustavus Ericson, who was one of the hostages, was placed under the surveillance of his relative Erik Banner at the fortress of Kalø in Jutland but escaped the following year. The "disinterested Dane" is Banner, described by Vertot as Gustavus's "friendly Jaylor" for allowing him some relative freedom of movement (77).

6 *Steen Sture, the Regent, or rather the lawful Monarch of Sweden*: although elected administrator by the Swedish national council in 1512, Sten Sture the Younger (1492-1520) never gained the title of king. He died in January 1520 after a wound received in battle when he met king Christian's army at Bogesund.

7 *an old copper-mine*: there were several copper mines in Dalecarlia, the largest and most famous being Stora Kopparberget at Falun.

8 *amor patriæ*: love of his country.

8 *His ideas of liberty . . . monarchical rights and privileges*: writing on the topic of rebellion in the wake of the French Revolution, and alert to the fear of a French invasion rampant in Britain during the Napoleonic wars, Mackenzie takes great pains to show where her own loyalties lie and to avert any suspicion of political radicalism.

8 *his own illustrious descent from her ancient Sovereigns*: here Mackenzie obviously follows Vertot, who claims that Gustavus was "descended from the antient Kings of *Sweden*, and particularly from King *Canutson*, who was his great uncle" (59). Karl Knutsson Bonde, thrice elected king by the Swedes in the second half of the fifteenth century when the Kalmar Union was torn by internal conflicts, was the half-brother of Gustavus Ericson's great grandmother. As Vertot also points out, Gustavus was related to Sten Sture the Younger, who was his uncle by marriage. Gustavus Ericson's supposed descent from any unspecified "ancient" sovereigns of Sweden must, however, be regarded as mythical.

8 *Gothland*: Sw. Götaland, the southern part of Sweden, although in this context not necessarily including the Island of Gothland (Sw. Gotland) in the Baltic Sea.

10 *epigraph*: the quoted lines are not from Brooke but from James Miller's (1706-1744) and John Hoadly's (1711-1776) play *Mahomet the Impostor. A Tragedy* (1744), Act III.i, adapted from Voltaire. Mackenzie may have confused this play with Henry Brooke's (c.1703-1783) play on the same theme, *The Impostor* (*The Poetical Works of Henry Brooke*, 4 vols., Dublin 1792, vol. 3).

10 *the animal spirit*: the component in the brain and nervous system which, in older medicine, was thought to be responsible for sensation and motion.

11 *you was in distress*: the ungrammatical speech of the peasant functions as a class-marker, a common device used by eighteenth-century writers to indicate a character's belonging to a lower and hence uneducated class.

11 *Van Melen*: Mackenzie apparently borrowed the surname for this ficti-

tious character from Berend von Melen, an important person in helping Gustavus Ericson to negotiate military support for his campaign from Lübeck in 1522. A fictionalised version of the historical von Melen, in early histories of Sweden referred to alternatively as Bern van Melen (Swart), Bernard de Melen (Pufendorf) and Bernard de Milan (Vertot), appears in later chapters of Mackenzie's novel under the name of Bernard Milan.

12 *some prodigious larches*: a misdirected touch of local color, as larches were not found growing wild in Sweden until the nineteenth century.

12 *rubbing it with snow*: rubbing the damaged area with snow was long considered an effective cure for frostbite in popular belief.

12 *the frigid zone*: technically speaking, the area which lies within the north (or south) polar circle; Dalecarlia is however not that far north.

13 *Peter*: apparently Van Melen's son.

13 *enthusiasm*: a controversial term in eighteenth-century discourse, connoting passionate ardor sometimes viewed favorably but sometimes, especially in religious and political contexts, with suspicion as bordering on dangerous fanaticism.

13 *usurped the lineal succession of Sweden*: the accusation is not correct, as Sweden was formally an elective kingdom until Gustav Ericson made the succession to the throne hereditary in 1544. During the Kalmar union, the Danish monarchs laid claims to the Swedish crown as well, and the only Swedish monarch appointed during the period, Karl Knutsson, owed his elevation to skilful politics rather than ancestry. Christian II claimed the throne of Sweden after the death of his father, the union king John (Danish name Hans), against whom the Swedes had been rebelling since 1501. After the death of Sten Sture in 1520, Christian negotiated with the Swedish national council and was formally elected king of Sweden in exchange for a promise of amnesty to his political opponents (a promise he would not keep).

13 *murdered its Monarch*: the reference is to Sten Sture the Younger, although he was not formally a "monarch." Sture was not assassinated but died after a wound received in battle (see note to p. 6).

14 *phlegm*: one of the four bodily humors, the internal balance of which in a human being was in Greek and Roman medicine thought to decide that person's temperament. A person with excess of phlegm was thus thought to have a somewhat stolid and not easily excitable disposition.

14 *epigraph*: Thomas Otway (1652-1685), *The History and Fall of Caius Marius. A Tragedy* (1680), Act III.i, lines 420-423. (Line 421 misquoted: "The throat of death . . .").

14 *Hedmora*: Sw. Hedemora, a town in the mining district of Dalecarlia, granted its town charter in 1459, but hardly the "chief village of Dalecarlia" or of particular historical significance in the Gustavus Ericson story.

15 *Marienburg*: a fictitious character, as is his daughter.

16 *Sweden's lawful Monarch . . . the Prince*: by having her characters call Gustavus Ericson a Prince and refer to him as the lawful monarch of Sweden, Mackenzie apparently wishes her readers to assume not only that Sten Sture the Younger was formally the king of Sweden but also that Gustavus Ericson would be next in line to succeed him, neither of which assumptions is historically correct. Although belonging to the upper ranks of the nobility, there was nothing in Gustavus's background to single him out as an obvious heir to the crown, even had Sweden been a hereditary kingdom at the time. When Gustavus Ericson was elected king in 1523, this was rather owing to his success in conducting the war of liberation against the union king, Christian II.

17 *public weal*: the welfare of the community as a whole.

17 *Nyhopping*: Sw. Nyköping, a town south of Stockholm, whose medieval fortress Nyköpingshus was famous for its dungeon.

17 *Gottenburg*: an anachronism, as the city of Gothenburg (Sw. Göteborg) was not founded until the early seventeenth century. The fortress of Älvsborg had however been situated at the site of present-day Gothenburg since the fourteenth century.

18 *to Hedmora*, for the purpose of sounding its inhabitants: Mackenzie may be confusing Hedemora with a similar-sounding village in Dalecarlia; for the place where the historical Gustavus Ericson first persuaded the population to rebel against Christian was not Hedmora but Mora, situated at lake Siljan.

18 *epigraph*: Hugh Blair (1718-1800), Sermon XIV on the theme "Rejoice with trembling" (Psalm 2.11), in *Sermons by Hugh Blair* (London 1784).

18 *Ulrica*: a fictitious character. Christian is known to have had a mistress, a woman of Dutch descent called Dyveke, and to have kept up the liaison even after his marriage in 1515, but Dyveke died as early as 1517.

19 *Catherine Sleswie*: although the character of Catherine is turned into a historical personage at the very end of the novel, the narrative of the orphaned Miss Sleswie up to that point is of Mackenzie's own invention and has no factual basis.

21 *Madam Schewellen, at Upsal*: apparently a fictitious character, never appearing in person in the novel.

22 *plantations of beech*: a minor misconception on the author's part, as beech trees would not have thrived as far north as Dalecarlia.

23 *visiting the mines . . . under the borrowed appellation of Linden*: that Gustavus Ericson should have worked in the copper mines under an assumed name is an episode in the mythologizing of his Dalecarlian adventures that seems to have originated with Vertot (cf. Omberg, 23). The name Linden seems however to be Mackenzie's own contribution.

24 *epigraph*: William Havard (1710-1778), *Scanderbeg: A Tragedy* (1733), Act I. iii, lines 46-50.

31 *the river Dala*: Sw. Dalälven

32 *Magnus, Duke of Saxe Lunenburgh*: as becomes obvious from Mackenzie's references to Magnus of Saxe Lunenburgh later in the novel, she confuses the region and town of Lunenburg (Germ. Lüneburg), part of the Prussian province of Hanover, with the duchy of Saxe Lauenburg in lower Saxony. The confusion may be understandable, as both place names figure in the ancestry of Britain's Hanoverian kings. For after the death of the last duke of Saxe-Lauenberg in the late seventeenth century, that duchy fell to the duke of Brunswick-Lunenburg (Germ. Braunschweig-Lüneburg), and then to his nephew, the future king of Britain, George I.

33 *Baron Bock*: the long footnote referring to Baron Bock is Mackenzie's own, and constitutes a summary of an "Essay, On the Secret Tribunal and its Judges, formerly existing in Westphalia, Extracted from the second volume of the Miscellanous Works of Baron Bock," included in the first volume of Benedikte Naubert, *Herman of Unna; A Series of Adventures of the Fifteenth Century . . . ,*" 3rd ed., 3 vols., (1796). The tribunals and free judges described in the summary are those of the medieval so-called fehmic courts (Germ. Vehmgericht or Fehmgericht), originating in Westphalia but active also in other parts of Germany. Their influence was at its strongest in the fourteenth and early fifteenth centuries, but was considerably reduced at the end of the 1500s. Having been delegated extensive powers by the Emperor, including the right to pronounce death sentences, the fehmic courts were greatly feared, and at the turn of the nineteenth century they became a popular topic in German-influenced gothic novels of the so-called horror school.

34 *epigraph*: James Thomson (1700-1748) and David Mallet (c.1705-1765), *Alfred: A Masque* (1740), Act II.iii, lines 31-33.

35 *Fitzer . . . the son of the murdered King*: Mackenzie probably based her fictitious character of Fitzer on the historical "Daljunkern" (meaning "the young man from Dalecarlia") who, claiming to be Sten Sture's son Nils, got the support of the Dalecarlians for an uprising against king Gustavus in 1527.

36 *citation*: a summons to a court of justice.

37 *Hernosand*: an anachronistic statement, as the town of Härnösand, situated on the north-western coast of the Baltic Sea, was not founded until the mid-1580s, by order of Gustavus Ericson's son king Johan III. The misunderstanding probably derives from the fact that in the eighteenth century it had become the second largest town in northern Sweden.

40 *a lady . . . her father's sister*: apparently a reference to the previously mentioned Madam Schewellen (see p. 21).

42 *epigraph*: John Dryden (1631-1700), *Don Sebastian* (1690), Act IV. iii, lines 363-368. Dorax's words in line 363 ("Till time discover what I have deserv'd") are rewritten, one line is left out, and the rest of Sebastian's answer in 364-368 is partly misquoted ("More then [*sic*] reward can answer. / If *Portugal* and *Spain* were joyn'd to *Affrica*, / And the main Ocean crusted into Land, / If Universall Monarchy were mine, / Here should the gift be plac'd"). A formulation very similar to that cited by Mackenzie appeared in a collection of mottoes published some sixty years later (Henry Southgate, *Many Thoughts of Many Minds*, 3rd ed., London, 1862, p. 619), and it seems not impossible that Mackenzie could have had access to some similar publication from which she may have quoted Dryden indirectly.

43 *defalcation . . . from*: failure in

44 *Eroson*: Västerås, later in the novel referred to as Westeraas, a town c. 65 rather than 40 miles from Stockholm by the lake Mälaren, and a bishop's see. The appellation Eroson appears to be a garbled form of Fr. "Arosen," the name used for the alternative Sw. name of the town, "Västra Aros."

45 *the . . . Maelar*: Sw. Mälaren.

46 *the Saxon language*: the language spoken in early sixteenth-century Saxony was Low German.

47 *boors*: country people of rude or unsophisticated manners.

49 *epigraph*: Thomas Otway, *Venice Preserv'd, or, A Plot Discover'd. A Tragedy* (1682), Act I.i, lines 210-211, 216-217.

50 *the linen . . . richly embroidered*: this episode is part of the lore surrounding Gustavus's Dalecarlian adventures. Peder Swart claims that it took

place in the house of Anders Persson (Pederson) at Rankhyttan, information which however is omitted in Vertot's version of the story.

50 *Von Hemert*: fictitious character, possibly remotely based on Anders Persson at Rankhyttan, who according to Swart, Vertot, and Scott (in whose book he becomes Andrew Lakintta) received Gustavus loyally and kindly, but was too afraid to support him openly.

53 *six noble hostages sent to Copenhagen as pledges of his safety*: in Gustavus's story of his father's murder, told in the following pages, the hostages demanded by Christian include not only Gustavus himself but, unhistorically, also his parents and sisters (cf. notes to p. 6). Gustavus Ericson's father was not executed in Danish captivity but during the massacre in Stockholm in 1520.

54 *the offspring of the illustrious Gustavus Ericson*: the father of the historical Gustavus Ericson and his sisters was called Eric Johansson, not Gustavus Ericson. The "–son" name was a patronymic and not a family name, Eric Johansson hence being the son of Johan and Gustavus Ericson the son of Eric.

55 *our royal master*: refers to Sten Sture the Younger (cf. note to p. 6).

55 *the Swedish dominions . . . black event*: *i.e.*, the territory controlled by Sten Sture the Younger and his supporters, including parts of present-day Sweden and Finland. Increasingly in conflict with his political opponents and, from 1517, under open attack from Danish troops under Christian II, Sture's regime came to an end after the battle of Bogesund in 1520 and the subsequent reinforcement of the Kalmar Union, when Christian II was installed as king of Sweden.

56 *Augusta*: the historical Gustavus Ericson's mother was called Cecilia. Mackenzie may have got the name Augusta from Henry Brooke's tragedy *Gustavus Vasa: The Deliverer of his Country* (1739), where Gustavus's mother appears under that name.

56 *Banner*: see note to p. 6

57 *Calo*: Kalø. See note to p. 6

57 *On the third of my departure*: *i.e.*, "on the third day since my departure . . ."

57 *Flensburgh*: a town at the present-day Danish-German border, in the early sixteenth century belonging to Denmark.

57 *Lubec*: Lübeck, a German city on the Baltic Sea, during the Middle Ages an important trading centre and the leading member of the Hanseatic League.

58 *the Triple State of Sweden, Denmark, and Norway*: *i.e.*, the Kalmar union.

58 *Calmar, a city garrisoned chiefly by Germans . . . I disdained any further development of my plan*: this episode agrees tolerably well with the accounts given by Swart in his chronicle, and Scott in her *History of Gustavus Ericson*. Kalmar, defended by a garrison of German soldiers, still held out against Christian, but the soldiers were apparently less than keen to put themselves under Gustavus's command and even threatened to kill him if he remained in the town.

58 *the late Administrator*: Sten Sture. "Administrator" is the term used in Vertot and Scott for Sw. "riksföreståndare".

58 *an old family castle in Sudermania*: Rävsnäs, a property belonging to to Gustavus's father. In Swart's chronicle, the peasants so unwilling to take up arms against Christian were encountered by Gustavus when traveling through the province of Småland, before temporarily retreating to Rävsnäs.

59 *epigraph*: Samuel Johnson (1709-1784), "The Winter's Walk" (from *Samuel Johnson: The Complete English Poems*, ed. J. D. Freeman, 1971), lines 9-12. (Misquoted: ". . . / Scarce frighted love maintains her fire, / . . .").

59 *Flensburgh, where I was left wounded by the Swedes*: in hinting at early sixteenth-century Flensburg as a scene of Swedish-Danish hostilities, Mackenzie seems to relocate events from the wars between Sweden and Denmark in the 1650s and early eighteenth century to the previous century.

60 *Lincopping*: Sw. Linköping, a town c. 130 miles south-west of Stockholm.

61 *arrived at the inn which Catherine occupied . . . hastened back to the abode of his friend*: an example of the author's rather relaxed attitude to geographical distances. The inn where Gustavus liberates Catherine is said to be located within two miles from Västerås (46), and given the distance of c. 118 miles between Västerås and Peterson's place at Linköping, the day trip back and forth undertaken by Gustavus would be quite a feat!

62 *Madam Peterson waited to take her coffee*: another anachronism, as coffee was not introduced as a drink in Sweden until the seventeenth century.

62 *Beware of Peterson*: the story of Peterson and his honest wife is based on an episode related by Swart and retold by both Vertot and Scott. It involves a man whom Swart calls Aren Pederson, living not at Linköping as does Mackenzie's character of Pederson, but at a place called Ornäs in Dalecarlia. On perceiving that her husband was about

to betray Gustavus to Christian's men, Aren Pederson's wife is said to have warned Gustavus and helped him to escape to a more loyal supporter.

63 *Count Struensee*: Mackenzie borrowed the name for this minor character from a well-known figure in Danish eighteenth-century history, Johann Friedrich Struensee (1737-1772). A German-born physician to the mentally ill Danish king Christian VII, Struensee rose to a position of more or less absolute political power and became the lover of the young queen, the British-born princess Caroline Matilda of Wales, before he fell victim to a conspiracy and was arrested and executed.

66 *a fleet horse*: a fast horse

68 *epigraph*: John Langhorne (1735-1779), "Hymn to Humanity," lines 76-77, 68-69, 80-81, from *The Effusions of Friendship and Fancy* (1763), vol. 1, letter XXVII.

68 *epocha*: a point in time beginning a new era.

72 *he removed them . . . from Copenhagen to Stockholm*: the historical Gustavus Ericson's mother and sisters died in Danish captivity, having been brought there after the Stockholm Bloodbath. That they should have returned to Stockholm as Christian's prisoners is Mackenzie's own invention.

75 *Augusta had mounted the funeral pile, while her lovely children*: the story of the dramatic death of Gustavus's mother and sisters given in the novel is fictitious.

76 *epigraph*: Queen Elizabeth I of England (1533-1603), "On Monsieur's Departure" (c. 1582), lines 1-4. The manuscript version preserved in the Ashmolean Museum was reprinted in John Nichols' *Progresses of Queen Elizabeth* (London, 1823), 2: 346. Mackenzie partly misquotes the first four lines which read: "I greeve, and dare not shewe my discontent; / I love, and yet am forst to seeme to hate; / I do, yet dare not say I ever meant; / I seem starke mute, but inwardly do prate."

79 *an annual feast . . . to be held at Mora*: this is the novel's first mention of Mora, which was indeed the village in Dalecarlia where the historical Gustavus Ericson managed to win the support of the population for his rebellion against Christian.

84 *the Convent at Eroson*: the hint that Sigismunda might be confined in the convent St. Croix at Eroson is the last we hear in the novel of this particular monastic institution, as its role as potential detention place for young women is in subsequent volumes taken over by another establishment, similar to St. Croix, but differently named and situated.

86 *epigraph*: lines 5-8 of "a Lapland Love-Song," ascribed to Ambrose

Phillips and quoted in *The Spectator* no. 366 (where line 6 reads, however, "I'd climb that pine-tree's topmost bough").

87 *The mines resounded with—"Gustavus for ever!"—"Down with the tyrant Christian!"*: the scene echoes the cheering peasants in the first act of Catherine Trotter's tragedy *The Revolution of Sweden* (1706) and the Dalecarlians crying out their praise of Gustavus at the end of Act III. iii in Brooke's *Gustavus Vasa*.

88 *Mora . . . return to Dalecarlia*: a geographical slip: the village of Mora is situated roughly at the centre of Dalecarlia. Possibly Mackenzie may have confused Dalecarlian Mora, which figures so importantly in the Gustavus Ericson story, with the famous stones on a meadow about six miles south-east of Uppsala (Mora stenar), where Swedish kings used to be formally elected during the Middle Ages. In Gustavus Ericson's history the place is however marginal, as he never went there to be elected.

90 *gone to Mr. Marienburg's*, as he turned towards Mora: in Mackenzie's geographical vision, Mora is apparently situated on the road leading from the assembly point of the army ("in a plain near Mora") to the Stockholmian suburb where Marienburg was said to have settled at the end of chapter 11.

92 *Gustavus led his warlike band . . . that province*: according to Swart, Gustavus Ericson began his military campaign in early 1521 by a successful attack on Kopparberget with a force of 400 men, who plundered the place and took the governor of the mine prisoner. The story is further elaborated by both Vertot and Scott.

93 *Bernard Milan, a noble Lubecker*: see note to p. 11.

94 *Epigraph*: James Fordyce, "Virtue and Pleasure: An Ode," from *Poems by James Fordyce* (1786), lines 43-48.

95 *the whole race of Marienburg*: all Marienburg's kinspeople or relations.

98 *Blanch*: the queen of the historical Christian II was not called Blanch but Elizabeth. She was the sister of the emperor Charles V, and had married Christian in 1515. The name Blanch might be suggested by an earlier Scandinavian queen, Blanche of Namur, who married the Swedish king Magnus Eriksson in 1335.

105 *epigraph*: Oliver Goldsmith (c.1730-1774), "Edwin and Angelina," a ballad included in chapter 8 of *The Vicar of Wakefield* (1766), lines 5-8. (Line 7 is misquoted: "Where wilds immeasurably spread.")

109 *Munster*: Münster, city in western Germany.

110 *First Cause*: used as a synonym for God. The underlying argument is

that since everything in the world has a cause, there must be somewhere a first cause, to which everything that exists ultimately owes its existence.

111 *unvitiated*: pure, unsullied.

116 *epigraph*: Philip Francis (c.1708-1773), *Eugenia: A Tragedy* (1752), Act V, lines 132-135.

118 *deserts*: wild regions, in this case of uninhabited forest land.

119 *Westphalia*: region in north-western Germany.

124 *epigraph*: John Dryden (1631-1700) and Nathaniel Lee (c.1653-1692), *The Duke of Guise. A Tragedy* (1683), Act III.i, lines 429-432 (misquoted: "Greater than Fame: Thou eldest of the Passions, / . . . / . . . / Wing me to my Revenge, . . .").

127 *Telga*: present-day Södertälje, until the early seventeenth century called Telje, a town about 19 miles south-west of Stockholm.

132 *My Liege*: a manner of addressing a liege lord, i. e., a lord to whom the speaker owes feudal allegiance. Also used in a wider sense, as here by a subject to address the king.

134 *felt excessive obligation . . . unsuspecting King*: Fitzer is grateful to Christian for planning to remove to Copenhagen with Ulrica, as he expects this to further his own plans to gain the throne of Sweden.

134 *epigraph*: Nathaniel Lee, *The Rival Queens, or The Death of Alexander the Great* (1677), Act III, lines 173-177.

134 *Westeraas*: a town approximately 65 miles from Stockholm by the lake Mälaren. See note to p. 44.

134 *Nericia*: Närke, a province in central Sweden.

134 *The Archbishop of Upsal . . . opposed his designs*: Gustav Trolle, appointed archbishop by the Pope in 1515, was a keen supporter of the Kalmar union, and used his private army to fiercely resist Gustavus Ericson's rebellion. Deposed and imprisoned by Sten Sture the Younger in 1517, but reinstated to his office by Christian II at whose coronation he officiated in 1520, he was thought to have been instrumental in instigating the massacre at Stockholm following the coronation festivities.

135 *laying siege to Stockholm*: Gustavus Ericson's siege of Stockholm lasted from the summer of 1521 to June 1523.

135 *Claude Lorraine*: French artist (1600-1682), famous for his landscape paintings.

135 *that soothing hum*: an allusion to Shakespeare's play *King Henry V*

(1600), Act IV, Prologue, lines 4- 5: "From camp to camp through the foul womb of night / The hum of either army stilly sounds."

135 *nervously*: powerfully.

135 *rein-deer*: a stereotyped touch of local color. Reindeer would hardly be found in the Stockholm region, however.

136 *reconnoitre*: to survey

137 *countenance*: patronage

138 *the means of amends are in your power*: Gustavus is hinting at the possibility of Sir Bernard challenging him to a duel.

144 *North Malm*: at this time still a suburb to Stockholm.

144 *epigraphs*: James Thomson (1700-1748), *The Tragedy of Sophonisba* (1730), Act V.vii, lines 8 and 14 (the last line misquoted: "It is to me perfection, glory, triumph") ; and, William Mason (1725-1797), *Caractacus, A Dramatic Poem* (1759), "Ode 1.1," lines 1-4.

144 *armed cap-a-piè*: armed from head to foot. (The placing of the grave accent on the last word is Mackenzie's).

146 *corps de réserve*: reserve troops, kept out of the action until needed.

146 *Von Hemert*, the protector of his child: the 1801 text reads "Van Melen, the protector of his child . . . ." As the context makes it quite clear that the person referred to is Conan Von Hemert, this obvious error has been corrected.

151 *Egill . . . his Treasurer Thunno*: according to Snorri Sturluson's *Ynglinga Saga*, included in his *Heimskringla*, Egill was a king of Sweden in what would have been the fifth or sixth century. His slave Tunni, Egill's father's former treasurer, fled into the woods where he lived as a robber with other escaped slaves, whose leader he became. Having defeated Egill in battle eight times, Tunni was finally slain. Pufendorf (who uses the name form "Thunno") reproduces the tale in his *Compleat History of Sweden*, but neither there nor in Snorri's version is Egill's adversary confined anywhere for life.

152 *Syren*: in Greek mythology, a siren was a sea nymph thought to lure sailors to destruction by their enchanting singing.

154 *epigraph*: William Congreve (1670-1729), *The Mourning Bride. A Tragedy* (1697), Act III.i, lines 290-294 (line 291 misquoted: "There, there, I bleed; there pull the cruel Cords").

155 *Wismar*: a town on the German coast of the Baltic Sea, between Lübeck and Rostock.

155 *Wrangel*: Mackenzie probably borrowed the name for this peasant

from Karl Gustav Wrangel, Swedish military and naval commander during the Thirty Years War (1618-48).

156 *to the fortress of Calo*: Mackenzie seems to forget that Kalø in Jutland was a Danish fortress, and would not have been under the immediate control of Magnus, a North-German duke.

159 *equerries*: officers in charge of the horses in a royal or noble establishment.

164 *John, King of Sweden, prior to Steen Sture*: Christian II's father King Hans, king of Denmark from 1481 to 1513, Norway (1483-1513) and Sweden (1497-1501). His official name as king of Sweden was Johan II.

166 *epigraph*: Shakespeare, *Othello*, Act. III.iii, lines 106-108. (Misquoted: "... thou echo'st me; / As if there were some monster in thy thought / Too hideous to be shown.")

169 *Sundercoping*: Sw. Söderköping, a town about 115 miles south of Stockholm.

169 *sent Sir Bernard . . . Lubeckers attached themselves to his cause*: an incident related by Swart, Vertot, and Scott, said to have taken place in 1522.

173 *a small and apparently deserted monastery . . . unprovoked brutality*: this episode, although set in a fictitious convent and at a different location, seems to draw on the 1521 massacre at the Cistercian monastery at Nydala in the province of Småland. On traveling back to Denmark, Christian II had the Abbott and several of the monks executed by drowning on suspicion that they had actively supported the local opposition against his regime.

179 *epigraphs*: Edward Young (1683-1765), *The Revenge, A Tragedy* (1721), Act II.i, lines 254-256 (line 256 slightly misquoted: "And he who knows not that, was born for Nothing"); and, Osborne Sidney Wandesford, *Fatal Love; or, The Degenerate Brother. A Tragedy* (1730), Act III.

181 *Christian's cruel and impolitic behaviour in Denmark*: in 1523 the Danish nobility in Jutland rebelled against King Christian and deposed him. According to Vertot, the clergy were equally dissatisfied with the king as were the nobles, and supported by Lübeck, Christian's adversaries appointed his uncle, Frederick, to be their new king.

181 *Admiral Norby*: Søren Norby (d. 1530), Danish admiral in charge of Christian's Baltic navy based on the Island of Gothland. Norby's attempts to relieve Stockholm from the sea came to nothing after Gustavus Ericson had received military assistance from Lübeck in 1522.

185 *trepanned*: enticed.

192 *epigraph*: Charles Beckingham (1699-1731), *Scipio Africanus: A Tragedy* (1718), Act II.iv, lines 63-68. (Line 67 slightly misquoted: "Love feels with rival Pride . . .").

192 *Sigismunda received in return*: I have added the name Sigismunda here to the 1801 text. Without it, the grammatical subject of the clause would have been Catherine, which would have rendered the sentence nonsensical.

202 *Stregna*: Sw. Strängnäs, later in the novel also referred to as Stregnez, a town on the southern shore of the Lake Mälaren approximately 50 miles west of Stockholm.

202 *being duly elected*: Gustavus Ericson was formally elected King of Sweden at a national convention in Strängnäs on June 6, 1523.

207 *epigraph*: from William Mason (1725-1797), *Elfrida, A Dramatic Poem* (1752), lines 109-113.

210 *Stregnez*: Sw. Strängnäs, earlier referred to as Stregna (see note to p. 202).

214 *Phœnix*: a mythological Arabian bird said to periodically burn itself to death after a long life, only to rise again from the ashes young and vigorous.

215 *his new palace*: Gustavus Ericson did not build a new palace, but he added fortifications to the already existing fortress known as "Three Crowns," which now became the major royal castle in Sweden.

216 *epigraph*: James Thomson (1700-1748), *Britannia. A Poem* (1729), lines 107, 126-127, 129, 136-137, 141-142.

218 *the German dominions*: an anachronism, as Sweden had no German dominions before the 17th century.

221 *eclaircissement*: éclaircissement, an explanation or clearing up of something that has been obscure.

221 *enlargement*: release

222 *relation*: from the reference to Hunsdorf as "the true fabricator of Sigismunda's relation," it appears that the word is used here as synonymous to citation, or summons. (See p. 126 for Ulrica's persuading Hunsforf write a fake summons, calling Sigismunda to the tribunal at Munster).

222 *No sooner . . . which this unexpected interview had interrupted*: there seems to be a gap in the text here, as we are told of no "unexpected interview" involving Ulrica in the context immediately preceding this paragraph. The summarizing character of the previous paragraph seems to indicate that it replaces a longer stretch of text now

cut out, and the dangling "interview" may thus be a result of this cutting-down process.

225 *Dortmund*: city in Westphalia, Germany.

229 *epigraph*: Henry Jones (1721-1770), *The Earl of Essex. A Tragedy* (1753), Act II, lines 192-197 (line 196 slightly misquoted: "How hard to turn the fond deluded Heart").

231 *Halden's Cross*: a fictitiously named Cross.

234 *"Cold was the north wind . . ."*: not identified.

234 *Margaret of Arensburg*: not identified.

238 *The Princess*: the sister of N——, in whose honor the tournament is given.

241 *epigraph*: Aaron Hill (1685-1750), *Merope: A Tragedy* (1749), Act IV. iii, lines 12-17 (misquoted: "No, there is none; no Ruler of the Stars, / Regardful of my Miseries———What Crime / Has drawn these Tortures on me? . . .").

252 *epigraph*: William Shakespeare, *Macbeth* (1606), Act I.vii, lines 21-25.

261 *epigraph*: not identified. The lines could possibly be Anna Maria Mackenzie's own.

272 *epigraph*: these lines are not by Whitefield but from William Whitehead's (1715-1785) *Creusa, Queen of Athens. A Tragedy* (1754), Act IV, lines 222-225.

280 *caparisoned*: decked with richly ornamented coverings.

284 *epigraph*: William Congreve (1670-1729), *The Double-Dealer, A Comedy* (1694), Act V. i, lines 592-596.

289 *take the child from its treacherous attendant, Sir Gottsler's before-mentioned female confidant*: apparently referring to Sir Gormund's former mistress who, having also become the confidant of the unsuspicious Catherina during her pregnancy, helped him intercept the letters between the latter and Duke Magnus (284-285). Whether Mackenzie added the duplicity of this minor character as a new idea at this stage of the narrative remains unclear; for although there is nothing in Alexa's previous account of the child-snatching scene to indicate that Christina, as she is called there, should be part of the kidnap plot, this may be due to Catherina-Alexa still being the dupe of her attendant (245).

291 *Phedora . . . Jacob*: presumably referring to Sir Gormund's two assistants in deceiving Catherina. The lack of explanation for the change of name from Christina to Phedora (see note to p. 289) for his female confidant adds to the impression that her duplicity was a second thought.

292 *manes*: spirits of dead ancestors.

293 *epigraph*: not identified. The lines may possibly be of Anna Maria's own hand.

298 *Christian . . . all Sweden wait only for his arrival*: Mackenzie seems to forget that Christian had by this time been deposed as king of Denmark, a fact already referred to in connection with Ulrica's return from Germany (222; see also note to p. 181).

299 *a powerful insurrection . . . the pretended son of Steen*: cf. note to p. 35.

304 *epigraph*: John Milton, *Paradise Lost*, Book 4, lines 750, 753-757.

304 *an union with Catherine*: the historical Gustavus Ericson married Catherine, daughter of Duke Magnus of Sachsen-Lauenburg, in 1531. Theirs was a politically arranged union; the bride was seventeen years Gustavus's junior, and the couple had never met prior to her arrival in Stockholm for the wedding.

306 *that comparatively infant city, which, founded only in the preceding century*: Mackenzie is mistaken here, as Stockholm had existed as a town since the mid-thirteenth century.

306 *several antique statues . . . that city*: the first Swedish monarch to acquire a major collection of antique statues was Gustavus III, who traveled in Italy in the 1780s.

307 *Right overcomes might*: the motto chosen by Gustavus Ericson for his reign was not "Right overcomes might," but "All power is of God."

309 *the Edda of Saemund*: *The Elder*, or *Poetic Edda*, a collection of Icelandic mythical stories found in a thirteenth-century manuscript, and possibly erroneously ascribed to the twelfth-century Icelandic scholar Sæmund Sigfusson. Mackenzie is apparently drawing on an English adaptation by A. S. Cottle, *Icelandic Poetry, or, The Edda of Saemund* (1797): her "The Traveller, or Descent of Odin" would be Cottle's "Song of the Traveller, etc.," and Rinda, Odin, Dager, Friga and Balder are mythical characters appearing in various songs in this volume.

312 *Christian's . . . death*: the historical Christian II did not die until 1559.

312 *died . . . on the 22d of September, 1560, aged 70 years*: according to recent historians, Gustavus Ericson was probably born on 12 May, 1496, and would thus have been sixty-four years old when he died on 29 (not 22) September 1560. Both Vertot (276) and Scott (395) claim, however, that he died in "the seventieth year of his age."

www.ingramcontent.com/pod-product-compliance
Lightning Source LLC
Chambersburg PA
CBHW030810310726
48980CB00006B/447/J
9781934555477